THIS IS THE ROUTE OF TWISTED PAIN

NEITHER THIS, NOR THAT
Book #1

MariaLisa deMora

Edited by Hot Tree Editing

Cover design by Debera Kuntz

First Published 2016

ISBN 13: 978-0-9967486-6-7

DEDICATION

Heroes get remembered, but legends never die. ~Babe Ruth

Because we all know every great story has at least some basis in experience: Thank you to those who provided me exceptional adventure opportunities, allowing me to spin these tall tales.

Contents

ACKNOWLEDGMENTS

Honestly? I don't know what possessed me to write this character. The genesis was a submissions call for a short story anthology to support the Semicolon Project, where all contributing authors would be attending the same signing in Mississippi. Since that signing was the Outlaw Author Motorcycle Convention 2016, the theme was bad boys. I'd just finished a great run of three short stories about bad girls, and at first it felt as if this story had started down that path.

We've got Penny Dane, who drives a truck, and even in the dead of night isn't afraid to invite a stranger into her bunk to get what she wants. But to me it seemed our Penny lacked the swaggering self-confidence needed to make her a bad girl. My muse must have agreed, and since someone had to be in control (clearly I wasn't) George Bell came into his own, filling my head with so much bad boy, it spilled over the short story length and well into novella. Welcome to the world, *Twisted Penny*. Booyah! What a pretty little standalone story! Submission complete, movin' on. Back to other books already on the schedule.

Yeah, naw.

Fast forward two weeks, and Bell hadn't stopped talking.

Two months later, and we were well on our way to the book you hold in your hands, *This Is The Route Of Twisted Pain*.

George, aka Twisted, wasn't an easy character to write. He is so unabashedly an outlaw; totally upfront about it and completely unapologetic regarding the things he does because everything he is, everything he does, supports his chosen family. His brothers. He has been all about the brotherhood since introduced to the motorcycle club life at sixteen, and even describes his hell-on-earth prospect period as one of the proudest times in his life. So he was totally focused on how to make life better for his brothers and the club.

That is until he met Penny. Once he met her, all bets were off, and he found his mind consumed by this woman. Obsessed. He calls

it addicted, and I suspect that's how it feels, because I found myself obsessed by Twisted and his life.

This book is different from all the others I've written in another way, too. As it turns out, there are a couple of different ways to write. One is by following an outline, where the plot is known, and the outcome is pretty clear. The story might waver one way or another along the path, but, especially in a series where much of the storyline overlaps, the destination is preordained (except when it's not /looks sideeye at *Gunny*/). The other way to write is literally flying by the seat of your pants, affectionately known as pantsing.

Twisted's book? Pantsing alla way, baby. To write, I would sit and locate the end of the previous chapter or scene—or sometimes find I'd stopped in the middle of a sentence, wherever exhaustion had overtaken me the previous day—and I would reread. Then, I'd have barely enough time to take a deep breath, put my hands on the keys, and close my eyes before we were off again.

Twisted directed every word, each movement, all aspects of the story. This is the first one where I have less than 10,000 words of deleted scenes. Shoot, some of my books, I have about half as many words in discarded dialogue and action as remains for publishing. For Twisted? There was only one section of the book where we had two false starts on a scene. Just the one place where I had to circle back around and listen more carefully to what he was telling me, watch for those forks in the path that had led us astray, and avoid them. In the end, I was happy with what we put down, and I doubt you'll ever know it, but there WERE alligators and pit bulls in the story at one point.

So here we sit, and there you are, ready to begin to dive into his world, set in the humid swamps and canals of southern Louisiana. I'll let you go play in the bayou in a minute, got just a few 'thank yous' to toss out.

Big thanks to the readers of these stories I pull outta my head. Y'all are amazing, straight up. For true. Love alla y'all. I do this writing gig for me, but jeebus I really get off on the fact that you like these folks in my head, too. Makes me kinda partial to you, 'cause I'm already partial to them.

Thank you to Kristen, Andrea, Jamey, and Jesse for allowing me to experiment on them with this story. Your involvement and perspective was, as it always is, spot on and fulla the goodness.

Thanks to Becky at Hot Tree Editing for her keen insight and guidance along the way. Love you, woman.

Thanks to Debera Kuntz for the fantastic cover you see on the front of this book. With very little guidance from me, she took what I had to say and ran with it, nailing it so well, I don't think I could love a cover more. I am in awe of your talent, woman.

Shout out to my family and friends, for putting up with me while I dealt with Twisted bein' all up in my head. You support me in ways you don't even know, and I love y'all hard.

To my personal motorcycle men, those who wear patches from so many different nations and clubs, thank you. You not only help keep my head on straight, at times you help me keep my head on my shoulders, period. Thanks for putting up with my bullshit, and you need anything, lemme know. Where y'all are concerned, my door is always open, and the table is always set. I might not wrench but, I'll fry up some oysters, make us some po boys.

Woofully yours,
~ML

Chapter One

GEORGE, AGE SEVEN

"Georgie, honey. Can you come here a minute?" From where he played with his plastic soldiers in the cool, oily dirt underneath the back porch, seven-year-old George Bell heard his mama call for him. He sighed and rolled onto his back, staring up, and blinking at the strips of sunlight making their way between the boards of the porch.

Footsteps ranged through the house, back and forth, telling him the occupants were busily getting ready for the night's festivities. He could hear bare soles whispering, high heels clipping, and the sedate and solid clunk of Miz Oleander's cane pacing room-to-room. "Georgie?" Miz Oleander would be chivvying them along, hurrying the girls, few of them women, in their quest to ready themselves before the onslaught poured through the doors. He tipped his head to the side, locking gazes with Teddy's black ones. "Georgie?" His mother's voice lifted again, emphasis on the last syllable, the joined sounds of "iieee" calling him from his hiding place.

"I'll be back," he whispered to his friend. "Watch the men and don't let 'em be stupid. Everybody gets to go home." He didn't get anything back, no response, no acknowledgment of his words. He never did. That was okay. He trusted Teddy to do as he was told. "Good man."

Flipping to his stomach, he turned in the tight space, his careful feet held over the soldiers' heads. Threat of a certain doom suspended aloft, but something he would never act on. His men were loyal, and so was he. Squirming, wary of the webbing spun overhead and watching out of habit for snakes and other varmints, he made his way to the tiny passage leading to the backyard. Removing the mesh jammed into the opening, he wiggled through, then leaned back inside to bring the covering back into place. Everyone would be safe and secure, and he'd be back to his friends as soon as he could. After he found out whatever it was Mama wanted him to do.

Standing at the edge of the porch, noise from up the way caught his attention, and he turned to see men already making their way down the lane and through the gate. A party thrown by Miz Oleander was not something to be missed, and the house would soon be filled to overflowing. From the side-to-side staggering gait of some of the men, they'd already started their own party. Men who'd been to the house before would be careful not to be too many sheets to the wind before arriving, or they knew Miz Oleander would gently turn them away. She took care of her girls; often called them that in public, "my girls" as if they were family. He'd seen and heard it, many a time.

Georgie knew the private side of things, too. Saw the ice-filled towels lifted to swollen lips, trembling fingers pressed to bruise-darkened cheeks, frightened glances quickly lowered from Miz Oleander's chilling blue stare. Around here, family time wasn't always fun and games, like the other kids in school talked about. To those children, a party night was the family gathered around a dining room table playing euchre or cards. Dominos if their parents felt a little racy. Dad with a beer to hand, Mom a creamy mint drink. One for her, maybe two for him. Kids bathed and tucked into clean-sheeted beds not long after the sun went down. Darkness was time for recharging the body, letting the mind sink into slumber. Not at Miz Oleander's house where there were more beds than you could shake a stick at, whose occupants would enter, leave,

and enter again before the clock struck midnight, and where the women weren't afraid to smoke, drink, and kiss their cares away.

Noise from inside the house brought him back to himself, and he stepped to the window, clambering easily to the top of the bricks stacked there for just this reason, bringing his eyes high enough to see inside. It looked like a dust devil of color and movement, the speed at which the occupants of the house moved dizzying. Lola, dressed in a tight-fitting costume that covered her armpits to thighs, frilly lace making a tail high on her butt to drape down the backs of her legs. Jeanine, adjusting her knockers in the tight brassiere that matched her underpants, that coordinated effort seen through the swirling splits in the scarves tied to a belt at her waist. Maribelle, youngest of the girls, wore a full uniform like he'd seen the rich girls in Slidell wearing as they marched by rows into their school. His mama stood behind Mari, fingers flying fast in the girl's hair, creating bouncy braids on either side of her head.

Mama was still in her dressing robe, cigarette held between her lips, head tilted to keep the smoke from stinging her eyes as she focused on what her hands were doing. He knew as soon as she finished with Mari's hair, she'd remove the cigarette and call him again, so he jumped from the bricks to the porch, reaching and opening the door, running through the kitchen. Grabbing a sweetmeat from the tray on the table, he dodged the slapping hand halfheartedly aimed his way from Mister Nondall, Miz Oleander's husband.

Oleander Nondall ran one of the most expensive and exclusive cathouses in southern Louisiana, right here in Mandeville. Her reputation brought in patrons from as far away as Hattiesburg, Mississippi, and Beaumont, Texas. Her girls were consistently pretty and well-spoken, with educated accents, and were always kept up-to-date on events by Miz Oleander's frequent quizzing. And Georgie'd heard her say often enough how clean they were. Lord knew they spent enough time in the bathrooms, so he reckoned they should be clean.

Stuffing the sweetmeat into his mouth, he charged into the parlor, dodging between the dozen women collected there, the strong scents of perfume and cigarette smoke setting up a racket in his head. A pounding headache was always his fate on party nights. The men who wandered down the stairs in the mornings complained of headaches, too, and he reckoned being up close to the perfume was what done it for them.

"Yes ma'am, Mama," he greeted when he reached where she stood, hand to Mari's face, tipping the girl's head back and forth to study her handiwork. "You called me?"

Coralie "Coral" Bell looked down with a smile. His mama was the most beautiful woman in the house. Coal-black hair framed a delicate face untouched by the sun. Pale, she was proud of her skin and had him rub lotions and creams into her shoulders and backside, anywhere it was hard for her to reach.

Her belly was round and firm, his little brother or sister needing another couple of months to cook. Her bun in the oven was the main reason for her lack of preparation this night. Few customers would be interested in a woman like her showing off an ability to breed. It reminded the men of where they were, and where they weren't, and highlighted how easily they could risk losing what they had at home if they made a misstep. Keeping this baby had been her choice, whispers in the night carrying the story to his ears, unsleeping on his pallet in the corner of her bedroom months ago, back before she was even swollen and showing.

"Coral, honey. You already have one little brat, and I'm feeding and clothing him. The goodness of my heart only goes so far, honey. Take the drink." That had been Miz Oleander's voice, cajoling and stern at the same time.

"Ollie, I can't. Not again." There was the echoing sound of glass sliding across the wooden table. He'd seen this drink before, smelled it

up close when it was cooking in the special pot in the kitchen. Reeking of turpentine and castor oil, it smelled most sickening when it rolled hot and boiling in the bottom of the copper pot. That had been back in the early spring, and in the cool air drifting through his mama's bedroom, the drink smelled more medicinal, like the pharmacy on a busy day. "Last time was bad."

"We caught it late, last time." Miz Oleander had been still cajoling, but the stern had chopped a larger hole for itself. "Nice and early this one." The glass slid again.

"I can't." Material moving, and a chair pushed back, legs scraping on the wooden floor. "And you know Georgie is my world, Ollie. I'll do extras, one a week if you need me to, whatever you say." Knees hit the floor and material moved again. Georgie squirmed to his stomach, hands lifting too late to his ears to block the words. "Let me make you feel good, Ollie. Lean back, darlin'. Leave it all up to me, Ollie. Let your sweet Coralie work some magic."

After that night, Miz Oleander hadn't come back with the drink. She wasn't happy, but Mama kept up her end of the bargain, working at least one trick a week without taking her percentage. That built up her bank with Miz Oleander, so George knew when it came time for the baby to be born, the midwife would be here and paid for, and his little sister or brother would have a roof over their heads.

"Georgie," she cooed, bending her knees to squat gracefully in front of him, fingers working across his face dusting and brushing. "How in the world do you get so dirty so fast, baby boy?" Not really a question, more of a reminder that he needed to not make her life harder.

"I'm sorry, Mama." But Teddy waited, and he knew that sorry or not he'd be back underneath the porch as soon as it was possible. Soldiering didn't happen without his hands to move the men; their battle suspended during his time away.

"Oh, baby." Soft lips brushed his forehead, fingers raking the hair back, her subtle scent enveloped him. Lilies and sweetness. *Mama*. "The men will be here any minute."

He broke in, "Already in the lane." Eagerly nodding, he was happy to give her good news. "A lot of men, Mama. Some of 'em already juiced up."

"Well now, that's good news. Thank you for bringing it to me, baby." Touching her forehead to his, she smiled, her cheeks lifting as tiny crinkles appeared at the corners of her eyes. Crow's feet, she called those, pressing her fingers firmly into the area every night, massaging in bitty circles. "So the men are nearly here. What does that mean for my baby boy?"

"Stay out of sight and out of mind. Don't leave the back rooms of the house." It didn't quite work as a sing-song, but he tried, knowing she would laugh. She did.

"Exactly right, baby boy. My Georgie boy." With a firm kiss to his forehead, she steadied herself on his shoulders as she stood and he accepted the weight and pressure gladly, happy to help in even such a small way. "Such a good boy."

"Coral," a man's voice called from the front room, and he watched as Mama's sweet face changed, a secret smile lifting one corner of her mouth. She stood there, silent and patient, only responding when the voice came again, more frantic at the wait. "Coral, honey. Where are you?"

"I'm here, Freddie," she called, fingers giving Georgie's shoulders a gentle squeeze before she stepped around him, and she walked to the front room, her dressing gown billowing out, body proudly naked underneath. "Right here for you, doll baby. Ready for you."

Chapter Two

GEORGE, AGE THIRTEEN

Georgie stood in the corner of the room. A silent sentinel, his job for the night was observing. When it was first brought up, Mama had argued against it, but Miz Oleander had been adamant. The john in bed with Mari had wanted an audience, the younger, the better, and was willing to pay big money for such. "Coral, thirteen ain't too young. He's got a willie and will learn how to use it soon enough. Grover is a gentleman, treats all the girls right. Your boy could do worse than learning from this man."

Mama had made some vague noises beyond that, but Miz Oleander cut her off. "During the war between the states, we had thirteen- and fourteen-year-old soldiers. If a boy of thirteen could fight a war then, he surely can watch a man takin' his pleasure from a pretty woman in my house."

Freddy had picked that moment to stumble in, bleeding from a scrape on his leg. Mama gave up the argument to tend to her baby boy, passing him the old hand-me-down teddy to quiet his screams, Georgie having given up comforting toys long ago. He still played with his soldiers sometimes, wedging his way underneath the back porch, arranging his men just so in lines meant to master every enemy. The

best part about those games was he could leave them and come back, sure in the knowledge that all would remain the same between visits. Mute lookouts, waiting for his hand to direct them.

Miz Oleander's eyes had cut to Georgie, standing silently nearby, almost like he was here tonight, and she called him over with a tilt of her head. He had left Mama with the nearly five-year-old crying baby and followed the woman of the house into the parlor.

A heavy hand had landed on his shoulder, and she'd leaned close to whisper. "Tomorrow night, you be in Mari's room at eight o'clock. Corner by the bed. Stand quiet, boy. All you do is watch. You wanna touch yourself, put that shit off until you hit your pallet. If you pop a boner, say your willie wakes up and wants to play, and you see Grover wants some of that, you stand there, and you take what he gives you. But, you do not touch." Her breath made a fetid cloud around him, stuffed full of ashtrays and old meat, choking him with the foul that rolled from her mouth. "All you do is watch and be quiet. You do good, I'll pay your mama for her extra tonight."

So he had been ready to stand and watch. Had watched an empty bed for an hour before Mari led Grover into the room. Turning into the room, she stared at Georgie and shook her head, her expression sad for a moment before she looked over her shoulder to the john, going back to work and lighting up the room with her smile. Fingers walked their way up Grover's shirt to the top button. Her voice low and sweet, rich in a way Georgie hadn't heard from her before, she said, "Tell Mari what you want, baby. Tell me what makes you feel good."

Grover stared at him across the top of Mari's head, reaching back a hand to quietly close the door. Without taking his eyes off Georgie, he told Mari, "Strip, honey." Firm. His voice was not sweet, and not mean. Just firm. No nonsense. "It's lesson time."

Positioning a now-naked Mari sideways on the bed, head away from the corner where Georgie stood, Grover tugged her legs until her

bottom was right on the edge. With her feet to the rail holding the mattresses in place, he spread her legs wide, exposing her to Georgie's eyes. "What's your job, boy?"

Having been coached while Mari undressed, Georgie answered quickly, "To watch and learn, sir."

"Exactly right, son." For the next three hours, Grover instructed him on the proper names for every part of a woman's privates, their faces side-by-side hovering over that sweetly-scented flesh. Showed him too, how a woman might like to be touched and why. How that would change given the situation. Taught him how a man could learn to read the desire and adjust their approach accordingly, giving everything that was needed.

Mari's crimson-nailed fingers slid into view and, as instructed, held her intimate lips open, flower petals spread wide so Georgie could discover the beautiful secrets he'd suspected lay underneath all the coy playacting the women did for the men who came to the house. Allure beneath the coarse familiarity with the other women when it was just them in the house. When the man finally smoothed on the lambskin condom he'd brought himself, Georgie's willie—*cock, his mind provided, using the word Grover taught him*—woke up, as Miz Oleander put it.

And it was staying awake. Throbbing, pulsing, brushing against the fabric of his undershorts, he knew what the man was looking for. He'd looked for it often enough himself in the last couple of years, lying in his pallet or a bed if one was available, fingers working his flesh. First two fingers, then as he grew up, and grew, a handful, then more than he could span. With a grip that dragged and teased by turns, he'd discovered things about himself as he imagined it was the hands of the women parading in front of him every day.

Now he was watching the act itself, Grover's ass muscles tightening and releasing, pushing his hips forwards like the dogs did when they got knotted up in the front yard. Georgie's cock demanded something he'd

been told not to do. Ordered to ignore. He could barely see Mari underneath the man, she was enveloped by his mass, only her thighs, and lower legs visible, splayed wide while he moved against her.

Inside her.

Grover had pulled him close to watch the first time he stuck it in her. Glistening in the lights left burning on either side of the bed, her sex had closed accommodatingly around the man's member. Him enveloped in her, her enveloped by him. Joined at the hip in a way Georgie hadn't ever considered.

"Watch her face." The hissed words startled him, and he pulled himself from the wash of recent memory to see Grover had straightened his arms, lifting himself off Mari, while still wedged into her hips and moving. "See that look, son?"

Mari's cheeks were flushed, mouth open, lips making a perfect "O" that her smeared lipstick distorted. As Georgie watched, her neck extended, pushing back and he looked down to see one of her hands shoved between the two bodies, moving with purpose where Grover was pushed into her. "See that look?" Georgie nodded, instinctively knowing in his role of observer that his voice at this moment would break the spell Mari'd cast over herself.

"You know how it feels when your cock spills over your hand? When you can't breathe for the beauty of the thing you do to yourself? When your entire being compacts down to the heat of your hand on your cock, tension in your fingers around the rigid shaft, the explosion of goodness that shoves itself out of you?" Georgie nodded again.

"She's there, son. Watch her come. Women are beauty incarnate when they climax." Grover muttered, his voice soft, crooning almost. "The most intimate thing they can give a man is this knowledge. You'll know her in ways most of her clients don't when this is through."

With a cry, Mari's other hand flew up, fingers flexing around Grover's shoulder and her entire body stiffened, it seemed her muscles were tensing to the point of pain. She cried out again and jerked. Then Grover put his head on her shoulder and moved faster, the familiar slapping sound echoing around the room, seen in action for the first time and understood. The power behind the movement, the need to finish, physical demands bringing bodies together violently in a way that didn't seem to hurt at all. Grover grunted once, then again, and then rammed hard against her body, holding still. Georgie held still, too.

Minutes passed, and Grover slowly relaxed, Mari's hands moving up and down his arms as her breathing became labored for a different reason than before, this being the weight settling on her chest. Finally, she wheezed, "Shitfire, he went to sleep." Georgie watched as she wiggled sideways, letting Grover slide off and face-first into the mattress.

Seated on the edge of the bed, she looked at Georgie, and he knew what she saw. Knew it and was embarrassed because while he hadn't touched, his willie—*cock*—didn't care, spilling in his undershorts instead of his hand. "You okay, Georgie Porgie?"

God, I hate that nickname, he thought as he nodded.

"You sure?" She peered into his face and seemed satisfied with what she saw. "Okay. You can go on now. Go get cleaned up." Said matter-of-factly, this took the sting out of her seeing the wet spot on the front of his pants. "I'll tell Ollie how well you did, Georgie..." she paused, then changed it, "George." Giving him ownership of an adulthood he didn't know he wanted. "You did really well. He liked it a lot." Chin up, he grinned at her. "He'll want you here again." At the thought, his willie—*cock*—jerked in his pants, and she saw the movement, giving him a wide grin before tilting her head at the door. Her legs closed, cutting off his view of her sex—*pussy*. "Go on now. No free shows tonight."

***

GEORGE, AGE FOURTEEN

George stood over the boy lying on the ground underneath the swing set, seats and chains still moving wildly side-to-side from the scuffling activity ended only moments before. Jaw throbbing, he gritted his teeth in an attempt to hold the tears at bay. George needed to not get into trouble again, or Mama said she'd make it so the job at the pharmacy was history. Him working was how he kept himself in school clothes these days, with all Mama's advances that went for booze and Freddy cutting deep into her earnings.

At least he'd won. That might be as usual, but this boy was way bigger than him and rumored to be the meanest badass in town. Or at least in the seventh grade. *Coulda went down either way, and no chance would the pharmacy want me on if I was sportin' a shiner.* Still shaking out one fist, lessening the sting in his knuckles, he glared down, watching the boy's eyes flutter as he came back to himself.

"Hey," George barked, and the boy cringed, shoulders rounding down. *Yeah, he's beat*, George thought. Now to make sure he wouldn't be coming back for seconds.

"Told you once already. Gonna tell you one more time. You do not. Lay hands. On a woman." Sabrina Rotain sobbed over near the slides; her girls had circled around her, cooing over the bright red outline of the boy's hand on her face. Leaning in, George tried to channel some of the asshole his mom's most recent good time boy brought to the room. He hissed, "You don't remember this lesson, and we have to conduct a second conversation regarding these issues, then boy,"—he toed the boy's ribs and shook his head when that provoked a high-pitched squeal—"we will have a problem the like you've never imagined." He toed the boy again, the boots he wore having enough point to be uncomfortable. "Now, need to know. You get me, boy?"

Angry eyes glared up at him, mouth bloody from a leaking lip but it hadn't taken much to take his opponent down. George knew being held

back a year helped a lot, making him the oldest in their grade. His raising also helped, weekends of moving disruptive johns along having given him ample opportunity to hone these skills. He pulled back his foot in a threat and the boy yelped without being touched, then said, "Yeah. Hands off. I got it."

Taking a step back, George lifted his gaze and glanced at the ring of faces pressed close. No friends of his in this group. The son of a whore didn't get invited to sleepovers and birthday parties. But, it didn't look like this boy had a posse, either. Every face turned his way would have been just as pleased to see George on the ground, and he made a split second decision, sticking his hand out, ready to help the boy up if he would only accept. It hadn't been a beat down because George didn't like the guy, just needed him to understand his actions weren't acceptable. If the boy could get past that, they might find things in common.

After a moment, then another, the boy gripped his hand and George hauled him up, then retained his hold, using it to pull the boy closer. "I'm George. George Bell."

"Ralphie Lewis," the boy said, pumping their hands up and down once.

"What the fuck did she do to rile you?" George asked as if they were alone on the little kids' playground. "Sabrina don't normally do anything wrong. Head down, watches her feet as if she's walkin' across hot coals most of the time. Takes care of her sister."

"Called me a faggot." Ralphie's face screwed up, flushing red as he remembered to be pissed off.

"So?" George's hand dropped to his side, and without thinking, he fingered the outline of the knife in his pocket. Four-inch switchblade, lifted from asshole's pants two weeks ago, still not missed. Not returned. Wouldn't be. Taken in trade for the man laying hands on George, throwing him against the wall when he'd stepped between the

asshole's fists and his mother. A life lesson in self-preservation because George could have laid a hurting on the man, but had held back when he saw his mother's frightened face, pulling his last blows, so the dickhead only needed ice and rest, not a breathing tube and hospital.

"She called me a *fag*got." Voice raising in pitch, Ralphie sounded incredulous at George's ignorance of the insult's impact. *As if the worst thing a woman can do is undermine the confidence of a man*. "Me."

"You a gay boy?" George tipped his head, his hard gaze around the ring scattering their remaining audience. He watched them retreat, most already having gone back to their regular cliques and in-groups, chattering voices detailing how things had gone down for those unfortunate few who had missed the actual action. "Suck cock, or take it up the ass?"

Ralphie's eyes widened in shock. *"NO!"* This was shouted, and if the kid had fallen down dead of a stroke like Mister Nondall last year, George wouldn't have been surprised. With a red face, and an angry expression twisting his mouth sideways, the kid looked more pissed now than when he'd been beaten and on the ground, groveling in the dirt at George's feet.

"Then what the fuck does it matter what that little bitch says?" George was quiet when he spoke, keeping his voice guarded, making Ralph pay close attention to hear him. "Insults are just that, a little kid's way to poke a dog. It's up to the dog how they want to counter that poke. Or if they even wanna react. Such a small thing." He tipped his head to one side, looking Ralphie up and down. "One little poke with a little stick that, if the dog can get to it, could be broken in two easily. A swipe of a paw, or the snap of jaws, stick's gone, but kid stays, now maybe looking for a bigger stick. Damn dog ignores things, and that kid goes away. No reaction means no fun, and that kid's out the door, looking for a good time somewhere else."

He leaned closer before continuing. "Dog doesn't ignore those little pokes, those little jabs? Well then the kid might pay the price, earning a chomp or butt whipping in the middle of the fight, but that dog is gonna lose the *war*." Straightening himself, he still stood half a foot shorter than Ralphie. "Don't be the dog that gets put down because of a little kid unable to control herself."

He gestured at Sabrina, then back to Ralphie. "Don't worry about getting into trouble for smackin' her. She'll leave it because she likes me and won't want to get me in hot water for fighting again." Leaning closer again, he confided with a sideways grin, "Don't know if you caught this, but I fight a lot."

Ralphie laughed, a startled yelp escaping him when his split lip stretched, the burn of that showing in his face. "Yeah, you got moves. I suck, though. You didn't have to do much."

"Shit happens, I take care of it." George shrugged. "Back to the dog and the stick and the little kid that don't know better than to poke that happily sleeping dog. Don't be the dog, dawg. Be the bigger man." He reached out, gripping the boy by the shoulder and shaking him gently to-and-fro. "Ralph." Renaming him, giving him that taste of adulthood granted to George last year by a whore. "Ralph Dawg." He winked, leaning close as if to whisper a secret. "Watch the master, man. Leader of the pack."

Walking over to where Sabrina stood, he reached out and looped an arm around her waist, tugging her perky knockers up against him. She took a breath that swelled her chest, rubbing those sweet things against him again. "You okay, baby?" His question was soft and quiet, for her alone, and at her nod, he smiled slowly, watching her eyes widen slightly. "Good, baby. That's good. You still wanna hook up tonight?" One stunned nod later and he gave her a full-on smile, her lips parting involuntarily as he pulled a gasp from her. "Pick me up at the pharmacy? Six o'clock?" She was a sophomore, drove a pickup, and at fifteen had a hardship license.

She nodded, and he gave her a squeeze, changing the trajectory of their encounter with three words. "It's a date." When he said those words, they were a promise, whether the girl knew it or not. Dates weren't hookups; they were more. "Don't be late, baby. Don't be a bad girl. Be my good baby." That got him a shiver, and he gave her another squeeze before turning back to Ralph. With a wave, George steered Sabrina across the dirt and grass towards the high school where he'd kiss her stupid before leaving her and heading back to the junior high building. Tonight, whether she was good or bad, she'd be sucking his cock, so he could give her his mouth like this now.

***

GEORGE, AGE SIXTEEN

Tense, George held himself still as the man leaned into his mom, forearm in her neck, holding her immobile where he'd forced her against the bedroom wall. His mom shook her head in response to a question hissed close to her ear, and then closed her eyes tightly when the man roared, "What in fuck were you thinkin', Coralie? What in actual fuck were you thinking? You know better, woman. You don't party with the enemy."

Her head shook again, the movement weaker, as were the pushing motions of her hands against the man's barrel chest. Short and powerfully built, with arms bulging in the middle like whiskey kegs, the man held her there a moment longer before releasing her, holding a hand to her shoulder to steady her as she leaned over, coughing. Twisting to look over his shoulder at George, the man gave him a chin lift before asking, his tone casual, "Georgie, how you doin', boy?"

James "Jimbo" Bell was his grandfather. The man didn't often visit, only two or three times a year. His life was entirely consumed by the biker club he'd founded after getting out of the army, taking up with the men he called brother in the Incoherent Motorcycle Club. Their main base of operations wasn't far away, over in Hammond, but they also

had clubhouses and businesses all along the interstate, running from Houston all the way to Florida. The man loved his daughter in his own way, and George's belief in that was the only reason Papaw was still standing in this room after what he'd just done.

Ignoring his question, George instead asked one of his own. "What'd Mama do, Papaw?"

Cold as steel, gray eyes raked him up and down. "She fucked up, son. Ollie contracted to provide entertainment at a private party, didn't check to see what party that was. Dealin' with someone she knew, but didn't realize they were just sub-contractin' pussy out. Vicar's Wrath." Sucking in a breath, Papaw continued, "Me and their president, we got a beef goin' back years. Decades." He glanced at Coral. "We've figured out how to coexist in these parts because they stay on their side of the lake, and I stay on mine. Your momma crossed the causeway. Bad enough." He shook his head in disgust. "But, after they got there, she found out who the party was for, and she stayed. Birthday party for Leswayne. He picked his pussy out of the line. Wanna give me two guesses who he picked?" George shook his head.

"Yeah, bet not. Your momma ain't the sharpest stick, son. Jesus, Coral, what do you think he's gonna do when he finds out whose legs he slid his dick between? When he finds out what you've been hiding? Ain't the first time you been dumb like this, and you can't hide your head in the fucking sand, you stupid bitch." He hated hearing Papaw talk about his mom this way, how he'd spoken to and about her for as long as George could remember. It wasn't that she was a whore or at least that wasn't most of it. It was that she was a woman and therefore second class to start with. Then she'd lowered the bar by her profession.

Forget that Papaw turned her out of his house when she was fourteen. Forget that he'd set her down this path with his own decisions, making her believe she had no other choices but to eke out a living on her back, walking the only path fate seemed to have for her, twisted though it was. Her whole life had been a precarious day-to-day

existence, never knowing what would be coming down the road next, her survival and means of support subject to the whim of men. The same way her mother had lived, governed by the rages Jimbo brought home from overseas.

George had heard the stories, seen evidence of brutality on his grandfather's knuckles more than once. Stories were told of how Mama's Ma suffered in silence for years before finally dying in childbirth, taking Jimbo's son with her into that grave. Any chance at life choked out of the boy by the cord snaking around his throat in the womb, her life pouring crimson from between her legs. Coralie was four when that happened. George wondered if Jimbo thought she should be thankful he'd kept her on for a decade. Kept her alive at all.

For years, George had helped Mister Nondall take care of unwanted litters of kittens and puppies, picking the squirming bodies up by their back feet, slinging them against the side of a steel barrel before tossing them into a half-filled water bucket, stunned and drowning without a fuss. Unwanted, unneeded, less cruel to kill them than to leave them alive to starve a slow death. Maybe Papaw felt he'd given Coralie a running start at life by not ending hers and burying her alongside her mother and brother.

"Fucked Leswayne real good. Exhausted the man, let him play his rough games. Hell, I got told that she gave it so good, she fucked him to sleep." The grizzled old man snorted derisively, lifting his top lip in a sneer. "Fucked him so good, he wanted a second taste. Tracked down the house. Talked to Ollie. Ollie called me, thank fuck, and didn't tell him the bloodlines of the bitch he had in his bunk. Didn't give him any cause to look this way because even Ollie knows if he found out what was waiting here, with the kind of mistakes Coral's made in the past, he'd fucking kill your momma, boy." Coralie made a noise, and he swung her way, planting an angry fist against the wall beside her head. She froze in fear, nostrils quivering with tiny sips of air. "You let him get that close, Coral. So close, he fuckin' talked to Ollie." Shaking his head, without looking around, he said, "Georgie, your momma fucked up."

"George," he corrected Papaw, watching as the man turned to him and blinked. George decided he'd heard enough. It was time to make a stand, make sure Papaw learned he couldn't come in and do this again. Make sure he knew that Mama wasn't going to be his punching bag, not ever.

"Mama, come here." Holding out his hand, he gestured with a curl of his fingers, calling her to him. Before her father could react, Coral retreated from the wall and to George, taking his hand and shifting behind him, letting him stand solidly in front of her. "Papaw. Love you, old man. But you don't get to talk to my momma like this anymore. The time for this is done." Papaw didn't respond, just narrowed his eyes, staring at George's face.

"It wasn't you in Leswayne's bed, making choices. You had so little to do with her raisin', there's hardly even any of your blood running through the veins of this woman. She's lived here more than half her life, so I figure unless you're kin to Ollie, you got no cause to take a stand like you've done today." George shook his head, feeling the trembling hands of his mother resting on his back. "You bein' the man you are, won't ask you to apologize to this woman behind me. But me bein' the man I am, you'll respect her from here out."

Papaw nodded once, then bent over and smoothly pulled a knife from his boot. He didn't hide the action, didn't posture or gesture with the knife, just popped the button on the handle, letting the soft snick of the blade locking into place do his talking.

George stood without moving for a moment, then lifted his chin. "You want it like that, old man?" Disbelieving, he shook his head sharply, once, asking again, "You sure you want it to go down like this, old man?" When Papaw still didn't respond, George reached behind him, thumb flipping the leather strap from over the butt of the pistol wedged into the holster there. Another five-finger discount piece, he'd picked this one up in a pawn shop in Slidell, using Ralph for distraction,

having him ask a million questions about a modified assault rifle the shop owner had while George long-armed his way into the display case.

Bringing the gun out and around, he allowed it to rest alongside his thigh, making no other movement. A second later he jerked, shocked when Papaw burst out laughing. Unlocking the knife, the old man folded the blade away and then stooped to put it back into place in his boot. He straightened and looked at his grandson. "George," he said, humor flooding his voice, still shaking with laughter. "Never thought to see the day when Jimbo Bell would bring a knife to a gunfight."

Papaw's eyes swung to look at Coralie, still holding her position behind George. "It's time. Told you it was comin' last time I was here. Told you I'd take him. Boy's comin' with me, Coral. Too old to be livin' in a cathouse anyway, shoulda done took him years ago. Showed his mettle today, needs to hone that hard he's found inside him. You haven't done a bad job with him, but George's comin' with me."

"What are you talking about?" George was confused because not only wasn't his grandfather pissed at having a gun pulled on him, now he was talking crazy.

"You're coming back with me to the clubhouse. Got a woman can help see to you, but mostly you need a man around you. Need to get yourself equipped to live in the world, boy, and your momma ain't gonna give you that. Hell, the sissy boys she favors won't show you squat when it comes down to it. You been bestin' them for years, makin' your own way while carrying her on your back. Doin' your own brand of back work, boy." His grandfather shook his head, holding out one hand as he questioned, "Are you tryin' to tell me you *want* to stay here?"

No, George thought, fighting against memories threatening to surface. *I hate it here*. He did. Hated everything to do with the whorehouse. He couldn't wait to get out, and he and Ralph had been putting together a plan, saving and scrimping to bankroll their escape.

Ideas they'd been tossing around to get them both out of the parish. Papaw throwing this up in his face wasn't a plan, and the voice George listened to inside himself was screaming caution. This whole thing seemed to be jumping from the frying pan into the fire.

"No, ain't sayin' that. But, Papaw, I got school," George moved, and his mother's fingers clutched at his shirt, holding him in place, hiding behind him. *All my life*. "And Mama needs me. Needs me to keep the johns in line. Ollie uses me for muscle sometimes, making sure the heavy-handed ones go light on her girls."

Papaw scoffed, not looking at George but staring instead at the door where a large form had appeared, blocking out a portion of the light. Slowly, seeming to choose his words with care, Papaw said, "Ain't all she uses you for, boy." At that, George sucked in a breath because it was true.

Content for years to just have him watching from the shadows, listening to the murmured instructions and explanations, once George hit fifteen, Grover wanted more active participation in his sessions with Mari. Insisting George direct Mari at times, always quietly requesting he "take care of business, son" while the man stood nearby and watched George jacking into a tissue. Now that George was sixteen, that participation had become *participation* in every sense of the word.

First had been Grover sitting on the edge of the bed, watching over George's shoulder as he jerked off on Mari's face. Chin lifted, mouth held wide open in a silent scream, she had patiently waited for him to come. It had taken a while with the close audience, feeling the man's hands brush his hips occasionally to shift him to one side or the other, each time startling him. Every interruption broke George's concentration so that he had to build it again, thoughts of the junior cheer squad captain riding him in the backseat of her car working in his favor. Her pussy tight and hot as she bounced over him with as much enthusiasm as she'd used during the football game the night before. Big, round titties he could bury his face between, and he had. So it was

George swung in place, twisting away from her hands as he stared into the face of his mother. He took his time, gaze sweeping her features up and down, his chest tightening as he finally came to believe what he read there. She knew what Ollie was doing. Knew and would support those plans because it would mean less back work for her. His voice was choked, sounding small as he whispered, "Are you shitting me?"

Voice raspy from decades of cigarette smoke, Ollie called from the hallway, "Let's all calm down now. Ain't nothing happening you don't want, boy."

Ignoring Ollie, his eyes drilled into his mother, locking her in place, keeping her voiceless with the pain and anger he knew flooded his face. Flat and toneless, his voice sounded foreign to himself. "You knew." She flinched at this tone, cutting and bloody with disillusionment. "You knew." Hissed and harsh, he bent forwards at the waist. "You knew."

A dark chuckle came from behind him as, using two canes to move her bulk through the doorway from the hall and into the bedroom, Ollie started to crowd close to George. He smelled her, that unmistakable scent that filled his nightmares. In his gut, acid churned and bile rose in the back of his throat. She needed to not be close to him, needed to not touch him. *Not now, not ever*. Without conscious thought, his arm moved. She abandoned her advance, standing stock-still when he lifted the pistol. From Papaw, he heard a low, warning, "Boy, consider yourself."

With great care, because his hands were shaking as with a palsy, George jacked the slide on the gun, forcing a round into the barrel. The gun seemed heavy, somehow weighted down with his crippling fear. He'd used it more than once, killing varmints that threatened to hole up under the house. Used it shooting empty cans from the top of fence posts with Ralph, the two boys trading jokes as they pretended to be quick-draw gunslingers. He knew how the pistol worked, knew how it

felt, and still the gun felt foreign in his hand. Intent meant everything. From behind him, sounding slightly closer, his Papaw said, "Boy."

Twisting to glance over his shoulder, George shook his head, saying, "Sorry, old man." He found that the cautioning words of the bastard who had been choking the life out of his own daughter not ten minutes ago just didn't matter. "Sorry, you don't carry much weight with me right now." *Might be easiest to end this for everyone,* he thought, *because I for sure ain't letting Ollie make bank off me. Off my ass like I'm one of her girls. I'll die first.* Lifting the gun, he pointed it at his own head first, then his mother's head, then Ollie's, knowing exactly where she was without looking.

Holding the gun still, he waited for a moment to see if he could bring himself to pull the trigger, then shook his head. Speaking to his mother, he commented dispassionately, "I kill her, she's your means of support. Can't do that, take away the only thing you think yourself capable of doing. That falsehood his fault, the man standing behind me. You're capable of so much, Mama, but you've stuck with what feels safe. Stuck me right here alongside you, not giving a shit what that means for me."

He shrugged, pointing the gun at his mother again. "I kill you, I'm killing Freddy's chances. Because I see where he is your life, Mama. And I pray you'll do right by him. I can leave you alone, knowing his daddy will step in if needed. Hell, at least you know who fathered him, right?" Ripping up from his chest, laughter left bloody ribbons in its wake, razored from the sides of his throat.

Tapping the end of the barrel against the side of his head, he waited, and after a moment saw a look of relief trail across her face. *What I thought. At least I know her druthers, now.* "I kill me, I'm doin' everyone in this room a favor." She made a noise, and he shook his head again. "I kill me, you got no excuse. I kill me, she's got no ticket to ride. I kill me, he ain't got no reason to return here. I kill me, I got no more shit to eat, no matter what. Because, Mama,"—he shook his head, feeling the barrel knock against his temple—"I've been eating shit for years, trying

to make it worthwhile for you to keep me. You kept me all this time, kept me close, kept me fed and clothed. Working as best you thought you could, you kept me. But I've been eating shit since I can remember."

Coming to a decision, he dropped the gun to his side and slid his finger from the guard, resting it along the barrel. He was leaving here today, one way or another. "Done eatin' shit, Papaw. You thinkin' to feed me a steady diet of it, you should just kill me now."

The answer came immediately; it was reassuring that his grandfather didn't have to give it a second thought. "Promise you a shit-free table, boy. My hand to God. You're done eatin' shit if I can shovel it away from you fast enough. You bring your own shit with you, then that's shit you'll have to figure out how to chew." A hand fell on his shoulder, gripping and shaking him side-to-side like he was wont to do with Ralph. "Got belongings to gather?" George shook his head, watching tears pooling in the lower lids of his mother's eyes, feeling nothing. No pain. No anger. No resentment. She was how she was, end of story. There was nothing from here he wanted to take with him, damn few memories, even. Life upended, his value a lie, nothing in his past worth the effort. "Let's get in the wind, then, son."

Within minutes, they were headed out of town, barreling along the interstate, seated astraddle the bike, in what Papaw offered with a lifted lip was, "Nuts to butt. You're gonna have to sit on the queen seat. Fuckin' shit. Hold onto the rack behind you, boy."

An hour after that, George was installed in a room over the bar of the clubhouse. Only a thin door with a weak lock stood between him and a dozen men he'd never met. Each of them staring as he walked through the main room, trailing behind Papaw uncertainly. Big, imposing, bearded giants who gawked at him as if he were a foreigner.

Men who might have heard what Papaw had about his participation in the whorehouse. Men who might look to gain a pound of retaliation in the form of flesh. Or who might be seeking to advance their station in

the club using him as a stepping stone to get past Papaw. Each figure in the room unknown, an unmappable obstacle course.

Up the stairs, he followed and then wordlessly entered the room Papaw pointed out. Scanning it, he saw a bed and a dresser, both better quality than anything assigned to him at Ollie's house. The door shut behind Papaw, closing him in, and rudderless, George stood in the middle of the room, not sure what to do next.

That dilemma resolved after a few minutes when a woman brought a plate filled with pulled pork and slaw, and George made himself a sandwich with the roll that sat alongside the meat. He ate standing, leaning against the wall beside the door. Without thinking about it too much, he reached out two or three times, trying the knob, just to make sure it hadn't locked itself in the interim.

The woman smiled at him when she came to retrieve the plate, telling him in a soft voice to, "Rest now, honey." But he couldn't. His mind wouldn't let things go, and knowing that Papaw seemed to know what had been happening was steadily eating away at him. He turned the scene in Mama's bedroom over and over again in his head. Maybe Ralph would have an idea what he could do; George could try to call him tomorrow.

Right now, however, he needed to get through the night.

George sat on the floor opposite the door, gun resting in a loose hold, forearms propped across his knees, waiting for the worst. He waited a long time, but no one else came. Raised voices sounded from the room under his feet, waves and crashes of anger and outrage beating their way up the stairs to bounce off that unlocked door.

At eight the next morning, with dry, burning eyes, he opened the door to Papaw's insistent pounding.

"Fuck, boy. You sleep at all?" A headshake his only response, he was stunned to the core by Papaw's next words. "You're amongst real family

now, boy. No need to guard your back because every man in this house will defend it for you. I called a couple of the ole ladies to take you shoppin', get you some jeans, but I'll put 'em off a spell. George, you gotta rest. You need me to, I'll stand here all day, let you get what you need. But if you trust me...if you believe me, you'll know you can rest easy here. I am Incoherent, and Incoherent has your back."

A quick hand to his shoulder, a reassuringly tight grip, and then Papaw pulled the door closed, and George heard the latch click into place as it seated. He stood, frozen, shocked by his grandfather's words. *Maybe I can do this,* he thought. *Maybe this is where everything changes for me.*

"Rest, boy." The instructions came through the wood, accompanied by a creak as Papaw leaned against it, doing what he said he would. Guarding George. Having his back. Making him feel safe. *I'm among real family now*. George moved to the bed and fell down exhausted, asleep nearly before he shoved the gun underneath the pillow.

***

"No," George whispered incredulously, gaze glued to his grandfather's face, waiting for Papaw to continue with his story.

Solemnly, Papaw gave him a single nod, his hair rustling against the back of the swing. They were in the clubhouse's backyard, Papaw in a porch swing hung from an oak branch, heels of his boots digging into the soft dirt, holding the swing motionless against the whipping winds. Foot crossed on his knee, George sat slumped into a metal chair at the outskirts of the flickering light from the bonfire. Incoherent members had been feeding the fire for hours, periodically placing new logs into it, laughing as flames licked up around their hands, scorching the hair from forearms.

"Truth, son. Wasn't for the club, I wouldn't be here talkin' to you right now. Wasn't for Whitewall, I'd be a dead man, and this after he saved my life a dozen times in Nam." Papaw had just told him a story

about the early days of Incoherent, a moment in time so far removed from today that it seemed eons ago.

"Why'd you name it Incoherent?" Papaw didn't have his own home. He had lived in the clubhouse for years, at least since Coralie moved out. Listening to stories, George had found out that transition had been less Papaw throwing her out, and more her moving out to be with a man she'd fallen for. That man had turned her loose after only a few months, at which time she'd migrated to Ollie's house and stayed.

Without a home, and never really having had one, it didn't seem odd to him that he'd been living here in the clubhouse for the past several months. After that first night, George hadn't lost any sleep over the changes in his life. In time, he had settled in like he'd been born into this huge extended family to which his grandfather had introduced him.

"Long story." Papaw laughed, and matching laughter came from near the bonfire. George turned to see one of Papaw's friends standing there. He knew most of the Incoherent members regardless of their chapter affiliation, but this stranger was from a different club altogether. Papaw's voice was spiked through with tolerant humor when he replied, "Shut it, old man. It's a long story, and you fuckin' know it."

"Yeah, but it's a rich one, and one well worth telling." The old guy's beard hung halfway down his belly, full and white, framing his teeth when he smiled as he was now. When he moved, George saw the back patch was a raggedy man, stick and a poke over his shoulder: Caddo Hobos. "Kid deserves to know you're a fuckin' hero, James."

"Another time, Michael." Papaw stood, stretching with a quiet groan and looked down into George's face. "Bed, young'un. Party's about to get loud." Leaning in, he told George quietly, "Lock your door tonight, son. Bagger's a friend, but we've strangers in our house. Incoherent'll keep you safe, but you do your part, too, yeah?"

That was one of the things he loved most about his grandfather. The man pulled no punches. He told it as it was, told it like you needed to hear it. This was him treating George like an adult. Giving reassurances that everything was the same, and the club would protect him, but just in case, "Under my pillow, Papaw."

"Good," Papaw nodded. "Just right, you gotta watch out for your own ass sometimes, too." He stood straight again, and George watched as his gaze swept the clearing, assessing and evaluating everything as if he were still leading men on a battlefield. "And, we'll never know when I'll need you to watch my back, George."

"I got you, Papaw." George's voice never wavered. "You need me. I got you."

"Know you do, son," Papaw looked to his friend. "Next generation, Michael. Standin' right here, this boy is my future. Couldn't ask for better."

"Keep him close, James, he's a good'un." An unfamiliar sound came from the other side of the bonfire, and both men came alert.

Papaw repeated himself, not taking his eyes off whatever it was he saw. "Night, George."

"Night." Without looking back, George took himself into the clubhouse, earning a few "goodnights" called from groups around the yard and backslaps from the men as he passed nearby. As he had every night since that first one, he slept deeply, secure in the knowledge that he was safe.

Chapter Three

Ralph, age sixteen

"You get the best pussy." Ralph laughed as he whispered this to George, leaning back to look at their dates sitting on the hood of his truck. They were waiting for him and George to get the snacks and make their way back down the aisle of cars parked on the back lines at the drive-in theater.

George slapped his shoulder and nodded, finishing paying the cute blonde at the window. She took a minute, scribbling something on the ticket before handing it to George. As they moved to the next window to wait for the food, Ralph looked at the piece of paper in George's hand, leaning over his shoulder to do so. "Shee-it, man. That's Sabrina's little sister. Tell me you ain't goin' back there?"

"How about I say I ain't goin' back there…again?" George's grin was sly, pulling his mouth sideways, and Ralph laughed hard. "Papaw'd have my ass if I fucked anyone in that family again. He said we're done with the Rotain's rulin' this parish. Judge lost his last election, so they'll be movin' soon anyways." Leaning his shoulder against the wall, George stared at him. "Tell me what you think about the club."

Incoherent. Something George was full-on certain about and Ralph was draggin' ass, pulling in last place as usual. "Man, I don't know. If it

were just ridin' bikes, that'd be one thing. They do a lot of shit, George. Not even a little bit legal." He looked around, verified no one was near enough to listen, and still lowered his voice to say, "Shit that needs doin', in some cases, but they do a lot of different shit."

"So? You do that same shit, but you're out there swinging on your own accord. At least club has patches at their back." George waited, then continued when Ralph didn't have anything to say in response. "I'm gonna do it. Next year, when I turn eighteen, Papaw said he'll let me prospect. Then I'll be IMC for true."

"You want it that bad, I don't understand. Why you waitin' if you're that sure?" Ralph heard the sounds of the movie starting up behind him, glanced over his shoulder at the enormous screen, seeing the wavering blue and green images were just fading away. Cartoons would be up next, plenty of time before the show. "Why not just join now?"

"Papaw wants me older. Wants me to be sure about everything. Said it gives me time to grow into my balls, learn what not to do with 'em." They both laughed at that because neither had been known to back down from a fight. And they hadn't lost in a long time; alone, or together, the George and Ralph team seemed unbeatable. "I can't wait, Ralph."

At the longing running through his friend's voice, Ralph made a decision. "Think he'd let me come in at the same time, or will he make me wait, too?" They were a year apart in age, but of a similar place in everything else. *Maybe in this, too.*

"Won't know if we don't ask," George shrugged, feigning indifference, but Ralph saw the glitter in his eyes, knowing it meant something to George that Ralph wanted to stick with his friend.

Their number blared over the speaker, and George was getting ready to move when Ralph stopped him. "We'd be brothers, finally." He stuck out his hand, wrapping his fingers around George's thumb, receiving the same grip in response. "Brothers for life, man."

"Brothers for life." George agreed, then grinned. "Now, let's grab our food, then go get some o' that pussy you were talkin' about. Did you see the titties on your girl? Pretty titties."

***

George, age eighteen

Hissing at the pain, George looked down at the tattoo artist's hands moving across the inside of his bicep. *My first tattoo*, he thought, without realizing he'd just promised himself more ink, even as he lay in the chair, rigid with pain.

He watched as the club-sponsored guy wiped away excess ink and oozing blood, revealing the lines and whirls of the marks left behind from his rattling gun. *Ride or Die*. As a biker's motto, it could mean so many different things. Riding was living, freedom and being in the wind all rolled into one. Ride or die could mean turning your back on the citizen world, leaving their rules and laws in the dust. In his case, it was a promise to Ralph, someone he considered his true brother.

The week before had seen them in a situation, and Ralph had once again proven beyond a single doubt that he had George's back. They'd been strolling up an alleyway over in Baton Rouge, working their way along the docks that lined the Mississippi River. One wrong turn and they wound up facing down half a dozen men, each looking meaner than the next.

There hadn't been any need for words between them, he and Ralph had moved as one, backs pressed together, protecting the other with their life. And together they had cleared the alley of all opponents. Each man presenting a different challenge, but one that they bested. Their hours spent sparring together paid off, and George had been surprised at the ease with which they dealt with the danger. In the end, he and Ralph were the only ones left standing, and when they walked out of that alley, it was with the confidence and understanding that together, they were so much stronger than they were alone.

Papaw heard later that one of the men died. Evidently had a heart condition, was taking blood thinners and Ralph's pounding of his head into the wall had him bleeding into his brain. George had determined he wouldn't be passing that knowledge on, would keep it to the grave because if Ralph knew, it would throw him off. He was set to be voted on this weekend, the officers all gathering around the table in the back room to see if they wanted to bring Ralph into the fold as a prospect. George didn't want anything to derail that, wanted Ralph to be where he was more than he'd expected. Only three months since George took up the prospect mantle, and he already knew Ralph would take to the life like he'd been born to it.

The artist slid his stool back, and George watched as his broad swipes with dampened gauze revealed the entirety of the tattoo George had picked from the front counter sketchbook. Embedded within a tangle of blood-tipped barbed wire were the words, Ride or Die. *For my brother*. Standing at the counter after paying, he was tucking his chained wallet into his pants and listening with only half an ear to the practiced aftercare jabber from the artist when the door behind him dinged, announcing a new customer. Out of habit, he moved, putting a wall at his back while he swung to see who was walking in.

A young man stood in the doorway, short sleeves showing a plethora of tattoos on his arms. George was studying them and was about to offer the guy a chin lift when he heard the artist's panicked voice saying, "Don't need no trouble, man."

George's gaze raised and focused on the massive pistol the gangster wannabe had in hand, watched as he flicked the end of the barrel at the room in general and demanded, "Gimme everything you got."

Oh, fuck no, George thought, moving on frantic instinct to duck behind the counter next to the cash register. *He's standing in my house. This is ours*, he thought, as only halfway committed to the action, he changed his mind and bent to pull his piece from his belt instead. Standing straight, George calmly leveled his gun at the kid. "You're

standin' in Incoherent's tat shop, dude. You wanna live? Turn the fuck around and walk. Step out like a man, because you don't know where you are. Guaran-damn-tee you don't want to buy this trouble."

"Fuck you," the guy said, not looking around as he tipped the barrel of his gun down towards the register. He ignored George, focusing on the artist when he ordered, "Empty the fuckin' thing."

"Dude," George said, reaching up with his off hand to pull the slide on his gun; his stomach churned, but he couldn't let this go unanswered. *My patch, my family*. That included the ones under their protection, like the tattoo guy who owned this shop. Incoherent got a rate break but didn't take any skim. Their role was to safeguard, and he'd damned sure do his part today. "You do not need the flash that bad." Sweat had broken out across his shoulders and back, he felt a stinging burn under the bandage, salt mixing with the still oozing blood. "Turn around."

The guy shifted, his eyes coming to George and in an instant, he saw it was a kid. Not a man but a kid decked out to look older, his eyes terrified and shining with tears. "I gotta. Gotta nut up. Man's gonna kill me if I don't." *This guy's younger than me. Maybe even younger than Ralph, and probably got no idea what he's doing*.

"Naw, kid," George drawled, trying to hold on to cool and keep things from spiraling out of control. "Don't matter who you're afraid of outside this shop, because in here? I'm gonna kill you if you do." He shrugged, the gun rock steady in his grip. "Needa turn the fuck around and walk away while you still can, man. I don't gotta nut up; I'm Incoherent, and you're in my house. You wanna walk away breathin',"—he leaned forward, the gun steady and on point—"then you need to walk the fuck away." He drew in a deep breath, then said, "Now."

Their gazes locked, the kid stared at him for a long minute before whirling and running out the door. As it squeaked and squealed on its way back to its place in the frame, he told the artist, "Call the house,

man. Let them know what's going down." The guy obediently picked up the phone and George was already on the move, catching the door and pushing it open wide, stepping from the chill of the shop into hell.

He was just in time to see what happened next. In time to experience it, really, because he was too close for comfort, caught in the blowback as a man not much older than the kid lifted his shortened over-and-under scattergun and pulled first one, then the second trigger, hitting the screaming kid square in the chest with each blast. Without thought, reacting on instinct, George lifted his gun, sighted, and squeezed the trigger twice, the first shot going wide as the shooter lunged for cover, George's second bullet clipping the man's arm.

Downed boy on the sidewalk was now silent and still. The bleeding man hunkered behind a car parked at the curb, yelling, but the words were incomprehensible through the ringing in George's ears. A growling sound penetrated and George shifted position to turn and look up the street, where he saw a vehicle approaching fast. Near where the guy was crouched out of sight, the lowered luxury sedan scarcely paused as its back door opened and closed, gunman escaping with help. *Motherfucker*. George stepped to the center of the street, lifted his gun again and pulled the trigger in rapid succession until he was out of bullets.

Fuck, he thought, watching as the sedan disappeared into the distance. Police sirens wailed from not too far away, and he heard the tattoo guy call with urgency in his voice, "George, you gotta get gone."

Tucking the gun into his waistband, he threw a leg over his bike parked one space away from where the kid lay bleeding. One glance at the sidewalk and George knew the boy'd bought it, so didn't bother to look beyond that. He also didn't acknowledge any of the bystanders beginning to filter out of the shops on either side of the tattoo parlor. They didn't matter. Only getting away before getting tagged did. Papaw would be way beyond pissed if George got picked up. Not only didn't he

have a license to drive anything, much less the bike, but the guns on his person would also be an automatic trip to Angola.

Two kicks later, his bike roared, and he shoved his toe on top of the shifter, pressing down. Twisting the throttle hard, the bike skidded sideways on the street as he gave it too much gas, then settled down. Toe to the bottom of the shifter, lifting, he twisted the throttle again, lifting. Jamming the brakes on so he could angle around the corner as he downshifted, gaining blocks of distance between him and whatever the cops would be wanting to know.

Shit happened, I dealt, he thought and then barked laughter he could hardly hear over the sound of the wind. *Coulda used Ralph today, but, he'll be in tomorrow, as in* in, *and we'll track this asshole down. Ride or die.*

***

PRINCESS

Face lifted to the star-riddled skies, the girl stepped in a small circle, toes of one foot planting near the arch of the other as she danced to the traditional music of the region. Zydeco music was raucous and lively, perfect for a distraction on a softly warm spring evening. The music was powering out of the windows of her uncle's house, so loud that if she had looked up, she could have seen the fabric of the speakers moving with the sound being projected into the backyard.

Eyes closed, she continued to move in her circle, knowing every inch of the ground she trod, unafraid of falling. Her lips moved to the words, mouthing phrases that only people living in the bayous truly understood. A seafood file gumbo was boiling on a nearby gas ring, rich scents rising from the huge stainless pot filled to the brim with the savory dish. Poke salad would round out the meal; the weed, tender and tasty now, bitter when later in the season. There would be crisp bacon crumbles and minced onion greens to mix in with hot grease and vinegar to make a dressing designed to partially cook the greens on the

diner's plate. *Wilted salad and file gumbo*, she thought, pausing her movement for a moment as the cassette tape advanced to the next song, silence hissing through the speakers.

"Hey." She heard a soft male voice nearby and opened her eyes to see a handsome boy, not much older than she was, standing at her side. Looking up, she watched as his smile hit his eyes, warming them and giving him an intense look she didn't know how to take. "You eatin' soon?"

Tipping her head to one side, she grinned at him. "Imma eatin' gumbo, don't know what soon is. Don't sound too tasty."

"Princess," her mother called from a seat near the back of the house. "Mind your words."

They'd known each other all their lives, and knowing how she would hate that correction the boy winced along with her. She flashed him a "thank you" smile before turning to answer her mother. "Yes, Mama." Looking at the boy again, she repeated herself, slightly changed, "I'll be eating gumbo. I've never heard of a dish called soon, but it doesn't sound very good."

He laughed aloud, and she took a breath as his face changed with the humor, a lock of hair falling over his forehead. Older than her by five years, he was turning off handsome, and when he smiled or laughed, she caught a glimpse of the man he would become. *Don't get stupid, gel. That age difference is huge*, she thought, turning away when the music began. Eyes closed, she tilted her chin up, trying to lose herself in the movements again. Those efforts were stymied when he reached out and gripped her hand. Flashing an annoyed look at him, she tugged but he refused to release her, so she eased closer to him and hissed, "Hey, let me go."

"Never," he said so softly she nearly had to read his lips. "Like you here, honey." At the affectionate words, she gave up her efforts to extricate her hand, allowing him to pull her even closer, his other hand

going to her hip. Steering her with their joined hands, he used his fingers on her waist to maintain the small distance between them. A moment later, he pushed at her, and with a grin she flew backwards, twisting and turning at the end of his arm, twirling back in as he pulled, and they danced.

Too soon the music stopped, and she looked up into his face, smiling. "That was fun." It was. He had made the dance relaxed and sweet, moving them away from weird and back to comfortable. *Always my friend.* "Thanks."

"My pleasure," he said, his voice low and rough. An expression swept across his features, another one she didn't recognize, but it looked both pained and angry. Before she could ask the boy what was wrong, she heard her uncle calling her from across the yard, and she turned to look at him.

"Get your ass over here, gel. Want to talk to you about that covered monstrosity in my driveway." She stuck out her tongue, knowing he was teasing. The classic sedan that had been parked in front of his garage as long as she could remember was his baby. He didn't want to talk to her as much as he wanted an audience willing to listen to the stories about the car. Then, surprising her, lifting his eyes to the boy, her uncle spoke to her again, "Princess, I'm serious, hon. Get over here. You all need to learn when it's time to move."

"I'll be right back," she said, looking up at the boy.

"No, you won't." His quiet response was confusing, and she glanced at him over her shoulder, already on her way to where her uncle stood. He looked disappointed and gave her a half wave as he turned his back to her.

Then she was in the middle of the small knot of grown men standing near her uncle, each of them wearing a vest with the same patch on the back. For the next two hours, she bantered with them, listening to their stories and turning some of those stories back on them, drawing

laughter with each quip. A favored child, the men in the club all treated her like glass, but lately she'd found she wanted more from them. She knew her uncle had shown her something she could never have because she was a girl. The club was all about brotherhood, and being there for the men who shared the patch with you. She could never be that, but she could at least have this, a natural kind of camaraderie with the men.

She looked for the boy after they'd eaten, but he was gone from where they'd stood. Grass all around the bonfire had been beaten flat with stamping feet, but he wasn't dancing anymore, either. She scanned the crowd, still not seeing him.

A little while ago, she had seen her uncle talking to the boy across the yard, hand on the young man's shoulder, and whatever their topic had been, the conversation had looked serious. Turning to her uncle, she asked, "Did you see where he went?"

"Need to learn when it's time to leave things alone, honey." He shook his head, wrapping his arm around her shoulders and turning her with him. Pacing towards the bonfire, he put her back into her spot from before. "Dance, hon. Don't worry about him. Just dance. He'll sort himself out."

Glancing around the yard again, still not finding the boy, she looked up at her uncle and nodded. Eyes closed, she listened to the music and found they'd moved on from Zydeco to southern rock. *I like this, too*, she thought, feeling the cushioning give of soft earth under her feet when she stomped hard. *I like a lotta things*. The boy's face flashed through her head, and then her next thought was, *Eighteen isn't a boy. He's a man*.

He's a man, she thought. *He's a man, and he likes me*. Her grin, this time, was small, private, and pleased. *I could like him, too*.

Chapter Four

TWISTED, AGE TWENTY-THREE

Tossing his cards onto the pile of cash and markers on the table, Po'Boy laughed when he said, "I'm out, brother. You either got the best hand in the world, or the worst, and I can't fuckin' tell. Either way, I'm fucked, so I'm out."

Twisted smirked, his head tipping back, teasingly flashing his cards. "Wanna see my hand, brother?"

"Fuck no." Po'Boy pushed the pile of winnings across the table towards Twisted, laughing harder when some of the money and papers fluttered to the floor. "You're a rat bastard, you know that?"

"Yeah," Twisted said fondly, pausing in his efforts to scrape things together. "Ralph," he said, hoping the other man understood the emotion behind his words, "fucking pleased you chose to come on this journey with me, brother."

Ralph Lewis, Po'Boy, shook his head. "Wouldn't have it any other way, George."

Nearly seven years ago, Papaw had come to the whorehouse and torn the blinders off George's eyes, forcing him to see the layers of

wrongness that surrounded him. How his mother didn't take the part a parent should, not protecting him from anything. Loved him in her way, but her way was so far off the beaten track, sane folks couldn't see her from where they stood.

He and his grandfather had tried several times to pull Freddy out of the mess at the whorehouse, but his younger brother was resistant. And, even from the outside, it was clear that his life was very different than what George had experienced. The favored son, Freddy had cars and flash to toss around, money earned by the women of the house on their knees and backs, and him uncaring. Using and spending, and going back to the well for more.

At eighteen, George had patched into the club as a prospect, proud as fuck of the emblem on his back from day one. It had taken him the two intervening years to convince his grandfather he knew what he wanted. Two years of listening to stories about the brotherhood until the desire to belong was like a living thing in his gut. Two years of seeing how each man supported the whole and wanting to have that even more than he wanted to breathe. Two years of preparing and training for that moment when he would finally belong.

Prospect patch pinned into place by Whitewall, his grandfather's second and the vice-president of the club, George was warned from the get-go that his path would be harder than any other prospect because no member would be willing to give an inch just because of who he was. It had been a fucking miserable ten months, but he'd done it. Done everything asked. Clubhouse cleanup after parties, scrubbing up puke and piss, and worse. Done to breed deep respect for the house, not tasked as punishment and he got that, an understanding that helped to lighten the load.

Each thing asked of him he approached the same way, twisting it in his head until he could see the good. He became whatever his brothers needed. If a member needed someone to ride in the back of a truck to help hold a bike upright, George was your man. In the rain. During a

thunderstorm. With a leaky bucket of mudbugs beside his ass. It didn't matter. None of it mattered, because George would be there. Doing it not to brown-nose, but because it showed he had that member's back in anything. Wanting the brotherhood that came right alongside the responsibility to assist wherever possible.

Incoherent's normal prospect period was a year and a day, with that last day promised to be hell on earth. Papaw pushed for the full time served, but his own officers overruled him, making it their choice to bring George into the fold early. George hadn't understood what was up when Whitewall had called him into the big room behind the bar during what should have been an officers-only meeting.

The room was huge. Vaulted ceilings lifted overhead, no rooms above so less chance of listening ears. The high ceilings meant they had room to install fans in here, and had, George balancing at the top of a wobbly ladder while wielding an electric drill and screwdriver. Comfort for the people in the room meant they could spend less time thinking about the heat, and more time applied to solving problems and issues within the club. A willing service, from him to the patch holders, flesh dues paid eagerly.

Whitewall called him in, but didn't give him a reason or a task, so George waited, standing alongside the door, shoulders to the wall, trying hard to ignore the arguments flowing back and forth across the table. Highest ranking members at the national level, the men were discussing the merits of raising their member dues. As someone voiced an especially lame argument for the increase, George couldn't help the shifting expression on his face. Startled when his Papaw barked his name, he ripped his gaze from the floor in front of his boots to lock onto the old man's face.

"George. You got somewhat to say, boy?"

"No, sir." The honorific of brother didn't sit right in his mouth when it was directed to his grandfather, not after the two years just past, where

he'd found what an excellent mentor the man made. Wise and patient, his grandfather could show a person the way of things without saying a word, leading them from lesson to lesson and letting them drink their fill from each along the way. He was always willing to give a body time to consider, time to distill those lessons, letting them settle deep inside where the teachings could be found as needed, waves of wisdom washing over the shores of their soul.

"Spit it out, George." Now every set of eyes in the room was trained on him, and sweat prickled along his shoulders, down his back, slicking his forehead.

Fuck. *"With respect, Prez, I don't have a place in this room for this discussion." He could and did call Papaw by his title. Could and did call him Jimbo on occasion. Just couldn't pull a brother out of himself for that man, because Papaw had come to mean so much more.*

Lip lifted, Papaw slipped the national officer mantle into place, changing from easygoing older man to the most dangerous threat in the whole fucking room, and that room filled to the brim with intimidating men. The Incoherent MC national president stood, pushing up from the chair, palms flat on the battered table in front of him. "Brother," this word growled deliberately, "you need to rethink what you believe respect is if you intend to give me a fucking non-answer to a fucking straight-on question. Now,"—he leaned forward, muscles in his arms bulging and rippling with the movement—"I asked you to spit out what you were thinking." He straightened. "We were talking about a dues increase, and you have somewhat to say. Spit it out."

"It's a mistake," George said straightaway. There was no more beating around the bush. That wasn't respectful, not in the face of the demand laid upon him. "If we need more money, there are other ways to raise it. Ways to bring in flash without breakin' our brothers' backs. If we need money, raising dues by five or ten dollars each month won't give us what we need. The amount we'd have to increase could push it to a decision time for some members. Men with wives and kids. Got school

comin' up and those families needing clothes and supplies, lunch money. Then there's hurricane season upon us, and storms brewin' every direction." There were three named storms churning in the Atlantic and Gulf right then. "Men will be lookin' to tide themselves over, not boost the club for unknown reasons." None of the men tonight had mentioned why they needed more money, just talked about it as if it were a foregone conclusion.

"What other ways?" That was Scot, their sargent at arms.

George turned his head, scanning all the men in the room. In for a penny, in for a pound. *"Other clubs have cash-heavy businesses."*

"Whorehouses," his grandfather said derisively.

"Strip clubs, private casinos if they carry tribal under their cuts. Bars. Tattoo parlors. Pawn shops. Cash business is good for a lot of reasons." George knew he was right, and this conviction gave him courage. "Doesn't have to be skin, no way. But yeah, whorehouses can be lucrative to run, Prez."

"Who'd run it?" Dropsie spoke up for the first time; he was Incoherent's road captain.

Uncertain for a moment if the question was directed to him, George waited for a beat before responding. "T-Bone and Kodiak would be my choice. Both are smooth talkers, think fast on their feet, and they'll do well with the necessary rub for the boys in blue. Pretty enough the women will be happy to have them around. And still badass enough to keep customers in line." He mentioned two full members, not officers, but his reasoning was sound, and he knew it, no disrespect intended for any man in this room.

Whitewall scooted his chair back and stood, leaning over facing Papaw, fists knuckled into the table. "Still think I'm fulla shit, Prez?" That question didn't make any sense unless Whitewall had already suggested the business route, but he hadn't spoken up during any part of the

discussion, so that was unlikely. Which meant his topic change wasn't to do with that, but with what else he'd introduced to the room. Me.

"Sixty-two days ain't much to wait, White." Papaw didn't look at George, just stared at Whitewall. Sixty-two days happened to be the time remaining on his prospect period if everything went well and these men wanted him to share in their brotherhood. Shit.

"Is if it's unneeded. Is if things are so right even a child can see the rightness." Fuck. *He knew he was one of the youngest prospects the Incoherent had patched, didn't know Whitewall thought him a child. "Man standing in front of you is righteous. You know it, you're just afeared of showing favoritism, and we love that. Love that you wanted shit to go hard for the boy. Prove the mettle you saw and told us about, making us all proud of him as if we were his fathers. Man don't have a father. Let us give him brothers. Give him a family he needs. And we need him, Jimbo. Dju hear how he twisted that shit to show us the underlying strength of his ideas? Smart motherfucker, we need him at the table."*

Papaw made a noise at that, and Whitewall lifted one hand, patting the air. "I know, that ain't for today. But let us put a foot forward. Begin as you intend to continue." The emphasis on this phrase wasn't lost on George, but he didn't understand the significance until Whitewall went on, "Ain't that what you said when you and I were stuck in-country, sitting in the heat, watching our toes start to rot from the wet and shit? Begin as you intend to continue, and you'll right the boat every time."

George watched as Whitewall stood silent, fists to hips, staring across the table at the man he'd known since they were young kids playing in the canal, teasing little girls on the playground. George had heard more than a handful of stories about their growing up together, signing up together, serving together, and then starting this club together. Brothers for life. Ride or die.

The room was silent, three men on their feet, the rest seated in various poses, attentively studying the actors in this scene. With a heavy sigh, Papaw nodded once, and Whitewall's head came up, chin lifting in response. These men knew each other so well, words weren't required. Without turning around, Whitewall spoke to George. "Take off your cut, George."

Fuck. *"Can't do that, veep." He backed up, putting his back to the wall, protecting the colors on his vest. They didn't want him. He swallowed hard, fighting back emotions.* They don't want me. *"Won't." After everything Whitewall said today, and then they didn't even want him anyhow. He crouched slightly, prepared for a fight. "Nuh-uh. No, sir. You want my colors, you're gonna have to take 'em from me."*

"What?" The barked question held laughter as Whitewall's head swung his way. "No, son. Not like that." He reached out and laid his hand on a piece of fabric George hadn't noticed. A foot long, curving, ends arching upward, the letters sewn into the fabric spelled out **Mother**. *The main chapter of the club was called the mother chapter, where the rest had been birthed from. Mother was an honor few men had, even the ones assigned here mostly had the city, or at most city and state, not the designation. "You feel you need a beat down before you sew this thing in place, well, hell yeah. That we can provide." Laughter came from the men, who one at a time pushed to their feet. "But, that ain't our intention, son."*

That night had seen a celebration in the clubhouse that rivaled anything Ollie ever thought to throw. Worn leather on his back held stiff by the unbroken bottom rocker, George accepted backslaps, shoulder punches, and gripping shakes that carried much more emotion than the few words uttered. Pussy falling over themselves to fall on his dick, he got sucked off twice before he even made it to bed with a third chick.

It all fell to shit the next morning. That third chick'd thought to work her way up the club, and abandoned the bed of the newest member for

an available and willing officer as George slept. Then she walked out of Scot's room and stumbled into the man's ole lady.

Caterwauling and squalling the two women set at each other, rolling up and down the hallway. Members stood in the doors to their rooms, woken by the mess. Sleepy and pissed off, George stood watching until Whitewall shoved him in the back, sending him stumbling towards the women with a brusque, "Clean up your shit, brother." Even with the swell of emotion the word gave him, he still eyed his duty with distaste. Snot and blood, nails flying everywhere, shirts ripped and showing skin—not how he'd wanted to spend the morning.

Gained his name at the end of it, when he'd had Scot's ole lady suckin' his dick while the man shoved his own cock down the party doll's throat. Eyes closed, chin lifted, Scot had been steadily gagging the bitch when he abruptly stilled, looking at George. Watching his own ole lady's head bobbing over George's lap, Scot laughed aloud, the edges of his humor not resting easily in the room. Fingers still twined in the bitch's hair, he asked, "How in the hell did we get here, George?"

"No fuckin' idea, brother." And he didn't, not for sure, but something that could have been damaging had worked out not so badly for him.

"Twisted your way through the shit, came out the other side smelling like a rose." Scot thrust once, twice, then snarled down at the woman, "Mind your fuckin' teeth, bitch." Looking back up at George, he said, "Twisted that shit, bent it around to where you needed it to be." He gestured to his woman, "Got the good shit wrapped around your cock." Fisting a hand in her hair, he pulled the bitch off him, shoving her around until George had to look at her. "Twisted your way away from this shitty piece of ass. You're twisted in the right way, brother."

Not the worst way it could have ended up, but he learned a harsh lesson that night. Separating the two women, neither of them mattering to him, he didn't give a fuck who ended bloody. Neither was a bitch he wanted to be accountable for, and he'd determined right there that he

would not be bringing pussy back to his room, to his bed, ever. Not ever again. And, he hadn't since. He'd fuck 'em in the party rooms in the front of the building, fuck 'em outside in the yard of the compound, but his room was his, untainted by pussy. He wouldn't ever be putting his patch brothers into a position to have to clear his shit with pussy, or with anything. He was determined at that moment to be the kind of brother they'd want at their backs. Want at their sides. Someone they deemed worth the effort, someone they understood would hold the line for them. Die for them.

Now sitting here with Po'Boy, he reckoned all the time and effort worth it. "Worth every penny of anything we have to pay," he muttered.

"You know it, brother." Po'Boy stood, stretching his arms over his head, reaching for the ceiling with every muscle tensed. There was a lot of mass to the man because he spent a fuckton of time in the backyard hauling on the makeshift weights they'd stashed there a few years ago. No time for a gym, even if there'd been money for it, so they made do to get what they needed. Honing their bodies for service to the club. "We goin' to Trudette's tonight, Twisted?"

A club favorite, Trudette's was a local bar; biker-friendly, meaning they didn't give you shit about wearing colors inside. Good food, cute barkeeps, rutted-as-hell dirt and gravel parking lot, but a decent place to spend a couple of hours. "Yeah, sounds good."

Half a dozen brothers trailed them into the lot, and Twisted sat straight and proud on his bobber, leading the way as the ranking club member among them. Only five years in, and not an officer yet, but he and Papaw had talked about the next church being the right time for Scot to step down. His health wasn't good; he was spending more time in the VA than at home with his ole lady, so SAA was a definite in Twisted's future.

Another reason he spent hours working those weights, doing side-to-side pull-ups, hanging sit-ups, and ran five miles nearly every day. When his club needed him to stop trouble, it wouldn't matter he wasn't big and bulky like Papaw or Po'Boy because he had his shit together in a way that few men would mistake. It helped stop shit before it even started. When he put the SAA patch on his chest, he'd need that sway even more.

Backing his idling bike into a spot at the edge of the gravel lot, he scanned the patron's vehicles and grinned. "Jimbo's here," he called to Po'Boy, getting a distracted nod in response as the man backed in next to him. Turning to see what his friend was looking at Twisted scowled. "Shit," he muttered, recognizing the bitch's car.

Sabrina hadn't aged well and hadn't gotten any sweeter than she was back in school. Twisted had dropped out his junior year, not seeing the need for a diploma in his future and having about a dozen more things to do in a day than he had time for with classes. Po'Boy had finished, which was good. Meant he had the head on him to help out with the various businesses the club dipped their toes into. Sabrina had gone to Tulane for secondary but never got past being tossed over for her younger sister. Trudette's wasn't her typical kind of watering hole, so just her being here gave Twisted a sour feeling in his stomach because the bitch held a mean grudge.

"Wanna leave, boss?" Po'Boy offered him an easy out, telling him his stare at her car had been noted, but Twisted shook his head.

"Jimbo's here, need to talk to him anyway. We'll just steer clear of the pussy." Nods from the men already off their bikes and waiting. Twisted stood up, swinging his leg over the seat. "Pretty packed in there. Might need to vacate some tables." More nods of understanding. If there weren't enough seats for them around where Jimbo was holding court, they'd turn folks out of their chairs, dumping asses on the floor if need be.

He continued, "Gonna be colors in there. Watch your backs until we scope the club." There were a dozen bikes at the other end of the lot, not ones he recognized, which meant not Incoherent and maybe not friendly. Or at least not a club near enough to have frequent contact. The only real rivals they had were still the Vicar's Wrath, but that didn't mean they wouldn't see shit from other bikers, even if they were ones just rolling through on a coastline ride. Shit happened. A man just had to be prepared to shovel as much shit back as got thrown at them, to keep things evened up.

Inside, the atmosphere was heavier than Twisted expected, but he ignored that and arrowed straight to where Jimbo sat with half a dozen Incoherent members in two booths near the back corner. With a jerk of his head, Po'Boy started the process of clearing two tables in front of the booths while Twisted walked to his grandfather, arm out in greeting.

Hearing one word, "Son," rocked him on his heels because his Papaw didn't pull that out except in private, so him using it now meant there was family business to deal with on top of whatever club business had the other men seated with him looking mad as wet hornets.

"Freddy's here, boy." Twisted schooled his face to impassivity, not wanting to give his feelings away. Freddy had turned eighteen recently, celebrated in style in the cathouse from what Twisted had heard. Times had changed in the seven years he'd been with Papaw. Clientele had changed. Ollie had stroked out, was warehoused in an old folks' home wearing diapers, which meant his Mama was in charge at the house now, and she didn't have a mind to whose money she took. So that changing clientele meant trouble for her a lot of weekends, as the Mexican green river flowed their direction, sweet smoke and other things replacing the harsher cigarettes in the parlor. Stoned men led to soft dicks, which resulted in further pissed off. Stoned girls meant bad judgment calls. Freddy didn't have it in him to be the enforcer the teenaged Twisted had been, and Mama's latest fuck toy wouldn't ever step up. It meant the girls weren't covered, most of the time, which they didn't like.

Discontent in the girls led to a turnover, which pissed off regulars. In the basic scheme of things, Mama was running the cathouse into the ground, riding that bitch down along the way. It sometimes made him sad to remember the opulence and splendor that Ollie offered, and see it brought low, women he remembered fondly turned into nothing better than two-bit whores.

Freddy being here wasn't trouble by itself, but Papaw's demeanor led him to believe that whoever Freddy was with might be. "Yeah?" He waited a beat, but nothing was forthcoming, so he asked, "So?"

"He's with a catty bitch." Twisted felt his mouth shift sideways, knowing what he'd see when he turned around. Sure enough, there was Freddy, in a booth near the door, sucking face with bitchy Sabrina. "Been goin' at her in the booth, figure they'll be headed out to get his hose siphoned soon. Hold your shit, brother."

Sabrina had a knack for getting under his skin, but he could keep cool for his brothers and nodded firmly, reassuring Papaw that the message was received. Twisted's arm was bumped from behind; he turned to see a draft beer, water dewing on the sides of the glass. With a muttered "Thanks," he accepted the offering and turned to face Papaw, giving the room his back, knowing that every man wearing their club patch would watch out for him. Gaze trained on his grandfather, he asked, "Who else is here? Saw bikes on the lot. We got goodness or trouble?" The irritation flashing across Papaw's face wasn't reassuring.

"VW, but it's an unannounced core from the 9th, not Leswayne's crew, unknown." So, Vicar's Wrath had rolled into their territory without a call. The bikers weren't from the Metairie chapter, which meant no immediate beef, but, even within the relatively small area within the bar, they hadn't made an approach to offer respect, leaving their intentions unknown for now. "They roll out without recognition, I'll place a call to Ragman, clear up any misunderstandings about boundaries." Ragman was Leswayne's son, someone Twisted hadn't met yet, but heard stories about.

"Sounds like a plan," he said, nodding. Twenty minutes passed, talk shifting around the group about upcoming runs and events, along with various kinds of other surface business. Out in the open like this was never the place for any essential club dealings, and every man knew it. They all worked at keeping the topics as light and cryptic as if they had ears under every chair.

"Watch your back, brother." Po'Boy's mutter came from beside him, and he turned to see an obviously drunk Freddy stumbling their direction, arm slung around Sabrina's neck.

"Fuckin' shit," Twisted said, knowing his lip curled at the sight. "Why can't shit just not hit the fan once in a while?"

"When the shit hits the fan, the fans start shitting." Po'Boy laughed at his own quip. "When the fit hits the shan, the shine gets blurry."

He turned to look at his friend, laughing. "What in the hell does that even mean, brother?"

"So, he's your brother now?" These slurred words were a blow he hadn't expected, the tone a whining echo of long ago days at Ollie's. "Blood ain't good enough for you?"

He let his eyes sink closed for a moment, then sucked in air through his nose, shifting to look at Freddy. They were about the same height, but Freddy carried more bulk than Twisted. Not a lot, Freddy wasn't fat, not by a far reach, but he was thicker through the middle, his shirt fitting snug around his stomach rather than his chest.

"Hey, Fred." Twisted offered this greeting quietly, not sure where his brother wanted to take this conversation, never sure anymore. Half the time they ended in silence and the other half there was shouting. He knew the club wouldn't want trouble brought to their table, brother and grandson or not, so he was preparing to walk outside with his brother when the sounds started.

Heard over the pounding volume of the jukebox, they were distinctive. No one would mistake them for anything other than what they were.

Pop. Pop. Pop. Outside, from what sounded like a distance, gunfire raced up the road alongside the growing rumble of bikes headed towards the bar. *Pop.*

Hand to his back, he pulled his pistol out and let gravity draw it down alongside his thigh. A careful thumb pushed at the safety while his eyes scanned what he could see of the parking lot. Lights were glaring, shining up and across the front of the bar as forty or fifty bikes raced into the lot, dust flying up around them, swirling, and obscuring details. Half the headlights abruptly turned off, while half stayed shining, and he could see dark forms moving through the shadows and lights, approaching the bar at a run.

"Oh my God." This scream came from the bar area and Twisted half turned, keeping an eye on the front entrance but looking towards the swinging doors leading to the kitchen. He was just in time to see the owner of the bar staggering through, hand to his neck, and a flood of red gushing between his fingers.

Before the batwing door could complete the return swing that would close it, the surface was hit from behind and shoved wide, three men pouring through. The leader wore a leather vest and had a machete in one hand, the signature weapon of the Vicar's MC. The blade whirled around his wrist, held there by a leather strap. The bartender who had screamed ran towards the injured man, who had landed on the floor, flat on his back, blood in dark puddles surrounding his shoulders. A split second later, the big knife connected, sliding through flesh as if it were butter. A section of her face flew away, white bone exposed in its wake, teeth sheared off and broken, then all that empty filling with red as she landed on top of the body in the aisle behind the bar, her shriek cut brutally short.

With a cry of anger and outrage, Twisted leaped forwards, lifting the gun. Before he could fire, an explosive blast came from the front of the bar, the concussive wave taking many of the nearby men off their feet and throwing them onto the floor. Glass in two of the windows broke, shattering and scattering the width of the room, raining down on everyone. Bits of burning paper drifted through the air, adding to the acrid smell from the blast. Deafened and disoriented for a moment, Twisted dove for cover behind one of the overturned tables.

It was from that position that he saw his world torn apart; watched as blood and flesh were ripped from bodies of men he called brother, from family. Through it all, Fred stood and watched, fucking watched with a shocked expression as everything went down around him. Untouched by splatter or blowback, he stood there, arm around the neck of the woman beside him, a woman with a wicked smile on her face, one that said she had secret knowledge. One that showed she had no fear, even standing in the middle of a raging firefight.

Gun an extension of his arm, Twisted lifted and fired, then fired again. Lining up shot after shot, he worked to take out the men from the kitchen first, then began targeting the crew now trying to beat a fast retreat.

Blood mixed with broken glass to cover the floor, making the black and white tile slick and treacherous. That uncertain surface taking the feet out from under a man who held a shotgun to his shoulder, the recoil from a blast causing a stumble that turned into a slip and fall, his skull bouncing off the floor while the gun landed near the door. Twisted climbed to his feet and, in a crouch, ran to the back wall, boots leaving a bloody path of footprints behind him. Ass to the floor, he got back down, propping his elbows on his bent knees, pulling the trigger until there was nothing left to fire with, or at.

Ringing silence settled onto the building, ears echoing the sounds that had so recently filled the air. That silence was broken by the barely-heard wheezing breaths of the injured, and the louder cries of shock

and fear escaping from the citizens, men and women forced to watch. A burst of static, then the surreal sound of a rock anthem flung itself from the speakers on either end of the room, the words screaming through and between the people standing around in shock.

The grating scrape of a boot sole on the glass-strewn floor drew his attention, and he turned to see Fred staring at him. He was alone; Sabrina had fled in the chaos. "Go, Fred. Get out," George shouted, seeing understanding dawn on his brother's face. With a nod, Fred carefully walked towards the door, all the weaving drunk having left him, his steps now steady and straight, arrow-true as if he waltzed through the grocery store instead of pacing between the lakes and rivers of blood covering the floor.

"George." He thought he heard Papaw, but the voice was tormented and hoarse, as unlike Papaw's gruff warmth as anything he could imagine. At sixteen, he'd found the person he wanted to be, seeing it every time he watched as his grandfather dealt with anything. Problem or goodness, Papaw handled it all with care, the anger of his youth having burned out when he buried his wife and son. Turning, Twisted scanned the men still standing, seeing Po'Boy with a hand to his upper arm, blood running over his knuckles. "Son."

Whitewall stood propping the outer door wide and through that opening, Twisted heard the roaring of bike engines, then the noise dissipated as the bikes moved away. Whitewall was nearly as good a mentor as Papaw, his job to balance the hard line the national president sometimes had to walk. "George." Whitewall stayed put, attentively watching out the door, so Twisted knew something else was going down in the lot, something worthy of attention, that attention something he didn't have time to pay right now. He turned away, trusting their veep to have everyone's back. "Twisted."

Scot was seated on the floor near the booth, a dazed look on his face, fingering a hole in the front of his vest. Twisted watched as Scot pulled the garment away from his chest, exposing a growing red patch

on the shirt underneath. Wordlessly, he lifted a hand, stroking the crimson mark, bringing his hand away and staring at his stained fingertips.

Half underneath the table was Papaw, head torqued around at an uncomfortable angle, wedged up against the bottom of one seat. On hands and knees, Twisted crawled, uncaring of cuts received, focused on traversing the distance as fast as he could. Shock seemed to stretch time, so it felt like he traveled miles in this fashion, aging and near dying before he reached Papaw's side. Eyes open and staring, Papaw was lying still. Not a sound, not a gurgle, not a breath.

From the blood and matter splattered across the seats and underside of the table, Twisted knew what he'd find when he lifted his grandfather into his lap, arranging the man's loose limbs with care. Cradling the ruined head in his hands, he was shocked at the sounds filling the bar now. Rising and falling, there was a keening cry that snaked through the crowd. The sound of pain repulsed any advance from the gawkers, denying access to the few who thought to ogle the fallen, making their continued presence abhorrent, even to themselves.

"Kill the fuckin' juke," he heard Po'Boy shout and a moment later, the undertones of music ended, but the wailing continued. "Twisted." Definitely not Papaw's voice, and he knew what he'd heard before couldn't have been either. Just his mind working overtime to make sense of the commotion surrounding them. "Twisted." This came from Po'Boy, and Twisted took a breath as a hand gripped his shoulder. "We gotta go, brother." Shaking his head, denying the demand, he remained where he was, cradling his grandfather. "Brother, we can't be here."

Absently, he noticed the sound had stopped, and knew logically it had been him, the burning in his throat testimony to the force of emotions churning through him. Looking up, he saw Scot had fallen to his back, watched as one of their members crouched, one hand sliding to cover the old man's eyes. Whitewall had his gun out, keeping the

mass of patrons pinned to the back wall of the bar, away from where the Incoherent bodies lay, but there were bodies back by that wall, too.

He glanced around, seeing the five behind the bar, knowing in addition to the three he'd dropped there, he had six more potential convictions scattered around the room. *Self-defense, or manslaughter?* Shaking his head, he looked up at Po'Boy. "Where we goin'?"

"Fuck, man. You tell us. We just can't be here when the po-po come, brother." Po'Boy had released the grip on his wounded shoulder, the flow of blood slowing. "Got a slug to dig out of me, another six of us who can ride. That's eight, counting you and me. Some of us got family close. We can go to ground, huddle up with them."

Twisted knew they had to be gone to avoid interaction with the police. Unwritten as a rule, it still ruled. Nodding, he scanned the area again. One breath in, then out, and he was dialed in, running it through his head, knowing step-by-step what came next. Lessons learned from stories passed down by the men he looked up to.

"Arrange and cover." They wouldn't be leaving their fallen for long, and even for a short separation, he would not allow them to be left disrespectfully. First order of business was respect for the dead. He eased Papaw off his legs, sliding him gently to the floor. Twisted put an open hand up and didn't even look to see who threw the tablecloth to him. He just gripped the fabric when it hit his open palm. Flipping it out, letting it bell through the air, he heard a half-dozen others doing the same. Crisp, clean fabric settling over their dead; starched white rapidly turning splotchy, stained with the spilled blood.

"Wipe and drop 'em." Every man with an Incoherent patch immediately did as ordered, pulling bar rags from behind the counter and tossing them to each other, or grabbing bandanas from the fallen, using the fabric to wipe down the pieces they'd fired. Leaving the guns meant one less search risk, but there were other ways for prints to remain. "Pop the clips. We'll take rounds with us." Cartridges weren't

traceable, so many made in a single batch, thousands at a time. Those batches sold in huge stores to a vast array of customers. "Grab the casings, too." Citizens purchased recreational ammunition, as well as men like him. But those bitches held prints, and a smart man didn't leave easy info behind. Two men bent at the waist, their fingers gathering up the spent casings.

"Go ahead and let 'em roll." That order was for Whitewall, and Twisted watched as the man stepped out of the doorway, waving his pistol at the crowd, urging the silent sheep into movement. Whitewall barely managed to get out of their way as the men and women stampeded to the parking lot, piling into cars and trucks, uncaring of the bumper strikes against parked vehicles on their speeding way out to the road, giving all the bikes a wide berth. The other club that had been on that side of the room still stood. Shoulder to shoulder, they had no bodies at their feet. A piece gripped in each hand, one of the men stepped forwards, tipping his head towards where Twisted knelt on the floor. Not understanding the silent communication, Twisted barked a question at the man, "What?"

"Ain't my gig, man." Hand sweeping wide to indicate the entirety of the clusterfuck surrounding them. "You're gonna find the patches on those vests behind and in front of the bar aren't official." *Fuck*. That meant the Vicar's Wrath patches he'd seen on the fallen didn't indicate real members. "Name's Pony, and it appears someone's lookin' to stir a war, didn't expect to find me and my boys here." Someone was drawing false trails in the sand, trying to lead the waters to a polluted pond. Pony continued, verifying Twisted's thoughts, "I'm Vicar's Wrath, man. SAA for 9th, and I'm tellin' you, this ain't VWMC business."

A single nod to indicate he heard and understood released the man and the group at his back. Twisted watched as they made their way to the door and through it. Bike engines turned over outside, and headlights swept the woods at the edges of the parking lot. Then the engine noise diminished, fading to nothing.

"We ready?" He directed that to Po'Boy, who glanced at the men, and then nodded to Twisted. He looked down at Papaw, then around the room at the other covered bodies. Incoherent wasn't huge. Not by a long shot. As an entire club, they carried about fifty full members and no more than five prospects at any given time. Losing seven, with three of those dead being officers at the national level, was a hit that would stagger the club.

"Y'all see where Fred went?" Nothing about the bitch's attitude rang true. She had been expecting this, had kept his brother here for a while with her mouth. Waiting around until Twisted showed, then within fifteen minutes of him walking through the door, she was strolling out, leaving blood and bone and a very confused Fred in her wake. "Bitch that was with him, I want her."

"Got a name?" That came from a Picayune member, and Twisted looked at the men carefully, marking the different chapters. Picayune, Hammond, Lake Charles, Baton Rouge, all men he knew from joint runs and parties, the wisdom of Papaw finally exposed, because in making those things mandatory, he'd ensured Twisted had brothers, no matter the house.

"Sabrina Rotain. Bitch is from Mandeville." With a jerk of his chin, he pulled all the men towards the doors with him. "But, that's gonna have to be for later. Mandeville, however, is where we're headed now. Let's split thirds, meet up at the house there." Nods from all sides, and behind him he heard Whitewall assigning rides. He knew without listening that he and Po'Boy would be riding with Whitewall, running protection for their veep, the man who would probably be their new president. They had three voids to fill: president, enforcer, and sargent at arms. *Fuck*. So much wisdom and knowledge lost in minutes, gone. Wiped off the earth, their lives snuffed out, leaving behind only blood already drying to maroon streaks on the dirty floor. Straddling his bike, he unstrapped his lid from its place hanging on the handlebars, not aware he'd lost himself in thought until he felt a hand settle carefully on his shoulder. Looking up, he found Whitewall staring at him.

"You cool, brother?" The only question that mattered couldn't be asked, not here, and while he wanted to howl at the heavens because he had just lost the only family member who ever gave a shit about him, he couldn't do that, either. So he gave the only answer he could.

"I'm cool." Quick, jerking movements secured the helmet on his head, a shift of his shoulder unseated the hand while Whitewall stared at him another moment, then moved to his own bike. In less than two minutes, they were on the road. As the first group to pull out of the lot they went left, and Twisted watched in his mirror as the next group turned right, and saw the final group cross the highway to head straight up a country road.

***

"We got coverage." That was intended to be reassuring, and coming from Dropsie, it should have been, but Whitewall evidently wasn't feeling enough of it because his response demanded more.

"Tell me what kind of coverage, and who." Coverage meant they had at least one man inside the investigation of the shootout at the bar. Coverage said greased palms and passing envelopes, powerful men in their pocket, and their asses shielded in the best way possible.

"Boss, you know we can't talk names here." No one was surprised that the president tag had been withheld so far. That could only be voted in, but Whitewall made an impatient noise and Twisted didn't know if it was that or at being blocked from the knowledge he wanted.

"Go private, then." Pushing to his feet, Whitewall gestured at Dropsie and walked towards the back room. Once there, he turned and again made an impatient noise, gesturing at Twisted. Their stares held for a long time across the room, long enough that Dropsie turned to face him, too. Gaze darting between the two men, he saw the same look of anguish and anger on their faces, along with irritation at his reluctance to trust them on this. That expression was what gave his feet

permission to move, following them into the room and waiting while Dropsie closed the door.

They stood in silence a minute, standing and staring at the chair where Papaw used to hold court. Where he had handed out praise and punishment. Ruling with an iron fist, he had steered the club through rough waters, building a membership with an undeniable strength. Growing the ranks in a slow but patient way, he was adept at driving the men into situations where brotherhood could be birthed. My brother: The phrase no longer rote but written in blood and faith. Twisted had stood in this room often, watching as his grandfather interacted with members, the family he built from nothing to become a force in the outlaw world.

Whitewall drew a breath that sounded shaky and...old. Twisted turned to see the man's eyes on him. Already alert, he became more so, his back straightening. Something was coming that the man felt he needed to prepare for, needed to steel himself to say, which meant Twisted would need to brace to hear.

"Ain't talked to anyone," Whitewall began. "Ain't anyone said shit to me, but we're all thinking it. Every one of us is feeling it." Pausing, he turned to look at Dropsie, who gave a short, cryptic nod. Swinging back to Twisted, he said, "Jimbo was proud of you, son. Proud in a way that ran deep, like the pull of the Gulf current through the lake. Immovable, his pride and belief in you. Every man wearing the patch feels the same. You've worked hard to earn your place, never taking anything for granted, never expecting shit just because of who your pappy was."

Twisted nodded—this was good to hear—but he knew how Papaw felt. The man told him every day, had spoon-fed him that knowledge with breakfast, lunch, and dinner. Papaw never explained, but Twisted always assumed he was so open because their relationship didn't really start until he'd moved into the clubhouse, and Papaw felt guilty about how remote he had been before. Twisted opened his mouth to respond,

but Whitewall beat him to the punch and filled the silence with pain-drenched words.

"Jimbo passed today from the handiwork of your blood. His blood." He leaned back, shoulders hitting the wall, all three of them still huddled near the door. "Whether Fred meant it to happen or not, it did. Shit like this..." Voice trailing off for a moment, it was stronger when he continued. "Shit like this cannot stand uncontested."

Twisted again opened his mouth, but it was Dropsie who cut him off this time.

"Bitch set shit up. We know her. Know her family. She's got the money and the right amount of stupid to think she can get away with this." Palm up, he reached out between them, his hand steady as he thrust it upwards. "Gotta send a message."

"Find her for me. Bring her to me." The first words Twisted had uttered since entering the room, and they were a death sentence. With a sharp nod, Dropsie turned and walked out, closing the door securely behind him. Twisted looked to Whitewall to see his gaze again directed to the chair positioned at the center of the long table.

"Prez," Whitewall said, and Twisted jolted to hear it, the loss ringing through the short word in no way conveying the weight of the true feelings ricocheting through him at that moment. Then Whitewall called his name, pulling his eyes away from the chair and to the veep's face. They stared at each other in silence for a moment, then Whitewall spoke, "Not a title I'm aimin' for. I ain't right for the job. Never was. Know my place. I'm not the man behind the lines, directing the action. I'm the man on the front, elbow-deep in blood when it's called for. Clear conscience because someone else made the call. It's weak, but it's also a weakness kept in check because I know about it."

Another moment of silence broken when Whitewall's next words shocked him. "Means that shit's gonna fall to you, Twisted."

"Oh, hell no." His blurted reaction pulled loud laughter from the man. The laughter turned into a hard, hitching breath, then another as Whitewall struggled to keep himself together. Twisted couldn't believe Whitewall would even suggest such a thing. In no way was he prepared to follow his grandfather's reign over the club. This had to be grief talking, and he'd easily be able to make Whitewall see the fallacy in his statement. "Every man out there, every man in a clubhouse with our emblem on it will follow you, Whitewall. Don't matter—"

"No." The word, loud and firm cut him off. "They might follow me, but brother, I won't lead them. I know my limits, pushed past them more than once, had to circle back to find the edges of where I belong so I didn't fuck up too badly, but I still fucked up. Thank God, I had Jimbo to back me up, settle my shit. No, brother. It's gotta be you."

"No fucking way." He offered this in just as loud and firm a voice, but Whitewall didn't let him get any farther.

"Only thing that will keep this club going is strength and a belief in what Jimbo built. That's you." Head shaking, he held up a hand, halting Twisted's words. "Hear me out, brother. Wasn't me nor Dropsie who took control tonight. Wasn't Po'Boy or any of the others. You kept your shit under control and powered through a hard situation. Kept your shit in a way that allowed us to keep ours, too. Showed us your pain, and then dialed it back, showing us your strength, too. You kept yourself under control and *in* control in a way that got us away from there, dealt with the situation in the best possible way, and I could see, fuck, I *watched* as you learned a fucking lot along the way. When given a choice not five minutes ago, you didn't take the easy road, didn't ask to let someone else deal with retribution. Balls deep, you'll lead from the front like Jimbo did. You'll do whatever is needed. It's what you've always done for us, and we...the club, Incoherent demands no less now."

He reached out, putting one hand on Twisted's shoulder, gripping hard, and grabbing his wrist with the other, holding on tightly.

Whitewall said, voice clear and ringing, "When we vote you in as president to fill Jimbo's seat, that shit's an honor and an anchor. Man you are, you ain't gonna turn us down. Man you are, that honor will fill you up and hold you firm. But, man you are, that anchor will also weigh at you, pull at you, keep you in place. This won't be a selfless decision on our part."

He shook Twisted slightly. "Man you are, you could go anywhere and be pulled into the inner circle in weeks. Man you are, you could find a club that would take you places, international, give you a seat at large tables where policy is laid down that supports the whole community. Man you are, you'd take that on and best it, all of it, make it your fuckin' bitch." He paused to take a breath, his eyes burning into Twisted's as he confessed, "Man I am, I want that for my brothers here. Want you. Want to keep you close. Anchor you. Keep you for Incoherent, keep you for us."

His grip relaxed, and he moved, pulling Twisted into a one-armed clinch, pounding his back with a hard fist. "Prez. Love ya, brother. Honored to be the first to call you that." In the words whispered fiercely near his ear, Twisted heard the emotion Whitewall was battling. "Honored, and fuckin' hate it at the same time. Jimbo was more than my friend. We were brothers."

"I know, brother. His love for you was not buried. He loved you right back." Twisted spoke truth, because while every brother was loved by his Papaw, there was a special affection for the men he had served with, and Whitewall had been with him the longest. "I think you're wrong about what the officers are gonna do, but brother, know that *I'm* honored to hear how you feel." Twisted pulled back, releasing his counter hold on Whitewall. "Gonna go out, see what we've heard from the po-po. Let you talk to the men you need to, get things in the works to pull brothers in for a meeting because, in any case, we cannot be headless. Not in this climate. You'll get my vote if I'm given one because I think you are the best man standing in this room. But we cannot be headless, twisting in the mud. We don't settle the shit from today, we'll

bleed members. I won't stand for that. This is Papaw's legacy, and I'll do whatever I have to in order to keep shit right."

"That right there? That steel in your spine? That's what I'm talking about," Whitewall said immediately. "Man you are, you won't say that without feelin' it, and how you feel it, you'll handle it." He scoffed. "Man you are, won't ever think you're up for the title, even if you're already doin' the fuckin' job. President will sit on your shoulders like a custom suit from the Garden District. Love ya, brother, but you're dead wrong."

Three hours later, Whitewall had been proven right, and the ending of the officer's meeting had Twisted's ass planted in his grandfather's chair. Seat shaped and broken in through the years, he found it more comfortable than he would have believed.

***

Twisted looked down at his hand and flexed the fingers. In and out. In and out. Bruised and bloody, his knuckles ached, and he could feel the swelling beginning to interfere with the way his joints worked. Clench and release. In and out.

Shifting focus, he looked beyond his hand, again fisted tightly, and into the face of the woman on the floor. They were in the back room of the clubhouse. A room with a sloping floor that led to a drain set near the wall. With cement floor and walls, it was a space designed for a quick cleanup and intended for the use it was being put to right that moment. Intelligence acquisition.

Through the clubhouse walls, he heard the muffled beginnings of a party outside. The funerals had been today, the club bearing the cost of everything, so the families didn't have money struggles laid on top of their loss. A wake worthy of the men they'd lost would be rolling strong in another hour. These tentative sounds from the open area behind the building were the initial arrivals. Mostly prospects who lived at the

house, eschewing a rental or apartment in town in order to remain on-call for the club they were earning their way into.

Guitar music rang out, an energetic strumming of the six-strings, followed by a rhythmic pounding on the soundboard to add percussive tones. A moment later he heard the distinctive sound of an accordion's wheeze, the bellows expanding and contracting with the movements of the unseen musician's hands. Harmonica blues bled through the walls as he leaned down, gripping the bitch's throat with one hand, pulling the other back, cocked and locked for action near his ear.

"Tell me," he growled and watched as Sabrina's eye rolled in her head, trying to see a way out of this. Blood matted the hair on the side of her head, and one eye was swollen shut, giving her the look of a deformed monster. *Outsides match the insides now,* he thought. Her bottom lip was split in two places, blood-smeared front teeth showed as her mouth gaped. He knew her breath was a scarce commodity and every movement from her tried to buy more. "Tell me, bitch. This can end now, if you talk to me." He heard an agonized gasp from her, and then another while she writhed in his hand.

Rattling noises from the party outside filled the room. That was followed by the bright hiss-and-scrape sounds of steel thimbles dragged in a bold movement across a galvanized scrubboard. Zydeco music was more delicate when performed by fingertips than the broad bowls of spoons, this choice meant their brother, Busk, would be playing tonight. There was a *tink* of a tuned triangle being struck, punctuating the melodic phrase of the song the musicians were beginning. Sabrina gasped again, and he tightened his fist around her throat, watching as red bled into the white of the one eye he'd left her.

"Fucked my brother." His thumb slipped in the blood coating her skin, and he adjusted. *Tink*. "Killed eight good men." One of the men who'd ridden away from the bar had died after rolling up to the house in Mandeville, blood leaking down his leg until his tank hit empty. Staggering as he stepped off his bike, falling facedown to the gravel,

he'd been dead before he toppled over. *Tink*. "Killed 'em sure as if you pulled the fuckin' trigger." Wheeze. *Squeeze*. *Tink*.

"You ain't gonna make it, honey," Twisted said quietly, not surprised she didn't react. Gauging by the purple in her face and her fluttering lid, she was nearly out of it. Relaxing his fist, he looked over his shoulder to where Po'Boy stood near the door, hands jammed into the front pockets of his jeans, his stance uncomfortable, but the look on his face resolved.

They'd traced Sabrina down easily, too easily. She hadn't even tried to make herself scarce. Nabbed and hauled her out of the back door of a beauty salon when she'd taken a bathroom break from gabbing with her clique, they'd brought her to the club the day after the shootout. They hadn't located Fred, however, thank Christ. Twisted didn't know what he'd do if he found out Fred had shit to do with Papaw's death.

His brothers hadn't found the shooters yet, either. Those imposters were so far in the wind not even a breeze of their passage remained. Yesterday, he and Leswayne had pulled out chairs from a table, sitting down opposite while each had a dozen men fanned out at their backs. Each man in the room had bristled with anger and rage, for very different reasons. Leswayne and the Vicar's Wrath because someone had impersonated them; charlatans going so far as to have cheap knockoff patches made and sewn onto vests. A lot of trouble to set-up a story, even for a pissed-off bitch like this one. Twisted and the Incoherent angry because they'd lost so much. Life's riches stolen away in a moment for no reason they could lay hand to. No reason except a bitch who had a vengeful streak.

A soft voice joined the ebb and flow of the music building in the backyard of the clubhouse. Words and melody coming together to create beauty, offering comfort to those grieving. *Squeeze*.

He took two steps forwards and slammed her back against the wall, knocking loose what little air she had left in her lungs. *I'm done with her*.

With his fingers tightening again around her throat and without looking away from her ruined face, he spoke to Po'Boy. "Get a barrel, brother." No reason for him to be here for this, Twisted would send him away, and he could pick a disposal vehicle. A scrape of the door, and then the room shared its empty vibe with Twisted, and he knew Po'Boy had eagerly taken his instruction.

"Can you hear me, Sabrina?" Eyelid fluttering, he took that as a sign that she had regained enough of her senses to pay attention. "You're dyin' here today." He knew she'd heard him when she jerked, trying to get away. With her wrists secured behind her back, and lifted to her toes as she was, there was no leverage she could find to wrench herself away. "You choose the way. Easy or hard, darlin'? Happenin', you got half a zeroes chance of leavin' here any other way. But, you can choose."

Tink. Laughter. A woman's voice made him wince in sudden fear, staring at the blank wall until he recognized it as Junebug, Busk's ole lady. Cool as ice, and club to the core, if she heard or saw anything, she'd hold it close. Knowing it wasn't just her life on the line, but her ole man's too since he'd vouched for her. *Tink*. Whispered words, "I can..." Tipping his head to one side, he looked down at Sabrina.

"You say something, bitch?"

"I can stop..."

"What can you stop, Sabrina?" He let up the pressure, giving her a tiny bit more air, but maintaining control. Total control. *Wheeze.* This from the bitch in his hand. *Squeeze.* His hand to her throat.

"Re...tribution."

"The fuck you think you're orchestrating, bitch? You do not pull the strings on my brothers and our shit. Count of five, what can you stop?" Bikes in the distance, closing in on the clubhouse, riders coming to pay respects. *My brothers*. The scent of wood smoke hung in the air; he

knew there'd be a pot already boiling, ready for the mudbugs to be dumped in, seasoning rolling through the water, lifting to the surface, then sinking underneath, still there, just unseen. In his head he saw Papaw, lying on the floor, his only real family, gone because of this bitch. "One." A beat on the drum box followed by the sound of the thimbles dragging up and down the rubboard. *Tink*. "Two." *Wheeze*.

"Big Nico." Her voice rattled on a ragged exhale, her pulse jackrabbit fast under his thumb. "RICO." An involuntary squeeze of his hand made her eye widen, pupil dilating. "Blamed...Jimbo."

Fuck. That meant this ran much deeper than he had thought. Than any of them thought. He'd hoped it was just this bitch wanting some of her own back, feeling put out that he'd taken what she gave away, then took the same from her sister. This information put an entirely different twist on everything. "You sure? Big Nico bought today's action?"

Eager to please, she nodded as best she could with his fist wedged up under her jaw as it was. "Nico...wanted you...there. Fred..." Voices raised outside, an exchange too far away to make out the words. "Fred was my call." Twisted ran what he knew through his head, pulling in all the details.

Big Nico was president of a single chapter club based from Georgia, the South Coast Devils, a name Twisted always thought was fucked-up since any map could show you that where they were based, Valdosta, wasn't near the coast. Nico's club had pulled a fuckton of fed notice over the past year, and no one knew why. Nico couldn't seem to dig his way out of the hole he found himself in. His costs kept going up. Then he made mistakes trying to sort *that* shit by being aggressive when Twisted could have told him to pull back. At that point, it would be time to reduce any points of failure, make it so those places were reinforced by trusted brothers, or just pay frequent visits to shore up the men's belief and faith in the leadership.

Sabrina didn't have anything to trade. Involving Freddy was her play. *This is on her. Tink.*

Men's trust had to be earned; their faith would be unwavering only because the object of that belief never faltered. If you falter, you lose everything. *Can't stop now.* Twisted stood, eyes closed tightly because this wasn't something he wanted to do, definitely didn't want this fucking vision stuck in his head. *Squeeze.* He wiped the sweat from his face with his forearm and held on. It didn't take long. By the time Po'Boy came back with a barrel strapped to a mover's dolly, it was done.

Twenty minutes later he was behind the clubhouse, standing with a wall at his back, brothers surrounding him. No one asked about the woman who'd been brought here in a van. No one mentioned his battered hands. No one introduced business to the conversation; that would be his to bring up, and for now, he wanted to remember the fallen instead. Wanted to immerse himself in the melancholy sounds of squeeze box and rubboard, wailing mouth harp, singing strings on a fiddle, and the shuffle of soft steps. It might take a while, but he knew eventually he'd stop hearing Sabrina's heels drumming against the wall. Stop feeling the convulsive jerk of her body at the end. Stop remembering the moment her pounding heart slowed and stopped, flesh growing still under his hand.

Fake it 'til you make it. Gotta give a good show. Knowing he wouldn't be unaccompanied long, he made his way to the area near the bonfire where the grass had already been beaten flat by stamping feet. Chin up, eyes closed showing a deep trust in his brothers, Twisted gave himself to the music, turning and stomping to the familiar rhythms. Sure enough, before they were halfway through the first chorus, a hand settled on his waist, defining the space between their bodies and he opened his eyes to a brown-eyed mulatto girl swaying next to him. *Pretty little thing. Struttin' her stuff. Box lookin' to catch the eye of the club's new president. She just bought her evenin' with that play,* he thought as he reached out and slipped his arms around her.

Not giving one fuck who the bitch belonged to, when the mood struck him, he took her off to one side and bent the bitch over the back of a bench seat. Removed from a van and placed on the grass near the bonfire, it was the right height for a quick standing fuck. Shorts to her knees, her booted feet close together, he opened the front of his pants and pulled out his dick. Rolling on the condom was quick, and then he slammed into her. Hot and wet, she was loose as fuck, but he could make that work tonight. *I'm livin'*, he thought as head back, he stared at the stars wheeling overhead while snapping his hips forward. She jerked and moved unexpectedly, and he glanced down to see Po'Boy feeding his dick into her mouth, her head angled to the side.

"Live it up, brother," Twisted said, right before the girl's eyes shifted sideways in her head and then all he could see was Sabrina's one unruined eye, rolling frantically while she tried to talk around the constrictor of his hand. *Fuck*. Looking down, he concentrated on watching his dick slide in and out of the bitch's box. "Live it up."

Chapter Five

PRINCESS

Her entire body trembled. She was able to make it out of the car and to her front door, somehow managing to hold herself together and stay in control. But, when she fumbled the key a third time in the lock, that grip slipped, and she barked a harsh, hoarse, "*Fuck*." Her voice sounded foreign to her ears, pained. She closed her mouth with a snap, cutting off any other words she might have said, not wanting to hear more evidence of her pain. A deep breath strengthened her, and she leaned her elbow against the door, using that propped angle to steady her hand, forcing the key into the slot. Once inside, she thumbed the lever on the deadbolt, locking the door behind her with a deep sigh. *Safe*.

Dropping her messenger bag to the floor, an empty water bottle inside clashed against something and she flinched at the noise it made, muscles all over her body screaming as she tensed to run. *Safe*, she reassured herself, *I'm safe*, doing her best to ignore the speeding pounding of her heart. When she was certain she could stand on her own, she pushed herself away from the wall. Dragging footsteps changed to soft padding as she clumsily kicked off her shoes on her way across the room and headed towards the hallway leading to the back of her house.

Sagging to sit on one corner of the mattress, she rested on her bed for long minutes staring at nothing, wrapped in the visions pouring through her head as she relived everything. Images and smells, touch that bled into pain rising to levels she never knew existed, the last twenty-four hours ran in an unstoppable loop through her head. Unable to close the doors on her memories, she sat blind to everything around her, sinking deep into the agony of the things she'd endured. Her breathing gave evidence to her rising emotions as it hitched and shuddered at irregular intervals, never quite turning back into sobs, but the threat was present.

Finally exhausted, her eyes sagged closed, the darkness allowing the images to slide away, bringing her back to herself. Sore all over, she hurt, found that even breathing was agonizing, and knew a hot shower would help make it not hurt so much. A shower would require undressing, and as she moved to accomplish this, she found it was a chore to make her arms move, those reluctant limbs making it a struggle to lift the hem of her shirt, pulling the stained material up and over her head.

The shirt snagged on something, causing pain to shoot through her face, and suddenly she was fighting the fabric half hooding her head, struggling to breathe as she ripped it off, flinging the shirt as far away as she could. Now the sobs returned in earnest, no longer threatening but overwhelming, crashing in on her as she dropped her face into her hands. Feeling the wetness dampening the dried fluids on her face, the slickness sickening as it reminded her of so many things she'd rather forget. *All for nothing*, she thought, twisting her hand and wiping across her face with one wrist.

She reached up with her other hand, fingers gingerly tracing across the artifact she'd taken away with her. The physical reminder of a mistake so damaging, she might never get past it. The souvenir that would serve to keep her safe going forwards. *Please, God*. Pain followed her touch, less sharp this time, the small piece of metal moving in small circles in response to her prodding.

Standing, she slowly stripped out of her jeans, groaning as she used the toes of her feet to edge them off her legs, leaving them on the floor next to the bed. In her underwear, she tottered to the bathroom, heat from the raised, red marks on her skin exaggerating the chill in the air, making her shiver. Lights still off, legs as exhausted as the rest of her, she stumbled over nothing. Arms flying out to catch herself on the sink, she took the last step forwards while leaning on the basin. A dark shape hovered in the mirror in front of her, the silhouette unfamiliar and she nearly screamed before the figure moved with her flinch, and she realized she saw herself.

Dragging in a deep breath that spread agony through her ribs, she closed her eyes and reached out a hand, fingers fumbling a moment before she flipped the light switch. Illumination bloomed in front of her eyelids, and she stood there, chin tipped down, waiting for the time when it would feel right to look at the woman in the mirror. Saliva flooded her mouth as her mind ran back through the events of the past few hours. Arriving at the arranged meet, forcing herself to walk through the door and into his house, knowing she would be forever changed when it came time to exit. *I'm alive. Upright and breathing.* Swallowing convulsively, she lifted her chin and opened her eyes.

At first, her gaze didn't know where to pause, what to look at, what to focus on first, and her eyes jittered, darting back and forth, tracking and tracing and marking the changes in her appearance. Blood and bruises darkened her pale skin, and her short-cropped hair was matted to the side of her head in places. Fingerprint-shaped purple marks dotted her throat and jaw, the unmistakable outline of a hand raised in a red welt on her cheek.

When she could no longer take it in, no longer stand to look at herself, she let her eyes sink closed, blindly reaching out for a washcloth from the stack on the counter. Hands to the taps, she ran cold water, dampening the cloth, and then, beginning at her hairline, slowly and methodically cleaned her face. Her lids flickered open periodically,

allowing her to check her progress, moving mostly by feel until she came to the unfamiliar outline at her brow.

He saw me like this, she thought, flinching as she understood the look of concern and confusion on the face of the man behind the piercing gun. *It's a wonder he didn't call the cops as bloody and bruised as I am.*

Gleaming in the lights, the bar glinted golden as it flashed with her movements. Bright and shiny, it stood out against her skin, emphasizing the bruising on her face. Eyes constantly returning to that beacon, she worked faster, rinsing the cloth, cleaning a small section of skin, then rinsing again. The rust-colored water swirling down the drain became less noticeable with each cycle. Finally, features clean, she stood facing the mirror and forced herself to meet her gaze, staring. "I'm the same person," she told her reflection. "No different, it's just me."

One hand lifted to her head, she ran her fingers through strands of hair, wincing as they tangled on dried blood. She whirled, turning on the bath taps and without waiting, stepped into the tub, flipping the lever to activate the shower. Cold water hit her back like a physical blow, and she gasped. Her spine bowed away in reaction, the movement setting her ribs to complaining again. Stripping off her underwear, she roughly scrubbed every inch of her body in the gradually heating water, only slowing as she carefully worked her fingers into the soreness between her legs. After the first downward glance, she studiously ignored the pink that stained the water. Staying in the shower until the hot water ran out, she then remained for a time until shivering from the intense cold woke more pain.

Again in front of the mirror and ignoring the pain, she roughly dried her hair with a towel, staring at her reflection. *Still me*, she reaffirmed, her hand going to her hair once more. Digging scissors from the messy vanity drawer, she tipped her head this way and that, running her fingers through, grasping onto strands and pulling them straight, evaluating what needed to be done. With tears in her eyes, she lifted

the scissors, watching as they shook in her trembling hand. *Snip*. Another strand. *Snip*. Methodically, she worked her way through, evening out the length, ignoring the tears flooding down her cheeks, dripping to the porcelain where short bits of hair lay. *Still me*.

Chapter Six

TWISTED, AGE THIRTY-TWO

"It ain't fuckin' with you to explain the situation." Twisted shook his head, flattening his palms on the table in preparation to stand up. A move, that if he made it, every man in the room knew meant these talks would be over in a way that said they were *over*. Meaning this conversation wouldn't be revisited.

As expected, his counterpart at the table backpedaled. Fast. "No, no. Jesus, man. Fuckin' chill. No disrespect intended."

"Tellin' me to chill don't 'xactly sound respectful." Twisted flexed his arms, pushing harder against the table, enjoying the fear and panic that flooded the face of this numbwit when the fabric of his jeans finally cleared the chair. Twisted bent over the table, putting his face close to the pasty features of the man still planted firmly in his seat, false hope keeping him there.

"So, followin' up on my previous statement, explainin' the situation to your stupid fuckin' ass ain't fuckin' with you." He jerked his head, smiling coldly when he heard the clicking ratchet of Po'Boy's pistol cocking behind him. "This? Now *this* is fuckin' with you." Another nod and the room filled with deafening echoes of gunshots and screams. He held himself steady, not even flinching when blowback splattered his

face, the hot liquid mixing with the sweat on his brow and creating a stinging rivulet of red that covered one eye.

Po'Boy spoke, "Fish in a barrel." He turned to look at his brother, watching as his veep's eyes intelligently swept the men standing around the room, taking in everything at a glance. "Guess it's too late to say I think he really was tryin' to be respectful. He just didn't have it in him. Terminal cranial rectumitus." That pulled a snorted laugh from Twisted, and he reached up, wiping with the pad of his thumb across his eye, cleaning the blood away. "Fuck, brother." Po'Boy winced. "You look like that kid from that fuckin' cannibal movie about that scary-as-fuck island." He pulled a bandana from his back pocket, flicked it open and offered it, the crisp folds proving the unused state of the fabric. "Here, clean your fucked-up face, man. Gonna scare the kiddies."

"You carry this shit for me?" Twisted reached out and took it, pressing it to his face with both hands, wiping firmly, clearing the splatter away as best he could without water and a mirror. "I'm touched, brother."

"You know it, Twisted. You're my main man. Ain't got no side men, but you my main, bro. Straight up." Po'Boy grinned, but the humor didn't reach his eyes, and he let Twisted know why in the next breath. "Big Nico ain't gonna be happy with this. We cleanin' up or letting him deal?"

"Let him deal. His mess, all day long this is his mess. We put this shit on pause for him. He can clean up the trash." To that end, Twisted pulled out a phone, connected the battery and dialed a number. One ring, then a well-known and much-hated voice sounded in his ear, the one-word greeting of "Well?" not sitting easy with him. *Fucking Gollum.* Fiddler was president of the Guanyin's Shield, a semi-local MC, run much along the line of Leswayne's Vicar's. Gollum was Fiddler's son, a ruthless man well known for holding information in a tight fist. He was playing go-between for Twisted and Nico right now, but just hearing his voice made Twisted's skin crawl.

"Tell your boss his leaky plumbing is plugged. He's got some cleanup, but nothing his housekeeper can't handle. I don't expect more flooding, but might be some foundation damage he'll need to look at." The dead jackass sagging backwards in his chair across the table was a cousin to Nico's ole lady. He'd been positively confirmed by their fed contact as the sole witness against Nico who had not gone into WITSEC. There was no doubt the asshole gained his knowledge through his blood connections, which meant Nico had more trouble than he knew. Twisted would explain that to Nico next time they met, but it wasn't something he needed to lay out over the phone, even on a clean burner like this one. "Let your boss know I can do an inspection tonight, if he wants."

"Ain't my fuckin' boss, asshole." Scorn thick in his voice, Gollum responded, "Plan on that inspection, though. He'll want to control any additional damage." The click and null of a disconnected call released Twisted to lower the phone, retracing the movements needed to remove the battery and stow the device.

Turning, knowing every man in that room would follow without question, he strode from the room, bloody footprints in his wake. Glancing down, he grimaced, seeing his shirt and vest were covered with the same gore his face had been. Riding through downtown Metairie would suck like this. "Got a tee?" He looked up at Po'Boy, seeing him nod silently in response to the question. They'd developed their own shorthand over the years, even more so in the past half-dozen after Whitewall stepped down, leaving Twisted room to bring in new blood loyal only to him. It had been a full decade since Papaw passed, the officers working hard to ladle protocol and knowledge down his throat every day. Force feeding him from a fucking firehose until Twisted, even more than he had ever thought possible, lived and breathed the club.

"Bitch." Standing by his bike, he grabbed the fabric sailing his way, laying his vest across the seat so he could tug the sodden shirt over his head. Covered again, he adjusted the weapons strapped to his torso and

legs, straddled the bike and kicked a dozen times before the engine caught. *Need a new fuckin' bike,* he thought, *item number fifty-three on today's coulda-woulda-shoulda list*. Glancing down to check his bags, the officer patch sewn to the front of his vest caught his eye and he reached up, fingering the edge. There was a half circle out of the lower left corner, the bullet hole from a shot that hit Papaw. He'd had one of the club's bitches sew around that ragged edge, keeping the President patch from fraying more, and then put that goddamned bloody rag on his vest. *Ends today, Papaw,* he vowed.

Looking up he saw a question on Po'Boy's face and elaborated. "Nico's bitch." Nodding understanding, Po'Boy got on his own bike, whirling his finger in the air to send the rest of the men on their way. Just him and Twisted for this run, one that would end again with death, but not by his hand. Not directly.

***

"You get it?" At Twisted's words, the bitch rolled her eyes up at him, and he had a flash of a face he couldn't forget. Another voice sounded in the room, and she pulled her mouth off his dick in fear, slobber stringing between her lips and his cock.

"Oh yeah, brother. I got all that shit. Fuckin' choice spank bank material." Fingers tapping on the face of the phone in his hands, Po'Boy stepped from the shadows as she gave a cry.

Twisted reached out, gripping and pulling the straw-dry bleached blonde hair on the bitch's head, putting her mouth back to work on his cock. Hands on his thighs she pushed, trying to pull back but he powered into her face. Lightly tapping her cheek when he felt the threatening edge of teeth, he shook his head, lips pulled back to bare his own at her. "You know how this goes, honey. Just take it."

Eyes rolling again, she finally squeezed them shut and gave up, opening her mouth wide, offering her throat and he took that. Felt her convulsively swallowing around the knob of his cock when he pushed

past the back of her mouth. From this angle, he could see the way her throat expanded around him with every thrust. "Fuck." His mutter hit the air while in the background he heard recorded sounds from their earlier activities, ones in which she was participating eagerly, not like now. Po'Boy was watching the playback, making sure they had everything needed.

She swallowed again, and he felt her pull against his hands, but now it was in counterpoint to his movements. Enhancing not evading. *Bitch is getting into it again. Even Nico deserves better. Goddamned fucking slut.* "Get the camera ready," he muttered.

Pulling out, he watched as she settled on her heels, face lifted, mouth open and tongue lapping the end of his cock. Hand moving fast, he worked himself, watching her as she waited. Hair in a tangle around her head from his tight grip, her hands folded on top of her skinny-as-fuck thighs, she was nothing but a receptacle and knew it. *Might as well have cumbucket written on her tits*, he thought, and with that, he started coming, shooting line after line of white across her face and hair, aiming more at her breasts. Watching as her hands came up, massaging that shit into her skin as if it were the finest creamy lotion, licking her lips, using the edge of one finger to loop more into her mouth.

"Fuckin' porno," Po'Boy muttered. "Got it all, boss."

Her eyes flashed open. She had forgotten their audience of one, about to become an audience of hundreds. Catching and holding her gaze as he tucked his still hard cock back into his pants, Twisted waited a beat and then gave the order. Pulling the trigger without lifting a single fucking finger. "Post it."

***

"So which of them do we want?" Dropsie asked the question every man at the table was wondering. One of the old school members still willing to challenge the national president and Twisted loved him for it. He loved that Dropsie never forgot he'd been a snot-nosed piece-of-shit

kid when Papaw dropped him into the clubhouse for the first time seventeen years ago. George Bell a rapidly fading memory even for himself. Mother dead for eight years, brother estranged for ten.

"I'm lookin' for club mentality, so anyone who defended the bitch ain't fit. Club first, and you all know we *need* that attitude. We can build loyalty in a good man, craft their trust. But, a brother who gets it and lives it? Those motherfuckers are a lean crop. Need to harvest what we can, when we can. Patch properly, but fast-track those select few."

There were nodding heads all around; he had a consensus for this, at least. Twisted leaned into the table, taking in each officer with his gaze. "We need fodder, too, so officer-loyal or loyal to a brother, we'll look at them and evaluate. Feds are sniffin' around, all up in our ass. We fucked their case good, leavin' them knotted up in the front yard, a cold hose directed their way that doesn't feel too fuckin' sweet. Reality struck for Big Nico when that video surfaced,"—he grinned at Po'Boy who grinned back—"and his shit imploded all around the feds. We all know that Nico had a play but didn't take it. Didn't man up, least not in time. Now we got a chance to scoop the cream."

Through the years, Twisted had reached an uneasy détente with the clubs of the area. Not by choice, but because too many fights would leave Incoherent weakened, and Twisted wouldn't allow that. The feds were enough to deal with and they were all over the area, looking for any slips that let them slide inside a club. They were enough of a threat that he'd stayed his hand from action, focusing instead on investigating Nico's past. He'd found some interesting things that confirmed the intel Sabrina had offered, but not enough of an opening to exact the vengeance his heart called for. So he and the club had bided their time, waiting. That wait had ended today.

He'd met with Big Nico before the shit went down in Metairie. First time he believed he had the right questions, he'd sat down with and been disappointed in the man's responses about the action ten years

ago. So, Twisted started digging deeper. He dug and found gold, and then once he knew the full lay of the land, he'd taken action.

He'd dealt with the leak because a statement had to be made about snitching. He and Po'Boy used the dead cousin's phone to lure Nico's ole lady to a bar where the back room was used for much more than meetings. Got her past any initial discomfort easily, mostly by pulling his half-hard cock out of his pants while he smiled at her. He snorted as he thought, *Didn't take much. Had her panting for it in under a minute.*

He'd fucked her standing while she shimmied on his pole like she was still working professionally. Fucked her from behind, not wanting her face anywhere near his, letting her rear back into him, doing nearly all the damn work. Her taking his cock and moaning like it was the best fuck of her life. Then fucking her face, using her as his tissue, getting off on her play at rejection.

Still using the asshole's phone, Po'Boy recorded the necessary parts, highlighting her face and making sure she was unmistakable on the video. Making it clear whose cock she was sucking, too. Huge fucking insult, national president of one organization fucking the ole lady of another's president. Bigger affront to Nico was her getting her rocks off, eyes closed, facing the camera as she said clear as fucking day, "Never had bigger. Never had better, baby." *I couldn't have scripted it better, baby.*

So, not only had Nico's bitch taken Twisted's cock, literally gagging for it, but she'd told the whole world that her ole man was a little-dicked sad sack in bed. Big Nico no more. Using the asshole cousin's online access to the secret group for that club, they uploaded that shit and then emailed it to every single person on the motherfucker's contact list. Distributing it far and wide, they made it impossible to ignore by shoving it in Nico's face and in the face of every man who followed him. Every man who called him president or brother. Twisted and Po'Boy's job had been to shovel that shit, and then stand back and watch who fed from the table.

Bitch had been dead inside of twelve hours. No surprise there. The big surprise had been how long Nico had held out. It was another thirty-six before the dust settled, an entire club gone. Toasted by a single fucking woman by first exposing Nico's shit to the feds through her loose lips talking to family, then by wrapping those lips around Twisted's cock to add insult to injury.

Retribution, he thought, his mind supplying Sabrina's despairing voice when she realized she wouldn't be walking out of that room. Honesty came from her lips because while she didn't know she'd wind up as gator bait, she just grasped that her breaths were numbered. It had taken a long time—so much longer than he wanted—but he'd gotten what he vowed that day in the bar, sitting on his ass in his grandfather's blood, watching his brother walk out after that bitch. Twisted had gotten what he'd vowed to himself when he'd folded her up to stuff into the dark barrel. Vowed when he used every wedge he could find to wreak havoc on the foundation of Nico's club, on his life.

Feels empty, he thought then shoved that aside. Another thought popped up in its wake, one of his brother. There was no fault to be laid at Freddy's feet over Jimbo's death, other than being stupid enough to trust Sabrina. They'd infrequently talked over the years since Papaw's death, barely staying in touch, only making sure the other had new numbers or addresses and sharing the occasional life event that defined them. Mostly that was on Fred's side. Him cleaning up his act, landing a good job driving a truck. Marrying a decent woman. Having kids with her, talking about seeing his eyes in their faces and how that made him feel.

"Feds are no joke," Dropsie warned, and Twisted nodded, bringing his attention back to the room, feeling the tension running between the men seated around the table.

Time to move this meeting forwards and the next piece of business was one that Twisted never thought to have to deal with.

"Know that. Also, know we got a man inside." He raked the officers at the table with his gaze again, coming to rest on the face of their road captain, Chip. "And, from him, we know they got one on the inside here, too." Face blanching, Chip pushed back from the table, not bothering to deny what Twisted implied. No words needed, one glance at Po'Boy and his veep was on the move, cornering the larger man and keeping him contained without laying a hand on him.

"Chip," Twisted deliberately withheld "brother" from the man. "Pains me to say this, but I gotta ask. You wired?" He hadn't anticipated the man would give it up like that, had expected to have to wade through a weave of bluster and lies, and Chip's quick retreat meant he might have more to hide than associations. *Fuck*, Twisted thought, going over the conversations they'd had here today. Plenty to chew over, but he doubted they'd given the feds anything to actually play with.

"No, Prez." Twisted gave him a quick headshake, revoking permission to address him by title from the man he'd known for a dozen years. Chip had been Scot's prospect, earned his patch under that old man's tutelage, and been a steady and stable member since. Word was this wasn't his play, but that didn't matter in the end. You either were the club, or you weren't. If you were, you didn't snitch on your brothers, on the brotherhood. Chip sucked in a breath, then breathed out what sounded like an oath. "No wires."

"Good start. Now let's see if the reality backs up that promise." At a brusque gesture from Po'Boy, Chip quickly pulled his shirt up, turning in place to show a naked torso. Inked up, but otherwise blank. Club colors etched on the skin of his back; the man had planned on being a member for life. *Fuck*. Twisted clipped out, "Check his pockets and seams."

With a muttered, "Sorry, brother," Po'Boy stepped in to conduct a search by touch on a compliant Chip.

"Nothing." That came nearly five minutes later as they all watched Chip pull his boots back on, wisely leaving his cut lying on the table where Po'Boy had placed it.

Twisted ran a hand down his face, smoothing the beard he'd started growing when Papaw passed. At first, shaving had been just one more thing to do, and he only had so much energy. He'd cast aside the things that didn't matter, and scraping his face with a bare blade had been one of the first to go. Now, his beard was a trademark. Intimidating to men, titillating to women. Part of him in a way he got off on.

Looking at Chip, he took a breath. "Let's see how much I get right, yeah?" Without waiting for a response, he powered on, "Heard your ole lady got pissed about you dippin' your wick in club pussy. Heard she went to her sister's house where they decided she was gonna scrape you off. Heard she started scraping you off, but wanted all your shit. Shit you rightly didn't give her. So she started takin', and how she started takin' was by going to her sister's husband. Pussy-whipped fella, hell bent on making his woman happy. And how he made her happy was by working his connections to help out her sister."

Twisted shook his head. "That man was a clerk at the courthouse who knows a judge. Aw, yeah, we're getting to the meat of it now. That judge smelled himself a campaign opportunity that was liable to get him to Baton Rouge and doin' that not by wearin' a robe. And that judge knew a fed. This bit's important, see. That fed was a fed who saw hisself an opportunity for advancement that meant he wouldn't be takin' the long-time career route."

Chip sucked in a breath to speak, but Twisted raised his voice, talking over him. "That fed spent hours talkin' to your bitch. And her? She sat there, layin' her mouth wide open, spewing every fuckin' thing you'd ever told her. And you talked a fuck of a lot, Chip. Fuckin' pillow talk was what it took to keep that pussy happy, so you had fuckin' *talked*. That fed told her to work on gettin' a meet with you, and you fell for her shit. Fuck yeah, that was you sitting down with her, takin' that meet. Her

layin' her mouth wide open there, too, talking you into 'lessening your sentence' by rollin' on us."

Voice changing to a sneer, Twisted swept his long hair back from his face and continued, "Us. Your brothers. The men who had your back when that bitch started takin' your shit. The men who had your back long before you had the bitch on *her* back, takin' your cock. Rollin' on us, and tryin' to fuck us in the ass, seein' as you didn't have pussy to fuck anymore." Each sentence seemed to smack Chip hard, driving him into the wall, pressing him against the surface as if he were in a gigantic crusher, the sounds holding him in place while squeezing the life out of him. "So, Chip. Tell us. How'd I do? Did I get it right? Miss anything?" Leaning forward at the waist, he roared, "Tell us."

Nostrils flaring wide, the big man stared at Twisted. That was the only indication he was feeling anything, the only indication that Twisted had the right of it. Every bit of it, right, and damning. *Time to move this forward*, he thought.

"I got it right." Twisted's whispered words dropped into the room, followed by chair legs scraping across the cement floor. "All of it. Every bit." He felt men at his back when he stepped away from the table. "Disappointed in you, Chip. Scot would be pissed as fuck you turned. Snitches at the table? One sittin' in his goddamned chair? Fuckin' disappointed." He took a step and heard the shuffle of boot leather behind him. "You didn't think we'd have your back? You think we'd let you go inside for the *club* and not take care of you? Let you go inside at all and not take care of you? Was that your fear?" That was the crux of it all, the lack of faith Chip had in them.

"Even a week ago, if you'd come to me and fronted that shit, we'd have worked it out." Twisted shifted his hips sideways to get around a chair without blocking any of the men from advancing with him. "I'll give you one thing because of who you've been for us in the past." Chip stood straighter, pulling his shoulders back, that invisible vise still pressing him deep into the wall. "One thing. You call it. How you wanna go down?"

Gazes never breaking contact, Chip hadn't closed his eyes since this started, and Twisted's own eyes had started burning. He took a breath and blinked, surprised to find wet gathering there. "*Fuck*, Chip. How the hell did you get so far off track, man? Huh?" Footsteps shuffled at his back. He knew every ear was tuned to his words.

Reaching up, he smoothed his beard again, needing something to do with his hands. Stomach clenching, it felt like he was unraveling inside because what was about to happen would kill another part of his soul, and he was desperate to do anything to stop it, even turn the gun in his other hand on himself if it came to that. "Fucking shit." He was within reach when Chip's legs bent, knees giving way, letting the man fall heavily to the floor. Kneeling in front of Twisted, Chip bowed his head, finally ending their stare.

As he moved behind the man he had called brother, Twisted tried to make sense of how they'd gotten here, to a place where his brother was surrendering to him, accepting. Before the traitorous pussy got her hooks into him, the man had been married, his wife dying birthing their second child. *Like Papaw*. Chip had gone off the deep end, his woman's people taking in their granddaughters to raise, the club taking in their brother, but only in a perfunctory way. They hadn't taken care of him, hadn't lifted a finger to derail his shit, just watched as Chip imploded. *Papaw had the club.*

"This is on me," Twisted whispered. *I failed my brother.* He laid a hand on Chip's back, resting his palm on the man's neck, fingers digging into the sides and holding tightly. "On me." He paused, lifting his head and looking at the men standing in the room. Men he knew. Trusted. "I coulda done better." He looked back down, remembering Chip's wife and ole lady, memories surfacing of eating at their table, seeing Chip's easy and comfortable teasing of his woman, seeing the love for him on her face. "This is on me," he repeated, and then continued, fingers squeezing hard as he lifted Chip back to his feet, pulling him into an embrace, hearing the sobs as disbelief and then relief hit Chip, "brother."

Chapter Seven

TWISTED

"Three ball, corner pocket." His muttered words were accompanied with a thrusting gesture of the pool stick, indicating the particular corner out of four at which he was aiming. Simple shot from where he stood, a straight lineup with the pocket. He just needed to pop a little lower right-hand English on the cue to pull it back to where he wanted so he could position for the next shot. *Spin to win, folks.* He straightened and took a step back, which rapidly turned into two additional half steps before he righted himself, killing the stumble's momentum. *Well, it should be a simple shot*, he thought, tongue in the corner of his mouth as he tried to recover gracefully.

Undrunk would equal simple. Drunk as he was right now? Not a fucking chance in hell he would be hitting that hole. His gaze crossed the two identically-dressed girls sitting on stools along the wall, tight tanks pulled low, crimson lips, shorts sagging around their hips. *Or any holes*. He squinted, the two women resolving into a single female form, wreathed in cigarette smoke. *Or any hole, singular*, he thought. *Not that I'm lookin' for skank, but pussy is pussy.*

Wrapping his hand around the edge of the corner closest to him, he bent and angled himself into position, bringing the stick down and

resting it on his hand in the notch formed by his jutting thumb. *Hold on*. Stroking back once...twice...then forwards with a soft crack. The tip hit the white ball, careening it into the red ball, and he watched as both moved exactly how he saw in his mind. Before the solid had finished falling into the netting, he called the next shot, striking the cue with the stick again just as it drifted to a stop. Shifting a half step to his left, he called the next shot. And the next.

Surprisingly, he won, and that game turned into another. And another, which he also won, the wooziness slowly fading.

"A man drunk as you are, how in the hell does he still win at pool?" Bills thrown on the tabletop were a contemptuous insult, but he didn't care. Right now those bills were a tank of fuel, a good meal, and hot shower. A haven purchased by a little overlooking was still a haven. It wasn't that money was a problem, just that his self-righteous little brother didn't want dirty money. He didn't know him well, but suspected that to Fred, earned would be acceptable, and it'd feel good to offer something to ease an unspoken burden. *I'll just have to convince him that hustlin' pool is work*.

Leaning crookedly, he put his stick on the table for the next player. *Pretend to be a little slow, promise 'em a chance at recovery*, he heard in his head and felt the grin falter on his face. That was a blast from the past he didn't need. *Papaw, go back to sleep*, he thought, shoving down memories of bullet-riddled bodies falling around him, holes appearing in leather vests like movieland stunt props, but these had blood and bone, breathing souls behind them. Everything that mattered stripped away in a moment. Some lost to family crypts, some to a rift nearly as final. This trip the first accepted overture in over a decade of attempts, giving him renewed hope of restored connections.

"No freakin' idea, man." His mouth moved without his request, but at least it had the right idea. "Same time, same place tomorrow? You can win it back?" He wouldn't still be in town tomorrow. Not a chance in hell he would still have the money, so there wouldn't ever be a

rematch. Fred's load was supposed to deliver in the morning, so they'd be out of here by six o'clock at the latest. As he scraped the cash together, pushing the thick fistful deep into his pants pocket, he glanced around and noticed the woman was gone. She'd escaped the stench of the smoke-filled atmosphere. *Prolly already walkin' the lot.*

Hand to his head, partly to hold the pounding thing together, partly to obscure his face, he made his way to the door. The giants standing there gradually resolved down into a single figure, and he was glad. It was hard enough to bullshit this one. There was no need to ask for trouble by bullshitting two of 'em. "Fred," said the man in the blue shirt, white patch with black letters spelling out "Paulie" over the pocket. "No." Which he knew was giant-speak for "I can't let you on the road like this. If troopers pull you over, it's my ass in trouble."

Startled at the name the bouncer handed him, he wondered, *Was Fred who I said?* Responding smoothly, he shook his head, saying, "Paulie, my man. I'm not drivin'. Partner is behind the wheel next shift. I'm just sleepin'." Giving up with a grunt and a lifted chin, Paulie reached out and opened the door for him, seeming to know the effort would have been beyond him at this point. "Thanks," Twisted muttered, getting a second chin lift.

And as easily as that, he walked out of the bar masquerading as a truck stop and into the lot, the occupants never knowing who they had hosted tonight. He shrugged, missing the leather vest that normally rode his shoulders like the voice of reason. That loss eased by the knowledge that tonight he could do anything without worry about dire predictions on the part of his officers. Twisted shook off the feeling, trying to beat back vertigo that threatened to upend his stomach. *Might shoulda left the vodka off the menu.* He grinned. *Might shoulda left the tequila off the menu, too, stuck to whiskey.* He shrugged, done was done, and tonight, as far as he was concerned was done.

Standing in the glare of the sodium lights, his gaze swept the parking lot. Row upon row of gleaming paint and chrome. Amber and white

lights gave the area a shimmering glow, red lights flashing at intervals, blue and green and purple under lights creating pockets of illumination amidst the hulking shapes surrounding him. Exhaust hung like a cloud over the oasis, the smell of diesel fuel thick upon the air, flavoring every breath. *Now to remember where my ride parked. Oh, Freddy boy, ready or not, here I come.*

He made his careful, weaving way through the lines of massive vehicles, looking for the company logo on his brother's truck, studying the windows to see greater than expected numbers of silent sentinels. Dark forms in their tall seats, living coals hanging from fingers propped on wheels sized to give leverage and advantage to a human, regardless of height. Searing brands carried from resting position to just below the glint of eyes in the darkness; countenance lit from underneath when the cigarette flared brightly for a moment, the inrushing air sucking back chemicals and flavor and nicotine given life with a troubled permission to rush towards extinction, the cigarette burning down to nothing in minutes. Reduced to ashes.

Finally, he thought, seeing familiar territory ahead in the form of Fred's truck. Cold and still, the engine wasn't idling, but the creak of suspension spoke to restless sleep inside the cabin attached to the chassis. *At least, I won't be waking him up.* Lifting a fist, he pounded lightly against the bottom of the driver's door, glancing behind him to ensure there weren't any pool-losing followers bent on retrieving their mistake by force. Creaking and shifting, then the sound of the window lowering. Surprised the door hadn't opened, he turned to look up at the same time a soft, feminine, so-*not*-Fred voice sounded.

"Interesting, but no thanks." Short hair, ends going a hundred different directions. It was impossible to tell the shade in this lighting, but that unruly mop surrounded a tiny triangle of a face, petite and pleasing. She lifted a hand to rake the mane away from her forehead, scratching for a moment at a barbell piercing her eyebrow, then allowed the fall of her bangs to cover the exposed skin. Not much, in terms of body modification, but something curious to catalog. The only thing he

really knew at this point was she wasn't his brother. "Try the next truck over. He had something to smoke earlier, might be receptive." The window began to raise back into position.

Unexpectedly, because he was normally as tightlipped as a cop in lockup, his mouth blurted exactly what he was thinking, all his filters apparently having reached their capacity tonight. "You're not Fred." *This round of ignorance brought to you by alcohol.*

She snorted, shaking her head and tilting it the slightest amount as the window stopped in place, halfway up and halfway down, committed to neither. He stared at her and decided to go with it. She evidently thought him a prostitute, might as well play the part. "Hell, for you? Half-price."

The window powered down to the fully open position, and she leaned an elbow on the metal frame. Amused, she asked, voice two octaves higher than previous, "Say what?"

She's curious. The remains of his drunken fog receding in light of this puzzle to solve. *Curious equals interested.* Interesting. "Half-price. I didn't realize you were a chick." Downplay everything. "My favorite kinda chick."

Chin to her palm, head tipping the other direction, she waited for a beat. Then, with that thread of humor still present, she asked, "What does that mean?" *Nice fuckin' voice. Nice package of pretty sittin' here in front of me.*

"My favorite kinda chick? A hot chick." He'd known whores in his life, knew one of them since he'd been birthed, since that had been his mother's chosen profession. So he knew the patter they preferred and made a split-second decision to find an edge there to walk. Lowering his voice, he pitched it sexy-sweet for his spiel, letting the truth roll off his tongue knowing it would be more believable than anything else. "Hot chick like you, I'm surprised you're not already laid up with a man. But

you ain't, and here I am. Give me a chance. I'll rock your world, baby. Rock you all night long. Make you feel so good."

Lips he hadn't realized were so generous stretched in a beautiful smile, giving her face additional dimension. His cock twitched, the first sign of life from that rat bastard all evening. Low and smooth, in a level tone, she asked, "What's the cost of this hypothetical connection?"

Ho-lee shit, she's goin' for it. Chin up, he pushed his bottom lip up and out, creating that pouting, bearded smile the girls seemed to like so much. Confident for the first time since before he broke the last rack of balls, he held her gaze as best he could in these indifferent shadows on the edge of the lot. "Man's gotta make a livin', but you're so pretty..." He trailed off and made a show of looking at what he could see of her. "...you name your price, and you got it, baby."

The rolling rumble of a hundred truck engines surrounded them, quietly vibrating the air, coiled power exploited for the drivers' comfort, keeping the cabs cool or warm according to preference. Her truck was silent, the window already slightly open before he'd knocked on the door. She took things as they came, without forcing things into a mold. He wondered suddenly if she could take him the same way and felt a shiver of fear trickle down his back, not sure how far he should push this farce.

He cast that thought aside as his chest settled, heavy with disappointment at her continued silence, and was a half breath from turning away when she spoke. "Payment after services rendered." There was no way a whore would go for that arrangement, rightly assuming they'd be stiffed. The way it worked was payment up front, like what you get or not, the goods were the goods. No way would a whore climb up in a truck without seeing the green. "Got a condom?" she asked, giving so much away with her two short sentences.

She couldn't know how whores worked. He knew that tidbit for a fact, now that he was paying attention. The inside of her cab reflected a

quiet femininity, more like an anti-masculine than anything specific or pointed towards the fairer sex. A quilted pouch on the dash to hold small things, the fabric would muffle any annoying rattles. Cute and functional, there was a ladybug-shaped air freshener clipped to the visor. Those things identified her truck in such a way that there'd be no whores for her. The typical truck stop lot lizards avoided female drivers like the plague, like sweetbottoms at club parties avoided ole ladies. Like cottonmouths and copperheads, knowing the other by the stench emitted, each giving the other a wide berth.

Her question, well, that gave away a lot. A woman without condoms meant she did without getting dick regularly, or at least never brought it home. He knew from his brother that truckers considered their rig a home as much as he looked at the clubhouse the same way. You only brought into that what you were willing to defend. Sweetbottoms didn't come inside, not past the outer rooms. Relegated to the party spots and common areas, they were never allowed back where the members lived because bitches didn't rank if the shit hit the fan. So this woman not having condoms meant she didn't shit where she lived. Which made her willingness to let him in suspect and odd.

Such a nice package of pretty, appealing and sweet. *Why would she be looking for paid company?* A beautiful woman alone on the road learned to be safe and cautious early on, or they didn't stay good-looking long.

Twisted, road name earned years ago, the only name his club members knew, didn't like odd. He liked to understand odd, dissect it, and see what made it tick. The why mattered.

Decision made, he nodded, reaching for the grab bar anchored to the side of the truck. Hand out, he caught the door as she threw it open before disappearing into the back of the truck, headed towards the sleeper. It took him two false starts, but he managed to climb up and into the seat. He powered the window shut and made a show of locking the door before turning to look into the rear of the cabin.

The pass-through between the seats led to a condo sleeper, dim lighting from the built-in cabinetry illuminated the area as well as the woman perched on one end of the mattress. A pistol was lying on top of a table next to her, within easy reach of her right hand.

Palms lifted in front of him, he shook his head. *Shit. Shit shit shit. Shoulda known too good was too good.* He imagined seeing his winnings from the night going up in a quick puff of smoke. Seeing the hit he'd take when the boys found out he'd been taken in by a slip of a chick who was hardly old enough to hold the license her current vehicle required. "Hold on," he said softly, feeling a cold ball of steel settle into his belly. *Calm and cool. There we go*. He was good in challenging situations. His responses never quite what people expected, twisting the fabric around him until everything of benefit came to him. "Hold on."

"Just so there aren't any misunderstandings," she said, reaching over and picking up the gun.

Shit shit shit. Hand inching down his leg, he split his attention. Half remained on the woman, watching the movement of her fingers and hand, fixated on the flexors and tendons and muscles in the arm holding the gun, and half transferred to his own hand, feeling the outline of the gun in his boot. Judging the time it would take to flip it out and into his palm, evening the numbers. He had another weapon in a holster on his six, but his position in the seat made that one awkward to reach. *If you can't win with one gun, you're fucked anyway. Wait,* he thought. *Wait and see.*

With a practiced flip of her thumb, she engaged the safety and then dropped it back to the surface with a clatter. Twisted refused to give her any reaction, not even the satisfaction he felt that she had so misjudged him. *Happens all the time*. With a pretty face and a lean, muscular body he preferred to think of as wiry, he found himself underestimated all the time, especially by men who felt bulging muscles were the measure of a man. And now, by a woman who didn't know the kind of viper she'd

allowed into her home. Her propping the door open, that invitation offered and accepted, slithering in, forked tongue flicking inside the smile forced into place. *Oh, darlin', your mistake. My pleasure.*

"So, how's this go?" She trained her eyes on him, fixing him in place, but he could see the edge of uncertainty there, too. She was rethinking things; probably already sorry she'd rolled that window down. Time to pour on the charm again, ease her into things. If he wanted to take this all the way, it seemed he'd be able to, and he found himself still intrigued. *Would be good to fuck someone just for fun for a change.* Most of his rendezvous were calculated for club advantage.

His last three encounters had all been like that, unsatisfying fucks that were more work than fun. First, the wife of a rival club's president, a video of her active participation emailed to the man's club that night. Twisted stood back and watched the implosion, members not willing to follow a man who couldn't keep his bitch in line, freeing Twisted to scoop the good ones right up. There was the offered daughter of a sweetbottom looking to trade up to ole lady status. He'd verified the age and willingness before tossing the bitch on a table and drilling into her hard and fast. Even without priming her, finding to his distaste that at just-turned-eighteen, she was already sloppy—*he gave a silent snort at where his mind went*—as a truck stop lot lizard. Then the party doll who'd sucked him off at a joint gathering three weeks ago, her reluctant man forced to watch the head-bobbing action. Prospect patch for the other club on his back, the hookup as much a discipline for him as a tradeoff with Twisted. He'd come with slitted eyes watching the crowd, listening to the bitch gag as he wrenched her hair, thrusting down her throat.

This cute thing in front of him was looking for more than a quick fuck. An offer of an all-night gig was on the table, and those words had triggered an involuntary tell, an eye flare suggesting he'd piqued her interest. It meant she was looking for a partner, not an encounter. Maybe she didn't know there was a difference. She'd be looking for sweet. *I can do soft tonight,* he decided on the fly. *I can give her sweet if*

that's what she needs. Tipping his head towards her gun lying on the table, he tipped his hand at the same time.

"This goes a couple different ways, darlin'." Using a gentle voice, soft and quiet, reassuring, he adjusted the tone until he saw the muscles in her shoulders relax a bit. "First, I need to know you don't plan on robbing me."

"What?" The question was forced out by her surprise, a laughing negation of sound that he was happy to hear. "No, of course not."

"Man can't be too careful." He gave her the smile again, and her face softened, brightening in enticing ways. He found this up-close view of her reaction intoxicating. *I know I'm good-lookin', but I do believe this chick is into beards.* Testing his theory, he lifted a hand, stroking downwards from cheeks to tip, over the point of his chin and down his neck the short distance to where his beard ended. She watched the entire motion without breathing. Not once. Mouth open partway, she would be embarrassed to know she licked left to right across her entire, lush bottom lip. *Fuck yeah, she'll be willing to ride my beard, no doubt.*

"You never know what kind of people you'll find these days." Stretching out his arm, he rested his hand palm-up on his thigh—*not a danger*, he projected, *harmless to you*—concentrating on her as he said, "I've got my own protection." Spell broken, her chin jerked up, pointing directly at him, eyes locked on his as he continued, "I have two pieces on me, darlin'. And a knife in my boot." Still and quiet, she didn't glance at her handgun, which told him she knew exactly where it was in relation to her body. She didn't have to look at it to go for it. *Interesting.* "I wanted to tell you now, so when you see me take them out and put them up here,"—he gestured to the surface between the seats, a built-in sticking out from the wraparound driver's console—"you won't be surprised."

She nodded, the only movement he could see other than the jumping fabric over her heart. Every conscious reaction was clamped

down, but she couldn't control that tell. His gaze slipped to her neck, and he saw the same pulse leaping there, pounding. *In about two minutes, I'm gonna have my mouth there*, he decided, giving her the smile again. "So long as you aren't planning on robbing me, and I'm extending the same courtesy, we'll have everything out in the open, yeah?" He moved and the chain from his wallet jangled against the seat controls, reminding him of something. "And I have three condoms, sweetness. If we need more than that, one of us will have to get dressed and walk to the truck stop, make a purchase."

That pulled a reaction from her, startled surprise. *Hmm.* At the honesty, or the offer to go three rounds in the space of time she was offering him? *Maybe she's been with shitty men in the past?* Young as she was, that didn't mean lack of experience; he was a prime example of that. By the time he'd turned fifteen, he'd fucked his way through the entire senior class, and even tagged a couple of juniors. Not to say his freshmen peers hadn't wanted their turn, but he focused on the leverage pieces first. Access to booze and cigs, invitations to upperclassmen parties, girls with jobs who didn't mind spending cash on flash for him.

He'd taken his mother's advice to heart, though, even back then. *Georgie, you always take care of the woman first. Don't make her feel like a slut. Don't make her wait on you to get yours. Take care of your woman.* She'd told him that the first time she saw the trash can full of used tissues, back when he was twelve. Watching the women around the whorehouse had given him a unique window into what "taking care of the woman" meant. A practical application of knowledge had never steered him wrong.

"Then how this goes is I come back there and sit next to you. I'll kiss you if you're okay with that." A pause and she nodded, his head bobbing as he returned the gesture. She was all in on this. He eased his hand down, pulling the pistol out of his boot. She didn't even look at his hand when it came up to place the weapon in clear view on the console. Her gaze remained stuck to his face, taking in everything he said. "Then

we'll neck for a bit, stretch out, get comfortable. I promised you all night, sweetness. We don't have to hurry anything."

Hand behind his back now, he pulled the other gun from the holster, laying it next to its smaller partner. Barrel to barrel, the two guns looked like a parody of a tattoo. A gangster he once knew, Two Guns, had that image inked on his belly. Once knew the man, nothing to know now. Two Guns had met the fate foretold by his name, eating the end of a rival's gun, shadows in an alley devouring his pain.

She licked her lips, then, voice soft and low, sweetly unsure, asked, "All night?"

"All night long, sweetness." He retrieved his wallet, flipping it open and taking out the condoms. Palming the wrappers, he replaced the worn leather into the back pocket of his jeans, feeling it snag on the frayed hole in the bottom corner of the fabric. "All night," he repeated, legs pushing as he levered to a standing position, half bent over, shoulders rounded and bumping the ceiling. He glanced up to the space over her bunk, seeing the upper bed folded away. It was much higher back there, more room to maneuver. "Permission to enter the boudoir, ma'am?"

That pulled a grin from her, and he returned it, knowing his smile looked more self-satisfied than hers did. That was okay; they'd get there. *She just needs some confidence.* Startled at the thought, he wondered why the fuck it mattered to him. He was about to get his nut off in a sweet piece that had fuckall to do with the club. No business in this truck, just two people about to fuck like animals.

She gestured to his feet, and he glanced down then back up, waiting. "Can you take your boots off up there?" She pointed to the floor underneath the steering wheel, and he looked to see two pairs of shoes lined up beside the outer wall, up beside the clutch. "I try to keep the outside as far away from where I live as possible."

Me, too. With a scowl, he remembered the one time he'd let a woman into his space at the clubhouse. A newly patched member, he'd gotten shitfaced and hauled a drama mama to his room. She'd been looking to work her way up on her back, and left his bed in the middle of the night to crawl into an officer's rack. Fucking her way through the ranks, only to be discovered by that man's ole lady the next morning which meant she'd fucked up for sure.

Hair and blood had flown, and while that shit was amusing to watch when drunk or stoned, it was a fuckuva lot less entertaining at six o'clock in the morning, hungover, and feeling like shit. Still, it had been his to clean up, so he'd waded in, taking a rake of nails to the face for his efforts. That had been the only time he'd done that shit; made his personal rule mandatory in the first church after he took up the president's gavel.

She was frowning, so smoothing his expression, he gave her a dialed-back version of the cocky grin, pulling the veneer of civilized back into place. "No problem, darlin'. I like neat and tidy right alongside you." He bent over and lifted a foot in the same motion, something he'd been doing for decades now. Leather changed, habits didn't. One tug and he dropped the boot with a quiet thud, exchanging positions, propping his other ankle on his knee as he tugged again. Reaching down, he sorted his boots, lining the heels up with the edge of the rubber mat, keeping them off the carpeted area. "Better?" He reached, unclipping his wallet, pulling it out and laying it between the guns.

It was good she spoke up. It told him she was willing to ask for what she needed. Communication always made fucking more satisfying and just easier all around, so her asking for this boded well for him.

She nodded, and he moved, easing a knee to the mattress, shifting to a hip and gliding past her to put his back to the rear wall. Head in his hand, elbow propping him up, he grinned up at her. Where she sat, shoulders leaning against the sidewall, her ass was about where the pillows would go if they weren't scrunched up into the corner. He

wasn't surprised. By the restless movement he'd heard even before knocking on the door, she hadn't been sleeping. There was a book tucked under the edge of the pillows, face down, uncaring if she broke the spine.

He glanced around. There were a dozen well-worn books in one of the shelves over the top of the bunk, held in place by two fabric-covered elastic straps. From where he was, he could read the titles on some of them. *Jesus, fuck,* he thought, trying hard not to laugh aloud. Motorcycle club books. Every one of them. He'd stumbled on a closet club fanatic. Probably religiously watched that fuckin' show on TV, even now that it was over with. Hell, she probably watched the reruns, too. Got her ideas from a Hollywood version of the life, probably didn't know a single founder's name of the club that "advised" on the show, but she could tell you the statistics for the actors portraying bikers.

From the looks of the models on some of the book covers, she wasn't above smut for her bedtime reading, so hopefully she wouldn't be opposed to acting out some of her favorite scenes. Mentally he compared himself to the clean-shaven, mural-inked, and gym rat-fit bodies on display and had to fight laughter again. Full beard, mostly black tattoos with a little color when the ink called for it, a leanish frame with a hint of body fat to attest to his love of food and booze—about the only thing he had in common with the guys on those covers was he wasn't wearing his cut right now, either. That was in Fred's truck, wherever the fuck that was, stored so he wouldn't have to deal with shit solo. Not that he was afraid of an ass beating if it came down to that, but this wasn't his town, so protocol demanded he respect the dominant club in the area.

He patted the mattress next to her hip, smiling up at her, tugging a pillow over. "Come down here next to me, sweetness." Reaching out, he stroked up her thigh, traveling from knee to near the "Y" that housed one of his favorite meals in the world. Sweet, clean, tasty pussy. *Been a long time. Too long.*

The muscles of her leg flexed under his palm as she scooted down, responding to his suggestion without argument. *Compliant*, he mused, *not a bad thing as long as she's got the fire that hair promises, too.* A light auburn, with blonde undertones, he hoped it hinted at wild. "That's it," he encouraged her as she inchwormed her way to prone. "Come on down," he called in a singsong. Turning to a hip, she faced him, propping her head like his.

"This is the kissing part," he said, cupping a palm behind her head and tugging gently. She resisted for a moment. Then her stiffness wilted, and when she leaned in, he got his first inkling of what was in store for him. Winter fresh, minty with the flavor of the gum she'd evidently been chewing, he breathed in her scent, lips working across hers. Nipping and plucking at her bottom lip, he gained the advantage when she gasped in a breath. Tracing across her lips, he dipped inside until the tip of her tongue touched his, and he tasted her. *Addicting*. Head angling, he opened his mouth wider, forcing hers to reciprocate, giving him better access. He took that. Hell, he'd take every inch she gave him, every indulgence possible if it meant he got to taste her again. And again. *All night*, he reminded himself, loosening a grip that had tightened, fingers winding into her hair to hold her in place.

"I'm liking this kissing thing," she whispered, telling him something he already knew, thumb to the telltale pulse beating like a tom-tom in her neck. "But, what do I call you," she asked when his lips moved so he could kiss along her jaw, finding her skin just as delicious as her lips. "What's your name?"

"Bell," he said, thoughtless of lies. All attention was taken up by discovering each inch of skin covering her neck and shoulders, his nose pushing aside the collar of her shirt to gain access to the flesh underneath. "Call me anything, baby," he muttered, using his grip on her neck and jaw to angle her head away, staring at the beauty in his hands for a moment. Giving and easy, she molded to his demands, arching her neck to create lines of magnificence like nothing he'd ever

seen before. Pixie-featured, the sharp edge of her jaw exposed a vulnerability he hadn't expected.

"Bell?" This question came with a giggle, and he listened closely, liking it as much as he'd liked the tone earlier when she'd only been amused. "Like Tinker Bell? Is that like a...stage name?"

He froze, remembering she believed him a truck stop whore, someone who fucked men for money, playing bear or cub based on the client's need. Someone who found the novelty of a chick behind the wheel worth what amounted to a freebie in trade. Forcing himself to movement, he resumed kissing and caressing her, trailing his fingers down her throat to her chest, dragging the fabric of her tee against her skin as he moved. "Just Bell," he said, mouth moving along her neck. "My last name," he told her honestly, something few people knew. "What do you want me to call you?"

"Penny," she said, breathless as he cupped a breast, fingertips working along the edges of her bra before abandoning it to move farther south. She scooted towards him, slipping halfway to her back, trailing her fingers up his belly to the curve of his hip. Leather tail of his belt in hand, she worked at the buckle for a minute, chin lifting to press her lips to his when he paused to concentrate on the soft, delicate brushes of her hand against his rock-hard cock.

"Penny." He tried out the name, liking how it fit in his mouth. Locating the hem of her shirt and pulling it up, he watched as she arched her back, titties begging for his mouth. Finding a pleasant surprise underneath, he brought the fabric over her head and tossed it to the carpeting. "Mmmm, my shiny Penny." Fingers dipping into the cups of her bra, he pulled them down, framing her freckle-dusted breasts beautifully with the dark copper-colored material.

Lips and fingers paid homage, tracing and teasing as he focused on her responses, finding her wonder at the pleasure gratifying. *Yeah, she's been pegging two-pump chumps.* His lips curved into a smile as he fed

her titty into his mouth, feasting on her. Lace and pebbled nipples giving wonderfully different textures to play with, he moved from soft skin to tight tip and back again, switching sides in order to leave no inch neglected.

Curled up against him as she was, he experienced every breath, every quiver, the sounds torn from her throat surrounding him. Back arched, she wordlessly offered herself and he took...everything. Tangling his leg with hers, he pinned her to the mattress, rocking his cock against her hip. Her hands had stilled, but his belt dangled free from her forgotten attempts at undressing him. Sweeping one hand up her side, he plumped and cupped the breast not currently in his mouth, drawing her deep when her fingers tentatively ran through his hair.

Cautious of her fair skin, he tried not to rub his beard against her too roughly, but found the scent and taste of her alluring and couldn't stop himself from nuzzling softly. "Oh," she cried, and he pulled back, unsure of her reaction, but knew what she wanted when her fingers tightened in his hair. Letting her direct his mouth back to her titties, he nuzzled again, scraping his chin across her nipple, indulging her with a brief tease from his rough beard. Soothing the smooth skin with his tongue, he repeated the motion, reading into her stillness that she wasn't just enjoying this, but that it was new and novel to her. *Bearded for her pleasure. Something to experience fully.* He hoped she'd be interested, his mouth watering at the thought.

Shifting down in the bunk, he snuggled his cheek against her stomach, eyeing his next destination. *Button fly jeans, no belt, no shoes. Got this one handled.* He grinned. Hand behind her knee, he gave a squeeze and tugged the leg farthest away from him out and up, spreading her thighs slightly. He didn't intend to go fast, no need to strip her yet. Time to play, see how hot and bothered he could make her. Fingertips only, he made small circles on the back of her calf, not moving up or down, just touching, spiraling slowly, creating a sensory feedback for her. At the same time, he nuzzled into her bare belly, gently rubbing against her as he laid a line of open-mouthed kisses

along the edge of her bra. Lifting his mouth, he broke away before calling her name softly, "Penny, can you do me a favor?"

"Mmmm?" A humming question was her only response. He nuzzled her again, tickling along her ribcage to a chorus of sighs before lifting his head and sucking a breast into his mouth. Flattening his palm on her leg, he squeezed and massaged her calf, anchoring her in two places. Lifting up, he blew a fast stream of air across her wet nipple, watching the entirety of her breast break out in goose bumps.

"Penny?" Just her name this time was repeated a little louder. "Penny?"

"Mmmm? Yeah, Bell?" At least he got his name from her; she might be listening after all.

"Can you take the tie out of my hair?" Dipping his mouth to her, he rolled her nipple between his lips, tonguing it against the roof of his mouth. His stiffened fingers scraped blunt nails up the back of her calf, skimming the fabric and she jerked, pulling away, spreading herself wider for him. "Baby? Can you do that for me?"

She wiggled, pulling the arm trapped underneath him out, making him lift up to assist. Both hands on his head now, he felt gentle tugs as her careful fingers worked the leather cuff free. He saw the system of eyelets and hooks arc past, falling to the floor. Reflexively, showing she either had long hair not long ago or knew someone intimately who wore their hair long, she thrust her fingers into the locks falling around his face, massaging and scratching lightly at his scalp until he groaned.

He nuzzled into her appreciatively then set about doing what he intended when he asked her the favor. Fingertips to her leg, drawing small circles again while he indulged both breasts with kisses, licks, and tiny nips, he then moved his mouth back to her belly, dragging his hair across her titties. Trailing his hair back and forth, he moved his mouth from side to side, tonguing and mouthing her skin as he scooted down further in the bunk.

Nails dragging, hand sliding, he fondled his way up her leg, exploring new territory there, too. Each inch pulled a different noise from her, and he worked to separate the actions that carried the most response, repeating those, pushing the sensation for her. Above her knee was a soft gasp, tender and sweet to hear. Halfway up her thigh earned him a shuddering rush of air, deeper and more than a gasp, but just as soft. Fingertip tracing the seam of her jeans, thumb rubbing firmly at the muscles underneath gave him an idea to set aside for now, but he promised himself he would circle back to it. *Oh, yeah, this is fun*.

Determined to meet in the middle, he shifted on the mattress again, bringing his mouth that much closer to the prize. Bellybutton next, tempting tiny divot in the center of so much quivering flesh called for a dip and a nip, beard dragging back and forth as he traced the circumference with the tip of his nose. Her belly was jerking with each breath, hipbones holding her jeans up, a dark, inviting separation between fabric and skin that grew and shrank with each gasp.

Mouth to that strip of skin, tongue trailing and dipping underneath, teeth to the button fly flap. Pulling and tugging, growling playfully, he brought her laughter to the surface again. That same refreshing rise and fall of sweetness filling the cab for a moment before cutting off abruptly when the button slipped through the hole. Palm to her other thigh, he pushed high and rubbed the side of his hand at the edge of gloryland. Heat from her pussy radiated out from her. *Gonna be so fuckin' hot and tight*. Relishing the idea, he moved his body over her leg, hemming her in and settling between her knees, elbows to the bed.

Hands on both her thighs now, he toyed and fondled, covering her still-clothed mound with his mouth, giving her the heat of his outgoing breath until she squirmed. He rewarded himself with a sipping inhalation that carried the scent of her arousal. *Fuck, yeah*. So rich and thick he could already taste her, already imagine how the folds of flesh would feel under his tongue. Tipping his head, he ensured his hair covered her belly, hiding his face as he rocked back and forth.

Mouth working her jeans, teeth biting at the seams where they joined together to cover her intimate areas, hands moving and gripping, pulling and lifting, hair teasingly light across her belly—it wasn't long before her vocalizations were louder. Not yet loud, but, at least more than a barely-there inrush of air. Her *oooooh*, and *mmmhm*, and a shaky *aaaahh* were music to his ears, and he again worked to push her up the slope. Easing a hand underneath her body, he threaded his way across her ass and up to the bare skin of her back. Hot and smooth. Silk under his touch.

Splaying his fingers wide, he pressed firmly, letting her feel the power and strength of his hold. At the same time, he trailed delicate fingertips up her side, across the fabric that still framed and accentuated her breasts, finding and teasing the hardened nipple. The hand underneath pressing, lifting, reminding her she had a man in her bed, the other hand carefully plucking at sensitive flesh, skillfully pleasing. Leaning forward, he opened wide, taking as much of her into his mouth as he could, rigid tongue pressing against that hot pussy just out of reach, lips locking so he could suck and bite through the fabric. His efforts were proven worth it when she stiffened and shuddered, the low moan flooding the air around him just as bewitching as her laughter. "Bell!" *Fuck, yeah, I gave that to you, baby.*

Backing off, easing up, he gave a practiced flip of his head, settling his hair around his face and down his back. Mouth open, she was drawing in unsteady drafts of air, eyes squeezed tightly shut. Hands draped across her belly from when she lost her hold on his head. Twisted watched as her fingertips moved in intriguing circles, imitating what he'd been doing to her only moments ago. He grinned and then moved, pressing his chin firmly just above her pussy. With his palm settled over her tit, covering and protecting it, he had nothing but confidence in his voice when he reminded her, "All night, Penny."

"Oh, God," she whispered, turning her head to one side, chin tucked tight to her neck where it met her shoulder. *Hmmm. Not the enthusiastic reaction I expected.* Then she surprised him when she

asked, hesitantly stopping and starting, "Did you need me to...um...do...um...anything?"

"Penny." He adopted a tolerant tone, one you might use with a favorite student. "I'm a man. I only got so many chances at reaching those peaks. Now, I can bring you,"—he mouthed her pussy again, grinning when she writhed in place, pushing up against the pressure—"as many times as you'll let me. Make you come until your throat is raw from screaming my name." Hands gripping again, firm to the point of fierce, he pulled and tugged, reminding her he was all around her. "But, biology declares I only have so many chances." Easing off, he plumped and caressed her tit, other hand splayed wide across her back, covering as much skin as he could. "I got three condoms and all night. I plan on using all three."

Shifting, he lifted to his knees, moving over her on all fours. Suspended for a moment, he stared down into her eyes, noticing their color for the first time. A bright crystal blue that went perfectly with everything he could see. "All night." He made the words a promise, bringing his mouth down to hers, giving a hum of pleasure when her lips parted immediately, granting access that he plundered. Tongue sliding and stroking, he traced the inside of her lips, touched the tip to hers, then plunged deep, twining and thrusting, head slanting this way and that. Her chest arched up, and he rubbed across her, the fabric of his tee snagging and dragging on the lace surrounding her tits. "All night." He pulled back, leaving her panting and staring up at him. Those blue eyes locked on his face, dipping to his mouth when he said her name. "Penny."

He stripped his shirt off, shaking his hair out as he tossed it to the side. Settling back on his heels, he freed her arms from the straps of her bra, leaving her shoulders bare but keeping the confining fabric in place just underneath her tits. Tugging at the buckle of his belt, he felt the leather slip and catch in the loops as he removed it from his jeans, letting it drop over the side of the bunk to the floor, a muffled thud cushioned by the clothing already there. Unbuttoning his waistband, he

eased the zipper down and then left off there, reaching instead for her jeans.

Fingers working, he glanced up to see she was looking uncomfortable again. *Needs some confidence. Maybe a little direction will ease the way for her.* "Hands behind your head, Penny. Under the pillow is fine, but I want you to keep them there." Uncertainty was writ large on her features, so he paused what he was doing to smooth his hands up either side of her ribcage, cupping her breasts as he stared into her eyes. "That'll be a reminder that you don't have to work for this, darlin'. My pleasure to please you." Her hands lifted, shoving under the pillow behind her head, and he grinned, appreciative of the movement and how that showcased her tits. "Beautiful," he told her, earning a curve in her lips. Not quite a smile, but he could work for those. "So fucking beautiful."

Hands sliding down, thumbs tracing a double line down her center, he reached the waistband of her jeans and tugged. She lifted her hips obligingly, and he pulled, finding a pair of panties hidden underneath that matched the copper of the bra. Fingering along the lacy edge, he told her, "Appreciate the view, baby. Perfect color for you. My shiny Penny." With a smooth motion, he removed jeans and panties from her, dropping them in a tangled mess to the floor, then took off her socks one at a time, flicking them over the side with a grin.

Knees primly together, legs pressed tight thigh-to-thigh, her feet were splayed slightly, one on either side of his knees. Clean and sweet, he didn't have any doubt she'd turn away at his next question, but it was one he'd be asking anyway. His hands in constant motion, up and over her calves to her knees, there was resistance to a tug, so he slipped his hands back down, cupping her instep, thumbs rubbing in broad circles.

"Penny," he began, staring down into her eyes. Her gaze fixed on him, immovable and tense. He got it, understood her nervousness, knew she was aware of exactly where her pistol sat on the cabinet three

feet from her head. She was naked, unclothed and bare skinned and with just as bare emotions, the orgasm stripping her of anything to hide behind. He knew how she came now, one of the most intimate things a man could know about a woman, and she'd given that to him.

When he didn't continue, she ran her tongue over that plump and bitable bottom lip, and then whispered, "Yeah, Bell?" Muscles in her belly jumped and jerked, the peaks of her beautiful breasts tightened and stood firmly upright. Heartbeat in her neck pounding, she seemed to be holding her breath, waiting.

"You clean, baby?" Always best to ask directly; get any conversation out of the way so he could decide how to move forward. It had been ages since he'd been near pussy he wanted to eat, but having her flavor rolling through his mouth with every indrawn breath, he was hungry for her. Musky scent surrounding them in the close atmosphere of the truck's cab a reminder of what might be his tonight. Patience was never his strongest suit, and if she wasn't as untainted as he prayed, he didn't know what he'd be willing to do.

"I showered this morning." Her voice quavered, satin slipping through the air to run up his spine. "I don't do anything special." Slick as a freshly-waxed fender, ignorance of his real question wasn't unattractive, merely underscoring what he already knew: she didn't get regular dick and may have had a long dry spell. "I'm sorry."

"Nothing to be sorry about, Penny." He leaned in, pressing a kiss to one kneecap. "Shiny Penny." He kissed the other one, running his fingers up her calves, cupping her legs and slipping his thumbs between. He then kissed the inside of the first knee when she allowed him to spread her legs. "Beautiful Penny." Mouth to the other knee, Twisted's tongue worked at her skin. "You smell sweet enough. I got no worries there. I was asking if you had any STDs you knew about." Blunt had been the right way to go here, and he watched, enthralled as she reacted, red flooding up her chest and neck into her face, fair skin

flaming from her embarrassment. "I don't, but don't have any papers to show you."

"I do not." With her chin tipped to the side again, he lost her eyes when they closed, lips in a tight line, every move screaming retreat. "Have anything, I mean."

Mouthing her knee, he pushed forward with his head, feeling her muscles tense to hold her legs together, hold him out, keep him away. Avoidance. Aversion. She'd only allowed him to strip her because she'd still been woozy from coming so hard. Coming hard with only titty-play, pressure, and heat from his mouth on the outside of her jeans. Not old, barely old enough to have a license if he read her right. Glancing around, he took in the inside of her cab again. Tidy, she'd put a few touches on it, but the truck hadn't been hers long. Scuff marks on the interior where things had been removed. Maps and paperwork showed she was working a lot. This was a long-haul rig with a hard-working driver, loads taking her coast-to-coast. But young. Embarrassed, and a—

"That's good, darlin'." One hand slipped down the back of her thigh, his fingers brushing along the outer lips of her pussy. Slick and wet. Aroused. At the touch, she stiffened and started to pull her hands from under the pillow. He knew she was reaching down to pull him away. "Hands, Penny," he barked, and she froze, but kept her face averted and eyes closed. Amenable, but uneasy, it seemed.

"I'm gonna touch you again, darlin'. Touch your beautiful sweetness just waiting for me." Matching motions to words, he trailed a fingertip across side-to-side, then dipped inside, bottom to top, flicking across her hard clit. The moan escaping her lips surprised her and when her eyes flew wide, he grinned, repeating the action. "Touch you, finger and fill you." He stretched out on his belly, shoulders holding her legs apart now. "Eat you." Mouth to her inner thigh, he stretched, trailing the tip of his tongue up and up, her scent spicy and thick, arousal written in each of her gasping breaths.

Nuzzling deep, he licked bottom to top, flattening his tongue wide, covering everything he could reach. She jerked back, ass pushed deep into the mattress, and he chased her pussy, having only gotten the barest taste, but already hungry for more. "Let me in, baby," he murmured, tilting his head, seeing her mouth slowly falling open, eyes squeezed shut. Palm to each leg, he lifted her knees, bringing them up and pressing outward. Licking slowly, he repeated the path, bottom to top. The already swollen lips of her sex were beautiful, flushed and red. They begged him to go again, and he did, leisurely, taking his time. And again. Lingering, lazy. *Loving*. He pushed that thought aside.

The simplest graze of his upper lip against her clit was enough to send a full-body quake through her. When he followed that with a flick of his tongue, diving underneath the hooded beauty, dragging up and over the hardened nub, her slick wet flooded his mouth. Palms to her thighs, he curved one hand underneath her ass, lifting her to his mouth so he could latch onto her clit, mouthing and tonguing it gently, taking everything she fed him, rewarded with a soft and breathless, "Aaahhh, *Bell*."

Pursing his lips, he sucked her, focusing with his mouth and tongue. The blood pulsing through her pussy scorched as he teased her entrance. One barely-there fingertip, slipped up and down, circling the opening, circuit after patient circuit—mouth to her clit, sucking and tonguing over and over. His name gained syllables as she wailed, "Bell!" when he pushed that single finger inside. Halfway only, in and out, patiently thrusting in time with his mouth on her, feeling the tight walls of her pussy clamping down on him. *Fucking tight.* Staring up her body, he watched her ribcage rise and fall at breakneck speed. Her back bent, arching, and she called his name again, and again. Ripples of her orgasm were beautifully visible on her skin and seductively felt on his fingers and tongue.

Her face had gone from taut and strained to soft, lips parted, and relaxed. *Two*, he thought, moving both hands to cover her belly, slipping up to tease the slowly softening nipples into peaks again. Her skin

flawless, a virgin canvas touched only with God's brush where freckles dusted her breasts and nose, thicker across her cheeks. Dark lashes dipped and touched those flushed apples. In contrast, his inked arms and hands looked dark and erotic as they moved across her. Spanning her ribs, fingertips finding purchase in the dips between, counting idly as he pushed up to cup her breasts again.

Still air in the truck cab carried enough moisture to the windows to have set up a thick fog. Condensation from their sweaty bodies filled the glass and shone a spotlight on her truck as dramatically as if the suspension was singing like he hoped it would be in a few minutes. He was hard enough to pound nails, blood surging thick through his cock, rigid with need. Dipping his head, Twisted lingered, lapping at her one last time before pushing to his knees and shimmying his jeans over his ass. Cock in hand, he stroked himself, root to tip and back again, once. Just once, and with the feast laid out before him, it was enough to nearly bring him to the edge. Makeshift cockring of thumb and finger beat it back enough for him to unclench his jaw to say, "Hand me a condom, Penny. Time for me to play."

Eyes jerked wide open, and she stared up at him, his intent because he wanted her full participation. The writhing and shuddering she'd done as he ate her inflamed his imagination of how she would be under him. On top of him. In front of him. Plunging up, down, back...chasing his cock like he'd chased her pussy a minute ago. Her gaze dropped to his cock and he flexed, tightening, feeling the crown mushroom out, knowing without looking it was red edging to purple, the crest defined. Throbbing.

"I have to move my hands," she told him, and he smiled, supporting himself up on one arm, suspended over her. Reaching between them, he trailed his palm up over her pussy, circling her clit with two fingers slow, then fast, then slow again.

"Move your hands, baby," he told her, engrossed in the way her lips parted when he hit the fast speed. She gasped, then bit down on her

lips and then gasped again. Every reaction controlled by his hand on her. Leaning in, Twisted kissed her softly, letting the flavor lingering on his mustache and beard from his intimate exploration of her invade this soft caress of lips on lips.

"Ohhh." She breathed in, and he smiled against her mouth, fingers circling slowly, and then rapidly. Movement followed by a crinkle, and then her hand was between them. He took the package, angled down and kissed her again, hard. Sucking her tongue into his mouth before tangling his own with it, pushing back into her mouth, thrusting. Timing his movements, Twisted played careful pursuit of her arousal. Fingers circled fast, gliding across her clit while at the same time trailing slowly against her tongue with his. Changing speeds, his fingers circled slowly, diversion for a hard kiss, head slanting, biting at her bottom lip. A contest to see her finish, fingers circling fast, a brisk thrumming side-to-side, earning her crying gasp into his mouth as she came again, worked to the edge and over with generous kisses and attentive play. *Three.*

Ass to heels, the fabric of his jeans cut into his thighs as he rolled the condom down. He frowned when he realized it was the kind he used for blow jobs. No matter, she made enough lube for two fucks with only the first orgasm. Her panties were wet and soaked before he removed them, darkened copper center giving everything away to attentive eyes. Fingers to her pussy, he spread her lips and pressed the tip of his cock inside. Knees wide, he arranged her before him, the fire-red patch just above his target leading him forward.

Supported on his elbows, he glided over her, and slipped both hands under the pillow. Finding her hands, he laced their fingers together. She clutched him with desperate strength, and he wondered again, *Is she?* Slow push, two inches in, one inch back, slow and steady. Push until her fingers gripped him hard enough to bruise, then pull back slowly, fucking those few inches he had inside her. "Spread your legs wider, darlin'," he murmured, and the stranglehold her thighs had on his hips lessened. "Bring your knees up." This instruction was less

enthusiastically followed, but he felt the softness of her calves along his flanks, and the angle changed, "Oh, yeah, baby."

"Ohhh." He watched the sound leave her mouth, lips pursed in a sweet circle he would fucking love to have wrapped around his cock before the night was over. Tight as her pussy was, he would be ecstatic to stay right where he was, though. *I told her she didn't have to do anything*, he reminded himself, flexing his fingers around hers. In a near echo of his thoughts, she asked, "What do you want me to do?"

"Darlin', you don't have to do anything." Pushing steadily, feeling her parting before him, hot, soft, tight, sweet pussy, his for the taking. "All night," he promised again, pulling back slowly, the drag against his cock excruciating in its beauty. "No rush, no hurry. You just do what feels right, baby." Surging farther in, his hips sashayed side-to-side, rocking slowly. Her bottom lip disappeared into her mouth, and he watched as her teeth dented the skin, biting firmly. "Am I hurting you, Penny?" Ass and back tensing, ready to pull out entirely if she indicated discomfort. *Un-fuckin-like me.* He dropped that thought like a hot potato when her back arched, torso pushing up against him with a moan. Her shoulders rounded, lifting, head tilting to brush her lips against his, feverish in her wordless need. He gave her what she wanted, kissing her hard, pressing her hands into the mattress as, rocking side to side, he thrust slowly until he was firmly seated inside her as deep as possible.

Her fingers twisted, frantic in their need to get away, get close, get into him, get away from him. He held on. Held on and lifted up to watch as she called his name and he felt that fucking flutter and ripple that he'd experienced at such a distance earlier. All around him, fluttering, clenching, tight and hot. Neck curving, back bowing, she twisted underneath him, shoulders and ass pushing into the mattress as she came just from his cock being inside her, nothing else. *Mind. Blown. Fuck, she's hot.* He watched her titties strain, begging for a caress of their own. Mouth to one, then the other, he offered tribute to her beauty with sucking kisses, maroon blossoms dotted in their wake. The edge of his teeth provided a different sensation, one she liked if the

noises coming from her throat were any indication. *Four*. This thought giving him a deep satisfaction.

"Gonna fuck you now, baby. Keep yourself spread for me. Hands in position, don't let them roam." Reluctantly releasing his hold, knuckles catching on hers as he unthreaded their fingers, he shifted to one arm in the bed, the other hand trailing up her chest to her neck. Cupping and tugging, he tilted her head, and then leaned down, sucking her bottom lip into his mouth. Thumb caressing the apple of her cheek, then trailing down, his hand closed gently around the column of her throat, heartbeat underneath his palm. Teeth gripping her lip, he muttered, "Stay spread." Heat and pressure from her legs disappeared, and he clenched his ass, grinding into her, feeling the last of her orgasm leaving her, drawing a final gasp as he jerked inside her, head of his cock bumping and rubbing deep.

Hips flexing, he pulled halfway out, carefully and slowly thrusting in, testing the waters to ensure she was stretched enough to take him without pain. Out—drag of her pussy torture, losing the heat of her skin against his balls—in, back to heaven, hot and soft, willing, sweet. Out faster, frame underneath him shuddering, her hips pumping up—in, quick and hard, bottom and grind, then—out.

Mouth to her neck, he felt her rapid breaths gusting past his ear, transitioning into a little moan when he pumped into her, deep and ringing while giving her his teeth in the muscle where her neck joined her shoulder. It fit his mouth like made for him. Twisted laid a series of soft kisses interrupted by tight grips with his teeth, each different effort bringing a new reaction from her.

"Sweet pussy, Penny. Shiny Penny," he whispered to her, lips ghosting across her skin. "Sweet Penny." Hips and back working ceaselessly now, he thrust into her steadily, each stroke exquisite and glorious. Wet, she was so wet, their play having every good return he could hope for. This was a messy fuck, and those were the ones he loved the most. *Messy is good, so good. But having tight, hot, and*

sweet...better. So much better. Never had it like this before. Where the pussy wasn't afraid of him. Wasn't afraid of pleasure, taking everything he had to give, and giving him back...this.

Coiled need settled on his spine, shivering its way up his back and wrapping threads of desire everywhere along its path. Muscles jerking and flexing independent of his intentional motions, his sac drew up, contracting and pulling close to his body. His cock was so thick, the lips of her pussy pulled and tugged with each stroke, inner walls holding him close. "Beautiful Penny."

It struck him she was quiet, and he shifted minutely so he could see her face, pushing one knee down in the bed, approaching her pussy from a slanting angle, finding exquisite there, too. *Perfect*. Mouth open, she lay trusting and lovely in his hands, throat working with each gasped breath. A rare beauty in his world, *flawless* the only word he could think. With her head moving side-to-side on the pillow, a fall of hair draped across her brow with the piercing while curls and strands stuck to sweat covering her cheeks.

Hard, deep, fast. The mattress squeaked under him, and the truck rocked side-to-side with the movement, her hips rising up to meet each downward thrust. "Fuck," he said, the tingle hitting hard when her bottom lip disappeared into her mouth again, the sight of her teeth biting into the ruby flesh too much. Powering through, he thrust hard, grunting and feeling the heat hit the head of his cock, surrounding him. Deep, deep, deep. *Fuck*. Holding his breath, he grunted and then stayed planted, mouth to her throat. *Fuck. Pussy like this can't be bought*. Struck by the epiphany, he took the thought to conclusion. *Can't be taken*. "Gave yourself to me," he said, lips to her shoulder, head pressed into the pillow beside hers, the lumps of her hands moving underneath. *Has to be given, presented, offered*. "Gave me something so sweet, man would break his back to keep that."

Breathing hard, sweat slicking his skin, he slipped across her belly, staying root-deep. Burying his face into her shoulder, he licked and

sucked his way up her neck. Mouth to her jaw, Twisted nibbled up, pulling her earlobe into his mouth, surprised at the unmarked skin there. Pierced brow, virgin ears, no ink that he'd seen. Not a virgin between her legs, but damned close. He'd bet every dollar in his pockets she'd only been breached once, maybe twice before. *Sensitive and so fucking responsive, the things I could do to this woman.*

Lips to her ear, he whispered what he knew, words spoken soft as the wing sweep of a butterfly, "I ain't your first, but I'm your best." She moved under him, arms straining with the need to push him away, but still obediently folded out of the way. "Ain't nobody ever ate that pussy before. Gave me something sweet. So fucking sweet. Something *that* sweet. Now I know what I negotiated for, I will be using the whole night, darlin'. I got plans on what I'd like to do with you." He felt his softening cock beginning to slide out and reached down, anchoring the edges of the condom against his shaft as he pulled out slowly. "Need a tissue, Penny. And a wipe or towel, darlin'. Let me see to you. Tonight is all about you."

Panting breaths had dried her mouth; he heard her lips part just before she whispered, "Tissues up by my seat. Wipes in the drawer to my right." He sucked on the skin just behind her ear, taking all her air along with a few stolen nips. She cleared her throat, then softly said, "Shower stuff, with a towel, in the built-in on the other end of the bunk." Organized, like he already knew. Everything in place, so she could put her hand to it in need. "Bell?" Calling his name like he wasn't still on top of her, like they weren't slick with sweat and lying close. She called his name as if she were across a room, untouchable, out of reach.

"Yeah?" he answered, bringing his mouth down her throat, lips moving in tandem with his tongue. "Whasup, Penny?" Next her chest, kisses on every inch traversed along his way to her breast. Titty in his mouth on a deep draw, he sucked hard, flicking the tender, sensitive nip with his tongue. A gasp escaped over the top of his head, then her fingers threaded through his sweat-clumped hair near his scalp. A sweep of her hand cleared the long hair from one side of his face, and

he tipped his chin, dragging his beard across her breast, angling his head to look into her face.

"Thank you." Her words didn't make sense. Then he took a punch in the chest when she said, "Promise I'll make it worth your while." *Fuck*. Prostitute. *Right*. Not a supremely sweet connection like he experienced. She assumed his actions the work of countless practice sessions. His thoughts must have been evident on his face because she frowned, tipping her chin to the side like she'd done before and then whispered, "I'm sorry. I don't know what..." Rattling a breath in, shards of pain like broken china laced in her voice. "...I'm sorry."

Recovery might be possible if he were honest with her. *Not happenin'*. He rejected the idea. *Modified truth, maybe?* "This wasn't about that, darlin'. This is just me, with you. Tonight, I want to be just me." That was a truth that cut close to the bone because, in every second spent outside this truck, he wasn't himself. He was Twisted, president of the Incoherent MC, a man who had killed and cheated every step of his way to the top. Twisted wouldn't be lying here, holding a used condom to his cock, worried about the emotions of the woman underneath him. Twisted would be flipping her over, hand over her mouth as he fucked hard, takin' her ass because she wouldn't have been sweet enough to get him off. Not the kind of cunts he fucked. Bell was a memory. George Bell someone he knew in a past life, memories flowing through dreams at night.

But tonight, he could be Bell, could be what might have been if Twisted weren't birthed years ago by circumstance and events beyond his control. "Just Bell and Penny, exploring the boundaries of what we like together." Dipping his chin, he tugged at her nipple with his lips, kissing the curve of her breast and across to the other one. Lips to her skin, he murmured, "Can you let me just be?" Teeth to the clasp, he released the bra still confining her torso.

"Yes." This response rang clear in the cab, the swell of her ribcage expanding out with her breath. "Yes, of course."

"Then, let me thank you, Penny dear." Moving down her body, he folded, rising on his knees, sweeping her frame with his gaze. "You've provided me with a priceless opportunity I will not squander away. Turned me into a pinchfist, and me holding onto these minutes with miser's fingers." Winking at her, he grinned, deliberately lightening the mood by drawing the two words out long, "Aaaallll niiiight." Her laughter was a sweet reward, too.

Five minutes later he was stretched out beside her, having shed his jeans along the way. She had flipped a sheet over their hips, in modesty or out of habit he couldn't say, but he liked her cuddled into his side like she was. Head to his shoulder, her touch grazed around his nipples, dragging her fingertips through his chest hair, down his belly and back up, repeating the journey tirelessly.

For his part, he had one hand pushed under the sheet, fingers tracing interlocking rings on her hip in an endless loop of tenderness. His other was thrust under the pillow in mimicry of her earlier pose. Glancing down, Twisted let his eyes dance across her exposed breasts, liking how they pressed against his side. "Tell me about Penny," he said, finding a curiosity inside him about her, an interest nearly as broad and profound as his appetite for her. Even having just taken her, just fucked her until he came, and came hard, he wanted to be back inside her. Reliving of his fantasies from earlier had him dancing along the edges of rational reasoning. *Two more condoms.*

He'd had her under him now, every bit as beautiful as he imagined. Loving slow and sweet like that had been unique in his experience, and he found himself hungry for more of that feeling. That fitting together, the sense of giving something of yourself even while your partner gave you everything. "Tell me how you came to drive a truck."

She tipped her face to his chest, kissing his skin softly, hot lips with a sweet dip of her tongue. "My uncle drove. Had a regular route, LA to Boston and back again. Produce up east, seafood headed west. Needed a relief driver the summer I turned nineteen. He threw me up into the

truck and taught me everything I know." Her hand lifted, gesturing to the cab surrounding them. "He didn't have any kids of his own. This was his truck. Now...mine."

"What happened to him?" Something had, that was clear. Even with her holding it back, the sorrow in her voice was strong, the grief fresh.

"Old business caught up to him." She kissed his chest again, gently tonguing the flat, pebbled surface of his nipple and he gave up a groan to her softly giggling amusement, glad she could set aside her heartache momentarily. *Tease*. "About six months ago."

"What kind of business?" Old business didn't sound physical or accidental, which left only intentional for his death. *Intentional ain't good. A health hazard for those left behind, in some cases. Wonder if she'd know about any blowback her direction since she worked with him and was apparently favored?*

"He was an officer in a motorcycle club until a couple years ago. Gracefully backed down because his health was bad." She drew an uneven breath. "Bad. Cancer. He stayed a member, of course. Stayed in, just couldn't give as much time anymore. But something had happened in Baton Rouge years ago. A man came hunting him, and someone in his old club gave him up." Gaze to her face, Twisted watched as she blew the breath out from pursed lips, trying to control the shaking in her voice, her wobbling chin. Angry, she bit out, "He was going to die anyway. There wasn't any reason for them to come along and take their pound of flesh."

"Do you know what his club name was? What club he was in?" His questions skirted the edge of too much knowledge, but she didn't notice, thankfully.

Voice soft, she cooed the name. "Bagger." The smile that curved her mouth with the word fell away, a resigned look taking its place. "That was his road name. He was in the Caddo Hobos. In there for years, the

vice-principal." She shook her head, hair rustling against his beard as she corrected herself. "No, that's not right. Vice-president."

Shit. Who had he stumbled into tonight? "Baton Rouge, is that home?" He had intimate knowledge that Louisiana clubs ran fiercely loyal, her statement that someone gave up her uncle didn't make sense, especially if he'd served until health forced him to step down. He wondered if she had it right.

"Yeah. Red Stick." She gave the English translation that locals used for the town's name. "I'm Cajun born and raised." Her voice back to soft, something about those words triggered a memory for her, safe and sheltered. Floating light on the air, giggling laughter shook her frame, settling into his gut, warm. Sweet. "Creole through and through."

"No accent," he observed, and she giggled again, the sound changing to a gasp when he curled his hand around her hip, fingertips tapping her mound right above her clit. *Mmmm, quick to rouse*. Stiffening his middle finger, he swiped once across her hooded nub. Her instinctive push against his hip, the restless movement of her legs, these things told of her eager desire. Hunger. A swipe, a gasp, then he retrieved his hand, retreating to draw small circles on her hip again. He'd instigate another sneak attack in a moment, was just giving her time to recover. "You don't have an accent," he restated, making the unspoken "why" a question.

A shiver moved through her, and he relished the knowledge that he drove her to that feeling. "Hmm. Yeah. No. Daddy pushed me to be better than my raising. Started with a demand that I speak proper English. Movies weren't fun days. They were linguistic lessons where he analyzed everything the actors said, how they said it, and then bent those things into something that I could fit around me." She rolled her tongue across his flat nipple, her thigh lifting onto his legs, tangling there. Teasing herself as much as him. She shrugged, the motion moving her tits against him. "It stuck."

Palm to her thigh, he cupped and pulled, sliding her leg up his until her knee was nearly in his crotch. Fingers trailing back down her leg, tender skin under his touch, arrowing directly to his destination. He skimmed against her pussy once...twice...middle and ring finger met, creating a single shaft that pushed into her slowly. Her sweet accompaniment of sighs and moans was glorious to hear. Working gently, in, then out, he finger fucked her shallowly. Deliberately taking his time, going slow, waiting. After only a minute or two of these careful caresses, she arched back against his hand, which retreated with her movement, denying her the desired depth. She hissed, "Bell."

"Yeah, Penny?" Pushing in hard, he buried his fingers, then crooked them inside her before pulling halfway out, dipping his thumb to find her wetness. A moment later that thumb was poised at her pucker, fingers back into place inside her, working in and out deep, in and out shallow. Her ass retreated from the probing pressure, much as his hand had moments before, but he twisted his neck, pressing his face into her hair. Wanting this, his voice was guttural when he whispered, "Let me try, Penny. If it hurts, or you don't like it, I'll stop."

She stilled for a moment before nodding consent, and he ran with it, teasing, on a crusade to rouse her this way, too. Touching, circling, pressing, he kept a steady thrusting rhythm inside her with his fingers. Frowning when nothing pulled a reaction from her. Stiff and still, she rested at his side, but was no longer cuddling, not playing. All the fascinating charm was gone, her breathing tightly controlled. Not even indifferent, ass play was a turn off for her. She had switched off. Her enjoyment chased away.

Abandoning his efforts, he focused on her pussy, in and out, out and sliding up to finger her clit, then back inside. Within seconds, she was no longer locked in place, not yet animated in her movements, but at least not frozen. Provoked to rage, fighting the urge to howl in anger, he asked the question kicking at a tottering wall in his head. "Did someone hurt you that way, Penny?"

Her nod wasn't a surprise, but his bitterness was. It surged, and he withdrew, hand back to her hip, urging her closer to his side, wanting that cuddle puppy back that he'd had for such a short time, stolen away by his own eagerness to introduce her to...everything. So inexperienced, especially to have had that done in a way that left ugly, lasting pain was inexcusable. He wasn't successful in tamping his temper down and knew it filled his voice when he spoke. "Never let someone do something you don't like." A squeeze of her ass cheek, squeeze and lift, then a soft hand caressing her curves. "Never. Not even me."

"I liked the rest of what you were doing." Honeyed tones of pleasure told him he hadn't broken the spell woven by their play from earlier. Not completely, thank God. She moved, hand flattening on his chest, palm over his heart. *Can she feel how it sped up at her touch?* His hand on her ass moved again, squeezing and lifting, coaxing, then once she was persuaded to slide at his urging, pulling her into place on top of him.

More contact than before, breasts flattened against his chest, she snuggled into him. "I like your beard," she whispered, thinking she told him a secret. Quick fingers running through it, lifting from underneath, then smoothing it down again. "It's so..." Her voice dropped to a softer version of her already tender whisper, this one barely a breath, "...rough." This word came out as 'rruuuffff,' sound drawn into letters not used in its construction, but better conveying her emotions. His hand stroking her face felt her lips move, and without that, he would never have heard the last word. "Everywhere."

"Hungry, Penny." Stroking down her back, Twisted's palms settled on each cheek, pushing her up...up... Her head lifted in surprise, her crystal blues staring down at him. Eyes bright as the summer sky. "Feed me, baby." As she moved up, he shifted down until things were lined up exactly right, and then he fed.

Afterward, he handed her the second condom, and she inexpertly applied the raincoat. Her fumbling attempts causing his head to rear

back into the pillow, and she seemed to forget what she was doing at the sight, licking and nuzzling his neck underneath his beard. Hand to his cock, he adjusted things, rolling the rubber into place and pulling her down while he thrust up with his hips. Catch, slip, a slight adjustment, thrust...*homerun*. Her teeth bit into the side of his neck, and he groaned, lifting his hips again. Bent knees gave him the leverage needed for a gentle rocking motion he could maintain for a long time. His hands lifting and pulling, her weight taking care of the return trip that settled him back inside her.

She sat up slightly, and leaning far forward, rested her forehead against his. In territory so far from fucking, he didn't know what to call it. *Yes, I do*. Eyes open, breath mingling, her hands cupped his head. Penny's fingers wound into the hair at the back of his head on either side, her elbows brushing across his chest as her upper arms pressed her tits together. Her hair wasn't long enough to fall around them, but strands of it tickled his face, and those blues were staring at him. Looking deep and long, he watched her eyes haze and lose focus, knew she was chasing those stealthy sensations he stirred in her. When she sucked her bottom lip into her mouth, he knew she was close. Picking up the pace until her eyelids fluttered, her lashes playing touch-me with her cheeks as she came.

Not giving her time to recover, he rolled, positioning her under him and chased his own orgasm. He found it deep inside her, where it seemed it had been hiding forever. He heard himself grunting, flesh slapping loudly in the enclosed space. Hair streaming down on either side of their faces, curtained and shuttered from the world. Safe. Sheltered. With the sheet twisted in their legs, he watched as she came back to herself, staring up at him in wonder and then—*fuck him*—she threaded her hands under the pillow, giving him her submission again. Wordlessly he affirmed her instincts, raining rough kisses on her face, down her neck and back up, shouting her name when he came.

"Rest," he murmured, curling in behind her, arms crossed over her chest, holding her close. "Get some shuteye and dream, darlin'."

Cleanup had gone quicker this time, his knowledge of her living space expanding with every exploration. He found the wipes and made swift work of taking care of the messy evidence of their lovemaking—*fucking*, his mind corrected. In minutes, her relaxed, calm breathing told him she'd found sleep, resting easy circled about with his care of her. Safe. Held in the bloody hands of a man much like the ones who killed her beloved uncle.

He knew he should go, should leave while she was lost in sleep. Leave her with the fantasy of a sweet man who loved on her until, sated and exhausted, she'd forgotten who she was with. A real life charade to follow the storyline of her books. Pretense and playacting. Make-believe. Gaze flicking around the cabin, it snagged on the lone wrapper, a folded corner catching the light, giving a glinting reflection. *I should go, but I'm a greedy bastard*, he told himself, lip curling in a sneer. "Yeah," his muttered agreement was audible as he settled behind her and closed his eyes.

A stretch of time later, a truck parked next to hers in the line started, the rumbling roll of the engine startling him awake. Still dark out, the hour was early. Listening carefully, he heard footsteps moving between the trucks, the hollow thump of a tire knocker doing an old school pressure check. Thud, thud, thud, thud. Two axles, four wheels, moving on to the next set.

Penny was still sleeping, the only change in position was her hands had lifted, cupping around his wrists where he held her captive. There was so much skin in front of him, so much heat, so much to explore. With his mouth to her neck, Twisted worked up to her ear, running his teeth along the curve of the shell, nipping gently at her earlobe. The whole time he thought to himself he wanted to ask about the barbell on her face but then got distracted when her breathing changed, signaling she was rising from sleep.

"Penny." He called her name quietly, not wanting to frighten her but he shouldn't have worried because the first sound from her was his

name in return. Palm to her chest, he captured the curve of one breast, fingers plumping and caressing as he nibbled on her ear again. He hadn't been gentle the first time, had taken her hard, now finding the idea of hurting her as distasteful as it had been earlier, asked, "Are you too sore, baby?"

Her head moved, shaking back and forth. "Sure, sweetheart?" A different movement, up and down, which was interrupted by a gasp as he pinched her nipple lightly, rolling it between his fingers. "Okay," he breathed, "okay." His cock, already thick and hard, thudded against her ass. Releasing her breast, he moved one hand to her throat, sliding the other down her belly, cupping her pussy. He gave a squeeze with both, feeling her body move as she blew out a careful breath, skin gone to goose bumps under his lips.

Easing into it, stroked slowly along her folds, finger to either side of her clit, then across the top of it, then either side. Up and down, faster and faster, positioning and angling his hand. Biting down on her ear, without warning he thrummed across her clit hard and fast. Her open-mouthed cries of shock as much a reward as her body jumping, shoulders bowing back into him, hips thrusting forwards, seeking.

Rolling her stomach-first onto the mattress, he knelt behind her, pulling her up with him. "Knees wide, sweetheart." Hand to her jaw, he turned her head and—"*God,*" she cried—captured her mouth, silencing her scream. That was followed by a moan he ate down, lips locked to hers. Breaking the kiss, her head fell to his shoulder, her body curving back. Staring down her body, he watched as his hair swept across her breasts, curling around well memorized curves. Looked farther to see his hand working frantically between her legs, fingers moving fast side-to-side as they slipped back and forth along the length of her pussy, doubling the sensation for her.

With another cry, calling his name, she came, a teeth-grinding, rolling motion evidence of the powerful feelings storming through her. Clenched fists flew wide as her palms lifted, releasing into outstretched

fingers. Her hands rose as if to fend off a dangerous animal stirred to life.

Pushing her to the mattress, he settled a palm in the middle of her spine in a silent command she accepted as gospel. Knees bent, ass up, arms stretched over her head, her open palms came together, and he watched as she laced her fingers tightly, holding on. Behind her, he put an arm to either side of her legs to give her support and buried his face between her thighs. Nose to that tight opening denied him earlier, he ate her pussy hard and fast, tongue thrust far inside, feeling the quaking pulses of her orgasm still affecting her. Sweet, clean pussy, flowing with the sweetest nectar he ever tasted, he devoured her until her frantic movements matched the cries rolling from her throat.

Rearing up, palm to her hip, he reached with the other to gather the final condom from its resting place. Tearing it open with his teeth, he rolled it on, staring down. Positioned as she was, quiet as she was, controlled as he'd taught her in the short time together, she could have been anyone and he found he didn't like that. No fantasy needed in this bed. "Penny," he called, cock in hand, poised at her entrance. She turned her head, neck twisting back—*Twisted*, his alter-ego chuckled—and he had her crystal blue eyes in sight. Her freckle-dotted nose. The glinting barbell in her brow. No longer faceless, this was his—*"shiny Penny"*—woman. With one long thrust, he buried himself inside her.

Now he was the frantic one, diving deep, rocking hard against her ass, hands on her waist, dragging her backwards onto him as he rushed headlong. *More skin.* He needed more. Bending over her, hand to the mattress, taking more. Curving his back, he fucked her hard, free hand gliding under to find and cup a swinging breast. "Down," he ordered, and she slid forward, belly to the mattress. Compelled to chase her, he rolled and circled his hips. Deep, deep, mouth to hers, browns to blues locked in place. One arm encircled her waist, anchoring her, his other arm under, palm cupping the column of her throat. Pulse beating under his thumb, around his cock, her every breath gusting across his lips, life in his hands. *Hold on.*

Fuck. "Penny." She stiffened underneath him, tight and clenching, pulling him in and he gave into the sensations, deep, hard, once...twice...a third stroke. "Penny, sweetheart." Teeth clenched, forehead to her shoulder blade, Bell filled the last condom as she came for him a final time.

***

Four days later, Twisted stood in the backroom at the Incoherent clubhouse in Mandeville, just across Lake Pontchartrain from New Orleans, listening to the confession of the man who had murdered Penny's uncle. Bagger had been part of a crew more than a decade ago. He had seen the writing on the wall and didn't like what it said, trying to derail the infestation of their territory by drug gangs. The club had embarked on a successful campaign of destruction that had severe consequences for a Central American drug cartel. That cartel a family operation that, when it was failing, turned deadly for the ones who had backed the Louisiana expansion. It wasn't club that had talked about his whereabouts, just a chance meeting in the VA hospital where Bagger had gone for treatment. He'd been seen and recognized, knowing with the disease he had his days were already numbered, then he'd had that number divided down to nothing by filth.

"Tell me who else is targeted." With bloody knuckles curved into bludgeons, he urged the man kneeling in front of him to provide answers that would cut his suffering short. His end was already writ in stone. The blood tracing his lifeline running thin, but the suffering could end.

The answer provided ensured that wouldn't happen because he said one name. The one name that Twisted didn't want to hear.

"Penny."

***

Feet to the parking lot, engine idling, Twisted straddled his bike, eyes locked on a truck parked on the fuel line. Hair braided into a single-tail, he wore a bandana tied around his face, covering his beard, secure in anonymity.

He heard a whistle, then another, lilting and lifting, dancing through the air. Walking the long-handled window washer around the front of her truck, jaunty steps moving in time to the tune, the woman he watched swayed through her tasks. Huge nozzles cocked into the tanks on either side of the truck, hood propped up and out of the way, Penny climbed onto the front tires to better reach her windshield. Arms lifting, muscles in her back moving as she scrubbed, unaware of any scrutiny. Twisted scowled when he realized the driver of the truck at the next pump was watching her titties move under her shirt. Mesmerized by the show, the foolish man took a step towards her. Tipping his head at his second, he sent Po'Boy to explain the dire mistake about to be made. *Move on, mister.*

My shiny Penny, he thought, and at that moment she turned, scanning the area. He marked the instant when her gaze locked on him. Saw her lips part, knew what she whispered, heard it in his head as if he were lying beside her again. "Bell."

Not yet. But soon. He cast the words towards her with the same intensity used two weeks before. "Told you, darlin'. Gave me something so sweet, a man would break his back to keep that. I plan on holding on."

Chapter Eight

TWISTED

"Brother," Po'Boy began, but Twisted cut him off with a shake of his head. Mouth pulled to one side, Po'Boy ignored him, pushing forward, regardless. "I got a man goin' like you wanted. Told him to trail to PA, turn his ass at the line because I ain't hanging a brother out there for pussy." Moving closer, Po'Boy looked over Twisted's shoulder and out the front of the clubhouse, where he was staring at a nearly empty parking lot. "Brother, this, along with everything else we got rollin'? You gotta know, this stretched us."

Nodding, Twisted didn't turn, just kept glaring out the window. He knew. After the shit with the feds, they'd had a slice of their membership bail or ghost. Understandable, but a disappointment he hadn't expected. Bringing in nearly twenty new members swelled their ranks, but still meant they were so fuckin' thin you could see straight through them in places.

Every day presented another battle of some kind. It meant he kept his game face on twenty-four seven. Between him and his officers, they were always working at prospect herding and new member educating. That shit was exhausting. The never-ending cycle of getting people to

where you needed them to be, then pushing them past that, so you could see where they might go next. *Rinse and fucking repeat.*

"Any early fan favorites?" Po'Boy kicked a chair away from the wall, dragging it around and sitting while he asked the question. Wood scuffed across the floor, and he knew Po'Boy was probably leaning back, chair kicked up on two legs.

Fuck, go away. He might want to, but no way could he say that, not to Po'Boy. Not to the man who'd been with him since the beginning. The one man he knew had his back, no matter what. Ride or die; they had the same phrase inked on the inside of their bicep. Not like a stupid-ass BFF thing, but a promise. Funniest shit had been the way the tattoo dude looked at him when he went in. Man didn't say anything, but he'd had finished Po'Boy's ink not two hours before Twisted sat in his chair, even though Po'Boy had not even been in the club at the time. Neither of the men had mentioned it to the other. It was just something they did because it showed how bone-deep their connection was. From seventh grade to now, they'd shared a lot of their life. Shared women all the time because none of the bitches meant shit to either man. But now, with Penny—he took a quick breath, imagining for a moment he tasted her on his tongue—with Penny, Twisted had something he didn't want to share.

"You make sure that door's shut?" Po'Boy reached out, rattled the knob and grunted. "Catfish and Mosser. Those two seem fuckin' solid as shit. Hambone is another I'm likin' the looks of. Wildman ain't shit but thinks he is. Need to organize a backyard beat down for him, knock some real into his head, let him pull and push some iron with you, give him a fuckin' goal."

Twisted dragged his hand over his beard and in response, his cock started to fatten. Penny's face flashed in his mind, the look of surprise and excitement as she experienced the rough titillation of his facefur dragging across her skin the first time. The taste of her suffused his tongue, a well-remembered treat, as was her squirming when he

positioned her over his face. She'd been drenched for him, and he'd eaten his fill. Twisted had been using thoughts of her to jack off to for weeks, carefully edging along the blade of pleasure every time he took himself in hand.

Shaking his head to dislodge the memories, he continued, "Zoomer, Rowdy, Ruger, all of 'em gonna be decent foot soldiers. We've picked up some good ones, keepers. I can't see anything to kick yet. Catfish. That man's brainy, think he could be a leader. We'll have to watch and see where we need to bolster the ranks across the state, use him when we need him. Wildman, I'd say we keep him here for now. Attach him to your hip. Let him really learn the lay of the land, bond with you."

"Quack, quack." Po'Boy laughed. "Imprinting?"

"Fuck, yeah. If it's what we need. There's a certain power in educatin' a man. You'll play momma to the duckling for as long as it takes, brother." Twisted turned finally, looking down at Po'Boy with a quick grin. "Momma duck, gonna sit on your hatchlings? Wiggle your ass in their faces?"

"Fuck you." Pulling out a small metal case from his vest pocket, Po'Boy offered him a thin, hand-rolled smoke, but Twisted waved it off with a shake. Tilting his head to keep the smoke out of his eyes, Po'Boy lit the joint and drew on it delicately, his actions telling Twisted just how potent the contents must be. With a hiss, Po'Boy sucked the smoke in a little deeper and then asked on a slow exhale, "Sure?"

"Yeah, not feelin' it." And he wasn't. Not for nearly three weeks now. Not feeling the booze, either. *Addicted to pussy,* he thought with a grimace, wondering where she was right now. "Fuck," he growled, pulling out the chair at the head of the table and dropping into it. "I'm so fucked, brother."

"No, man." He looked up to see an indulgent grin on Po'Boy's rapidly mellowing face. "Pussywhipped, maybe. Fucked? Not for weeks."

"Jesus." Tipping his head back, he watched as the sweet smoke curling from the slow-burning joint lifted, getting caught in the downdraft from the fan blades spinning overhead, dissipating to nothing. "I ain't never been...fuck." Eyes closed, he let thoughts of his last hour together with Penny flood through his mind.

"I've never..." Her voice trailed off, then picked back up, still soft and full of awe. "That wasn't like anything I've ever experienced, Bell."

He was facing the back wall of the bunk, turned away from her, hiding the devastation he felt. Penny had curled into his back, one arm draped over his waist, other hand up by his head, fingers idly playing with strands of his hair. She had thoughtfully moved it before resting her head on the pillow, showing again that she had experience with hair much longer than what covered her head now. Nearly every muscle in his body was locked in place, trying to deny the need to roll and hold her, pull her close, feel her pressing against him, cuddle puppy to the bone.

"Was good," he responded quietly, downplaying that it meant every bit as much to him as it had her. Turning his face to the pillow a bit more, his lips contorted when he drove the first wedge in, knowing what his cruel words would do. "Thanks, honey."

He hadn't been prepared for her reaction, hadn't expected it. In no way could he ever be ready for what she did next.

"Don't do that." Lifting up to an elbow, she leaned over him, close enough every breath brushed gently against his cheek. Eyes locked to his face, she repeated herself, attacking his actions head on. "Don't do that. Don't downplay what that was. And don't try to tell me you didn't feel the same, Bell. Don't lie to me."

Turning to his back, he asked a question he didn't know if he really wanted the answer to. "How much of tonight you think wasn't a lie, Penny? It's all a lie, every breath I took in here with you, lies."

"Your name. You caring for me, not just after, but all night. What we just shared. Not a lie there. Those things aren't lies, Bell." One corner of her lips quirked up, and her eyes sparkled in the limited light reaching where they lay. "You and me, right here. This isn't a lie, either."

"My name's not—"

She cut him off. "People call you something else, I know. You think I don't know what that means?" She pointed to his club tattoo, inked over his heart. "And that?" Fingertips trailed across the lines x'ed on the inside of his wrist. "And that?" She leaned in and kissed the names written across his ribs, Jimbo, and Scot, a dozen others. "I told you Bagger was in a club, Bell. I knew what I was letting in my cab before I opened the door. People might call you something else, but you are *Bell."*

"Bell ain't nothing but a memory." He'd gritted out the words, teeth clenching through hopeful pain. If she got it, if she knew what I am and kept me here anyway, what could that mean for us? *"Penny, I'm not the man you see. Not the man you slept with."*

"Yes, you are." She smiled and leaned down, pressing her lips to his shoulder, his chest, his throat, tits pressed tightly to his side, soft and warm. Cuddle puppy. She moved to his jaw before murmuring, "Yes, you are."

He pushed away, shoving to a seated position, pain tearing through his chest when he saw the hurt look on her face at his rejection of her words, her actions. I could take what she's offering. *He shifted that thought away far more violently than he had her. "No, Penny. I ain't. I ain't nothing you want in your life. Trust me on that. This was a..." He searched for a word, then settled on something that was inadequate, a poor explanation but at least carried some meaning. "...pleasant interlude in my day. Thanks."*

Rocking back on an elbow, she stared at him, frowning, still trying to break through a wall she would never topple. "I don't sleep around, Bell,

but you already know that. You figured out a lot. You might know me better than anyone ever has." Moving abruptly to a seated position at the edge of the bunk, she ran impatient fingers through her hair before bending and picking up his clothes from the floor. "You want it this way? Well then, congratulations, I can't do anything about it. You gave me the illusion of control in here, I know. So you want to keep everything your way? Your way or the highway? Okay, there you go. Fine. Have it your way. I'm surprised, though. You don't seem like a coward." She set the bundle on the edge of the bunk, separated her shirt from the pile and pulled it on. "Your way, then. It's a shame because even with as little as I know,"—she shook her head, not looking at him—"even I know this wasn't just pleasant, Bell."

Without another word, she picked up the rest of her clothing, dressed and then stood. Turning to look down at him one final time, she shook her head before parting the curtains and crawling up into the passenger seat. Pulling the divider closed, shutting him in darkness, leaving only a narrow strip of light shining through, she told him, "You don't know anything, Bell. But we'll do this your way. Just get dressed and go."

He had done that. Had given her that. Given her more than she knew, by not staying. Broke something inside him, but he'd walked away.

Now he wished like hell he'd stayed.

***

"Again," Po'Boy shouted from the pull-up bar, yelling at Wildman, who was on the incline bench. "Do it the fuck again, fucktard." Not even winded, Po'Boy hadn't stopped doing his reps, eyes locked on the man struggling to continue with a new set of sit-ups.

With a shouted, "Fuck you," Wildman did just that, digging deep and pulling another full set of reps out of somewhere. From where he worked with dumbbells nearby, Twisted heard him grunt another faint, "Fuck you," as he finished.

Grinning, Twisted shouted across the yard, drawing everyone's attention when he told Po'Boy, "I like this one. He's sassy."

"Fuck. You. Too." These grunts came from the general direction of the incline bench where Wildman was now stretched out flat, breathing hard. "Prez."

The honorific was late coming, but it came, and that made Po'Boy whistle and shout with laughter, "Brown-noser. Need a scrub pad to get that stain off, brother. Nose deep in that stink."

"Fuck you harder." Wildman gripped his ankles, sitting up and glaring across the yard at Po'Boy, who had just dropped lightly to his feet, shaking out his hands and arms.

"See? Sassy!" Twisted bent and let the iron fall to the mat, feeling the ground underfoot tremble as it landed. "Not much on the vocab side, but he's playful. I like that shit." Footsteps crunched through the grass behind him, and Twisted turned to see Chip approaching.

Twisted straightened, smiling. This was something he counted as a win. They'd redeemed a brother, the general membership never knowing anything other than what they'd been fed. That story being Chip was targeted because of a shithead ole lady, her bein' scorned and pissed off, and mouthing off to the wrong people. Truth to that point and a lesson to every member that pillow talk could cost dear. The skim was that Chip'd brought it to the table immediately. The real continued with the knowledge that the feds had eyes on them, focused on him, but Incoherent was using those eyes to blind the feds in other places.

Chip lifted his head, raised one hand in a half wave at Po'Boy and looked at Twisted. "A word, Prez." With a shift of his body and tilt of his head, Twisted agreed, and they walked towards the double doors of one of the club's back rooms. Pulling the door open, Twisted reached out and hit the switch on the inside wall, turning on the overhead lights.

“Sup, brother?” As often as Twisted had offered the word since everything went down, he could see it still hit Chip hard, and did every time the word came his way. See first the denial, and then a grateful acceptance of the trust, belief, and honor that moved through the man. Twisted hated it had come to a point where all that was nearly stripped away, and loved that they’d made it back here with everybody breathing.

“Got some word. Heard from one of the boys. We got eyes on Dane’s truck.” He knew his sudden alert attention wasn’t lost on Chip, and it made him anxious when the man pulled a face. That expression told Twisted this wouldn’t be news he was gonna want to hear. “She’s back in the region, but she ain’t alone, Twisted.” He swallowed hard before continuing. “Picked up a man somewhere north. Ain’t got a name. Still working that angle, but he isn’t a driver. He doesn’t leave the passenger seat unless…” Trailing off a moment, Chip cleared his throat and seemed to select his words carefully, moving into dangerous territory warily. “Unless it’s bunk time, boss.”

Twisted froze, then asked, hearing the rage tearing his whispering voice to shreds, “Come again?”

“Prez.” Just the one word, that single word meaning Chip didn’t have to repeat himself. *Unless it’s bunk time*. After a moment of silence, Twisted finally gave a short, sharp shake of his head. Chip took a breath, was gonna try to say something to make it better. Easier to bear. The man had lost his wife and family, yet he was looking to quieten Twisted’s soul.

“Get the fuck out.” Eyes to the floor, he was glad he didn’t have to repeat himself, Chip gently closing the door behind him. *Unless it’s bunk time*.

“FUCK!”

Chapter Nine

PENNY, AGE TWENTY-FIVE

Four years ago, Penny Dane had laughingly accepted her uncle's invitation to ride cross-country with him, jumping at the chance to learn the ropes of driving a truck from a master. Bagger had been driving all his life, was old school, not giving two shits about log books or DOT regulations when it came to getting his loads where they were meant to go and making damn sure they got there on time. Steady and dependable, he'd been with the same company for twenty years, and was one of their top performing drivers. So she climbed up in the truck, and in the process found a profession she could love, so she stayed. The independence of the job was attractive, and it didn't hurt she enjoyed spending time with her uncle.

Then a year ago, he'd gotten sick, and she'd taken on the lion's share of the work, keeping the truck going as if there were two drivers even when he was out, sick at home, or at the VA doing his chemo. He couldn't afford for the truck to sit idle, and if she didn't run it, no one would.

Penny was thankful she'd reached an age she could test for the license, and Bagger was the only person not surprised that she'd passed the exam on her first try. But then again, he'd taught her to drive.

Taught her to ride a motorcycle, too, so she added that endorsement to her license.

When good weather weekends found them home in Baton Rouge, she and her uncle would roll out, riding the coast for as far as he had the energy to ride. Sometimes just the two of them, but often they'd ride with the men he called brothers. Members of the Caddo Hobos, the club he had helped found decades before she was born. The CoBos, as they were informally known, were nearly a half-century old. Many of the members were the second generation, raised in the life by their fathers, the club a true family. It was a heritage she'd grown up knowing and loving, that love profound and genuine, nurtured in her every time she saw Bagger's pride in what he'd wrought.

Then Bagger was killed. Two to the head while he sat in his car at the pharmacy, waiting for drugs that wouldn't be of any use to the wounds he took. He'd been sick, the tumors eating up his insides, caught too late to do much more than treat the painful symptoms, but even those last months' worth of breath stolen from him by a coward.

Penny heard the chatter at the wake. She'd been crouched behind the bar, hooking up a new keg when she overheard a conversation between Ace, the man who had been Bagger's lieutenant in Vietnam and then his president back in the states, and Peanut, a member who stepped into Bagger's old role of vice-president. What they had to say literally took her legs from under her, seeming to suck all the air from the room, stealing her ability to think, speak, or breathe. "Club business." And "Cartel." Finally, a name she recognized, something she could hold onto with both hands. "Fiddler."

She glanced in her mirrors, checking the lane beside her as she turned on her blinker in preparation of moving over. A small car pulling a larger-than-the-car moving trailer passed her, traveling about twenty miles an hour above what the trailer was rated for and she watched it sway from side-to-side as it entered the slipstream of wind ahead of her bumper. Changing lanes quickly, something Bagger liked to say wasn't

aggressive, just driving with authority, she mashed the accelerator harder, pulling another two miles per hour from the laboring engine.

The mountains and hills of eastern Kentucky were tough on her truck, especially when fully loaded as she was now. Inertia was both a boon and bane, allowing her to slingshot over the top of the next hill more often than not, she just had to be willing to push the shit out of the rig on the roll down to gain the benefit for the sling part back up. Glancing to the other mirrors, her attention snagged for a moment on her passenger.

Tyler Sawyer was the son of one of the CoBos, and a man she'd known for a long time. He'd never joined the club, never seemed to want to be far into the life, but had been around for enough parties that he knew all the players. After her first desperate attempt and failure at tracking Fiddler down, Penny bided her time for a bit. She took a month off, nursing her wounds, trying to regain both her strength and courage. Then, she'd reached out and activated her network outside of the CoBos influence. Ty being one of those connections she felt comfortable making.

Moving back to the right-hand lane, she waited for a beat, letting the truck settle into the ruts, hands smoothly handling the big wheel. Eyes front, deliberately not glancing his way, she started the same conversation they'd been having for the past two days, ever since she picked him up outside of Wooster, Massachusetts. She'd covertly been trying to engage him in her mission nearly since she'd tracked down his number, surprised it had changed since they'd last spoken. Ty not giving it to her himself made her wonder if he'd been trying to pull away. Maybe without Bagger around, the cement of their friendship was crumbling. *I don't want to lose Ty*, she thought with a shudder. Putting that aside, she asked, "So, Fiddler and Bagger served together overseas, right?"

"Penny, we aren't going to do this. Not now. Not ever. Might as well give up the line of questioning." Tone terse, he cut her off when she

started to interrupt. "Daddy would kill me if I dragged you into anything related to Fiddler. You know how protective the CoBos are of you, honey. I've told you too much already."

He really hasn't, she thought. *Only fed me parts that he thought had no value*. He was wrong, so she had some of what she needed, but she knew he held a lot more in his head. How to turn him to her way of seeing things was the question, and she had one last angle to play. Something she had hoped to leave in the past. Something that would be hard as hell to talk through, but at least she was driving in challenging countryside, had something to occupy herself with. "Fiddler's son. You know him?"

"Penny—"

Before he could get more than her name out, she cut him off with a fierce shake of her head and a harsh, "Shut it. You remember my hair?"

He nodded. She glimpsed the movement from the corner of her eye. He would remember it, having pulled it at parties when they were kids, and laughed at her when it escaped its bonds once, tangling and snarling during a ride. A smile hit her lips, but she knew it wasn't pretty. He'd extended an opened blade that day, offered to cut it off himself if she needed. Her hair had been something she was proud of, hanging well past her waist. "Yeah, I remember it. I didn't want to ask, and the short looks really cute on you, but why'd you cut it?"

"I didn't." She swallowed hard, heard the sound of the tires riding the edge of the fog line around a corner and smoothly pulled the semi back into the lane, correcting her mistake. She was walking an edge in the cab here, too, waltzing along a razor that threatened to cut her to ribbons. "Gollum did."

The breath he sucked in was agonized and loud, painful to hear and she nodded. "Yeah." Just from the sound she could tell he knew what that meant. A year ago, she wouldn't have. Hell, six months ago she thought she knew the darkness that lived in the bayous she called

home. She had been wrong. "So you probably know what else he did, don't you?" Turning the wheel in the other direction, she steered them around another curve in the switchback highway, taking them on down the road. Focused on her work, she muttered, "You know what he likes."

The curtains behind her seat swung with the movement of the truck and for a moment, she could have sworn she caught a trace of Bell's scent. Felt the weight of his forearm on her shoulder, hand up beside her head, stroking and playing with her hair, not knowing how much pain that brought her. A simple, gentle caress meant to be comforting but reminding her with each movement how much she'd lost.

I was wrong about him, she reminded herself, turning the wheel back to true, straightening out for the next curve. Preparing, readying herself, she lined the truck up for the twisting turns ahead. She had refused to look at Bell after he came out from the sleeper, didn't want to see him sitting in her seat to tug on his boots. Hearing the soft sound as his socked feet slipped into place. The gentle plinks of the chain on his wallet playing out along the edge of one of his guns as he retrieved his belongings. Looking out the side window, she had ignored the mirror, too, not wanting a glimpse of his beauty. Hoping it wouldn't stay with her, would exit the truck when he did, leaving her alone.

Swallowing back the tears that threatened to swamp her at the memory of his hand gliding over her head, the feel of his lips pressing momentarily to her temple, the tortured murmur of Bell's final good-bye, she cleared her throat. "Gollum offered information in trade."

"Trade for what?" Surely he wouldn't make her say it aloud. He knew what that bastard liked, everyone in southern Louisiana knew, his appetites were…legend.

"Tell me about Fiddler and Bagger. What were they to each other before they came home?" So much was tied up in the time the men spent in Vietnam. So much of their shared history lost now because she

couldn't ask Bagger. "Jimbo was in their unit. He and Bagger stayed brothers, but Fiddler was out on his own. Leswayne, too. Why?"

"What did you trade for the info, Penny?" The quiet question ate at her control until her hands were nearly cramping, holding onto what she could. "Penny. Doll. *Please*." His voice broke, and she knew at that moment he had loved her once. Growing up, she hadn't wanted anything to do with boys not in the club, but hadn't found anyone with it that she wanted. Hadn't found anyone out there in the wild, either, but she and Ty had been close friends once. "Tell me no. Tell me that's not what happened."

There was a pull-off about a mile ahead. She needed to stop the truck and get out, check the brakes to make sure they weren't overheating. She could keep doing this until then, and then fall apart for as long as she needed, as long as Ty didn't try to help her. She needed answers, not analyzing. Pumping the brakes, she prepared to downshift, slowing the rig. "What did Fiddler do that made everyone hate him? Why was he pushed out, hung out on his own?"

"Penny—"

"My virginity, okay?" The shouted words startled her. Her own voice racketed around the cab, rebounding off every surface, striking back at her with bruising force. "You know Gollum, I'm sure you've heard how he likes that." Rocking back into the seat with each word, she pushed through the pain. "I traded it for nothing in the end, because he didn't give me anything. Now you tell me, what did he do?"

"Raped and killed a kid. A little girl. Made her mother watch. Called it his own offensive. The Fiddler offensive. Made fun of the mother before he killed her, too." That was about what she'd expected, but that wasn't enough, not enough for a decades-long hatred to still be brewing between four families.

"What else?"

"He blamed a soldier. Got caught and threw the kid under the bus in a way the boy didn't think he'd get out from underneath it. A private in Bagger's unit." Ty made a noise deep in his throat.

She slowed the truck more, working the brakes and gearshift in tandem, drawing down their speed so she could pull into the wide graveled area on the side of the road. Rolling to a stop, she popped the parking brake, letting the truck idle as she listened, staring out the front windscreen.

"Kid didn't see any way out. Offed himself. He had a wife and son. Killing himself like that...Bagger was close to the boy. When he blamed Fiddler for the death, Fiddler laughed in his face." His voice broke, and she knew he was going back there even before he opened his mouth. "Penny, why?"

She knocked the truck out of gear with the heel of her hand and eased her foot off the clutch. Safely parked on the side of the road, now she needed to escape the cab. "Currency of the moment." She shrugged on her hoodie, keeping her eyes downcast, not wanting to see his face yet. Not wanting to see what she knew would be there. "Supply is apparently lean. Demand"—hand to the door, she popped the locks—"is high. Be back in a minute." Swinging out of the truck, she pulled the lever to open her equipment cubby and then slammed the door. Standing for a moment, she leaned heavily on the side of the truck, pulling in breath after shaking breath. He hadn't made her relive it, not yet. She knew Ty, though; he wouldn't give up. Knew she'd be hearing his questions drift down from the overhead bunk tonight, taking advantage of the quiet in the sleeper. She just hoped it wouldn't mean he thought of her differently.

If he knew of the man she took to her bed a month ago, he would have a far different opinion. Knowingly taking someone like Bell to bed, letting him initiate her into sex in a way she wished to God had been her first time. But then again, if she'd known it could be like that, she might not have survived. If she'd known that it could be that sweet, that

tender, that rich an experience, she might not have lasted following her single night with Gollum. The two encounters were so different, so far apart on a spectrum of anything, she couldn't even relate them.

Gollum had been all about pain. So excited at the prospect of popping her cherry, knowing who she was and knowing he was the first to get into her pants, he nearly didn't make it through putting on the condom she'd insisted on.

She'd insisted on the blood tests with the ER doctor the next day, too, and he'd been a lot more accommodating than Gollum, not taking any persuading. *Better safe than sorry*, she'd told him, and he nodded as they both had watched a nurse wrap her bicep with a strip of rubber.

At the time, Gollum working over the top of her seemed to take forever. Gave the impression it would go on for her whole life, seconds ticking by so slowly she could have sworn the clock broke between each one. The silence between each stroke had filled with his foul breath rasping in her ear, deafening her. It wasn't until she was with Bell that she knew it had been blessedly fast. One and done, and he hadn't spent any time inside her.

What came after was different. Probing her body with whatever pleased him, tearing at her in ways that left damage behind. Him hitting her, holding her braid wrapped around his hand to haul her back to her knees following each swing. Neck wrenching sideways, trying not to fall, she'd known instinctively that would be the worst possible thing she could do. Anticipating each swing, each blow, she'd still been surprised when it landed. Time after time. After time.

The terror rippling through her when he'd pulled the knife from his belt had been primitive. A trademark of the Vicar's Wrath MC, it was massive, broad and long, nearly a machete. He'd brandished it in front of her face, laughing when she cried out in panic. She'd never claimed to be strong, never claimed to be fearless, but kneeling naked in the harsh light of day in front of a madman, she'd plumbed the depths of her fear,

saw it running, flashing brightly along the keenly honed edge of that blade.

With one wild sweep, he had severed the braid at her scalp, dangling it in front of her like a trophy. She'd heard that he had his woman use the hank of hair to make a get-back whip for his bike, but since they didn't run in the same circles, she hoped she'd never know for sure. Then he'd threatened to mark her. She lifted her hand, fingering the barbell threaded through her eyebrow. *I took that back at least*, she thought. Memories of Bell swept through her, and with eyes closed she thought, *I took that back, too.*

With a sigh she dug in the equipment cubby, pulling out her flashlight. Time to check the brakes, time to verify everything was in proper working order. Something she could control, as long as she paid careful attention.

***

"Why didn't you call sooner, Penny?" As she knew he would, Ty started talking to her as soon as the lights went out in the sleeper. He couldn't let the topic lay dormant and would keep digging around the edges, trying to understand the dimensions of what he knew pained her. Ty'd want to make it better. He'd want to sort it for her if he could. Wrap her in cushions of his care and erase the pain, not knowing Bell had already been there, easing things with his own brand of care. That was until he took it all away, proved to her she wasn't worthy of the tenderness he'd shown her. *Ty will be the same*, she cautioned herself, digging until he'd categorized the depths of the mess she'd made of her life, then walking back to his world and out of hers, leaving her to sort through the mounded, muddied remains, the scars on her soul no longer covered by gentle memories.

They were just west of Memphis, and she'd stopped for a quick nap before driving on to the Dallas area where her load was bound. Fully dressed, she was resting on top of the covers, a light blanket thrown

across her jeans. Bare feet and shoulders, she had on a soft, well-worn camisole. A favorite, and after a day like today, comfortable and comforting were needed. When it was time to drive again, if she were chilled, she could pull on a flannel or sweater over what she had on.

Ty continued talking, and it felt a little as if he were lecturing a little sister when he said, "When you knew what happened to Bagger, you could have called when you learned what happened." *Oh, no, he isn't going to go there*, she vowed.

"You will not blame me for this." Her words were firm, tone unyielding, and he made a quiet noise of dismissal. "Don't start down that path, Ty. I knew what I was doing. Knew the cost. That's mine. You can't have it, can't take it, and I won't give it to you if you begged. It's done. Over and done. But you"—she swallowed, feeling her lips trembling and praying it didn't show in her voice, speaking into the shadows of the curtained bunk—"don't get to judge me."

"I wasn't," he said quickly, and she snorted. "I wasn't," he denied again, and she wondered if he'd do it a third time. *Before the cock crows*, she thought, *bet he will*. Turning to her side, she shoved her hands under the pillow, that action bringing memories of Bell to the forefront. His quiet confidence giving him easy mastery over her fears, she remembered how he led her to where she needed to be to respond to him. Gave her permission to feel, to take pleasure, to move beyond heinous acts he didn't have any knowledge of. Pulling her along with him, not afraid to show her what she gave him back. Empowering her even as he took her body. An intense connection she had never known could exist.

Twisting her head, she pushed deep into the pillow, sniffing and trying to fool herself that she could still smell his spicy scent. She must have made a noise, because, like Peter, Ty denied his own actions a third time. "I wasn't, Penny. I'd never judge you for that, doll."

WWBD? She wondered this, nearly breaking into an asinine giggle. Bell would tell it straight, make sure Ty knew she was okay, and then give him the tools to move on. "I got my question to Gollum through a man called Scorch. He isn't a Vicar's member, but he knows men in several chapters. I met him at a bar shooting pool one night. Purely chance." At a noise alongside the truck, she rolled onto her back, listening carefully.

"I didn't believe in chance, not at first, but he checked out." The noise stopped, and inside the truck was so still and quiet, she listened to herself breathing for a moment. "Told him what I wanted to know. He said he had a line on a guy who'd be in the way holding that knowledge. I didn't know at the time it was Gollum.

"Took a couple of weeks to get to where we were talking specifics." She curled her lip. "I didn't know what kind of a hornet's nest I'd be stirring up but wanted…no, I *had* to know. Bagger was dead, the man who was a second father to me. Saw my mom suffering because her big brother was gone. I couldn't stand it, Ty. I *needed* to get to the bottom of who hated him so much they'd kill him like that." Ty turned over above her, the movement gently shifting the truck's chassis.

The noise from beside the truck came again, and she sat up, pushing the curtain aside to lean into the front compartment. Using the mirrors to look down either side of the truck, she saw there was a figure near the driver's door, barely visible in the reflective surface. Her breath caught in her throat. "Be still," she hissed to Ty, knowing he wouldn't know what she meant. "Ty, be quiet, we've got a visitor."

As she watched through the mirrored image, she saw the figure moving. A man, closing in on the door. He passed out of sight and then came a soft hammering on the door, reminiscent of a night not long ago. Crawling out of the sleeper, she settled into the seat with her knees bent and, already knowing in her gut what was waiting for her, she leaned over and looked outside. That beautiful face looked up at her. The one she saw every night in her dreams, dreams where she

roused to waking with an empty ache between her legs. His distinctive beard, sharp cheekbones framing his gorgeous eyes, hair hanging around his face, casually tucked behind one ear. No smile, no change in expression, no indication of what he expected, he stared up at her. *Bell.*

With a fluid movement, he gripped the grab bar beside her door and swung up onto the steps bolted to the fuel tank. Never breaking their locked gaze, he leaned in, mouth inches from the barrier separating them, his breath fogging the glass with each ragged exhalation. With his chest heaving as if he'd just run a marathon, tension was written in every line of his body. He looked just as she remembered. Exactly as he did in her dreams.

The truck shifted, and he felt it at the same time she did. Penny watched as what had to be rage swept over his features, then Ty's voice came from behind her and that rage on Bell's face washed away, replaced by a murderous anger. "Oh, hell, no. This shit isn't going to keep coming at you, Penny. Club business isn't yours." Heat hit her as Ty leaned across her, finger to the window control, the electric motor in the door humming as the window lowered. "Just get the *hell* off her truck, asshole. You do not get to—"

Whatever Ty was going to say next cut off as his body jolted. With him in her space this way, she couldn't see the window opening, couldn't see what Bell was doing, only knew Ty was moving. Hands flailing, trying to grip onto anything and failing. As he was drawn through the window, a knee, and then a socked foot caught her in the face as he flew past. Dazed, she cradled her throbbing cheek as she looked outside to see the two men on the ground. They rolled left, then right, coming to a halt right up against her fuel tank. Bell, she knew it was him by the hair, reared up over the top of Ty, striking him in the face once, twice, a third time to the gut before she gained enough wits around her to shout at him to stop.

He paused, bent his neck so he could look up at her, and without looking back down landed another vicious punch to Ty's midsection.

"Bell, stop it!" He stiffened when she said his name, then his chin came up, and a profound pain flashed across his face. "*Please*," she pleaded, and he looked away, down, as his fist again found its target. His other hand darted to the small of his back and terror flooded her as she remembered he carried a pistol there.

Fingers working frantically to pop the locks, she pushed the door open with all her might, wanting to get between them somehow. With a loud clunk, the door's bottom edge clipped Bell's head, knocking him sideways. As she scrambled to get out of the truck, Ty lunged up to his knees, bringing his clenched fists around in a hammer swing at Bell's chest. "*Stop!*" He paused the swing, looking up at her panic-stricken shout and then Bell twisted, taking him down again.

Not even noticing when the ragged metal edges of the boot scraper abraded the sole of her foot, Penny bent her knees and jumped the last three feet to the ground, landing beside the two struggling men. From this near the conflict, she felt the heat radiating from them, and could hear the guttural sounds as they reacted to landed blows, pummeling with one hand, the other clenched around their opponent's head, holding tight so as not to give the other man leverage and room to do more damage.

On her knees beside them, she shouted again, no longer hopeful that her words would have an effect, these two men battling were too far gone to hear any pleas she could utter. "*Stop it!*" A loud groan of effort from Ty and he flung himself sideways, taking Bell with him, and in the process flattening Penny. This time, it was her head that hit the truck, clipping the fuel tank as she fell to her back. Immediately she lifted both hands, cradling her head as she curled into a ball, trying to avoid any more hits from the two men.

As if from far away, she noted the noises had stopped, then felt gentle hands on her shoulders. Tugging her sideways, her head was lifted to rest on hard thighs, and she felt the chill from a chain underneath her shoulder, knowing it was…"*Bell.*"

"Here, Penny." His voice came from right above her head. "I'm here, darlin'." Fingers probed the back of her skull, making her wince and pull away. "Shhhh, darlin'. Be still. Lemme see." Gentler now, he traced the edges of her pain, easing and drawing it out.

"Get the hell away from her." That was Ty, and she winced at his shout.

"So loud," she whispered.

"I got you, darlin'." He shifted, and she felt his arms closing around her, lifting, cradling her to his chest. Secure. Safe. In a quietly intense tone directed across the top of her head, he ordered, "Get the fuckin' door, numbnuts. She ain't bleedin', but she's already got a hell of a goose egg." Dropping to a whisper, he added, "And be quiet. She said you're loud." The soft clunk of the door opening, then a hissed, "Shit. I can't climb up holdin' her like this. Let me pass her to you. Then you hand her up."

Eyes squeezed shut against the pain again swelling in her head, there was jostling movement, and then different arms held her, a well-known voice whispered in her ear, "Penny, doll. Why'd you go and get hurt?" Before she could answer, she was moving again, lifted, chill air all around her before being enveloped in warmth again. More movement, then the door closing and the distinct sound of the locks engaging. From outside, thumping on the side of the truck and Ty's shouted, "What the hell, asshole?"

"Did you just lock him outside?" It seemed her voice did work, and she asked this while being moved again, Bell cursing when his head hit the edge of the top bunk. "It's cold." She wasn't complaining for herself, but that seemed to be how he took it since she felt the soft warmth of her plush blanket tucked around her within seconds. "Bell," she started, getting a grunt in response, and then she felt him stretch out alongside her, his fingers stroking her face. Softly caressing her. His touch moving across her features as if he were committing her to memory.

"Penny." With just her name, he gave her everything: longing and loss, the same emotions and aching she had felt for weeks. Joy and despair, heights and depths of which she had plumbed, thinking she'd never see him again.

"I saw you." She told him something he already knew because he sure as hell had seen her. Two weeks ago in Louisville, she'd felt the weight of his gaze and looked up to find him staring at her. "You were there." Her instant happiness changing to tears when he'd wheeled his bike around, turning his back on her and riding away. "You left without saying good-bye."

"Didn't need to." His voice came from near her head, and she cracked one eye open to peer up at him. Propped on an arm over the top of her, he was frowning down, fingers trailing across the sore spot at the back of her head, then the bruising on her cheek. "Good-bye ain't on the radar for us, Penny. Don't you know that by now?" He leaned in, tracing along her nose with the tip of his. "You can bunk all the pretty boys you want, but I'll always be here,"—fingers tapped her breastbone, resonating through her heart—"and you'll always be mine. Ain't sayin' good-bye, darlin'."

"Twisted." This came from outside along with another loud banging of a fist on the door. "Open the goddamned door."

Bell stiffened. She could feel his reaction in every muscle and knew it had to do with Ty using what must be Bell's club name. Reaching up, she cupped his cheek in her palm, ruffling his beard with her fingertips. Softly, with emphasis she hoped he understood, she told him, "Here—in here with me—you will *always* be Bell." He took a breath, and she breathed with him, but when he opened his mouth, she covered his lips with her thumb, stopping his words. "In here, the outside doesn't matter. We can keep it as far away as you need, Bell."

He swallowed and nodded, then rolled his eyes with a muttered, "Shit." She frowned her question at him, and he grinned, "Boots, darlin'. I'll take 'em off and let in Wrench."

Tipping her head to one side, she questioned, "Wrench?"

"Yeah, Wrench." He indicated the front of the truck. "Your pretty bunk boy."

"Ty." He nodded, and she said the name questioningly again, "Wrench?"

"Yeah, I'll let him in. Just lemme get these boots off. Gimme a sec, Penny." Moving, he climbed over the top of her and out of the sleeper. She heard the seat take his weight, the air suspension wheezing, then the thump of his boots. The locks clicked, and the passenger door opened immediately, letting in a blast of cold air cut off by the slamming of the door. "You stay right there, for now, Wrench." Ty made a noise and then the truck shifted violently as a loud thump sounded. Bell's voice was on the passenger side when he next spoke. "I said you need to stay here. Reaching for the goddamned fuckin' bunk ain't stayin' here." A muttered response, then, his voice low and dangerous, that danger sounding even in the pauses, Bell repeated himself, "Fuckin'. Stay. Here."

The truck moved again, and she opened her eyes to see Bell standing at the entrance to the sleeper area, looking at the top bunk. His eyes roamed side-to-side, and he appeared to be shocked. Head tipping down, he transferred his gaze to her as he said, his statement not quite a question, "Wrench is sleepin' in the top bunk." She nodded then winced as pain shot through her head. He sucked his bottom lip into his mouth for a moment. Then she saw his teeth scraping at it as he slowly released it to say, "Ain't sleepin' with you." More cautiously, she shook her head.

He lifted a hand to his neck, keeping his eyes on her as he idly ran it under his beard, then reached up and smoothed his beard back down. Thinking. He was trying to put something together in his head.

His knuckles were bruised, the skin broken in places and she wanted to— She interrupted her own thoughts with a scoff. *What? Take care of him? Why? Why is he here?*

She knew the moment he came to a decision because his body visibly relaxed, shoulders dropping two inches as he breathed in deeply. Angling sideways, he sat on the edge of the bunk and she shifted her hips to make room. His stare intense, he opened his mouth, then closed it, sitting for another moment in silence. Licking his lips, he swallowed and, with words that seemed forced, said, "You were right."

"What?" The question jumped out of her before she realized it. Then she froze when his lips lifted in a smile. A smile she'd seen on his face before, in the dim light of the bunk, four weeks ago.

"You were right, Penny. It wasn't a lie. Not here. Not with you. None of it was a lie. What we had...have...matters." His hand lifted, fingertips trailing down her arm to her hand where he twined his fingers through hers, holding on tightly. "I don't understand what this is, but it matters. You already knew that. You had it right. You're in..." He trailed off, eyes closing in what looked like pain. "Out there, all the things that are out there, none of them matter when I'm with you."

Ty made a noise and Bell's eyes opened. Bell made a face, saying, "Open the curtain, Wrench. Go ahead and join in the convo, why doncha?" He turned loose of her hand and moved to the other end of the bunk, leaning his back against the outside wall, and gesturing to her with one hand, the other gripping her ankle and giving a sharp tug. "Come down here, darlin'." She went there, crawling to him on hands and knees, letting him guide her to lay with her back to the rear of the bunk, resting her head on his thigh. Any self-conscious reserve she might have felt fell away as his hand stroked through her hair. *I bet he*

woulda liked my hair long, she thought, lifting her eyes to see Ty glaring at her.

"Wrench?" she asked, trying to knock a little of the anger out of him, but it backfired, and she cringed when his face darkened. "Ty, how do you know Bell?"

"Oh, no, Penny. That isn't the right question." He shook his head once, turning to look out the front windshield. Lifting a hand, he rubbed his already bruising cheekbone. Then without looking at her, Ty asked, "Question is, do you know who you have in your bunk?"

***

TWISTED

Fuck, Twisted thought, lowering his chin and frowning at the man seated in the passenger seat of the truck. He'd known Wrench for years, knew of him long before they met at a rally and the rumors hadn't held a candle to what the man really was. He knew if he didn't have the element of surprise by pulling Wrench through the window and letting him drop the eight feet to the ground, they would have been evenly matched.

If he'd known who was in Penny's truck, he might not have hauled his ass up here. Wouldn't have pounded on her door, but what Chip told him had fucked with his head. Twisted held it together for two days. Two days, and the whole time he'd been crawling up the walls, ready to chew off his own hands trying to keep them from reaching for the door. The phrase "*unless it's bunk time*" had burrowed inside him, leaving a sour taste all along its path, traveling a trail of destruction inside him that still burned. Even more than the first day after he'd left her, she was on his mind. Worse than seeing her and not having her was the thought of someone else taking what was his. What she'd given to him.

Halfway through the trip up here he'd texted Po'Boy his destination and gotten back a five-letter question: **Moron?** His response had drawn

a **lol** from Po'Boy, because for once in his life, he admitted a mistake, telling him, **Yeah. 4 wks ago I was**.

Pulling up at the truck stop had been nerve-wracking because he didn't know if she'd still be here. Didn't know if he'd have to chase her down the interstate like an idiot. But she was, and he knew it from the truck number. No mistakes this time, no miscues, no knocking on the door of someone not her. Then, seeing her climb into the seat, nearly close enough to touch, he'd forgotten the reason for the trip. Forgotten she had a passenger, an unwelcome rider, a man who, as far as he was concerned, would be turned out on his ass in a heartbeat; duffle and clothes thrown in a tangle after him. *Takin' out the trash*, he'd thought more than once; even that thought flying from his head as her eyes stared at him.

No matter that Wrench got a few of his own licks in. It had been a satisfying scuffle, bleeding off some of the rage that had built from before he even left the clubhouse. Each mile bringing him closer to her, but also bringing him closer to whoever was in her bunk. She'd somehow gotten caught up in their fight, and it had taken the sound of her head hitting the truck to pull him out of the dark red fog he'd been in. It seemed to be the same for Wrench because it had been a toss-up to see who'd get to her first.

Then, in the truck, when he caught sight of the evidence of their sleeping arrangement, he hadn't believed his eyes. Hadn't believed until she confirmed his understanding. What she'd given him was still his to have. *Still mine to take*. Twisted's fingers slipped through her hair, the pads of his fingertips finding tiny tangles and easing them out. Her touch on his face, her hand in his, every movement of her body called to him, told him she was right where he'd left her. Right where she'd been since the first time he touched her. Where she was now, curled up next to him, his cuddle puppy. Her fingers draped over the top of his knee, top of her head in his lap. Firmly in the headspace bordered by his name. *Mine*.

"Do you?" Wrench's voice ripped away the curtain of thought, and he looked into the man's eyes. Together they'd done some shit but separately, they'd done a hell of a lot more. Twisted knew all the skeletons, so this man wasn't safe behind a wall of innocence.

"Castin' stones, man?" If he could shut Wrench up, Twisted would have a chance to talk to Penny, have time to try to understand why she had the man with her. Knowing him wasn't a surprise; Wrench had been a nomad for the CoBos for years, easing his way into and out of various clubs' territory, scouting out profitable joint ventures. Wrench's old man and Penny's uncle had been friends, nearly as tight as Papaw and Whitewall, coming from the same era, their unrest and disillusionment with the America they returned to after the war creating an unbreakable bond. Something he'd seen in recent years with men returning from the sand wars. He'd never served but had been raised on stories of their brotherhood forged under fire, in strange lands.

"If you have stones to throw my way, by all means let's see them." Wrench held his head high, staring into Twisted's eyes, trying to intimidate, or maybe communicate. Before answering, Twisted held that gaze for a moment, deciding they needed to talk before either said much more in front of Penny. Wouldn't do to stumble into club business unaware.

"Just sayin', I might not be lily white, but neither are you." Giving a little, he waited to see if this was where they needed to go, his efforts validated with Wrench's next words.

"True, but you've dipped a bit farther into the inkwell than I." A shift in his lap and he glanced down to see Penny staring up at him.

"You know each other?" She lifted a hand, tucking a strand of hair behind her ear and then unconsciously, trailed her fingers across the knot on the back of her head. Penny squinted when she found the sore spot, knuckles flexing as she pushed, then retreated, leaving the pain to settle on its own. "How do you know each other?"

"Met at a rally several years ago." This was true, and so was the next thing he would say. "My grandfather knew his daddy." He watched as the little wrinkle that had appeared between her brows smoothed out as she accepted his answer. He gave her a bit more truth, reminding her at the same time of how it had felt when they lay together the last time. "You said you knew what I was, Penny. I found out after I got home that I knew your uncle, too. Met him once. Seemed a nice man." At that, her face lightened, pleasure suffusing her features that he had cared enough to dig and find a connection between them.

Wrench spoke up from the front seat. "Penny," his voice softened as he continued, "sorry about the head." From this angle, when she turned to look at Wrench, Twisted could only see part of her face, but the expression she gave the man was nothing short of loving, and that worm inside him bent, working back on itself, burrowing a little deeper. Wrench rolled his shoulders, settling into the seat and propping his feet on the driver seat. "Turnabout's fair play." He paused, his gaze flicking up to meet Twisted's. He then looked intently back at Penny. "How did you two meet?"

The smile that curled her lips lifted her cheeks, and he took in the look on her face when she shifted in his lap to look up at him. "It was kinda a mistake," she started, and then a full grin parted her lips. "A good kinda mistake, but still a booboo." Her eyes sank closed when he threaded his fingers through her hair, giving herself to the sensation of his hands on her. When his touch slowed, her lashes fluttered and opened until she was looking up at him again.

"Was looking for my brother's truck—" he began, and she cut in.

"But he knocked on my door instead."

Grinning down at her, he picked up their story. "She rolled down the window, chatted me up a little."

A blush gave her cheeks color as she delicately picked around the boundaries of what was truth with her next statement. "We talked for

what seemed forever. Talked and laughed. I could have spent all night just doing that."

Palm to her cheek, feeling the heat from her skin, he traced across the arch of her brow with his thumb, loving the sight of that sweet smile on her face. A soft, secretive look, all for him. "We did spend all night," he whispered.

"Yeah," she whispered back, and the longing look on her features now meant he wanted to kiss her so bad he could nearly taste her on his tongue. He lifted her hand, curling his around hers, bringing her knuckles to his lips for a soft kiss. "All night." When she repeated the phrase he knew how much of the night she recalled, that she remembered his repeated admonishment that they needn't go fast, that slow would do for them, because they had all the time in the world to discover each other.

Noise from the cab drew his eyes up, and he saw Wrench had turned away. He was slipping on a clean pair of socks before shoving his feet into the boots stored on that side of the truck. When he glanced over his shoulder at them, the pain Twisted saw there made that worm wake again, stretching and leaving poison with each movement. She might not have slept with him, but given half a chance, he knew Wrench would push it. His lust for her almost hidden under the affection, but it was there, raw and hungry. *She gave that to me*, he thought, glaring at the other man. *Not you. Knew you for years, didn't give that to you.*

"Where are you going?" Penny asked Wrench, lifting her head off Twisted's leg slightly. He slipped a hand around her shoulders but intuitively knew better than to try to restrain her. Instead, he used a light touch to stroke slowly along her back, gratified when she settled back into place. *Cuddle puppy*. He blew out a breath he didn't know he was holding, feeling her relax against him. Staying with him, curled beside him even as Wrench retreated to lick wounds she didn't know had been inflicted.

"Gotta pee. And I'm hungry. I'll grab a bite to eat and fill the thermos. Be back in an hour, Penny." He hesitated. "Get some rest, doll." Without looking towards them a second time, Wrench climbed out of the truck, closing the door with a soft emphasis more telling than a slam.

"He's mad." His worm gave a shudder, but he pinched off the movement. *Friends*, he reminded himself.

"Naw, darlin'." Bringing her knuckles to his lips again, he brushed them across side-to-side, feather soft, touching more than kissing, a long, lingering caress. "He's giving us a moment." With a squeeze, he let her go, scooting down on the mattress until she could put her head on his shoulder. His arm curved around her body, which was curved into him, and he could nearly hear the click in the universe as things aligned, maybe for the first time in his life. *Second time*. He grinned as he curled a knuckle under her chin, lifting her face to his.

Gently, he kissed her. Exploring and relearning. Remapping known territory. She didn't make it hard for him, wasn't holding back, no matter he'd been the one to walk away. "You gonna give me this again?" He didn't know he'd spoken the words aloud until she responded.

"You want this?" Her tone quavered, uncertainty warring with a frightened desire, and no wonder, the way he'd left things. The way he'd reentered her life. Time to offer reassurances, smooth things over in order to give her a secure landing place.

"Oh, yeah. Found something here I like a lot, Penny. Shiny Penny." In between words and phrases, he dropped tender kisses to her lips, to her cheek, on the tip of her nose. "My shiny Penny." The possessive growl in his voice didn't scare him, not anymore. He'd had weeks to get used to that feeling. "No pretty bunk boys, darlin'."

Her lips curved under his as she smiled. "Ty isn't like that. We're friends." *Fine. I'll leave her to her ignorance*. Tracing across her bottom

lip with the tip of his tongue, there was a quiet rush of air as she opened her mouth to speak again, but he pushed inside, taking her by surprise. Dueling with her tongue, velvety soft, sweetly addictive, he adjusted them so she was on her back, him leaning over her, leaning into her, holding her in place, anchoring her with his weight. *Not lettin' you go, darlin'*.

Pulling back, tracing the slope of her nose with the tip of his, he rained soft kisses on her face, determined to touch every freckle. "More than I remembered," he murmured, seeing her eyes open partway, then her lids sink back closed as he continued to kiss her. "Head okay?"

Her eyes flew open at his question, wide in shock. This response wasn't quiet. It was forced from her, quaking voice filled with panic and pain as her body stiffened in fear. "What?"

"Is your head okay, darlin'?" He elaborated quickly and felt her slowly begin to relax into him again, the hesitancy telling him she had been ready to bolt, had forgotten the fact they were in her truck. *Well. That was interesting*. "Does my baby have a headache?" *Give her an out, in case she needs it*. Might not let her take it, but he would make the offer. His cock ached, hard and awkwardly bent in his jeans. *If she doesn't want this right now, might as well put me in a cuckold's cage*. Waiting for her response was torture because surely she knew what he was asking, but took her time to respond, eyes tracking back and forth across his face, trying to read something. Then a soft smile, the barest curve of her lips enough to tell him she'd found what she was looking for.

"What head? No aches in mine because it's woozy. You're here." She'd been worried about giving him that much, exposing so much of her feelings, not knowing for sure if his matched. Whatever she'd seen was enough for now. He could work to set those worries aside for good, let her off the hook. *No niggling fears to give my cuddle puppy concerns*.

"My head's in the same place, darlin'." With a gentle brush of lips against lips, the demanding raise of her head to chase his mouth was not only agreeable but felt amazing. "I can't get you out of it." Press of his lips to the corner of her mouth. "Taken up residence." A nibble along her jaw. "Permanent like." Lips to the soft skin behind her ear, he felt her neck stretch, knew she'd be willing to give him more if he wanted it, so he took the offer, mouthing the strong muscles along that fragile column.

"Can't get you out of my head." With his hand on the move, he trailed fingertips up her side until he could brush the swell of her breast with his thumb. A swipe across the nipple timed with when his mouth hit her ear made her shiver, and he smiled as he told her, "You've dug in deep, darlin'. And I like it. Like it *beaucoup* much. Gonna keep you here a while." He touched his mouth to the skin of her neck, brushed his lips across her ear. "Don't want to get you out, Penny." Another swipe across her suddenly hard nipple was followed by another quiet whisper. "Nope. Not out. Want to get you off."

Titties are a hot spot, he remembered, teeth to the side of her neck as he palmed her breast, pressing into her thigh with his hips, letting her feel his cock. Palming and plumping, his finger and thumb met in a tug at the bud resting on the peak. Mouth moving on her neck, he tasted her skin, savoring the emotions evoked by her surrender to him. "Tell me what you like, Penny." A kiss. "Pretty Penny." A gentle bite soothed with his tongue and a tight, sharp pinch that bought him a moan. "My shiny Penny."

Her hips moved, lifting, chasing sensations not being offered. *Fuck yeah, she's hot. Titty play makes her hot*. He slipped his thigh up over her legs, giving her his weight and pinning her in place, thrusting rhythmically against her. Groaning at the combination of pain and pleasure, his dick still bent nearly double in his jeans, he buried his face in her neck, feeling her arch against him. Moving his other arm, Twisted slipped his hand up her back to cup her neck, holding her firmly. Secure. *You're safe with me, darlin'*.

Palm to her belly, he sneaked a hand under her shirt, wondering at her bra color, but not giving that first shit right now. Hot skin under his mouth, he nibbled at the side of her neck as his fingertips found the edge of the fabric and tugged firmly. He brought it down and under her tit. Shoving her little shirt up while he was on the move, he brought his head down to where his hand cupped her. Not playing around, Twisted latched on, drawing her deep and pulling a ringing, *"Bell!"* from her lips as he sucked hard.

Head moving while his mouth was working her, he made certain to let her feel his hair and his beard as he fed on her titty. *Addictive*. Everything about her burned into his brain again. Sounds. Scents. The way she moved. How she felt under him like this. Hand sliding across her belly, he wrapped his fingers around the far side of her waist, pulling her tight against him. He thrust his hips and rubbed while he cupped and gripped, his mouth sucking deep. Releasing her waist, Twisted slipped his hand between her legs and pressed firmly. Gracefully, her thighs fell open for him, and he rewarded her with the edge of his teeth across her nipple. Cupping her pussy through her jeans, he ground the heel of his hand in, pressing hard and gripping. She stiffened, the bow in her back arching her titty up into his mouth and her leg muscles tightened and tensed under his thigh as she came. Quiet, she didn't give him a sound, lost in the moment but not so far gone she dropped the tight leash she held on her control, and he didn't like that, wanting more. She held onto that silence until he set up a steady massage against her clit he knew would carry her up the mountain again. Switching sides with his mouth, working her nipple through the fabric of what he saw was a dark blue bra, he set about teasing and pleasing her until she gave him what he wanted. Acknowledging who was with her. *I gave you that*, he thought, remembering those were the words in his head the very first time he made her come.

"Bell!"

They lay like that for a time, then with one hand, he unbuckled his belt and worked the waistband fastener on his jeans, giving a silent

groan when he finally reached in to adjust himself. She stirred sleepily, and he remembered she'd been in the bunk when he'd approached the truck and had likely driven all day. Never having been selfless where sex was concerned, he wasn't sure he'd have it in him to turn her down if she offered, so he cut her off by quietly asking, "Did you have dinner?"

Her head moved on the pillow, and he curled himself around her. *Who's the cuddle puppy now?* With a mental snort, he angled his head beside hers, pushing close enough to press a kiss to her cheek, capturing her mouth when she turned to face him. Softly, gently, he worked his way across the stretch of her lips, side to side, chuckling when he made her giggle. The sound as sweet and light as he remembered. *Everything I remembered is right here*.

"Toasty," she muttered, her legs shifting restlessly. Twisted moved and shoved the blanket off her, then returned to his position. "Bell." She wasn't complaining, and he thought her slurring mutter was cute. "I'm gonna get sweaty."

"I got a sayin' for that, darlin'." He waited a moment, and she gave it to him, a soft inquiry of sound, more a whimper at the back of her throat than a word. "Don't sweat the petty things." A repeat of the sound, now descending in tone, she evidently thought it was interesting but not funny. "Pet the sweaty things." It took a second but her body shook with the giggles she gifted him, lyrical and sweet, filling the air around him. Moments later, she was asleep.

If someone asked two months ago if I could be content just watching a woman sleep, I'd have laughed at them. He lay beside Penny, head close to hers, close enough he could dip his chin and brush his lips across her bare shoulder. The thin strap of her camisole lay loose along the planes of her body. From the time Chip told him she had a passenger until he saw who it was, all he felt was anger. In the time since they'd come together, he hadn't fucked anyone. Hadn't gotten sucked off. Rosie palm had been his nightly companion, his mind filled with Penny. Asleep or awake, it didn't matter; she'd been on his mind.

At first, he'd thought maybe he needed to shake it off, count it an oddity in his world, because a man like him didn't get a taste of sweet and keep it. He'd get sweet and ruin it, but he'd never had anything...never met anyone like Penny. Then, when he couldn't get her out of his head, he'd found her problem and dealt with it. Fucktard hadn't died easy, not once he'd shared that Penny was on someone's menu. He'd died, though, a spray of water from a hose and a splash of bleach removing any trace that anything had happened, but Twisted couldn't leave it alone. Not after what the man had said.

So he'd started digging deeper. Finding a common thread between Papaw and her uncle. 'Nam, '68, the Tet offensive that created a lot of bonds between men as they struggled through swamped fields, village to village, dealing with people who hated them. Found another common thread, this one a surprise, because Leswayne had the same background, as did another man, Fiddler. Bagger and Jimbo seemed cut from the same cloth. Like Whitewall and Dropsie, their goal was a brotherhood. Clean and simple, they wanted to live a life surrounded by people they trusted, and who trusted them. Make a life to be proud of, and then share that with the people you love. Take care of your brother, take care of the club, and take care of your family.

Leswayne and Fiddler had a different agenda, one combining a vicious love of combat and an endless appetite for what they called "the good life." Their good life always seemed to come at a cost to others, and the clubs they ran shared similar practices. Their dues were high, fines were plenty, runs were constant and mandatory. Support patches came with a fee, lessened by a bounty if the RC or SC lured in another group. Flesh trade, drug trade, gun trade—if it had an illicit attraction, Vicar's Wrath and the Shield delved deep in those waters.

Leswayne's son, Ragman, seemed to be breaking away from his old man's policies. He at least was approachable—reasonable to deal with as long as you could keep things from hitting his old man. Gollum, however, was definitely the fruit of his daddy's loins. Some of the things Twisted had heard about the man were tough to believe, even when

he'd been unfortunate enough to see the aftermath. It looked like the bloodline would be ending with him. Word was he'd gotten castrated in a prison fight inside Angola a couple decades ago. *Probably one of the reasons he's such a mean sumbitch*, Twisted thought.

Penny huffed out a breath, her head turning slightly on the pillow, tongue slipping into view momentarily before retreating. *God, she's so fuckin' good-lookin'. How in the hell did she hold onto everything that's in her while hanging around a fuckin' club?* He wanted her, wanted to taste her again. His cock had barely stopped aching, but it was thumping back to life in a hurry at the thought of her wrapped around him.

A month, he marveled. *After only having her for hours, she's obsessed me for a month and right now, I'd give my left nut to be fucking her. But I'm just...holding her.* She shifted again, and in the next moment, she breathed out his name. "Bell?" Sleeping, questioning, calling his name as she stirred, it seemed his Penny had been wanting, too.

"Right here, Penny. I'm right here, darlin'." Curving one arm across her chest, he pulled her in, cuddling close until she settled again. Keeping hold of her, but this time, it was for him. When he was confident she was asleep, he whispered, "Thought about you all the fuckin' time, beautiful. I can't seem to lose this need for you. Under my skin, in my blood, I can't leave you behind no matter where I go. Ain't no replacin' you. Won't even start to try."

Shoulders shifting, she proved his assessment of her sleep wrong by rolling slightly away from him, but then her neck curved, bringing her face up in a clear demand. Eyes closed, lips curving into a gentle, pleased smile, she waited, and he leaned forwards, pressing his mouth to hers. A soft hum resonated from her, and he froze when she pulled away, nestling back into the mattress, head pillowed on his bicep. It wasn't her mostly-asleep movement that stunned him, but what she said while on the move. "I know, Bell. I love you, too."

Five minutes later, once he was sure she was out, he was dressed and standing outside at the front bumper of the truck, waiting for Wrench to emerge from the truck stop. Dealing with Wrench and the why of him being here was far easier than trying to decide how he felt about her words.

By the time the shadows moving between the trucks finally resolved into Wrench, Twisted was tired of waiting. Wrench made an impatient noise as, with a muttered, "Lemme set these inside," he moved to the passenger door, opened it and placed the bag and thermos on the floor there, then carefully closed the door. "She sleeping?"

"Yeah. Passed out about half an hour ago." They stood quietly for a moment, in an unconscious mirror reflection of each other, hands in the front pockets of jeans, heads tipped down. Wrench's hair was cropped short while Twisted's swung loose around his face, but their stances were identical.

"Smoke?" Wrench pulled a brand new pack from his jeans and Twisted shook his head. There was the crumple of paper and cellophane, then the pop and hiss of a match striking. The ember threw red shadows on Wrench's face as he drew hard on the cigarette, the smoke and scent of burning tobacco drifting across the space between them. "She...you really met her by chance?"

This seemed to be digging at the man, and Twisted wondered again about the expression he'd seen on Wrench's face earlier. He decided to give a little, see where Wrench took the info. "Yeah. She thought I was a lot lizard at first."

"No shit?" The startled laughter told Twisted that Penny hadn't talked about him at all, and that fucking stung a little.

"Shit free. I played along, weaseled my way into her cab. Then, like she said, we talked for a good long time." The emphasis he put on the word "talked" would leave little to the imagination and Wrench reacted, turning his head to the side, looking away, a dark scowl settling on his

features. "She's sweet. Mmhmm. Never met sweeter. Sweet talker." His words might be innocent, but his tone was not, and Wrench reacted again, lips curling into an involuntary snarl.

Flicking the half-smoked cigarette into the darkness between two trucks, Wrench lifted his chin, staring directly at Twisted. This kind of behavior would usually earn him an ass-whipping, but Twisted let the aggressive move pass, holding the man's gaze, willing him to talk. It felt like a fishing expedition, but Wrench had a lot of information in his head that Twisted needed if he was going to understand Penny. *With what she said? Do I want to know?* It had taken a long time before Wrench shook his head, finally looking away. "She needs someone who can protect her. Can you? Do you think you can fill that role for her?"

"What's she needin' protection from? From where I sit, it kinda looks like from you, if that shitty expression ain't lyin'." He waited, hoping Wrench would rise to the top of the pond for the lure resting there. The man opened his mouth and then closed it before squeezing his eyes shut, stupidly blinding himself in the presence of an enemy. Offering a trust Twisted wasn't sure he wanted. He braced, because whatever he was about to hear had hurt this man in profound ways, and he suspected it wouldn't go any easier hearing than saying it. There wasn't any way he could be ready for what he was about to hear, however.

"Known her all my life. We both grew up around the CoBos. Like an annoying little sister, she was always around, always up in my shit, giving as good as she got. Bagger, her uncle, was cool about it, but he loved that she wasn't afraid to jack with anyone. He egged her on, taught her she was invincible, because, with his backing, there wasn't anyone gonna fuck with Penny." Wrench shook his head. "Called her his princess, and we both know what that means around a club. Wrong lesson, but he couldn't have known. Got her a bike, taught her to ride. Fuck, man, she looks as at home on her bobber as she does driving Bagger's truck." Cutting his gaze to Twisted's face, he paused a minute before continuing, eyes again directed towards the toes of his boots.

"I had a thing for her."

Twisted made a noise. He couldn't stop it because that past-tense statement was a declarative lie. "No had about it." *Might as well push this into the light, shine some understanding on it now.*

"Have," Wrench agreed with a single word but then rocked Twisted back on his heels. "Wanted better for her. Want better. Wanted to keep her, somehow. Some part of her, anything to keep her in my life. I was afraid I'd fuck it up, lose her in every way. Talked to Bagger one night, probably six years ago. Figured out he wanted better for her, too. That knowledge sliced deep. The man was like family. He was a second old man to me. Finding out he didn't see me with Penny? That shit hurt worse than anything I could have imagined. But, you know what? He was right. If I had gone there and fucked it up?" He laughed softly. "Penny can hold a mean grudge. So I lost a chance that wasn't mine to begin with but gained a little sister. Love her to death, man." Twisted made a noncommittal noise.

"Then Bagger got killed. The club looked into it, found out the details on what happened." He glanced up at Twisted again before letting his gaze fall back to the parking lot with a heavy sigh. "Heard what you did a couple weeks ago. Grateful, Twisted. I appreciate it. The whole club appreciates it, man. It was way too long coming, but CoBos didn't have any kind of opening to make the same play." Silently Twisted tipped his chin.

"But, you didn't have the whole story. Still don't." Those words stopped the breath in Twisted's throat because they were discussing Penny, and if he didn't have the whole story and the story he had was all about Bagger, then what didn't he have? That shit seemed to hold his Penny inside, and even as he prayed the man would shut up, he willed Wrench to keep talking.

"If you knew the whole story...Jesus. After seeing the way you are with her, and knowing what went down? I know you don't." Lifting his

chin, Wrench stared directly at Twisted's face. "You'd have made it rain blood, man. You wouldn't have stopped with just the trigger man. You'd've pulled that weed out by the fucking roots. Dug deep, blood welling around every shovelful of shit you uncovered." Twisted's spine straightened, shoulders pulling back even as his hands balled into fists, nails cruelly digging into his palms.

Wrench informed him, "It's a fucked-up mess. Fucked up. FUBAR, and I didn't have a fucking clue what she was going through. Not until four goddamned hours ago. Not that first clue. No one knew what she was planning, so she executed it without any backup in place." He paused and Twisted heard the dry click of Wrench's throat when he swallowed. "Paid the ultimate price a woman can pay."

Teeth clenched, Twisted felt those words wrap around him, strangling him because he knew exactly what that meant. Remembered her sweetness. The charming naivety. Her unconscious sensuality. Heard his own words to her, *I ain't your first*. "That mean what I think?" No more than a growl, the question broke from him, his tone low and deadly.

Without breaking the stare, Wrench nodded, uncaring his broken emotions were on full display.

Quiet, intense, Twisted ordered, "Tell me what you know."

***

After Wrench was done talking, Twisted turned on his heel and stalked away. Down the line of trucks, out past where the lights stopped shining, trudging out to where he could look up and see stars. Mind racing a hundred miles an hour, again and again he ran over the facts Wrench had given him, coming up to the same conclusion every time. *I'd have done the same*.

He couldn't fault her, couldn't hold it against her, even as he wondered who it was. That was the one thing Wrench held back, said

the name didn't matter, just Penny did. Twisted couldn't argue against that, and if he were honest, he was better off not knowing the who, because knowing the what was hard enough.

I was the first in her bed to hold her. He knew his time with her meant he was probably her first in so many ways, just not that one. He could set that aside, her losing her virginity in that manner was like writing in the sand, the letters and words present in one moment, washed away by the power of the Gulf in the next. It didn't mean the writing hadn't existed, was just transient in a way that left a temporary impression.

Her and me? Carved in stone.

Chapter Ten

PENNY

Bit by bit Penny woke, the familiar rumble of the diesel engine and whine of the transmission creating a quiet blanket of white noise that had led to some of the best sleep she'd had in months. She rolled and stretched, feeling the sway of the cab as the wheels crossed the painted lines on the road, noise changing briefly. Hands over her head, she reached for the end wall and flattened her palms there, pressing, tightening her muscles and stretching again. Relaxing back into the mattress, she listened to see if Bagger was traveling with friends, their chatter over the CB radio an assistance in staying awake. She'd be able to tell from his voice how tired he was, and with...him...being so...

Her brain stuttered to a stop, events of the past months crashing back into her and she rolled onto her side to face the back of the bunk, knees tucked tight to her chest. Choking back one sob threatening to break free, she had to swallow another before she could clamp down on the pain. She felt movement in the vehicle, and her eyes flew open, belatedly remembering Ty and Bell had been in the truck last night. Remembering their battle. Remembering Bell holding her, touching her, kissing her until she lost her mind, his hands roaming her body with unfettered access.

As she was lifting up to look over her shoulder, a body fitted itself to her back. Heat and hardness enveloped her, an arm curving over her and across her belly, pulling her tight to the man's chest at her back. Lips hit her neck, along with the teasing brush of a beard, while a gruff voice asked her, "Sleep okay, darlin'?"

Bell. She licked her lips, carefully asking the obvious, "Who's driving? Ty?" Rolling away from him to her stomach, she lifted up on her elbows and had just started to move to a sitting position when she found herself yanked back down. His arms tightened around her, drawing in against him. In such close proximity, she couldn't help herself. The scent and feel of him was everywhere and with closed eyes, she nuzzled his chest.

"You went to sleep fast last night, Penny. Exhausted. You were beat, more than a single run's worth of tired." His voice, pitched low for privacy, rumbled around her. With emphasis, he asked again, "Did you sleep okay?" A hand slowly smoothed up and down her back, fingers playing with the hem of her shirt, glancing across her bare skin, leaving trails of heat in their wake.

Forget that. I need to ignore what I let him do to me last night, and everything will be okay. Disregard everything. Her thoughts weren't hopeful so much as despairing, because if he didn't move away, there would be no way she could ignore him. *Focus on the question*. "Is Ty driving?" She knew he could drive a rig, but in the days they'd traveled together, both this trip and others, he hadn't offered, so she assumed he hadn't wanted the responsibility or had the proper credentials. "Where are we?" She had an appointment at the dock to unload, and if she were late, there'd be penalties and fees taken off her trip payout. "What time is it?"

His fingers stilled, and she felt him pull back slightly, knew he was looking down at her, but she refused to look up. Her eyes open, she stared at his upper torso, the neckline of his shirt pulled out of whack, one collarbone and part of his chest exposed. Tattoos with a sprinkling

of hair showed on the skin she could see. A lot of tattoos, which she'd remembered, because his ink looked so striking, but she hadn't had the time to study them before. *I'd like to learn every inch of him*, she thought, then dismissed the idea. Without intent, her subconscious tested her resolve and her head dipped forwards, the tip of her nose traveling through the air only a fraction of an inch above his skin. *Stop it*. She pushed against him, moved back, gaining an inch, which he promptly reclaimed, and his arms tightened around her again.

"We're about thirty minutes outside of Sherman. And, yeah, Wrench is drivin'. He said there's a truck stop near your delivery that we'll hit, fill up the thermos and grab a bite. Two hours before the paperwork says you gotta be backed in and ready." He paused, and she felt him grow even more still where he was pressed up against her. She tested the waters again with another push, scooching down on the mattress a little to gain leverage. "Will you knock that off? Jesus." He yanked her back up, this time putting her face even with his neck.

She remembered he liked her mouth on him there when he'd had her on top. With his cock inside her and his hands first lifting her ass up, then pulling her body down firmly as he moved underneath her. Bell had thrust deep, to the root, rocking her forwards over his torso and she'd taken the chance to bend down, kiss his chest, then up his neck. He liked her teeth and lips so much he'd granted her the knowledge of how he sounded when he wanted more. Bell's throat had produced a series of long, low groans, his head rocking back into the pillows while she'd tongued and kissed his skin. He'd liked it. Told her so, told her she was, "A good girl."

His chin dipped, bringing his lips into view. They were curled up, lifting the corners of his mouth, the beard moving to accommodate. She lost the view of much of his neck, hidden behind his beard, but still saw the notch between his collarbones. The top edge of a tattoo skirted along the bones, lines and color covering more skin than showed through the neck of his shirt. Her palms were flattened against his chest,

keeping the tiny bit of separation she'd gained. "Darlin'." His lips moved, the word so gentle it was scarcely audible.

"Why are you here?" Last night she'd been so addled by the blow to the back of her head, she hadn't asked that question. Hadn't even thought it. Just knew she wanted to see Bell. She wanted to see him, had wished for him, and Bell showed up. Like magic. Wish granted. Things happened, and he locked them in the truck and made her come with his hand. Over her jeans. Mouth on her breasts. Then he'd held her until she went to sleep. Her dreams had been filled with him over the past weeks, but now he was here, back with her, going bare-fisted against a man she'd known since they were kids, in some caveman display of ownership. "Bell? Why were you looking for me?"

He rolled to his back, taking her with him so she was draped across his upper body. Her hands slipped to the mattress to support her weight, and one of his arms imprisoned her, pulling her down against him. The other went to shove pillows behind his head and then settled on his chest just in front of her. "You ever know someone addicted? Alcohol or drugs?" She stared at him a moment, then when he continued to wait patiently, decided it was a real question.

"Yeah. Why?" *What does this have to do with my question?*

"Seen the havoc it can wreak on their lives? How it starts out slow, a want instead of a need at that point. But then it grows, becomes that need. All they can think about, even if they don't talk about it all the time, it's always there." His hand lifted, palm cupping her jaw, thumb slipping along the edge of her cheekbone and back again in an infinitely tender touch. One she wanted to commit to memory, holding it against the time when he'd leave again. "Obsession sets in. They start to be consumed by whatever it is they're addicted to. Doesn't have to be a substance, either. You know that?" She nodded, careful not to dislodge his touch because she so liked what he was doing to her. His other arm had loosened when she'd stopped resisting, and the fingers of that hand were drawing circles on her back. Circles, loops, occasionally changing

to long arcing sweeps, but the pressure and sensation were constant. He'd done the same their first night together, touching her frequently, running his hands across her skin as if to reassure himself she was there. She liked that, too. The touching, the fact he enjoyed it as much as she did.

"Sex, power, money. Everything's tied to chemicals in the brain, and what gives the most pleasure is what becomes the focus. For some folks, all it takes is the tiniest taste, and they're hooked." His thumb paused its movement, fingers gripping her jaw. As he spoke, the muscles in his face had tightened, a jumping, pulsing beat in his jaw showing in between spoken phrases when she guessed he was clenching his teeth tightly. His next word was pushed out, a captive forced into the air of the bunk, truck still swaying along its way down the road. "Addicted." Angling her neck, she rested her cheek on his chest, seeing his face change with her movement. When she settled her head on him, his entire countenance softened. He dropped the guard he'd been holding over the past couple of minutes, everything about him telling her how much he liked that simple action.

The sound of the truck engine shifted as the vehicle sped up, changing lanes again, the noise of the car they were passing growing and then fading before she heard the soft shup-shup as they crossed the painted lines again.

The quiet spell stretched and grew, but it wasn't uncomfortable; it was just them, being together without talking. Bell sighed, the movement of his chest lifting her head and torso and she grinned, so he did it again, larger, on purpose, turning a smile her direction in response to her expression. That look bled away, leaving him pensive, seeming a little anxious and she wondered at that. Then when he spoke, she realized he had been answering her question all along.

"I'm addicted to you, Penny Dane. All I can do is think about you. Wonder if you're okay." His eyes cut left, towards the closed curtains separating the bunk from the cab. "Even when I shouldn't, when I have

shit to take care of, I can't keep you outta my mind." His beard rustled as he shook his head. "My focus is lost. I'm adrift, darlin'." He looked back at her and the lines at the corners of his eyes spoke of pain. "Without you, I'm only half breathin'. Felt like something was missing, so I set my boys to watch you. Caught up to you. Wanted to prove to myself it weren't nothing. Saw you from across that lot. Fuckin' saw you. Wanted you. It tore my heart apart just seein' you. You boppin' to some fuckin' tune in your head, pretty and good. My sweet Penny." He shook his head again.

"Didn't want to fuck you up. And I will. I can promise you. I can fuck up a sure thing that don't mean squat all day long. I'll most assuredly fuck up something that matters so much." His thumb glided across her cheek, down and back, soft and slow. "Boys told me you put a man in your truck." The fingers on her back contracted, digging deep, holding on. "My Penny." Those words were growled. His lips barely moved, but his chest resonated with the sound. "Got my ass to where I hoped like fuck you'd be. And you were." He sighed again, eyes closing briefly, palm flattening on her back. His voice was gentle when he whispered, "My Penny."

Gaze back on her, staring into her eyes, he looked confused and sad. The expression wasn't easy to read. She couldn't decide what it meant until he said, "I didn't know what it was until you said what you did last night. But like with everything, you already knew the truth, didn't you?" He paused, and she lay still, not sure what he was asking. "Telling me you loved me, too, proving you already knew what was happenin' to me."

She froze in place. *Oh, shit. Did I say that?* Her brain must have been more addled than she thought. It only took a moment before he barked a harsh laugh, pulling her attention back to him. *"Fuck me."* Turning away, looking towards the curtains again, he swallowed hard. "Sleep talkin'." He snorted a laugh that sounded no less painful. "Me layin' myself out there, and you don't even know what you said."

"Truth doesn't always require conscious thought," she told him, astonished at her mouth moving. *Go with it, reassure him*. "You need me to say it again in the broad light of day?" She waited for a beat. Then screwing up all her courage, she told him, "I can't get away from you in my head, Bell. You call it addicted? Yeah, I can see that." She nodded, feeling his hand moving, palm slipping along her jaw, fingers threading through her short hair. "I'd rather call it love."

His hands shifted to her sides, slipping under her arms and he pulled, tugging her up his body so she rested on his chest. His hands moved up to cradle her face, palm to each cheek, fingers curving around her head, holding her immobile. His eyes were fixed on her, darting across her features, and his attention was solely focused on her. Her face was reflected in his eyes, but he was all she could see. He drew her head down to him, lifting his lips to meet hers in a soft, wet kiss that was so good her toes curled, digging into the mattress. "You love me?" he asked with his lips pressed to hers, the tip of his tongue slipping out, caressing her mouth.

"Yes," she answered simply, and it seemed to be enough because he pulled her in for another kiss.

***

Po'Boy

"Oh, hell yeah." The man handed Po'Boy another beer, nodding vigorously. "I've seen that kind of shit before. Man, you better believe somethin' like that can tear a club apart, all over pussy." Po'Boy'd seen a bike broken down on the side of the road and stopped to help out. Together he and the rider solved the electrical problem and when they were done working on the bike, met up at a nearby bar so the man could express his thanks. They were relaxing on the patio, shooting the shit when Po'Boy had asked a casual question, and this man latched onto it like the outcome was important to him. *Interestin'*.

Twist top removed, the man tossed it in the general vicinity of the large trash can in the corner and then gestured with the bottle of beer. "Seen it happen to brothers. Good brothers. Good until they get pussy in their beds, and then that pillow talk shit starts to pull them in. A woman holds the keys to the kingdom if a man lets her." He gestured with the beer again. "Next thing you know, this brother'll be missin' church, askin' you to fill in his place."

Po'Boy studied him. Medium build, middle of the road looks, unremarkable voice. His tattoos all covered up once he put his shirt and plain vest back on after layin' in the dirt under the bike. This was a man it would be easy to forget, and he appeared to play that angle. The only distinctive feature Po'Boy'd seen so far on this self-proclaimed gypsy biker was a massive branded burn on his back.

"Pussy winds down to a brother missin' church, huh?" *Prick coulda been talking about Incoherent, thinkin' he had everything just right with what's been going on with Twisted. Prick'd be wrong, but this is...interestin'*. Po'Boy glanced down, not wanting to bring attention to his question, hoping it could run under the radar, but he needed to know. "Tell me, what comes next?"

Chapter Eleven

Penny

"Drop me at my place," Ty told her, leaning forward from where he sat, ass resting on the edge of the bunk. Bell was in the passenger seat, angled back against the door, socked feet propped on the dash. She glanced that way to find both men looking at her, and Penny grinned at how different the expressions on their faces were: Ty, tired and grumpy looking, ready to be home; Bell, attentive and watchful, focused on her.

She and Ty had done this routine a dozen times; he would tag along on a run when he didn't have anything else going on. This was the first time she'd picked him up out of state, and she frowned, thinking she never had a chance to ask him about that, or follow-up about him helping with her search.

"Can do," she responded, glancing over at Bell. The look on his face was intent. He seemed to be studying her, which made her oddly nervous. Looking out through the windshield, she waited a moment, then, hoping she hit the casual tone she was aiming for, asked, "What were you doin' up in Yankeeland, Ty?" From the corner of her eye, she caught movement and turned to see Bell had tensed, pivoting away to glare out his side of the wide windshield. Nervously, she reached up,

tucking a short strand of hair behind her ear, hating that the motion telegraphed the importance of her question.

She glanced at Ty, and he stared back at her, pain moving through the expression on his face, sharp and profound. He whispered, voice so quiet she could barely hear him, "Fuck. I miss your hair, Penny."

That hit her like a freight train, bowling her over, and her eyes filled with tears so suddenly she couldn't see the road, couldn't blink them away fast enough. In only moments they had overflowed, streaming wet down her cheeks. She whipped her head around to face front, turning away from the pain, trying to route around it, find a different pathway. Through these seconds, she kept the truck steady, hours and miles of experience allowing her to hold them in place. She heard Bell give a quick, clipped, "What the *fuck?*" He sounded shocked, but she didn't have any time for that, no time to manage him or what he might learn, because Ty's voice was low and growling when he continued, careless of their audience, "I'm gonna fucking kill Gollum."

This time, when it came, Bell's voice was no longer shocked. It was hard as stone as he asked, "What in fuck does she have to do with Gollum? And whaddya mean, you miss her goddamned hair?" Ty made a noise and from the corner of one streaming eye, she saw both men disappear from view, curtains swaying in their wake. Voices, low and quiet, but no less intense for that, came from the bunk. Swiping at her cheeks with a palm, she struggled to regain her composure, straining to listen to their muttered conversation over the whine of road noise.

Bell roared wordlessly, and the cab lurched, and—knowing what that might mean—so did her stomach. If they were fighting again...

I can't do this. Motions jerky and abrupt, Penny turned on her blinker and headed up the next off-ramp. She parked the truck on the broad shoulder, the sudden stop causing the empty trailer's tires to lock up, leaving trails of blackened rubber in their wake. "The fuck, Penny?" Bell shouted.

It took a single motion to knock the gearshift into neutral, and another to set the air brakes. Sobbing, she opened her door and was already jumping down before the vehicle had even stopped rocking in place. Ty yelled, "Get back—"

She staggered, slamming the door as she tripped over her own feet, making her way to the side of the road. Bent double, she had her arms wrapped around her body as if she were in enormous pain. And she was, anguish rolling over her in waves. With just a few words, Ty had torn away the protective wall she had worked so hard to build up over the past months. The knowledge crawled up her spine that she had given herself away for nothing, and to a man as vile as Gollum; it settled into place in her head, finding the home it had made for itself still waiting.

As she stood, heaving great breaths in and out, trying to keep her feet, strong arms wrapped around her from behind and Bell's voice was there. His touch, the sound of his voice: those were anchors she could use to beat back the pain. As he turned her, drawing her close, she wrapped her arms around his chest, holding on, taking what she needed from him. "I'm sorry," she whispered softly into his neck, feeling his beard scratchy against her cheek.

"For what, darlin'?" His answering whisper was just as soft, tender with care for her.

"For being such a dramatic wuss." She hated how her voice hitched in the middle of that short sentence, hated that they were standing on the side of the road on display, hated even more that he had seen her like this. All her life, she had done her grieving and healing in solitude, because feeling exposed like this felt wrong. Vulnerable. Made her a pathetic crybaby.

"Wrench told me, Penny. With what he said happened, you have every right to be angry and upset, pissed as hell. Don't be sorry. It ain't weak. *You* ain't weak." He knew what she meant, how she felt. "You

take your time, get it together. I got nowhere to be but right here with you. Take your time, Penny." His arms tightened around her securely. He held her, helping her brave the memories stirred by casual words. *Fuck, I miss your hair.* "I'm right here." His head moved, beard shifting across her face and she felt his lips touch her cheek. "Nowhere else I'd rather be." His hand moved, sliding up to cup around the back of her head. "Right here with you."

***

TWISTED

Twisted held her for a long time. Wrench came over, murmured he'd called a friend and then even before Penny could respond, turned and walked back to the truck. Twisted didn't look at the assclown. He wasn't sure he could right now without losing his goddamned mind. Yesterday the man had told him what Penny'd done, and with the awareness she was looking for her uncle's killer, Twisted understood it. Didn't like it. Really fucking didn't like it, but he could agree with using whatever leverage you had in order to advance a cause that meant a lot to you. He'd done it, time and again. He understood believing the cause worthy, making that calculation and then gladly paying the cost.

But that was before he knew what mother*fucker* Wrench was talking about. Without a name, it was easy to make the bastard faceless, mentally make it less pain-filled than it really was. With a name...shit was about to go down that Twisted wasn't sure his little slice of the world was ready for.

Gollum.

Twisted knew the depths of his own capacity for handing out pain. Knew he could be a mean son-of-a-bitch. Had destroyed lives without losing one moment of sleep. Squinted one eye as he sighted down the barrel, bracing for the sound about to come, ready for the spray of heat that would hit him when he pulled the trigger. Walked across the broken backs of his enemies to get where he wanted to be, grinning the

whole time, fingers poppin' and snappin' a jive, ready for thimbles to drag across a tuned rubboard.

Five years ago, he would have fucking roared. He would have laughed until he had tears in his eyes if anyone described the last twenty-four hours, and told him it would be his lot. No way would he travel 800 miles to meet up with a fucking chick. She'd come to him, or she wouldn't get his dick. No chance he'd ditch a club cage without a second thought, leaving it so someone else had to travel the same road to retrieve it and clean up his shit.

He would have flat refused to let a fucking bitch drive him around, even if it were her fucking truck. Never fucking fight over said bitch with someone he didn't have a beef with, other than the bitch herself. Get the bitch off, then lay there with a pounding, throbbing dick in his pants, listening to her sleep and fucking smile because she sounded content. Fucking exchange vows of goddamned love. Stand on the side of this damn road without his goddamned cut on and hold her because she was sad.

Jesus, grow a pair of balls, boy. He could imagine his Papaw telling him that on a laugh, even as he let one of the house's fender bunnies snuggle into his side. Grandma had been gone before Twisted met her. She'd died a long time before he was born. The story of her death etched on his soul because it started the path that led to him. Crooked and turning, but still a pathway he wound up treading. He didn't know her, but knew she wasn't club. His grandma had never set foot inside any clubhouse. She'd barely been Papaw's bride when he left for the military, staying behind while he proudly served his country. Then, still a young girl, she'd been unsure what to do when the man returned to her was so changed. Papaw didn't talk about her much, but when he did, the expression he wore was sad. Lost. After getting to know Papaw, as a teen Twisted would imagine seeing them together, wanted to have had the chance to see them, so he could learn more about them. More than the few pictures he'd seen.

Yeah, Twisted could be ruthless. Gollum, however, wrote the fucking book on it. Over the years, their paths had crossed. Neutral parties or gatherings, both of them in the background, circling the other like junkyard dogs, itching for any chance at a *sic 'em* command. Wanting it so badly they could taste it. The thought of *his* Penny in that man's bed curdled his stomach, sending bile racing up his throat.

Twisted had seen the aftermath of Gollum plowing through enemies. He'd admired some of the more efficient techniques, even while wincing at the brutality. Standing here today, holding Penny, he remembered laughing about the story of how the man treated one bitch who went willingly to his bed. Remembered telling Po'Boy she got what she earned, giving a man like Gollum her pussy. And *his* Penny had done the same, gone to the man's bed and laid down of her own choice. Her first.

Red. That's all he saw when Wrench said what he did. Twisted ran his hand up her back again, cradling and turning her head, pressing her cheek against his chest, fingers working gently through her short hair. Wrench's voice sounded again in his head. *Hair so long, she could sit on it. So fucking beautiful it'd take your breath away.* He knew what happened to it. Not two weeks ago around the burn barrel at a party, he'd joined in the laughter about a story told about Gollum. The man had his bitch take another woman's hair and make him a memento. *Stupid bitch*. That had been the consensus, but which woman it was about had been in question, the bitch who donated her locks, or his bitch for putting up with his shit.

My Penny. A vehicle pulled up near the semi and sat, idling. Wrench called out his good-byes and Penny stirred, her hand lifting from Twisted's back. He assumed she waved, but he didn't turn to watch the motherfucker go. Wrench's words continued to play through his mind. *You need to find out what he told her. She's not going to stop until she knows, and you can save her that because you already meted out justice, man*. Memories swam to the surface, and he saw her face, flushed, eyes half-lidded, smile languorous. Another vision started

bleeding through, his imagination painting her with eyes widened in fear, lips twisted in pain. Pale and drawn. *Fuck.*

She made a soft noise and pushed against his hold. Her voice was quiet when she said, "We should probably get off the side of the road. DOT will be stopping soon, see if anything's wrong. I hate to give them any reason to inspect."

He lifted his head and looked around, blinking against the setting sun as he watched the trucks and cars zooming past down on the interstate. Wordlessly he turned, started them walking back towards the truck, guiding her to the passenger door. She looked up at him, and he shook his head, not yet ready to trust his own voice. Their gazes held for a moment, and then she shook her head with a half smile that didn't contain any humor. "Of course, you know how to drive a semi."

Thirty minutes later, Penny stirred and took her socked feet from the dash and turned, sitting sideways in the seat as she murmured over the engine noise, "Tired." He nodded and jerked his head towards the swaying curtains before glancing over. A pensive look was on her face.

He directed a smile towards her and gave her the encouragement she needed. "You should lay down then, darlin'."

Eyes on his face, she sat there then said, "I'm just...drained."

"Happens when things come crashing down on your head. Get a nap in. We'll be home in a couple of hours." They hadn't talked about what happened, what caused her to pull over, why she fell apart. He wanted to get her to a safe place first; somewhere he could control her reactions better than in the bunk of a truck.

Right now, she was exhausted and compliant, but he knew from the little experience he had with her that it wouldn't last. So he needed to get her home, get her into his house, and get himself under control so he could work through this at her side.

"Home?" Her mouth pulled sideways, and he didn't know her enough to read that expression at all, so he studied her. Glancing between her face and the road, he tried to impress it on his brain so he could decipher another part of the mystery that was Penny. He wanted to hold every nuance of her.

"Yeah." Puzzled, he reached out a hand, gratified at how she immediately took it. Gripping tightly, she held on. Fingers folded around his hand, giving and taking the security of that connection. "Home."

"How do you know where I live?" Her head tipped to one side as she asked the question before she straightened as if giving something away she didn't want to. She wanted him to have looked that far into her, wanted him to already know, which he did. They just weren't going there today.

"*My* home." Tugging on her hand, he pulled her from the seat and across the space separating them. She stood beside him, looking down from her small advantage when he said, "Want you in my house, darlin'. Takin' you there." He tightened his grip when she would have pulled free. "Got plenty of space to park a rig, you'll see. More than. Go get some sleep,"—he squeezed and relaxed his fingers slightly—"but kiss me before you head to the bunk."

He thought she might argue, was ready for it, but instead, she simply bent, pressed her lips to his and tightened her grip on his hand before releasing her hold. A swish of the curtains, shift of the truck chassis, and she disappeared into the bunk.

Parking the rig beside the big barn to the south of his house, he thought the sound of the brakes setting might wake her, but when he looked into the bunk, she was still sleeping. Hands pressed palm-to-palm, shoved under her head, she rested on her side facing the front of the bed, but even in repose, her face wasn't relaxed, tiny lines creasing between her brows. He took a step towards her but paused when his phone buzzed in his pocket. Yanking it out, he saw Po'Boy was calling.

Torn and feeling guilty, it still only took him a moment to reject the call, sending a quick, canned text response that he'd call back in twenty minutes.

Easing onto the edge of the bunk, he traced along her hairline with his fingers, brushing the backs of his knuckles across her cheek. "Wake up, sleepyhead." She sighed and shifted, a small smile curving the corners of her lips upwards. "Penny, darlin'. We're here." He retraced the glide across her cheek, the softness of her skin mesmerizing. "Penny." He swept the short strands of hair back from her face, gritting his teeth when Wrench's voice sounded in his head again. *Fuck, I miss your hair.*

As if in response to his thoughts, her eyes flashed open and before he could react, she had shoved away from him, back to the corner of the bunk, a wild look on her face. "Hey," he called, not sure what had set her off. "It's just me, baby."

On a shaky exhalation, she whispered, "Sorry. I just..."—she lifted her hands and scrubbed at her face with her palms—"I'm not used to having folks in my space like that." Dropping her hands to her lap, she offered him a smile that didn't reach her eyes. "Sorry," she repeated.

"No worries." He waited for a moment, but she didn't move from where she had retreated to. "So Wrench didn't wake you up?" He didn't know where that came from and watched her blink in surprise.

"Well, yeah, he did."

"So it's just me in your space that freaks you out?" That came out rude and sharp and immediately he tried to soften it with a joke. "I'm not that bad-looking, am I?" Pushing his bottom lip out, he gave her his pouting smile, relieved when she grinned back at him and started scooting her way to the front edge of the mattress where he sat.

"No, Bell." She reached up, touching his shoulder tentatively, then stroked across his bicep with more confidence. *Your hands on me?*

Anytime, darlin'. "He didn't get in my space." With a giggle, she added, "He'd throw things from the top bunk, or the passenger seat. Holler at me to 'wake the fuck up, bitch,' which is his way of being gentle." She grinned. "We grew up together."

"Sounds like there's a story in there." Covering her hand with his, he gave a gentle squeeze. "Let's head inside. Stories are always better over beer, and that's something I've got plenty of. Come on, darlin'." He stood and tugged on her hand. "Get your shoes on. Let's head inside."

***

It took a while, but eventually she relaxed enough to talk to him about what happened. He had underestimated two things: One, her tolerance for alcohol, because, by the time she finished reciting events and tried to walk out the door and back to the bunk of her semi, she was staggering. Two, the unplumbed depths in the well of anger waiting inside him. After carrying her to his bed and arranging her sleeping body, head to the pillows, comforter drawn across her hips as her remembered preference, he walked back to the big room at the back of his house and picked up the bottle of whiskey.

Lifting it to his lips, he sucked in one welcome mouthful of sting, but stopped there. He had too much work to do to get plastered. Stretching out one hand, palm down, he studied it, finding that with everything she'd handed him tonight, he could still hold firm, unshaking. He was that far beyond rage. The boil in his blood was constant. Digging his phone from his hip pocket, he looked at the missed calls, seeing Po'Boy had not redialed, but there were four calls and a matching number of texts from Wrench.

Fucktard.

Swipe, delete.

Phone to his ear he waited, ready to cut his brother off if he answered in a mood. A mellow Po'Boy came on the line instead, startling him. "Bruh, sup, my man?"

What the fuck? "Brother, you rang?"

"I did?" A pause then a rough giggle. "Fuck, I'm baked. Thought you called me."

"I did, but only because you dialed first. You remember what you needed?" Twisted rolled his eyes, thinking, *ess-ess-dee-dee*.

"Imma 'member it tomorrah. A'ighty?" A sigh, then a self-pitying grunt. "Been gone a long time, brotha." Another grunt. "Brands said you'd do this shit. Pussy gets in the way."

"Pussy ain't gonna get in the way." He scoffed, "You know me better, brother. Who the fuck is Brands?"

"Nomad, rollin' through." A sigh. "See ya 'morrah?"

"Yeah, brother. See you tomorrow. Church before food." There was an open-door party tomorrow night, and before he left to hunt Penny, he'd mandated church before any of the officers got their drink on. There were things to sort out, business needing to be settled where it came to how they were going to deal with Fiddler and his kin, his club. He turned, glancing back at the door leading to where Penny lay sleeping. *Means I get tonight with her*. "I gotta go. Shiny side."

"Peace out."

From personal experience Twisted expected she'd be asleep for a few hours. This meant he had time to activate some connections outside of the area. He texted Wrench back, just a quick, **Home safe sleepin**. Got back a **Good**, did the same swipe delete before tapping into his contacts. Lifting the phone to his ear, he waited, then smiled when heard a drawling "Hello," from a man he knew well. "Retro, man. Got a minute?"

Chapter Twelve

TWISTED, TWO MONTHS LATER

It had been three weeks since he'd effectively moved her into his house. That was after it took him more than a month to convince her that what they had wasn't going to fall apart. More than a month of her going out in the truck by herself. It was something he didn't know would bother him until after she'd driven away the first time. It wasn't that he didn't trust her, but more the not-knowing things that ate at him. Was she tired? Hungry? Catching guff from a dockhand? Stuck on the side of the road? Lying in a ditch? The options were endless, and none he could come up with were good ones.

The grin she wore the next time he saw her should have tipped him to the fact he was acting like a crazy person. But, it wasn't until she showed him the more than 300 texts he'd sent her in five days that it sunk in. His habit of deleting things immediately after sending or reading them had masked the fact that he was obsessively checking in on her. At least from him. Not from her, having to deal with the nearly constant ding or vibration that told her he was asking another question.

Did you eat?

Where ya at?

How's it goin?

You good?

Where ya goin?

Is it goin' good?

When he stumbled for the words to explain, she covered his mouth with her hand, her fingertips brushing against his lips. "Shhh. It's okay, Bell. I think it's sweet." She ducked her head, avoiding his gaze for a moment. "I haven't...no one's ever cared like that." Her eyes met his and he watched as they darkened. He knew why when her hand moved, cupping his jaw, thumb sweeping across his bottom lip. "I like it."

"Glad you like it, sweetheart," he spoke against the pad of her thumb and then opened his lips, taking it into his mouth. Playing with her thumb, he gripped it between his teeth, traced everything he could find with his tongue, sucked on it like a teat. Everything he did pulled a reaction from her. A gasp, her mouth falling open. Eyelids dropping to half-mast, gaze fixed on his lips. A full-bodied shiver rippled through her when he bit down lightly, talking around her thumb, "I'll keep doing it then."

"Okay, then." Her whispered words were gasped rather than spoken, and he smiled, rolling his tongue around her thumb again. "Bell." At his name in her mouth, he abandoned his torture of her thumb, reaching up to cup the back of her head, bringing her close, waiting until his mouth hovered over hers to say, "Welcome home, Penny."

"Thanks," she breathed, and he grinned, sliding a hand down her back, wrapping around her waist and pulling her close.

"Want a proper welcome home?" He didn't have to wait for her response. The rocking of her head was immediate, and he rewarded her with a brief lip touch, brushing across in a barely-there caress with his mouth.

She groaned, and her disappointment was tangible, puffs of breath against his lips painting her desire on his skin. "Not quite proper," he whispered, feeling her shiver again. "Want me to try again? Give it another go?" Not trusting him this time, she responded with a hum and he rewarded her again, this a suitable reward, covering her mouth with his, head slanting.

Long minutes passed and her breath was as ragged as his when he pulled back. Forehead pressed to hers, eyes closed, he asked, "Want more?"

"God, yes."

That led to him kissing her again, which resulted in undressing her, and then him in a rush to find solace inside her.

Chapter Thirteen

TWISTED, ONE WEEK LATER

Well, that didn't go exactly as planned. He didn't have time for anything past the single thought before his head whipped to the side again. Blood sprayed in a fan across the face of the man with a fist in his hair, holding his head up. Twisted watched as the dead man licked his lips, then gathered enough saliva to spit to the side. *Points for not hawkin' in my face.*

Probing with his tongue, Twisted found the split in his cheek flooding his mouth with blood. *Lemme show you how it's done.* Biding his time, he let the bitter fluid fill his mouth, holding still until the man leaned deep, putting his face right in front of Twisted, getting ready to shout at him again, no doubt. The problem was, the guy was too close. Got close, stayed close, put himself in harm's way by staying within reach.

Stupid. He should have done things differently. Should have had a soldier holding Twisted from behind. Should have made sure the bonds hadn't slipped. Should have checked more than the obvious places for weapons. *Dead man,* he thought, just before he spat a mouthful of blood into the man's eyes, knowing the mixture of blood and saliva would burn like a motherfucker.

Twisted rolled, sacrificing his scalp to gain distance while he shoved a hand into his front pocket, coming out with a small pen. With a flick of his wrist, the concealed blade popped into place. He swept his keys from the ground where they were knocked during the initial scuffle, fingers folding around what looked like a cute kitty face keychain, now revealed to be a deadly addition to bare-fisted fighting. Coming up from the ground, he threw himself at the lone man he'd identified as a danger, the only one who hadn't holstered his weapon while Twisted was kneeling on the ground.

Sweeping right to left, the thin blade bit through the man's face, striated muscle visible through the hole gaping in its wake. Not sure if that would keep this guy clear, he followed up with a violent punch to the throat, knowing his kitty's work was done when the guy stopped making sounds. The keys went into his pocket, and in a continuance of the same motion, Twisted stripped the gun from the man's fingers. He turned, seeing no other weapons yet bared. *Flat-footed enemies*, he thought, lifting his chin as he stared into Gollum's eyes.

Shouts and yells rose around them, Twisted's delayed backup flooding from the woods surrounding the clearing he'd seemed destined to die in today. The men at Gollum's back countered finally, pulling their weapons. Bullets whistled past with sounds of pain filling the air. Meaty thuds of fists. High, wavering screams. Still the two men stood, locked in a stare.

On his side of the standoff, Twisted fought the urge to draw it out. *Make him pay*. That was what his blood chanted as it flowed fast through his veins. *Make him pay*. Shouldn't have cut her hair. *Make him pay*. Shouldn't have taken what she offered, knowing he didn't have anything to trade. *Make him pay*. Her tears as she told Twisted what had happened, tears as he held her. Buckets of fucking tears choking her voice, rusting his heart, staining the time Twisted had with her. *Make him pay*.

"Do it! Fuckin' *do* it!" Gollum screamed suddenly, bending at the waist, mouth open, cords in his neck straining. Fists clenched into impotent weapons with no nearby body upon which to impress their hatred, Penny would be forever safe from him. *"Fuckin' do it!"*

"Since you asked so nicely." Twisted wasn't even aware he spoke aloud until he heard Po'Boy laugh beside him. Sighting down the barrel, grip unfamiliar in his hand, Twisted focused on the still-screaming mouth in the face in front of him. *Squeeze*. A small, controlled kick but it meant the barrel lifted slightly, blocking his view of the bullet striking true, the body falling in a heap to the ground, white and gray and red splattered in a wide arc behind.

Twisted sighed, an ache beginning to set up camp in his head following the echoing report. He spat again, blood still welling from the gouges to his inner cheek. "Downed?" He and Po'Boy still used their own shorthand. They'd been through enough situations to refine what they'd started years ago, found from much use that a shared vocabulary and straightforward questions worked best to minimize misunderstandings when it mattered most.

"Nada." A short laugh. "Well, nada for the good guys." Twisted swept his hair back from his face, catching it in one hand, grimacing as he felt slick blood coating the strands. "Here." A nudge against his fingers and he glanced over, taking the hair tie from Po'Boy, who was choking with laughter. "You're always bitchin' about tangles after riding away from a fight where some fucker put his hands on you. They always go for the hair." Po'Boy shrugged. "Figured I'd get ahead of it this time." Twisted shook his head, took care of business and turned back to the field. "Yo, been weeks."

"What?" Scanning the field again, Twisted saw a couple of pockets of activity yet.

Po'Boy sighed. "I said, it's been weeks, brother. You gonna come clean about your pussy?" Teeth clenching, Twisted held his silence. "Oh,

come on, brother. You think we don't know about this shit? Bagger's girl. See? I even know her bloodline." Twisted threw a hard elbow his way and Po'Boy grunted. "Goddammit, brother. Tell me one thing. One thing, and I'll leave you and your pussy alone."

Twisted grunted, shaking his head, intonation different with this utterance of the same question, "What?"

"She suck good?"

With a roar, Twisted was on him, hand under his jaw, gripping tightly. Po'Boy laughed, reaching up with one hand to trail his fingers across Twisted's face, pulling them back covered in red that he painted underneath each of his own eyes. "You ain't whupped," Po'Boy wheezed, a grin still on his face. "You're mesmerized by pussy. Stupefied by the snatch. Feel ya, brother." Pushing against Twisted's hand, he leaned into him. "Oh yeah, I feel ya. But we still gotta talk."

"Yeah," Twisted drawled, dropping his hand and stepping back, feeling curious eyes on them. "We gotta talk, but you say anything like that again and you ain't gonna be able to talk through that mouth." He shifted, turning to look out at the remaining groups of men. "She doesn't factor."

"Fuckin' lie. I know it, you know it." Po'Boy stepped up to stand shoulder to shoulder with him. "I'll give you this once. Free pass, man. Mostly 'cuz you're beat all to shit, and I love ya." They were quiet for a minute. "You're my brother. I worry."

"Don't worry."

"I worry," Po'Boy repeated, his voice losing the teasing tone.

Twisted sighed. "I know, but don't. It's all good, brother."

"Home or house?" That distinction was Po'Boy's way of asking if Penny would be coming between Twisted and the club party later. This entire conversation had turned uncomfortable. Clearly Po'Boy had been

watching, had seen how tied up Twisted was in Penny, and was now questioning where Twisted was in his head. Hell, this might even be a final test, but he didn't give a fuck.

Twisted turned to face him and they locked gazes, the atmosphere surrounding them growing heavy and intense. Twisted decided to open up a tiny peephole for Po'Boy, let him in a bit. Ease his mind. "It's good, brother. Truly good. Like she's meant for me. Ours was a chance meeting, so you gotta call it fate. Nice change, she's different, Po'Boy. A really fuckin' *nice* change from anythin' I've ever had, man. She's my *lagniappe*, for true. But, I am who I am, *brother*. I'll either be there, or I'll be home." He shook his head. "Doesn't matter. I'm Incoherent, core. You know it."

"That I do," Po'Boy agreed. "Just wanna see your ugly mug around the house. Good joojoo. Now you tweaked me, 'n I wanna meet her, big time. Bring her."

"Not tonight." He paused, and decided to shift the talk away from Penny, and back to today. "I count eight." There'd been fourteen of them when they started. Eight still upright wasn't bad. They never bothered tallying the dead until after everything was settled. They'd learned long ago it was only the living you had to worry about.

A man broke away from one group and even before the gunshot splintered the air, Po'Boy had already counted him out. "Seven."

"True that." Footsteps sounded from his other side and even without looking, Twisted knew who it was. "Retro."

"I'm late, but not that late. You boys don't have any sense of hospitality. Didn't save anything for me or mine." The hippy-looking biker had hair longer than Twisted's, pulled back into a long braid, tucked inside the back of his cut. Probably tucked inside his belt, too, to keep the wind from stealing it. "You get what you wanted?" That was Retro being cautious, not knowing Po'Boy as well as he did Twisted, not

chancing what would have been shared, even between trusted brothers.

"You're in time, man. Shields started the party early. We're just catchin' up now." Twisted glanced back, seeing nearly forty men fanning out behind them. "You bring a bus? Fucking shit, man. That's a lotta bodies."

Retro was president of the Bama Bastards, out of Birmingham, and had been friends with Papaw for as long as Twisted could remember. The man had an easygoing demeanor, but that was intentionally misleading, because when he set himself against or for something, he went at it with everything inside him. Take no prisoners, giving not an inch from his planned path.

Papaw had leaned on the younger man a lot, mentoring in return, helping guide the Bastards into a place where they were profitable and, while not the dominant club in Alabama, they were well respected. For a variety of reasons.

When Twisted looked around the field again, he knew he was watching one of those reasons in action. Retro had gone all-in on his behalf, with no more than a single request. Some clubs would have turned him down flat, or at best phoned in a response, turning out only a limited number of disposable bodies.

Retro ignored his statement, asking his own questions. "Shields know why they garnered your displeasure?" He held out a thick length of what looked like rope. Woven into one end was a clasp, leather straps wrapped around the other. The material was a rich auburn color with sun-streaked highlights running the length of what Twisted knew was braided human hair.

"Not yet. And they won't," Twisted answered, reaching for the get-back whip he knew had been attached to Gollum's bike until Retro removed it. Penny's hair in his hands, the length astonishing, even having Wrench's words to warn him. Chin down, he squeezed his eyes

closed, scrubbing across his face with one hand, the other resting on his hip. He felt the weight of the whip as it brushed against his leg. Tangible evidence that everything she'd said, everything he'd heard unknowing of the identity, all of it was true. *Mine*.

"She's...hields aren't in a place to demand they learn anything." Twisted had been about to declare something that didn't have a place on this field, didn't have a place in club business. "They've been a thorn for far too long. It was time to cull the flock." He gestured towards the bodies littering the field behind him, not giving them the courtesy of a glance. "I've got a dozen other ops going down." As if on cue, his burner phone rang, and he bared his teeth. "As of today, Guanyin's Shield is no more. We burn cuts tonight."

"*Jesus*. Fiddler?" Retro's question fell to silence as Twisted answered his ringing phone.

"Point is done." That was Chip, and he was glad to hear the report because that meant things could be wrapped up today.

"Downed?" Same shorthand, same answer.

"Nada. There?"

"Nada. Fiddler?" Next to knowing if his boys were good, this was the most important question.

"I said Point was done, didn't I?" Chip took a breath, the length and raggedness telling Twisted that the fight hadn't been easy, and while they might not have dead to deal with, they surely had injuries. "Gollum?"

Twisted's gaze swept to the field again, landing on the body not twenty feet away. From here, he could see that half of the man's face was gone, the bullet having found its mark beside his nose, blasting its way through bone and flesh. "Way done."

"Good deal."

"Very good." His phone buzzed, and he looked at the display. "Got Catfish. See you at the house." Without waiting for a response, he disconnected, picking up the call. "Downed?"

And that set the tone for the next hour as the club checked in, touching base to let him know their part in the operation was complete, and telling him how things progressed, using as few words as possible on the electronic devices. Their full debrief would happen tonight, over beer in the back lot, stories growing with each telling until every man had to have taken out a dozen enemies alone. Legends in the making.

Twisted was standing in nearly the same spot an hour later, feet wide apart, stretching his back with hands to hips when he heard footsteps again approaching. "Yeah?" He didn't open his eyes, rolling his head side-to-side. One of the prospects had just left in a pickup, the bed full of pissed-off Shield survivors, their bikes and cuts left behind as spoils of war. Po'Boy had gleefully taken on the task of stripping each warm body of their vests, enjoying it most when they fought him, giving him a chance to go all out to bust knuckles on their heads in a way usually denied him. The outcome was preordained, but it was always hard to watch grown men fiercely defending their colors, still fighting on even after seeing their brothers brought low. *That's what we need in a member*, he thought, belatedly realizing he hadn't heard a response.

Lifting his head, he saw Retro standing there, staring at him. "Yeah?" he repeated. They might not have needed the Bastards fists or iron today, but it was good for his boys to see the support, good for the disbanded Shields to see it, too. "Respect, man. Know I already said it, but you showing means a lot."

Head to one side, Retro nodded. He stood in this position for a moment, then straightened and asked, "Who's your daddy?"

Twisted blinked. He hadn't been asked that since school. When he told the teacher the truth, he'd been kicked out for three days for using "inappropriate language." "My old lady was a whore. Don't know whose

jizz broke the barrier and knocked Mama up. Jimbo was my granddad, only daddy I really had."

Retro looked down at something he held in his hands. A wallet, chain dangling from the worn leather rectangle. "Was goin' through shit. Strippin'." Twisted nodded. It was something they'd all done at one point or another, removing IDs and pictures from bodies to slow down the identification process if graves weren't hidden well enough. "Found something I think you need to see." He didn't hold it out, just looked from his hands up to Twisted's face, then back down. "I don't know what it means." His glance traveled the same path, up and then down. "Might not mean anything." His gaze fixed on Twisted's face, locking on with an intensity that was uncomfortable. "Might mean everything." He took a breath, lifting the wallet an inch. "This is Gollum's." He hesitated, then held a folded piece of paper. "Found this inside."

Twisted took the thick paper, knowing before he unfolded it that it was a picture. When he saw the image, he couldn't stop the startled laughter that burst from him. "What the hell is this?"

"Don't know." Retro's voice sounded like it was coming from inside a barrel. "Look at the date."

Twisted flipped the paper over, seeing a processing date stamp along the edge. "Year before I was born." He flipped the picture back over, staring at the image. "That's my old lady. My mom." He heard Retro grunt in surprise. "You didn't know, did you?" Another grunt that he took for agreement. "That's my mama, so who's the man?"

"Twisted," Retro's voice was soft, searching, "look at him."

"Looks like me." He did. The man in the picture looked like him. Full beard, longish hair, curling around his shirt collar. The man stood, arm around a very young Coralie Bell. *Hadn't even turned fifteen when she had me*. She was leaning into the man, one hand resting on top of her belly. "Got more pics?"

Twisted didn't look up, just held out his hand, accepting the trivial weight of the pictures when they were pressed into his palm. Flipping through the images, they were organized oldest to most recent, and in them, he saw the progression of age on the man. Saw his hair long, then short, then long again. Saw sleeves of tattoos creeping up his arms; saw those arms cord and thin as the flush of youth left the man. Saw finally the face he most feared would be at the end of things. "You look at alla these?" A noncommittal sound, but he knew Retro had seen it all. "You show anyone?"

"No, man. Not mine to share." Retro's response was fast, and he took it at face value, believing in the integrity of the man.

"Don't." He shoved the pictures back to Retro, wanting free of them. He saw the man tuck the images into a pocket inside his cut, pressing the snap into place to fasten it shut. Ignoring what had just happened, he said, "Bring your boys to the clubhouse. We'll have a cold one waitin'." Twisted turned on his heel and stalked away, taking in the state of the field at a glance. Bodies all carried away, bikes being loaded into a cattle trailer, men standing around with nothing left to do. "Incoherent," he shouted to get everyone's attention. "Bastards are our guests tonight. Put on a good show. See y'all there. Done good, brothers."

He heard Po'Boy's voice in the distance, calling something but lost it in the roar of his engine. His ass was already on the seat, hands to the grips, and then he was out of the ditch and onto the gravel road, feeling the whip and grind of the loose surface underneath his wheels, controlling with some effort as the bike tried to slide out from under him. A moment later and he was straight again, rolling faster than was prudent to the highway that lay twenty miles away.

Three bikes pulled out behind him, the reflections in his mirrors showing unidentifiable men.

Another twenty past that highway and he'd be home, where he'd left Penny sleeping last night. He'd only texted her a quick message before he left his phone in the tech bucket at the clubhouse this morning.

Now he was on his way to her, need boiling through him. Not to fuck her. He needed her to know. Know she was safe. Know she was forever safe. Know what he'd done today, the events he'd orchestrated to bring about the death of one man, uncaring if another dozen lost theirs, so she'd be safe. Not what he'd found out. He wouldn't taint her with that knowledge. He'd take it to his grave. Twisted was filled with an almost overwhelming urge to ask Retro to destroy the pictures, filled with a premonition that they'd surface in a way that would tear away at him.

***

An insistent buzzing from his jeans pocket made him scowl. Gaze fixed on the road, the rider dug the thing out, his hand holding it level with his eyes. *Fuck*. Too many words to scan, but with what went down today, he couldn't go incommunicado, not now. The next bend in the road had a pull-off, a place where locals dumped bags of trash, and the parish came along once a month and cleaned them up, leaving trash scattered all along the ditch. A truck sat smack in the way, right where he needed to be, right where his planned trajectory would take him. *Fuck*.

Into the dirt, too fast, automatically correcting the slide. Tree coming up fast. He saw it and accommodated, another split-second adjustment had him pushing the handlebars, leaning to steer around it. *Easy*.

What he didn't see was the stone. Slate gray rock, earth's ancient backbone, once part of a Kentucky mountainside, ripped out of its place in the dirt with blasting powder and exhaust-belching machinery. Cold and gray, broad and squatty, table-sized to fit seven, if they were dwarves. Fallen to the side of the road in Louisiana, it had come to rest in a slant, wedged against a tree, entirely obscured by the trunk. Invisible until someone might be right on top of it. Too late.

Chapter Fourteen

PENNY

Penny sat in Bell's darkened kitchen staring out the window with unseeing eyes. Thinking. Turning things over in her mind. Coming to the same conclusions.

Three days.

He'd been gone three days. She'd woken to find him gone, not uncommon; a text told her he might be late, something she assumed had to do with club business. Something she knew a lot about, given Bagger's position, and her long-term association with the CoBos. She had laundry to do and needed to clean out the truck. There was lots to keep her busy in this place where she was still settling. While it was a change she hadn't expected, she found herself enjoying the sense of domesticity gained by moving in with Bell. It was nice to come home to a place inhabited by another person and even better when that person was Bell.

"Baby," he whispered, "just bring your shit here." She arched her neck, inviting an extension of the line of kisses he was pressing to her skin and he took her up on that offer, his beard scratching and dragging up her throat. "Then you won't hafta haul your ass outta my bed." Hand to her breast, he began the soft rolling movements she loved so much.

She'd gotten in about an hour earlier, first swinging by the truck yard to dump off the trailer, then to her house to pick up her bike and a change of clothes, leaving the bobtail sitting in front of her garage. The look on his face when she rolled into his driveway on her bobber was priceless, and she had barely gotten the kickstand down before he was on her, lifting her from the saddle and holding her tight. "Feed my baby," he'd whispered into her neck, the feel of him making her shiver. Now, they were lying in his bed, bellies full of the biscuits and gravy he'd made for supper.

His back arched as he pressed his hips against her, letting her feel the hardness of his cock against her thigh. She liked that, knowing he wanted her. Had wanted her since the first moment he saw her, staring down at him from the seat. He'd worked to get her, too. Not just that first night when he turned every fearful thought into dust, leaving it by the wayside as he taught her what passion felt like, but every time they'd been intimate since.

Bell nuzzled into her neck, beard rasping across her skin as his hand dipped to her waist, the chill of the room raising goose bumps on her skin when he dragged the hem of her shirt high. Fingertips trailing across her exposed belly, he adjusted in the bed beside her, scooting down slightly. Penny's breath sped up, knowing what this signaled, because as much as he liked touching her, he seemed to enjoy playing with her breasts nearly as much as the act of fucking itself. He could spend what felt like hours licking and sucking, teasing her until she was so wet, he could slide inside on a single thrust.

"Gonna be my good girl?"

With his murmured question against her belly, his head angled up so he could look at her. She met his heated gaze and nodded, knowing what he wanted, what she wanted to give him. Surrender. *She lifted her hands, fingers trailing through his hair from where she'd been cupping the back of his head, and tucked them underneath the pillow, threading her fingers together. Binding her hands together tightly, even if he*

couldn't see, compliant and suddenly on the edge of an orgasm, the anticipation building in her belly faster than he could bring it, clenching and tight. Knowing what he'd be giving her in time, knowing he'd let her touch him when he was moving inside her. She was still riding that wave of need when he moved to cover her, hearing his chuckle rattle through her as he arched into her, pressed tight...and she came.

Head turned to the side, eyes closed against the sensations, lips holding back the cries bubbling up her throat, she quivered and knew that gave it away when he said, "One." That voice, that word, his weight holding her pelvis immobile when she wanted to thrust up against him, his hands on either side of her ribcage, pushing her shirt high up under her arms. Then his mouth was on her, covering her breast, pulling hard, the suction an unbearable sensation, unbelievable that it connected to so much inside her, threads drawn taut. His beard was an entity to itself, trailing wickedly low on her belly, commanding a response as it swept across her sensitive nipples. Rubbing and scrubbing like a bristle brush one moment, it was soft as a kitten's fur the next. Teasing and pleasing, then gone. Her groan of dismay rang through the room, mourning the absence, even knowing he would bring it back, give her that again, gasping as she acutely anticipated the return.

"Good girls get what they need." His voice was hoarse with what she'd come to know was desire, and she licked her lips, feeling him tensing as he moved up, rocking against her. "My shiny Penny." His words were enough to pull another shiver from her because he exposed himself with every sound. Truth rang through the possessive words. "Mine." With his mouth to her breast, he drew deep again, and those threads lifted her spine, stringing her like a marionette doll, shoulders pressing deep, elbows as wide as her thighs, accepting him, taking everything he had to offer.

"Naked." His weight lifted, settled to the mattress at her side and she opened her eyes. "Now, Penny." Ass to the bed, Bell stripped. His eyes settled on her, and she scrambled to do as he demanded. I like that, *she thought as her fingers wrestled with her jeans,* him knowing exactly

what he wants from me. *It made her comfortable in ways that should have been uncomfortable instead, but he never took her power away. In giving her a framework within which to work, he actually gave her the freedom to fill the space completely. He wanted her naked, which meant she didn't have to worry about what panties she had on, or if she'd shaved her legs last night. She didn't have to think about makeup, or hair, or anything except giving him what he wanted. But if she balked, if she had a reason to say no, he listened. Sometimes not even listening, but more like knowing.* Mind reader. My magic man.

"Knees." The softly growled command gave her a shiver she felt inside, thighs slick with results from the orgasm she'd already been given supplemented by a renewed flood. "Swap ends, baby." She adjusted on the mattress, putting her head down towards the foot of the bed. "Hands, darlin'." Adjusting again, she slid her arms out, pressing her chest into the mattress as she stretched. Her last movement to bring her hands together, palm-to-palm, fingers threaded together. Holding firm.

Heat radiated against her backside, but no touch yet. With closed eyes, she mapped his movements by that heat. Bell became a furnace when they were in bed as if his blood ran hotter than hers by a fair measure. Up the outside of her thighs—that would be his hands—he glided through the air above her skin. Knowing he was so close, but not having that touch to anchor her, she trembled without knowing it, realizing only when he spoke. "Gone too long. Needy tonight." Cheek to the sheet, she nodded, feeling the barbell in her eyebrow rasp across the fabric, that momentary reminder of her history nearly enough to pull her out of the moment.

He noticed. Of course, he did, dammit. When did he ever not see my smallest reaction? *"Penny? Tell me." Demanding, as he was in every aspect of their encounters, he wanted to know her thoughts. She knew him well enough to know he might not give up on it but hoped she could derail the inquisition. A headshake earned her a swat on one ass cheek, light but stinging. "Give me that, darlin'." He'd take it, take it all on for*

her. Had taken it, nearly all of it, only a few things left that she'd held back. This was one of them. Every time he'd asked about the piercing, she'd been able to deflect. "Penny." Gruff, his gravel-filled voice came from over her, and she knew he'd moved while she was distracted. She felt his heat all across her back now. Covering her. Protecting her. He'd promised to keep her safe. Kept that promise with everything he'd done so far. "Give it to me."

Fear had weight. She'd learned this through the months since dragging herself to her car, leaving behind so much more than her virginity. Fear and dread could take you down, suffocating you under a growing swell of emotions and reactions. And shame? Shame could flatten you in an instant, grinding you to a pulp underneath the mountainous, ponderous burden it brought to bear. This was him offering to take it from her. He was stronger than she was, had lived through so much where he had to be. I could give it to him. *Without meaning to, her mouth opened and the words spilled out.*

"He said he liked me unmarked. Liked that I was a blank canvas. Said he had plans for my skin. Like my skin was separate from me somehow. He said that and all I could taste was the fear that had lodged itself in my throat. Bitter and biting, I was so afraid he'd follow through. Afraid that after everything, he wouldn't let me go, he wouldn't let me be. I left there, got in my car and drove to the nearest tattoo shop. I didn't think, just did. Didn't think that it would be a reminder that I'd come to hate. Didn't think anything except hearing his voice, lips to my ear, the stench of him in my mouth. All around me. He liked me being a blank canvas. So, I took that away. It's not much."

A touch on her shoulders caused her eyes to flash open. Bell's tattoos rippled in front of her. He was stretched out beside her, his hand on her back. "But, it's what I could do. So I did it," she continued. Propped on one elbow, he reached out, fingers working at the barbell. A click she felt as much as heard, it was nothing like the ratchet of the piercing gun. He then pulled back, thumb smoothing across her eyebrow. Staring into his eyes, she read the promise there. He had to know it wasn't enough.

"Taking it away doesn't mean I won't still feel it." He tilted his head, and she read that promise, too. "I know I'm safe with you. But I did what I did, Bell." He wrinkled his nose, and she sniffed. "How do you do that?"

"What, darlin'?" His beard moved with the sound of his words, the question that he surely already knew the answer to.

"Make everything better?" Now his beard moved again as his lips curled up on the corners. "I love you." It was the first time she'd said the words in this room, in this bed, and she hoped in affirming what she'd told him weeks ago, he would know what it meant. I'm yours, Bell.

"You just gave that to me." Not a question but a statement, and she nodded, no disquieting barbell to tug against the sheet. Just a smooth glide of her skin on the cotton. "I got you, baby." She moved slightly, adjusting one knee, and his eyes darkened, tension returning to the muscles of his face in a way she recognized. "Still wanna fuck?" Her nod was faster, and he made a noise far in the back of his throat, not quite a growl but a sure sound of desire. "You got it."

As he moved, she closed her eyes, feeling the mattress shift and then the heat of his hands hit her back, gliding up in a solid touch. Firm. Steady. Stroking up her skin, they curled around her shoulders, pulling back, nestling her ass against him, feeling his cock riding between her cheeks up and past her anus, blazing heat from his sac resting against the lips of her pussy. "Gonna play." This was a promise because it told her he would be teasing her, pleasing her, and eventually be inside her in the way they both loved. But first, he would see how hot he could get her to run, how heated her blood could get, stoking the furnace within himself with each movement.

It took some time, but he worked at it, inching her back to where she'd been before their heart-to-heart, before he took the final piece of fear lodged in her away. With fingers and tongue, he eased into it, lapping and tweaking until she squirmed on the bed, wishing he'd give

the command to move so she could wrap her fingers around her own pussy, thrusting and rubbing herself over that edge he had her riding.

He moved behind her, hair on his thighs bristly against her legs. Resting his forearm across her hips, he cupped one cheek, tugging and holding her open. Penny tensed; this was something they'd avoided since the nearly disastrous moment in the truck that first night. "No, baby." His voice was soft, caressing her as surely as his hands. "Wanna see, not fuck your ass." Assurances given, she trusted him and gave him that, relaxing against him and liking his chuckle as he recognized her compliance. "One day, but not tonight."

Her eyes opened, and she bent her neck, staring at him over her shoulder. He knelt behind her, tall and strong, head tilted to look down. One arm extended, holding her hips in place, holding her open as he said he wanted. The other hand between them and she knew what he was doing when she felt the probing, prodding tip of him at her entrance. He swiped across once, and then thrust slowly until the head of his cock was firmly embedded inside her, filling her, but only barely before he withdrew completely. The sound she made brought his eyes to her, and she shivered when he smiled, that smile so wicked she didn't know if she liked it or feared it.

"Fuckin' tight, sweetheart. Gonna play." So this isn't the fucking part of the night yet, *she thought, feeling the tip of him push in again, fractionally farther, then he withdrew completely.* God. *Again, and this time, her pussy lips were so sensitive she felt them fold around him, felt as the ridge of his cockhead slipped inside, felt herself stretch to accommodate, then registered the emptiness as he pulled out.*

"Tight." He groaned, his arm moving as his hips shifted back and she watched him stroke himself. Hand to her pussy, he trailed a finger down, circling her clit, pressing hard all around but not touching. Her turn to groan and he grinned wickedly again. "Wet." Finger to his mouth, he tucked it between his lips and sucked. She tensed all over, the ghost of

that pull echoing throughout her body. Threads drew taut again while nipples and clit tingled.

Hand back between them, the tip of him prodded, pushed until she felt the engorged head of his cock slip inside. "Fuck, baby. Breakin' through to you is heaven." A short stroke that stole the breath from her body, lungs suddenly airless, mouth gaping open, those threads pulled near to breaking. "What do you need, Penny?"

You, *she thought, unable to voice her desire.* Always. To be yours forever. *Pressing her forehead to the sheet, she squeezed her eyes closed.* To know I'm alive, to know I'm yours. *As he often did in this position, he called her name, patiently waiting without moving until she turned to look at him again.*

"Tell me what you need." Demanding now, and the shift from question freed her.

"To belong." Her torso bowed, curving so she could rest her head on the mattress and still see him. "Belong here. To know I belong here." He moved and she hated the thought of losing him again. Shifting without conscious intent, she shoved backwards, hands releasing their partner and pressing tight to the bed to anchor her efforts. Taking him inside on a single stroke, she watched as his neck tilted, head arching back on a long groan. Something he gave without fear of what it might say, never holding back on the noises or reactions she triggered in him. Back bowing his hips outward, towards her, inside her finally.

When his head righted, his eyes came to her, and she felt quiet laughter through his cock, still buried inside her. "My baby is bad." Then he proceeded to give her everything she needed, just as she knew he would. Moving inside her, forcing her to find the peak again, Bell's words rang through the room. "Two."

He snapped forward, hands on her hips pulling her back fast, the pace brutal and glorious and bringing her up a mountain she'd never climb on her own. Her fingers clutched tightly at the sheets. She was

desperate to be anchored because a blinding need coiled deep in her belly. Strong, so strong, the potential nearly terrifying with the strength of what he built in her. He held her suspended for long minutes before pushing her past, forcing her into freefall, knowing she was safe in his bed. "Three."

With one arm in the bed, the other curved under her, fingers to a nipple, pulling and tugging, pinching hard, drawing those threads taut again. Stroking deep inside, his hard thigh pressed tight to her legs, and the bed was shaking and rocking beneath her as he took her there again. "Four."

Pressing into her, the heat of him enveloped her back, pushing her to the mattress, following her down. Then the sound of his groans covered her skin in goose bumps as he found his orgasm, coming hard, bucking into her again and again, each reaction pulling a matching one from deep inside her and finally, what she longed for more than anything, her name graced with the title she loved. "My shiny Penny."

That was a month ago, and now...was now.

Texting and calling futile, his phone answered that first night by an Incoherent prospect at the clubhouse. With noise of a party in full swing in the background, the man had been more interested in how big her rack might be than telling her where Bell was, laughing when she couldn't remember his club name at first, disbelieving when she said she was waiting at Twisted's house, asking him to pass that message along.

Bell had been careful not to have her meet any of his brothers, keeping them at bay in a way she knew probably had to be strange. Evidence all over his house shouted that he had company over frequently, but since she'd been with him, it had only been the two of them. Just them cocooned in a world he created two days a week. Her off the road, him away from the club, just them, exploring this thing between them without outside influence.

It probably helped she was gone five days at a stretch, and that her runs were steady. Leave out on Sunday, back in on Thursday night or early Friday morning. Putting her at home directly in the way of what were usually club party nights. And he'd spent every one of them with her. Nearly two months, they'd only been apart the nights she was on the road.

She'd woken Saturday with him gone, which wasn't usual, but not unusual. Then she'd waited until the early hours of Sunday morning to call his phone, not wanting to be the bitchy ball and chain. Handing him space she thought he must need, since he didn't come home to her. She made a quick call to dispatch on Sunday night when he still wasn't home, to give away her load. *I'm sick*, used as an excuse, but it was true. She was sick to her stomach in a way that no pink liquid could soothe. Monday, more of the same, a longer phone call to dispatch filled with excuses followed by a day of nothing. Laundry done, truck clean, Bell's house was clean, even his garage straightened. A day full of doing, but no Bell. Nothing that mattered.

Last night she'd abandoned any notion of restraint, digging through his desk, his medicine cabinet, the drawers in his dresser and nightstands, sorting through the kitchen, compiling a list of people and numbers she thought went with the names. Having no sleep, she knew she wasn't in a good place in her head, but she needed to know why he was staying away.

There had been bikes rolling past his home for the previous two days, some rumbling fast, clearly on their way somewhere, but some had slowed. Slowed until it sounded as if they were going to turn in, but then they throttled up and rolled on. She wondered if they were scouts for him, checking to see if she was still hanging around. If she was still there, in his house, not getting the hint that they were done. That he was done with her. Something she didn't understand, couldn't comprehend, it just didn't ring true, not after the time she'd spent with him, in his arms, talking, laughing...loving. So she gathered names and numbers, trying to plot a path.

Jimbo. His grandfather, someone she knew was dead, but his name still on paper in the kitchen's junk drawer. Long gone, he would no longer provide a possibility to find out what was going on. That left her with two options. An Incoherent member named Whitewall. Retired from active involvement with the club, but still someone Bell had spoken of fondly. Or, Po'Boy, the Incoherent veep, and Bell's closest brother. This name recorded a number of times, old numbers crossed out, new ones written in, scraps of paper boasting even more phone numbers noted with *PB*.

Penny looked down, staring at her phone, willing it to ring. Nothing. *Ball and chain*, she thought, straightening her shoulders, deciding to take the chance that she was wrong. Tapping it awake, she got to the phone app and then paused. *I could call Ty*. He would know which of the two men she could trust.

"Hey, doll." Penny squeezed her eyes shut tightly, holding herself still. She'd abandoned her perch in the kitchen for this call, seated herself on the floor in Bell's bedroom. Knowing there wouldn't be anyone here to catch her if she fell, she needed to give herself firm footing, even if it came with memories. *Control what you can*, she thought, then heard Ty's voice again. "Penny?"

"Yeah, hey." She belatedly joined the conversation initiated by her. Ty had left her alone since she told him she was moving in with Bell. He didn't counsel her against it, just stopped texting or calling, and she suddenly remembered the pain he'd expressed when she told him about Gollum. "Got a minute?" She heard the quaver in her voice and scrunched up her nose in response, knowing he'd be sure to hear it, too.

"Anything." That one word was low and forceful, resonating in a way she knew was dangerous because she was about to break the hope it held. She knew if she broke him often enough, he would stop picking up, no longer willing to be party to his own pain. The threat of losing his friendship tore at her, but she needed to know, and he might hold information.

"You..." Stupid to think he talked to Bell on a regular basis, but he might have knowledge from friends. "...hear anything through the rumor mill about Bell?"

Cautious now, he asked, "What do you mean, Penny?"

"I dunno. Anything." *How much should I give him?* "I'm...he's been gone a while."

"Doll, you know if there's club business, he'll be focused on that. Did you need him for something? Anything I can do?" He must think she needed a jar of pickles opened or a lightbulb changed.

"No. It's not that. He's been gone since Saturday morning." Chin jerking, the last word took forever to make its way out of her mouth. She couldn't have kept the tremble out of her voice if she'd tried, and knew he realized she was crying when he answered.

Alert, but soft, so soft it broke her heart, he asked, "Saturday morning?" Then he followed with something that told her she had cause to be afraid. "Are you sure? You didn't see him Saturday night?"

If he'd expected her to see Bell Saturday night, it meant something had happened, and Ty knew about it. "What happened?"

"Doll, he didn't come back to you Saturday night?" Ty's voice was quiet, intense in a way that set her on edge.

"Ty, what happened?" Tears rolled down her cheeks and she no longer cared if he knew, sniffing hard and wiping at her nose with the heel of her hand. "Tell me."

"There was some club business. He left once it was done. The word is everyone thought he was coming to you, and when he didn't show for the blowout after, assumed you had your own," his voice hardened, and she winced, "private party."

"I got in Friday, everything was normal, went to bed. Woke up Saturday morning with a text on my phone from him, telling me he'd be late." She straightened, pressing her shoulders deeper into the wall, firming her spine. "He didn't come back." She swallowed hard. "He didn't come home."

"You're there now?" Ty's question was abrupt. It sounded like he was on the move and she wondered where he was. "I'll come to you."

"Yeah," she said, "I'm at Bell's place." Ty knew she would be, knew she'd moved in, which meant his question now was about verifying access. "Tell me what happened."

Tone curt, all he said was, "Business."

God, she hated that word. Something Bagger had used to keep her at a distance from a lot of his life from the time she was young. Club business held secrets he didn't want her to know, things she had no place learning based on her sex more than age.

"What kind of business?" There was business, as in the club owning things and funneling that money into member's pockets to support them or supplement what they could earn on their own. Then there were aspects of club business that never hit the edge of legal. Outlaw territory, a place Bagger warned her off again and again.

"Penny." Her name was a growled warning, one she chose to ignore, pushing harder for information.

"Tell me. Ty, tell me, dammit." She pushed with her legs, her back sliding up the wall until she was standing. "I'll call Po'Boy." She had a thought and took a chance, jumping without a chute. "Or Retro." When the suck of his next breath was audible, she knew she'd hit something. "Retro remembers Bagger. He'll talk to me."

"Penny, dammit." A roar, pipes burbling and echoing. She closed her eyes because that was Ty's bike. He'd parked it years ago—she assumed

he'd sold it—but the exhaust was distinctive. If he was riding to her, then that meant he was bringing business to her door. "I got an hour between you and me. You sit tight, hold on. I'll be there." His voice muffled, difficult to make out over the noise of the bike, but she heard him say, "Fuckin' sit tight."

The call disconnected and she was left alone again in the dark of Bell's bedroom. Her phone buzzed, and when she looked, Ty had texted, **Sit tight**.

She stood there a minute, turning over what he'd said, and what he hadn't said. There was business Saturday, something Bell felt he needed to protect her from. Business successfully concluded, so he'd felt safe. She knew that, or he wouldn't have left without every brother knowing exactly where he was headed. They assumed he was coming to her, which meant they knew about her, knew who she was to him. Knew enough that Bell being out of touch for three days wasn't worrisome, except maybe to those men who had been rolling past for two days, keeping watch. Ty didn't want her calling Po'Boy, but more didn't want her calling Retro. One she knew, one she didn't, and she suspected that was why. He wanted her here, alone, and wanted to control the information. *Yeah, right.*

Fifty minutes later Ty rolled in, but he wasn't alone. Forty bikes were at his back. Not what she expected, either, because they wore a mix of club colors. Some were CoBos she knew, some she didn't. Incoherent cuts were expected, but what she didn't expect were women on the back of two bikes. Property of patches. Ty wanted her to have someone here to help her hold it together and brought POs. It was a sweet thought, but she wouldn't be hanging back at the house like the little woman. *Bagger taught me better.*

She met them outside, leaning against the seat of her bobber, boots and leathers on, as ready to roll as any of the men looking at her sideways while they were heeling and toeing down their kickstands. Before she could move, there was another roar of bikes, and she

watched as Ty's neck turned, his head swinging to track the bikes pulling into the driveway. His chin dipped, and he stared at his boots for a moment and then turned to look at her. "Couldn't just fuckin' wait for me, could ya?" Interesting how his language changed given the audience. In the truck, he talked like the college-educated guy he was. Here, he'd developed an accent that blended Cajun and Texan. "Had to go and make that damned call."

"If I were missing, would you sit on your ass and wait for someone to come to the rescue?" That was the word she'd settled on. *Missing*. Bell was missing. "I called Retro. He didn't give me anything, just said he'd meet you here." She gestured to the long-haired biker swinging off his ride, "He's here." She gestured to Ty. "You're here." Tilting her head, she lifted her chin to a man standing nearby, watching her with a curious expression.

His nose had been broken more than once. There was a bruise shadowing one side of his jaw, and his bottom lip had a healing scab on a split from what had to have been a vicious blow. For all that, he was handsome in a rough-edged way, a dangerous way. He was broad, muscled, and powerful looking. Not someone you'd fuck with. Short hair, short beard, the battered aspects of his face spoke of his willingness to do battle, and she knew from Bell's stories they'd stood back-to-back through more than one fight where they'd come out the winners against overwhelming odds. She didn't know him but knew who he had to be.

"Po'Boy's here." Lifting one shoulder in a shrug she prayed looked more casual than it felt, she said, "Let's get this party started, because Twisted," she intentionally used his club name, "ain't here and ain't been here since Saturday morning. I want to find him. He matters to me." She looked back at Po'Boy, knowing this man was Bell's closest friend. "I need to find him."

***

“How much do you know about what he’s been doing?” Po’Boy’s stance was aggressive, taking up as much of the doorway as he could manage, standing with his shoulders spanning the opening.

Penny had led the three men into the house, finding it disquieting that all three seemed to be more at home than she was. Po’Boy, clearly having spent a significant amount of time there, went directly to the kitchen and retrieved three bottles of beer, pointedly not bringing her anything. *Bitches don’t get served,* she thought, remembering CoBos parties. If she wanted something to drink, she’d have to get it herself, but for now, she would overlook this opening gambit to put her in her place, focusing instead on his question. They were in the den; she’d thought it prudent to keep the conversation away from the large windows. Retro had his ass on the desk, Po’Boy to his left in the doorway. Ty had taken up a position on the wall to the right of where she was leaning. Waiting.

“Nada.” She watched in surprise when both Retro and Po’Boy reacted to that statement. They had expected her to know something. *What?* “I know better than to ask after club business. You know who I am,”—she motioned to Retro, and he nodded—“and I can educate you if needed.” Po’Boy frowned, a line furrowing his forehead. “But just understand I grew up around a club. I know better. I wouldn’t ask, and I respect his position. Would never make him compromise the brotherhood.”

“You expect us to believe you suckin’ his cock and ain’t asking where he’s goin’? Pillow talk is pussy’s favorite in on club business. Lick you a lollipop and get you an in. Pussy thinks takin’ dick means you got a fuckin’ say in shit that ain’t any part of your business.” Po’Boy spoke again, and his tone was no longer wading the edges of disrespectful. It was fully off the pier and into deep water, but because Bell hadn’t brought her around, he’d bought this for her, so she’d have to take it. For now.

"Yeah, I do being as I still don't know for sure you are who I think you are, which means he didn't pull out the fuckin' albums and share you." She pushed off from the wall and took one step towards him. "But I know you. Just from his stories, I know you. I know he'd die for you. I know you've had his back for most of his life. I know he loves you. That you aren't just a patch brother, you're closer than blood."

She swept out her hand, indicating Ty. "I've known Wrench all my life." She then pointed across to Retro. "This man was friends with my uncle." She flicked her gaze his way, seeing a smile on his face. "Friend of mine, now." She jerked her thumb towards her own chest. "I'm Penny," she offered her lineage, her association with men in the life the only thing that granted her space in this room, "Bagger's niece,"—she took a breath and then said what she hoped was true—"and Twisted's ole lady. I get it. I'm with it. But he's been *missing*," she emphasized the word in a way none of them could mistake, "for too long because I didn't make a call, not wantin' to be a ball 'n chain." Another breath. "Done with that. Only focused on finding him." She spread her hands wide, inviting them all to join her. "Help me do that."

None of the men moved. No one said a word. *Shit*.

She steadied her gaze on Po'Boy's face, focused on his eyes, holding them through sheer force of will. Slowly, Penny shifted to echo his stance, setting herself against him in a way no one could mistake, and still no one spoke. His gaze stayed on her, and he looked at her searchingly, his face impassive. Then his mouth stretched in a grin that threatened to reopen the split in his lip and he laughed. "Jesus, you're a fuckin' ball buster. I like ya. Twisted's woman. Fuck yeah." His body relaxed and he sagged into the doorframe. "Let your boy here tell the tale." He shrugged, flicking a finger at Ty. "Go on now, Wrench. Talk her through it."

She turned to look at Ty, who suddenly wore an expression that he'd rather be anywhere but here, and acid churned through her gut. Penny tipped her chin down and took a deep breath before leaning one

shoulder against the wall, then she looked up at him and said, "Least said, soonest mended. Get on with it."

"Not sure you want an audience for this, doll." That was Ty trying to be nice, trying to protect her, trying to help her save face. What he didn't understand was every minute that ticked past on the clock meant she had less to save. "Why don't we—"

"Ty," she whispered. "I love him." In those three words, she knew she'd killed her friend, watched him brutalized with a weapon she hadn't meant to wield. Denied him, pulling away something he'd been holding onto. But she didn't care. Couldn't find it in herself to care. Bell was missing.

"Gollum's dead." It wouldn't have mattered how he said it, that would have kicked the stuffing out of her, and it did. Her breath whooshed out in a rush, leaving a desert behind in her lungs. Dry and arid, airless in a way that would cause her to implode, her chest compressed hard. Her heart stuttered as her skin heated with a burn that had nothing to do with the sun and everything to do with the hatred she had inside her. "He died Saturday, a little before noon."

Club business. Bell had done this for her. And if he did that, then it meant only one thing, something she'd seen before, back when the CoBos ran the Mexicans out of their parishes. "War." Wrench nodded, and she turned to look at Retro, bypassing Po'Boy except to note he was staring at her, looking puzzled. "Your Bastards?" Retro nodded. Bell had called in the troops, had been ready for a battle, but that had happened Saturday morning, meant Retro had days of intel to share, if he would. "Ears?" Bagger's language slipped out, his phrase for informants and Retro shook his head.

"Nothing to report, or I'd have called Twisted, and if I couldn't get him, Po'Boy." So no retribution talk, not yet. How far would these men let her push before they shut her down? She decided to see if she could get a little farther down the road.

"Fiddler?" Retro stared at her a moment and then shook his head. She knew what that meant. This had been a comprehensive assault against the entire club. She tipped her head, staring at the edge of the oval rug, tracing it along the wooden floor. Both protection and soundproofing, the rug served two purposes. Could be a bitch to clean, but also helped in clean-up if you were in a hurry, unannounced visitors making their way up the walk, calling a hello to the house, giving you just enough warning to lift one edge and sweep crumbs or dirt underneath, to be removed after company left.

If they swept the whole club up, there might still be pieces drifting around, hiding under a protective covering, something or someone positioning them in such a way to keep them out of sight. "How many members did you fail to account for?" Po'Boy snickered, and she looked up to see him shaking his head. *Right*. Unless one of the members talked, the club's full roster would never be known. "No, wait." She tipped her head back down. You might look under ninety percent of that rug, and still not see what needed to be removed. "What parishes were the Shield members that you can't locate from? Where's home for them?"

"What you diggin' at, girl?" That was from Retro, his question softly voiced, tone honestly puzzled. She didn't blame him, but over the years she'd been privy to enough strategy sessions with Bagger and the CoBos that she believed she was on the right track. "There's not been any noise about blowback on this, honey."

"Let me ask you." She pointed at Po'Boy, knowing he was the one she had to convince. "Someone did this to your club, left you the only man standin', would you let it go? Walk away?"

"Fuck no." He straightened, denying even the thought. "Oh, fuck no. Take my cut and bike, kill my brothers? I'd go down in a fuckin' *blaze*."

"Right." *Hell yeah, he would. So would any Shield*. She swung to look at Retro. "How many, and which parishes?"

Ty spoke from beside her. "Twenty, most are Acadia and Evangeline." Westward parishes. She tipped her chin down, thinking again of the rug and the area it covered, where the edges fell, and what was beyond them. "What are you thinkin', Penny?"

"Allen." She named a western parish. "Rapides." She named another before lifting her head, staring at Po'Boy. "They belong to—"

"Vicar's Wrath," he growled out the information, something she already knew. He was beginning to follow her thread of thought.

"Leswayne and Fiddler were—"

"VietVets, same as Jimbo and Bagger." He supplied information she also already knew. "Fuck, you seriously thinkin' that, woman?"

"Yeah, I'm thinkin' that." She shook her head and looked at Retro. "Middle drawer behind you. Grab the road atlas. My old one from the truck, pull it out." Bell had given her a new one, laughing softly at her argument against the gift. *"Penny, it ain't a big expense, and your old one is tattered. My baby needs good tools to bring her safe home to me."* She pushed the thought away and moved across the room. In a moment, the four of them were standing around the edges of the desk, looking down at a map of Louisiana. She touched several cities and parishes she knew were run by Incoherent. "Y'all own all these." She pointed to the city where Gollum's home was, her trembling finger not able to touch the paper. "Shields had this, and all of this." Her finger swept along the north/south interstate. "You probably ran your sweep from east to west, which meant the western edge got a call, slipped the gauntlet somehow. If I was Shield, and I knew my leadership was dead, I'd be looking for friendly faces. Every Shield member knows Fiddler and Leswayne's history. That's where they went." She straightened. "I'd stake my life on it."

"Stake your ole man's?" Po'Boy tilted his head, looking at her from under the fall of hair over his forehead.

"He's my life, so yeah, I am."

Chapter Fifteen

PENNY

Penny tugged the bandana higher on her cheeks with one hand, the wind teasing and pulling it out of place. Riding whip on the line of bikes guaranteed eating dirt, and with every man trying studiously to ignore her presence, it irritated a bit. Black vest on her back, not even sporting a property of patch, which meant there was no place for her on the back of any bike in this line. If that wasn't enough, riding her own flew in the face of every piece of protocol Po'Boy and Retro recited, but she didn't care, told them so repeatedly, and then did what she wanted anyway.

A scowling Po'Boy thought he'd handled it when she came out of Bell's house to see him pocketing a sparkplug, but he hadn't counted on how much time she'd spent with Bagger growing up. Between teaching her how to fish with a cane pole, and working on bikes while sitting side-by-side on a stump, Bagger had shared a lot of himself with her. She could out-wrench Wrench, and he knew it, which is why he looked amused as the column pulled out, riding west.

Fifteen minutes later, she rolled up on the back of the mass of bikers, knowing when the riders caught sight of her in their mirrors by suddenly erratic paths. Word must have traveled up the ranks, because a few

minutes later, Po'Boy moved out from the head of the line and into the lane for oncoming traffic, slowing down before he slid in next to her bike.

He shot her a look so filled with venom it was a wonder she didn't expire on the spot, and she lifted her clutch hand to cover her heart in mock dismay. His hand signals were unmistakably dismissive, and she fought a smile when she pretended to misunderstand, settling into place and nodding enthusiastically. His shouted, "Fucking cunts," was distinct, as was the moment when he gave up on dissuading her. Left hand lifted in a bird, his bike surged out into oncoming, barely missing a car going the other way as he flashed past the line and back into his position on point.

Now they were coming up on the parish line dividing Lafayette and Acadia. There was a little restaurant there she and Bagger would frequently eat at when they rode, and their gravel lot would make a good jumping-off point for the rest of the ride today. With a sigh of relief, she saw lifted fists coming down the line of bikes indicating a stop was imminent, and then had a flash of panic wondering if she dared stop with them. Po'Boy might be angry enough to attempt other methods of keeping her under wraps. Penny shifted her hips side-to-side, feeling the weight of the knife on her hip and the slide of the leather holster at the small of her back. *I got more up my sleeve*, she thought. *Fuck it, and fuck him. I just want Bell home*.

She had barely gotten the kickstand down when the shouting began, and she watched as Ty stepped into Po'Boy's path. Not putting a hand on him, just putting himself in the way. Still, not smart. Po'Boy executed a takedown maneuver she'd never seen, and within only a handful of seconds, Ty was off to the side, rising to one knee, his back dusty from a roll on the ground to get away from Po'Boy's hands. An instant later and Po'Boy was in her face, mouth open, roaring, lips pulled back to expose his teeth. With cords and veins standing out on the sides of his thick neck, he kept shouting the same question, never giving her time to respond, not that she had any intention of doing so. "You wanna die,

bitch? You fuckin' wanna die? Huh? Wanna die? Got a fuckin' death wish?"

His hands shot up, but he seemed to have second thoughts because they hovered over her shoulders, not touching. His mouth didn't stop, though, and he shouted, "This ain't no fuckin' tea party. Ain't no hair-pullin' jello wrasslin' match." Already close, he leaned in another inch, heat from his skin pouring over her. "You got it in you to kill a man? Because that's what I'm aimin' to do. If they got my brother? They got him, and I find out they *got him?* I'll turn over every fuckin' stone to find him, kill anyone in my way. Break their backs, walk on their bones to find him. Strip off every piece of skin a man owns if he knows the least thing. You got that in you?" He ratcheted up the volume, screaming, "Huh? *Bitch?* You got that in you?"

In all this, she hadn't flinched, even though fear flooded through her. Heart pounding in her chest because this man was in her space, furious to a level she'd never seen, he made it very plain what he expected to go down today. But Penny held to the memories of Bell: his laughter, the amusement in his voice when he found her funny. Choked herself with memories of the pain she'd felt when she heard what happened to Bagger, knowing the loss couldn't be fixed.

She clasped tightly to her resolve in the face of his anger, just as she had the night she'd willingly gone to the bed of a man to get information. It steadied her because she knew if the details had been available, she would have used the information to find Bagger's killer, and murdered him. So in the face of Bell's brother's extreme love for him and witnessing that love turning to wanting to protect her, she held firm.

Her only response was to look deep into this man's eyes, holding his gaze, knowing her pupils were probably just as dark and filled with pain. *I love him, too.*

"*Well?*" His shoulders swung in a little closer, the name patch on his cut moving with his vest, catching her eye. *Po'Boy*. No one had explained his name, and she'd never ask, but suddenly she knew what it meant. The music Bell listened to was old school, older than his years, and one of his favorites was a song from the mid-seventies. Now that she had the thought, she couldn't stop it, couldn't have kept her mouth shut if paid to because she *knew*. And knowing, learned so much about this man.

"I get it. You've been down a road I haven't traveled. You've killed a man...men." She nodded, walking the edge carefully. "I wanted to but couldn't find him. Blocked at every turn, but I wanted that so badly. Wanted the one who shot and killed Bagger. God, *Bagger*. Loved that man. He gave me the world. The man who killed him took that away from me. I wanted my own back. Wanted that in the worst way. I gave everything I had to find out who it was." Sucking in a hard breath, she found it filled with the stench of Po'Boy's rage and terror. "Everything," she repeated in a whisper.

He grunted, the sound pained and guttural, and she knew he understood what her payment had been. It didn't matter now, a thousand men could know and judge, and she wouldn't care if it could bring Bell home. "Wanted that man on his knees in front of me." She nodded. "I'd do it. Still will. I will do it, in a New York minute. Will if I find him. I'll put a gun up to his head, pull the trigger without flinching." His eyes flared, and she noted it, knowing he recognized the cadence of her words.

"Twisted didn't tell me shit about Incoherent business, but he did tell me I was important to him." She pulled in a breath. "I'm just a poor girl." There was another eye flare, and she felt sure she was on the right track to him letting her do what she needed without fighting her every step of the way. "My family wasn't rich, in anything except love. I'm important to him, and he might be in trouble. Friend," she stayed carefully away from the word these men used among themselves, "if I did a single ounce less than everything I have inside me to find him,

then you'd know I'm not the woman for him. And you shouldn't want me for him."

He roared again, wordlessly, the sound so fierce it shook her bones.

Against every instinct, she leaned in, lips to Po'Boy's ear, and whispered, "He picked me. For some unknown reason, he picked me, and *I love him*. Can't breathe without him. Can't live. I have to do this. Don't take this from me. Let me in, Po'Boy. I have to. *Please*."

His hands settled on her shoulders, and she braced for a shove that didn't come. Instead, he folded her to him as if she were the most delicate crystal, as if she were fragile and breakable and precious, and she knew it was because Bell had talked to Po'Boy about her. Knew in an instant the riders rolling past the house for the last two days were as much sentinels on her behalf as lookouts for their brother. She shivered, feeling the power held in check in these arms surrounding her. Not an intimate embrace, it felt as if Po'Boy was taking as much comfort as he gave, together they were building reserves against whatever lay ahead.

While she and Po'Boy had their heart-to-heart, Retro worked to make good on the plans they had put into play while at Bell's house. Ten minutes after their group went into the diner, two pickups pulling trailers showed, and on those trailers were three dozen of the bikes confiscated during the skirmishes on Saturday. In short order, they were unloaded, then her bobber, along with fifteen other bikes had been loaded up, lashed down, and the trucks disappeared in a swirl of gravel dust. Another ten minutes and a whitewashed bus pulled into the parking lot, twenty men climbing off and going directly to those bikes parked in the side lot.

Retro, she had learned, was a master of organization; for all he looked like an old-school hippy with his apehangers and waist-length hair, he could work the hell out of a call tree. It started with the three calls he'd placed before throwing a leg over his bike at Bell's home, and then continued after they arrived at the diner. Once he'd verified things

were moving, he quickly sorted other things, too. He'd reached out to various connections, and with direct questions to ask his sources, found she was right, Vicar's Wrath was sheltering the remaining patch holders in Guanyin's Shield. They were holed up in a remote clubhouse, and the word was they weren't worried about the battle following them home. The Vicar's Wrath were arrogantly preening, having been told by Leswayne they'd be absorbing the Shield in its entirety, taking in not just the members, but taking over their territory and businesses. All the intel was Shield related, filled with bubbling rage against Incoherent for what was seen as an unprovoked attack and takeover move. Bell hadn't telegraphed the real reason, and Penny found herself glad for his discretion.

It wasn't until five minutes before the expanded group was set to get on the road that a call came through, changing all their plans. She'd been talking to Ty. Actually, he'd been talking at her, trying to get her to back down from the decision to accompany their group. Wanting to spare her involvement with a rescue mission that might not be a rescue, but instead, could be the opening salvo in a new war, one the Incoherent MC wouldn't face alone. They'd be standing shoulder to shoulder with their supporters, the Caddo Hobos, and the Bama Bastards, all the three clubs squaring off against Vicar's Wrath and the remains of Guanyin's Shield.

"You don't understand," Ty told her for the fifth time. "What we're about to ride into is going to be extreme, doll. I don't want that for you."

Penny stared at him, trying to decide if anyone would stop her if she reached out and thumped him on his head. Hard. With the butt of one of her pistols. Repeatedly. At least until he shut the fuck up. Fortunately, before she could act on the idea, Retro whistled from across the lot and waved them over. Both of them. She couldn't contain a small victory smile at being included.

Retro began talking as soon as they were within earshot, phone still pressed to the side of his head. "Waiting on the final word, but it sounds like one of my boys found a crash site." At the words, Penny felt the earth underneath her boots sway sickeningly as an uproar sounded all around them, every man shouting questions. She wasn't aware she'd staggered until Po'Boy reached out and gripped her bicep, holding her steady. "Plate on the scoot is Twisted's. The bike is fucked-up. Totaled."

Nothing in there was good and she felt the burning sick as it rolled up her throat at the news. *Bell*. There'd been an accident. That was why he hadn't come home to her. In her head, she heard the words of Ace again, standing in the doorway to Bagger's house, telling her something bad had happened, and she had known by the look on his face that her world had come to an end.

"Still waiting," Retro barked into the phone, and at the force of his angry frustration, she jerked her arm out of Po'Boy's grip, taking two steps backwards, feeling her legs wobble under her like a newborn foal. Swallowing hard, convulsively, she shoved her hands into the pockets of her jeans, suddenly chilled all over her body, even as a hard sweat broke across her skin.

"Got it." Retro's words scarcely registered. She was stuck back at the moment when she heard him say, *Crash site*. The place where a crash happened. One bad enough to total Bell's bike. *The bike is fucked-up*. She swallowed again, struggling to maintain her composure.

"Penny." She heard Po'Boy but wasn't listening. Nothing made sense. *Crash site*. "Penny." She lifted one hand, waving as if shooing away a bothersome fly. Closer, "Dammit, bitch." Chin down, she stared at the tips of his boots. Squared off, strap over the arch, round metal circles holding all the black leather together. *Those aren't buckles*, she thought. *What are they?* Snapping fingers in front of her nose. "Penny Dane, wake the fuck up." Lifting her head, she looked into his face. He looked as white as she felt, as near to losing it as she was. "Goddammit, you fuckin' lied to me?"

She shook her head, not to tell him no, but because his question didn't make any sense. "What?"

"You said you were ready for whatever it took." He waited, and she stared. "This right here? This's what's needed. You a liar or you got your boots on? Huh? You got your boots on?"

Another question that didn't make sense, so she offered the same confused, "What?"

"Got your goddamned boots on? Do you got your goddamned boots on? Do ya? You got those motherfuckers on?" He pointed to her feet, and she looked down, wondering absurdly if her boots had flown the coop in the past five seconds. "Fuckin' boots on your goddamned feet?"

"Yes, I have my boots on." She'd confirmed that first, of course. "What do you mean?"

"Got your boots on," he confirmed. "Lift your fuckin' leg up, bend that mother. Swing it up behind you, fast." She stared at him. *Twisted being missing knocked a few marbles loose*, she decided. "Kick your own ass and get it into fuckin' gear, bitch. Get it in gear and get going. Kick that ass, kick it hard, and get goin'. Fuckin' listen to Retro, Jesus. Five minutes ago, you said you needed this. Now you gotta put your boots on, kick your own ass, and get it in fuckin' gear."

"You talk a lot. Don't say much, but you talk...a lot." Her mouth had moved before she realized it, blurting her unfiltered thoughts.

"Yeah, and gonna piss you off, but I'm right a lotta the fuckin' time. So, get used to it." He paused, studying her. "You're ready. Knocked that loose right outta ya. You got it tight and right now, sister." She saw Ty stiffen at the word that was nearly a title for a woman around a club. She might not be wearing Twisted's patch, but Po'Boy had just given her status. "Now, bitch, listen the fuck to Retro."

When she turned, Retro was studying her, the expression on his face cautious. "You with me, gel?" She nodded. He studied her for another moment and then seemed to come to a decision that she was ready, so he laid it on her. "On a road running between what went down Saturday and his house, we found a crash. Twisted's bike is totaled. Looks like he cartwheeled off into the trees on a curve. The bike is wrapped around a trunk. He mighta hit a tree about thirty feet beyond." She winced and felt heat at her back, knowing without looking that it was either Ty or Po'Boy.

Retro took a breath and continued. "Cage tracks show someone picked him up. Penny, they weren't cautious about it. My boy says there's blood everywhere, but not enough to indicate he bled out at the scene." She bit down on the inside of her cheek, hard, swallowing back the flood of saliva accompanying a renewed nausea. "In and out, came from the same direction. I had one of my boys talk to a dispatcher he's bangin', she checked, nothing was called in. Blood, oil, everything supports it happenin' Saturday. I think members from Vicar's picked him up. Maybe forced him off the road, so they were right there with transport. Dunno why. I can't sort that shit in my head, but that's what I think." He bent slightly, staring into her eyes. "I'm fuckin' glad you done what you done, made your way here with us, because here's what I see going down next if you're game."

"Anything," she said immediately, forcing the word past clenched teeth. "Tell me what to do."

He stared at her a moment, then his gaze focused over her shoulder. She glanced back, seeing it was Po'Boy standing behind her. He glowered at Retro in a way that said he would be demurring on her behalf if she didn't step in immediately.

"You have a plan." She turned back to Retro, straightening as she took a breath. "Tell me."

***

Penny braked to a stop at the end of the road, looking left, then right and then left again before she pulled out. The heat was stifling; she could feel it through the soles of her boots even after lifting them to the pegs. Sweat plastered her tank to her body, and it tickled her skin, trickling down her spine. She was nervous. Riding an unfamiliar bike with the differences in weight, height, and basic handling were enough to make her more cautious than normal on their own. What she was riding into? So much more to fear than the possibility of dropping a bike.

Unbelievable, she thought, riding onwards. *Yet here I am, willingly riding into the enemy's camp on a dead man's motorcycle without anyone at my back*. Po'Boy and Ty were unhappy with the situation, and that was putting it mildly. Ty told her in no uncertain terms just how stupid he thought this was. He told Retro and Po'Boy this repeatedly, with a strong emphasis on everything he saw that could go wrong. She didn't disagree. It was crazy stupid. But Retro had a plan, and she trusted him. She, as he put it, was game.

There was stealthy movement in the woods to her right. She swung her head that direction and watched as men ran, pacing the bike's progress as she steered up the road, wheels turning slowly. It was hard to count individuals as they slipped through the shadows, but she estimated the numbers at about fifteen. Bending her neck to look to her left, there were fewer men, maybe four. Nearly twenty in total, and that was out here by the road, not even at the compound.

A wide driveway was coming up, turning off to her right and winding down through the trees. No signage, no flashing lights announcing a club lived here, no bunker or guardhouse by the road, but she knew this was her turn. The last chance to chicken out and leave Bell to the gentle mercies of Leswayne, a man who had hated Jimbo, and by extension her man, for decades.

She could do it. Could ride past. If there weren't any Shields standing guard—and there wouldn't be, those men wouldn't be trusted yet—no

one would recognize the bike she rode, and she could make her escape. She wouldn't, but she knew she could.

Bell's face flashed through her mind—the first time she'd laid eyes on him, his chin lifted, eyes fixed on her through the truck's window, that slow smile that curled his lips, lifting his beard. She'd wanted him right then and there, the heat between her legs at that moment rivaling the sun's efforts of today, boiling hot and wet for him, even before he said a word. Five hours later, she'd been falling in love. Now, months later, she felt the same. *I love him*.

Without another thought, she leaned, and the bike turned into the end of the drive, setting her course straight for Bell.

***

PENNY

Squatting in place, she stared up at the large man who stood in front of her. Turning her head, without taking her eyes off him, she spat, trying to clear the sand from her mouth. Running her tongue along the inside of her bottom lip, she tasted the bright copper of blood. "You busted my lip open. Busted my mouth." She knew he would understand the meaning of her words when she followed-up with, "That's two."

When she'd rolled to a stop in front of the only building visible from the driveway, the noise of the bike's pipes had drawn an audience, which wasn't surprising. That they at first kept their distance had been. No crowding around. No questions of her appearance. No words at all.

She'd met Leswayne only once, and that in passing more than a decade ago. Even in that small interaction she'd been shielded from the man by her association with Bagger, but still remembered him being a munt, as Bagger and the CoBos called him. It had taken half a bag of candy, but she'd finally bribed a teenaged Ty into telling her that was a man-cunt, someone who behaved in ways the brotherhood frowned on, namely being butthurt at nothing and causing a drama. That was how Ty

had explained things, and she'd suspected the meaning remained about the same even a decade later.

So when the bloated and ill-kempt man had finally walked out, nearly five minutes after she'd rolled up, she'd still recognized him right away in spite of the physical changes. Something in the way he'd moved, how he'd held himself as if he were more than anyone else in the place. *Munt*, she'd thought again, heeling down her kickstand.

By the time he'd gotten halfway to her, she'd swung her leg over and stood, stretching, giving a show. She'd needed to buy thirty minutes. No more than forty-five. Their plan called for thirty, but she'd mentally pushed that another fifteen, and she would gain that time for the boys any way she could. If that meant she bought five minutes because some stupid motherfuckers were thinking with their dicks and looking at her breasts instead of taking her for a threat, she'd shove the girls up and out a dozen times over.

"Hello the house," she'd called, somewhat belatedly. Standard protocol would have seen her making that appeal the moment she killed the engine, well before she made herself at home by getting off her bike. *Well, shit. Daddy'd be pissed at my poor manners*. She grinned, then had felt the expression die away as Leswayne had stopped ten feet away.

Ten, not fifteen. Not zero.

Zero would have meant he didn't know her, had thought she might be a sweet-cheeked gal looking for a party.

Ten feet had said he might be aware of who she was, and that could mean one of any number of things. Bagger's niece, Ty's friend, Bell's woman—in any case, it had spoken of a tad bit of respect, which she could milk and gain that extra fifteen minutes if it were needed.

Ten had meant he didn't think she was a threat.

Fifteen would have said he wasn't certain what her agenda was, wasn't certain if she were about to go psycho bitch on him for something. Fifteen should have put him out of reach, even with a lunge. Fifteen could have given him the advantage.

Ten had meant he was wrong.

Walking dick. But is he a thinkin' one, too? She'd tilted her head and used a soft, conversational tone as if sitting at a kitchen table with friends. "Hey, Leswayne. How you doin'?" Only a fraction of an inch, but she'd logged his startled reaction as his head jerked back. "I don't know if you remember me—"

"I 'member you, bitch." His words were not unexpected, but the lack of heat in his words was. "The fuck ya want?"

"Yeah. I'm Penny. Hoped you'd remember me." She'd offered a closed-mouth smile, knowing it would look as false as it felt. "Hey. I wondered if we could have a private sit-down conversation." She'd intentionally used language she'd known he would reject. The last thing she'd wanted was to be alone in a room with him, and said this with an expectation he'd react negatively to the idea of her being an equal, which a sit-down would imply. When parties pulled out chairs on either side of a table, the playing field was level, and this wouldn't fly for a man like Leswayne. *Or any of the men*, she acknowledged wryly. "I have a proposal—"

"One of y'alls, go open the cage," he'd ordered and one of the men moved. A moment after his footsteps faded, she'd heard a metallic rattle that made her blood run cold. He had a cage for humans. "Got your proposal right here." He'd laughed, grabbing his pants halfway down his thigh, gripping what she assumed was supposed to be the head of his dick. Before she could control her thoughts, her mouth had run loud and clear.

"Gettin' ahead of yourself, ain't ya?" Shaking her head, she'd finished. "Way ahead of yourself from the looks of it."

Shit.

She'd barely had time to think the word before he took three long steps towards her, hand drawn back level with his shoulder and then he'd brought it forward in a wide, descending arc, and connected on the side of her head, hard.

"There's your fuckin' proposal, bitch," he'd growled as she kept her feet with difficulty.

Ears ringing, she'd shaken her head, trying to clear her thoughts. Once again, her mouth had outstretched the bonds of prudence. "FooFoo, you had three chances. That's one."

A laugh and a muttered, "Bunny FooFoo," from the side had made Leswayne's face darken with anger. Penny had stepped away from the bike, realizing she and Leswayne had been surrounded by men, the leather-clad bodies formed a loose circle around their altercation.

Ignoring the pain blooming on her face, she'd kept after him. "You turning down my offer without even hearing it?" She'd swept her hand out, indicating all the men standing in the clearing. "Their lives not worth the words?"

"Who the fuck are you?" That came from the side again. It had been flat disrespectful of the man to respond to a question aimed at the president, and Leswayne's eyes had shifted that way, revealing a wariness she hadn't expected. *He isn't as in control as he'd like me to believe.*

She hadn't turned to look but answered all the same. "Penny you already know. Penny Dane is my full name." Waiting, she'd heard what she expected to hear from the men surrounding them: confusion. Leswayne wasn't big on protocol or history, not unless he was rewriting it.

"So? Who the fuck is Penny Dane, gel?"

Eyes locked on Leswayne's face, wanting with every fiber of her being to see if he really knew it all and still pulled his shit, she'd recited her lineage. "Niece of Bagger, former veep of the CoBos. Best friend of Wrench,"—a bickering mutter had come from the men. They'd known at least one of these names, and since Bagger was dead, she'd assumed it was Ty. This had made her wonder exactly what role he played in the club—"also of the CoBos. Friend of Retro, prez of the Bastards"—more muttering, and from the corners of her eyes, she'd seen the circle expand unevenly as some of the men stepped back in respectful reaction—"and ole lady of Twisted, nat prez of Incoherent." Leswayne's face had paled at Retro's name, but Bell's had bought her a different reaction, which brought her to now, knee to the ground as she probed the split in her lip caused by a second hard, inescapable backhand swing.

"Get the girl up." By not using her name, he was trying to minimize the impact her words had on the men. If they were willing to put their hands on her now, then she might not last the time needed for Po'Boy and the boys to make their way through the woods to the rear of the property.

Shuffling footsteps behind her sealed the deal. There were too many who were either ignorant of who their enemies were, or blinded by the lies spewed about what a victory Saturday had been. They'd be swooping in to scoop her up any moment, rush her, take her to the cage, something she couldn't allow. Leswayne hadn't moved back after he'd struck her. He was so close she'd brush against him if she stood, the idea making her skin crawl with revulsion. She threaded her fingers into the top of her boot, gripping the folded handle tucked there for safe keeping.

Knives had been a favorite way to pass the time when she was younger. She'd learned how to flare and flip a butterfly, wheeling blades around her fingers, sucking oozing cuts when she misjudged. Wielding needle and horsehair when she lost. Following Bagger from clubhouse to clubhouse, playing with the other club kids, she'd learned both

bishop and mumblety-peg early. Bagger gave her this knife, and she never lost a game with it. Never had one that mattered this much.

Orienting the handle by feel, she placed the bite in her palm, and pulled a breath, blowing it out slowly. Tugging the blade from her boot and flicking her wrist, she flung the tang. No flare here, no flash or show, just the security of feeling the safe handle slap into her palm while she straightened her arm, thrusting up and out, dragging it left to right as fast as she could move. *Butterflies in your stomach*. The handle grew slick and she pistoned it back and forwards a second time, dragging up through the resistance encountered, hearing the high-pitched squeal coming from Leswayne. "Three." The word escaped in a whisper as she felt hands gripping her wrists, slipping in the blood covering her as they worked to pull her away from the slowly toppling body in front of her.

"Jesus, fuck. You fuckin' killed him, goddammit." That came from right behind her and her neck bent as she tried to see who had her. Thin and dark-haired, this man was no one she knew, so she renewed her struggles to get away. "Penny, stop it." His use of her name surprised her. Then he grunted as the heel of her boot connected with his knee. "Twisted—" He grunted again and slumped against her, the dead weight of his body carrying her to the ground. Po'Boy's face appeared over his shoulder, and he grinned down at her, pistol in hand.

Like a guard dog, Po'Boy stood over the top of her, head on a swivel, watching to see if there were more threats imminent. Penny shoved at the chest of the unconscious man, heaving him off and to the side without help. "I think he was trying to say Twisted's here somewhere," she wheezed and watched as Po'Boy turned, scanning. Then he locked in place. Finally free, she pushed up from the ground and ran, aiming to where he'd focused, hearing Po'Boy pounding behind her as they approached the shadows around the clubhouse.

Chapter Sixteen

TWISTED

Twisted heard the roaring of a bike's pipes. The engine throttled up twice and then cut off abruptly. Not an uncommon sound at a club's compound, but for the past five minutes, he'd had chills. It felt as if something was on the cusp of happening. *Goose walkin' over my grave*, he'd thought more than once, barking a laugh the first time but that changed to a groan as it set off waves of agony through his body.

A scratching at the doors, the rattling sound of the chain they used to padlock it closed, then the cellar doors opened wide. Dirt and root steps leading down to the dank dirt floor where he lay illuminated by the bright sun coming from outside. Heat poured down the steps along with the light, and he shivered again. Where he was, stretched out between the two raised platforms on either side of the long, narrow room, it was cool, and he'd not been thankful for that until this moment. *See, it can always be worse*. He didn't know he'd smiled in response to his internal dialogue until he heard Leswayne's voice. "The fuck you got to be grinnin' at? You one stupid muthafucka."

Standing at the top of the steps, Leswayne took up a significant amount of room. Not because he was broad as much as he was wide. *Wide load, comin' through*. With a proud beer belly jutting out over the

top of his pants, he looked like he was beyond the delivery date of triplets by about two years. It was a pure wonder how his pants stayed up unless that belly hanging over cinched them into place like a chip clip. *Snap*. It had been years since Twisted had laid eyes on the dread outlaw, hadn't recognized him at first, with his puffy features and doughboy body.

Not recognizing him had brought pain because Leswayne didn't care about injuries Twisted might already bear on his body. He'd been free with his feet and fists when Twisted couldn't stop a laugh at his outraged shout, "What do you mean, you don't know who I am? I'm Leswayne, muthafucka." *Leswayne, you might be. But Samuel L, you ain't*, had been Twisted's stupid, stupid response, drawing laughter from half the men standing in a circle staring down at him. Even before he saw how that yanked Leswayne's features into an angry scowl, he'd known the men's reaction, each one of them a patched member of the Vicars, would cost him much more than his words, because a man like Leswayne couldn't be bested, not in front of men who didn't respect him.

"Lazy ass, get your fuckin' ass up these steps. Got something I want you to see." Twisted stared at him as the man coughed, hawked, and then spit on the first step before turning to walk away.

Get my ass up the steps. Right. He was fucked-up. Knew it. Had known it the first time he'd regained consciousness lying in a pile of brush and trash, staring at the sunshine filtering through the pine needles over his head. Left side useless, he was pretty confident his arm was broken up by his shoulder, knew the collarbone was definitely broken, mostly because part of it was sticking out of his skin.

When he'd forced himself to a sitting position, he'd passed out again, coming back to his senses slumped sideways. His arm hung slack at his side, shoulder drooping like a melting Saint's candle. He'd seen his bike then, and that hurt nearly as badly as the bones. Front wheel warped and forks collapsed around a tree trunk, it had struck with

enough force to break off the top of the dead pine, the fresh wood shining brightly where that deadly arrow had speared the earth not five feet to the left of where he sat. Attempting to stand triggered another woozy spell and he'd fallen hard when he tried to widen his stance to stay upright, left leg giving out from under him for no good reason.

After that, he'd stayed on the ground, digging his pocketknife out and opening it with his teeth to cut away the strangling fabric of his shirt. No phone, that motherfuckin' burner had been in his hand when he'd clipped the boulder he now saw hiding behind a tree, no doubt cartwheeling like the bike had, probably traveling even further than his body. The road he'd been on wasn't well traveled, and he knew from the angle of the sun in the sky he'd already been there for hours without being found, so was surprised when a vehicle slowed and stopped, driving off the road right in that bend. He'd thought it might be a local dumping trash. Or that he was delirious from heat and injuries combined with no water. But he wouldn't take a chance it was real, screaming out, "Hey." Again and again.

Only after he'd shouted the house down to bring the driver his direction did he realize he didn't have to expend the effort.

They were there for him.

Vicar's Wrath patches on their vests, hands like iron lifted and carried him to the truck parked in the ditch, then dropped him gracelessly to the bed. When he came to again, one man was riding in the back of the truck with him. It was someone he recognized as being a Ragman supporter, the man looking down at him, slowly shaking his head side-to-side. Oh yeah, he was fucked-up.

They'd brought him here. The wind of the truck's passage through the darkness keeping the heat at bay until they stopped in back of the compound, sweltering temperatures intensifying the pounding in his head. They'd dragged him out of the truck bed by the waistband of his jeans, Twisted unable to hold back the groans when his legs buckled

underneath him, sending him face-first to the dirt at Leswayne's feet. Then Leswayne went to town on Twisted, enjoying himself with every kick, hit, and blow he landed. Powerless to fight back, all Twisted could do was take it. Take it without flinching. Take it without screaming. Take it knowing in his gut for the second time that day that he was going to die.

During one of the times his body failed him and passed out, someone took him to the root cellar, locking him in. When he came to, he could see the links of the chain holding the doors closed, and laughed, knowing there was no way in hell he'd be headed up those steps under his own power. And now, here was Leswayne, asking the impossible.

A face appeared at the top of the steps, and Twisted stared, unsure if he was seeing things. "What the fuck you doin' here?"

"Shut up." Those two hissed words told him this was a friendly visit, and he nodded, giving the man the benefit of the doubt, watching as he moved silently down the steps. With the man's shoulder propped under his good arm, Twisted held onto the man, grimacing when the movement set his injuries singing with pain. "Hold on." A hand urged him to sit, and he did, stretching his legs out in front of him. "Gonna hurt," the man said, producing a bandana and whirling it into a makeshift rope. With it knotted around the wrist of his injured arm, Twisted leaned his head back on a groan as the arm was pulled across his torso, bandana tied to a belt loop of his jeans. With his vest buttoned around his forearm, it was secured as best as it could be without a sling.

"Holy hell, fuckin' hurts." Twisted ground these words between clenched teeth, feeling a sick sweat breaking out all over his body.

"We got maybe two minutes before Leswayne comes back to roust you." Ragman stepped back, staring down at Twisted. He hooked his thumbs into the front pockets of his jeans, his cut gaping open to

expose the pistol holstered at his hip. Twisted hadn't seen him for a while, hadn't cared to with so much shit swirling around. This sudden assistance surprised him. He'd never gotten the feeling that Ragman would be open to a direct strike against his old man, even if he'd made it clear he wanted to take the club in a direction opposite to everything Leswayne wanted.

"What's waiting for me out there?" By breathing in small gulps of air, he was able to keep the pain beaten back. Focusing on something else was helping, too, like trying to pick apart the puzzle standing in front of him.

"Woman rolled in about twenty minutes ago." That would be the bike he'd heard, the one that swept in carrying the feeling of deep unease. "Claimed to be your ol' lady." *Oh, Jesus. Please, fuck no.* "Said she was willing to trade for you."

"She give a name?" He lifted his good hand to meet the one offered by Ragman, pulling himself to a standing position with a grunt. He wouldn't be winning any footraces, but he at least wouldn't fall over.

"Penny." Ragman ducked under his good shoulder again, wrapping his arm around Twisted's waist. "Up we go, man." He tugged, and Twisted stood in place, unable to move. "Come on, we won't have long to slip out."

"Penny? Penny Dane?" *How in fuck had she found this place?* Why would she look here for him? He'd hoped she was looking, hoped she'd call Wrench and get a search going, but had not considered she'd make her way here.

"Penny was all she said. All she got out before Leswayne was on her." Twisted was stuck in place again, unable to take a step or a breath or even think for a moment, an image of the bloated misery of a man touching Penny—*my shiny Penny*—nearly breaking him.

"What do you mean?" His tone must have penetrated, finally, because Ragman turned to look at him.

"Holy fuck, she actually is your ol' lady? Oh, fuck. Fuck. *Shit*. Jesus." The horrified tone Ragman used conveyed everything.

"He hurt her?" Wouldn't matter. If he'd touched a hair on her head, looked her way, breathed her air...Leswayne was dead.

"He's not that stupid." That statement took Twisted by surprise, and he grunted, listening carefully as Ragman continued, "He hated your granddad, hates you, but there's a healthy respect for you in the Vicar's Wrath. Her sayin' she's your ol' lady, boys won't be down with fucking her up. Families are supposed to be off limits, but she rode in on a bike. Not just any bike, but Gollum's ride." Twisted's breath stuck in his chest and he stood, waiting for Ragman to continue, because he knew for a fact that bike had headed to Alabama, which meant Retro was somehow in the mix of whatever Penny was doing. "You know that shit cannot stand. She was holding her own. He was playing with her, but she'd managed a standoff." Ragman leaned forward, taking more of Twisted's weight. "Come *on*."

"Take me to her." They made their way up the crude stairs, one slow, fucking painful step at a time. "Fuckin' get me to her."

"Man, no. I gotta get you out. He's going to kill you." A noise drifted to them from the darkness. Ragman's voice fell to a whisper as he repeated his words, "He's gonna kill you. Then he'll kill me. Finally, God, he'll do what he's tried for so long. I can't give him that victory, Twisted. You gotta get out so I can deal with my blood."

"He doesn't get her." She could survive anything; she'd proven that, but he knew if something happened again, she wouldn't be the same. The confidence that was so much a part of her would be gone. She had come back from that before with grit and strength and love, but if Leswayne tore those gains loose inside her, she'd never be the same. "She's mine."

Flickering firelight reflected from the trees on the other side of the long, low building that sat in the middle of the clearing. It was a bonfire and from near the flames he heard shouted laughter and cursing, the sound of a mob of men watching something by turns entertaining and sickening. Ragman stopped arguing, steering them towards the end of the building. They rounded it, and as they pulled to a halt, Twisted saw what was happening.

***

PENNY

A form separated itself from the darkness, slowly resolving into the face she'd feared she might never see again. Standing on his own two feet, and breathing. Staring at her with a look that promised everything she'd ever wanted. She took in everything about him, the bruises, makeshift sling for his arm, him standing like he favored a leg. Not all of the battering he took was from the wreck. She saw clear evidence of fists and knew that could be laid at Leswayne's feet.

She assessed him, and on the fly made a decision. With how she knew Bell, and knowing the men who looked up to him, she didn't fawn over him, didn't coo over his wounds, but simply stared and spoke aloud, reminding herself he was, "Upright and suckin' air. You good to move out?" One corner of his mouth curled, and then he nodded once. *He's okay*. "Right. I'm on a bike, but some of the boys brought cages."

"Gonna be a hit to my manhood," he muttered, reaching out for her hand, not giving any indication he realized she was covered with blood and gore. She lifted and laced her fingers with his, then he tugged, pulling her closer. Tipping his head, he tenderly brushed her lips with his, tracing a tiny circle on her swelling cheek with the tip of his nose.

She took a breath that hitched hard and got it under control by running her own words through her head. *Upright and suckin' air*. "You ridin' bitch, big man?"

"Fuck, yeah." He pressed his forehead against hers, and she felt his next words resonate throughout her, reassuring and making all things right in her world again. "Love you, darlin'."

Her answer was just as certain, just as true. "Love you, too."

Chapter Seventeen

PENNY

On the couch in his den, Penny relaxed into Bell. Having draped herself partly across his chest, her fingers settled so her palm was positioned above his heart, feeling that reassuring thud and thump. Home. He'd spent two days in the hospital, complaining the entire time and she'd spent those days smiling. Not because he was in pain, which he was, the surgery on his shoulder had been massively invasive, and rebreaking the already knitting severely fractured collarbone wasn't all the surgeon had to do.

She'd been smiling because he was, as she kept reminding him, upright and suckin' air. She'd said it so much, Po'Boy took notice, and a few minutes ago, he'd shown up at Bell's house with a patch for her vest: USA. She'd been sitting on the arm of the couch, and after looking at it for a long time, then up at his widely grinning face, she gave up and asked, "U.S.A.?" Po'Boy had laughed and shaken his head.

"Yousa," he replied, which was what she'd said, sort of. He snorted at her scrunched nose and took pity on her apparent confusion. "Yousa. Upright, suckin' air. Yousa."

"You want to call me USA, but pronounce it yousa because..." She trailed off, catching sight of Bell's face behind Po'Boy. He watched their

interaction with an expression of such peace, it stole her breath clean away.

"See, then we can work it into shit. Like conversations. It'll be awesome. I can say shit like, Yousa gonna make sammaches." He shrugged, laughing again, and she wondered if this big, hard man had ever laughed as much as he had since they saw Bell walk out of the shadows next to that damned building. "Shit like that."

"I'm gonna make sandwiches? And you're going to use some lame-ass nickname to direct me like that? You think that's gonna happen, Po'Boy? Huh?" She shook her head, adopting a patois and an accent that her father would surely hate. "You flat loco, man. You wanna 'splain to me exactly when it was we became friends? I seem to remember lots and lots of hate and threats. Shoutin' and threats. Cursin' and threats. Why don't we go back to that? Huh? Back to you cussin' me out and yellin' at me, all up in my face? That dude? I didn't have to make that dude sandwiches." Bell turned to look at her and he slowly shook his head, the corners of his mouth lifting his beard slightly. She sighed heavily, dropping her gaze to her sock-covered toes. "Got a preference, friend?"

"Little sister, you gonna keep that shit up, I'll have to take offense; think you don't like me much. Fuck, bitch, I brought you a fuckin' present and you ain't even offered me a beer." He held his palm out, insistently tapping his fingers against his palm. "Gimme back."

"Fuck you, brother." She gave him what he wanted, and his hand shot out, gripping her shoulder. A squeeze of his fingers and she saw lines of peace settle into his face. This meant much more to him than she thought, and she wondered what the story was behind those emotions. "Oyster or mudbug?"

"Not that anyone apparently gives a fuck if I starve, but oyster sounds good to me." Bell, clearly done with his brother bonding with his ole lady, broke into their conversation. "And he can call you whatever

he fuckin' wants, but that ain't your nameplate, baby." He gestured to Po'Boy with his good hand. "Fuckin' give her the real deal, asshat."

Glancing down at Twisted, Po'Boy complained, "She's Yousa to me, brother. Best names have deep stories. You fuckin' know that." He reached into the pocket at the breast of his vest, bringing out another small, rectangular patch. Holding it in his palm where only he could see it, he asked, "You sure, brother? She gonna be pissed as fuck if she don't think this is funny. You might wanna wait 'til you can at least fuckin' run. She gonna be pissed like that."

Penny dipped her chin, looking up at Po'Boy from under her brows. She didn't say anything, just held out her hand. He dropped the small piece of fabric there, and Penny smoothed it out on her palm. She stared at it for a long time. *Shiny*. Just the one word, saying everything. Bright and polished, a new beginning for both of them. Eyes to Bell, she waited for a beat before pulling on a scowl. His brows flew up, and she barked out a laugh. "FooFoo?"

Bell's head fell back, and he complained to the ceiling, "Dude had one job. One."

She looked at Po'Boy, seeing an answering smile to her own on his face. "Love and respect, brother."

"El and ar, little sister."

***

TWISTED

He watched Penny and Po'Boy, feeling something warm grow inside him. Something he'd not felt in a lot of years. Movement in the kitchen caught his attention, and he glanced that way to see Ragman walking into the room. Fortunately for him, he'd decided not to hold a grudge for the conk on the head, the only anger being that Penny'd killed Leswayne, stealing the chance from him. From the debriefing they'd

done, the coup had been months in the making. It was unfortunate timing that Incoherent's beef with Guanyin's Shield happened when it did, escalating Ragman's timeline significantly. Then everything had gone sideways when Twisted had crashed, and Vicar's Wrath was there to scoop him up.

Time enough in the days and weeks ahead for the club to explore all the ways the power exchanges had shifted. The war launched meant every MC in the region was affected, all the way from east Texas to the Florida panhandle. For now, he had his shiny Penny, and they had the protection of their brothers while he healed. It would be a chance for them to see how they fit together, but he had no doubts that the way they suited each other would be pleasing, and satisfying.

Twisted watched her face, noting the soft expression that played across her features when she looked up at Po'Boy. There was a deep, genuine affection there, not something he'd expected, but he'd take it. Take it all day long, happy he had that between two people who mattered so much to him. Things could have gone so many different ways, but it had all sorted out right in the end.

The first night in the hospital he'd worried about her state of mind, unable to get the image out of his head. Her on one knee in front of that motherfucker, his hand finishing the arc of the swing that took her down. Leswayne shifting, readying for another blow, Ragman sprinting out from where they'd been but no way he could get there in time, then Penny exploding from the ground, arm moving, gutting the motherfucker. Ragman getting to her, pulling her away just as Po'Boy materialized out of thin air, along with about eighty friends. Riding to the rescue, literally, their three patches presenting a united and strong front.

It had been a rout from there. The smartest of the Vicar's Wrath members hit their knees where they stood, understanding they were relics of a club that was no more. He'd managed to stay on his feet long enough to see the confiscation of all the patches there.

Twisted had accepted a visit from Ragman while still in recovery after surgery, the biker showing while the nurses all wisely looked the other way. They'd come to a quick accord, dealing in Ragman as a second to Po'Boy in a new Incoherent chapter running out of that fuckin' clubhouse, after all the shit had been cleared. Uprooting members from all sides, throwing together combinations that would take a year to see if they worked. *Good enough for now*, he thought, gaze traveling up and down Penny's frame. Delicate but so fuckin' resilient, everything he wanted in one package. Someone to protect, but someone who could stand strong when needed. *Tough enough*.

She'd crawled up in the hospital bed with him and hadn't left even when the nurses came in to run her out, wordlessly refused. And when security came, one look from her ran them out of the room. Once they yanked the tube out of his throat, he told them all she had the right of it. She was his, and he was hers. Enough said in those words.

Doc had come in, frowned at her and then ignored her, something that pissed Twisted off, too. Not that he wanted the motherfucker to look at his ole lady, but she was there. It wasn't until later when she whispered part of her story into his ear that he realized Doc was keeping her secrets. He'd been the one to work on her after Gollum was done.

Now they were home, her face healing, and his shoulder as well. Po'Boy reported things were good in the club. Catfish was settling into a newly expanded role taken on when Twisted gave up his local office. Doubling their membership in a weekend meant he wouldn't have time to fuck around with politics once he was healed. Instead, he'd be needing to roll between houses, keeping track of everything.

Penny. He looked at her, assessing her for the hundredth time that day. She was solid. Even with all that went down, she was solid. Not untouched, but she was a woman who could run to him with the blood of his enemy coating her hands and take a moment to banter after assuring herself—albeit silently—that he was okay. That woman would

find her way to solid, even without him in her bed. With him there, she'd find her way there faster.

Retro had told him about the scene on the way to his rescue, how she had refused to accept any answer except the one she demanded, and how the moment had transformed Po'Boy. If he had an ounce of doubt in his body about his brother, he might worry with the way the man looked at her. Jealousy didn't live in him, however. He knew Penny better than that, knew Po'Boy to his soul. *Ride or die, both of 'em.*

She pushed up from the couch, leaned deep to brush her lips across his, and turned to saunter towards the kitchen with a shout over her shoulder, "Oyster comin' up. Ragman, you'll stay." Not a question, Ragman still gave her a nodding response, and she moved out of view. Twisted looked at Po'Boy, then Ragman.

"Brief?" He didn't offer to get up, didn't pretend to be anything other than what he was: recovering from surgery to reconstruct his shoulder. It would be weeks before he could ride again, at least according to the surgeon. Between the wreck and everything that happened after, it was a wonder he was standing.

"Bastards report no negative chatter," Po'Boy began. "Wrench had different news, but Ragman talked to him last."

"Mexicans are moving." Ragman's voice was quiet, pitched so Penny wouldn't overhear. "They've not recognized the shift in leadership nor the new players on the field." He paused, then glanced at Po'Boy. Slowly, he said, "Got more, but not sure how much you want to hear right now."

"Everything." He couldn't make decisions without information. He couldn't deal if he didn't know what aces might be still in the hole. "Gimme what you got."

"Gollum...talked." Ragman's lips twisted. "Motherfucker talked a lot. Talked to the wrong people about something that he got hold of a few

months back." Twisted tensed, the tender muscles in his leg protesting. The throbbing in his shoulder lifted from dull to sharp. "He found an audience in Nogales."

"Arizona?" That was news, but unless there was something else Gollum would have had to talk about, Twisted didn't have any ideas why a Mexi gang would have thoughts about Penny. "What the fuck is in Nogales?"

"Cartel. Straight line to Columbia. Do not pass go. Do not collect any fuckin' thing." This came from Po'Boy, and Twisted watched with unease clenching his gut as his brother glanced towards the kitchen where Penny could be heard humming and rattling pans. "Gollum talked a mean streak. Ran his mouth about everything that would gain him advantage with his suppliers." It wasn't until after everything had gone down that Twisted had learned how deeply the Vicar's Wrath was into running and dealing. Jimbo had always adopted an attitude that each club had to police themselves, kind of a "not my circus, not my monkeys" way of looking at things. But now, knowing what they knew from all Ragman had told them, that hands-off stance would have been the undoing of every group in the region. Vicar's Wrath was the sole reason the DEA had focused on southern Louisiana for so much of their efforts over the past months, looking for links and holes in the partnerships and friendships, trying to find an in with Leswayne.

Po'Boy asked, "You 'member what you said the trigger guy told you?" Twisted looked up at him, sorry he hadn't insisted on being at least sitting for this conversation. Relaxed, stretched out with his head on the arm of the couch wasn't how he wanted to do this. He pushed and struggled, dragging himself upright, grunting and wincing at the awakening pain. Po'Boy continued, "You 'member who he said was on radar?"

"Yeah, I fuckin' remember." The name had caused that man's death to drag out long and hard, blood and tears washed down the pipes for

hours before Twisted granted him peace. "What the fuck does that have to do with Nogales?"

"Gollum talked to the wrong people. See, the cartel has need of *Norteamericanos* who match a particular type, and they noted that the only living relative of a man they hated, that man being Bagger, was the same person Gollum claimed to have a line on if they wanted. Two birds, one stone. She's pretty, brother." Twisted jerked his head to the side, not wanting Po'Boy to see his reaction. "And they like pretty. They like untouched, too, and with what Gollum told 'em, they know she's nearly that."

"She's mine." He growled the words because this was true. *Fuck*.

"Know that. Soul deep, brother. Ain't dick happenin' to her." Po'Boy shook his head. "Won't let anything happen to little sister."

"The whole club is on alert, Twisted," Ragman put in, keeping his voice low and quiet. "But you gotta know, they have long arms, longer memories, and they remember very well how Jimbo and Bagger joined forces to run their asses out of the region. You being Jimbo's and her being Bagger's, and now her being yours? That's a big fuckin' target, brother."

"Retro ain't heard shit about this?" That was surprising because Retro's network ran coast-to-coast, and up into Canada. He was diligent about fostering relationships, building his network. His blood brother was in a club poised to go international, if rumors were true, an access to which would give Retro a broader base of intel than ever before.

"Nope, and I didn't beat around the fuckin' bush askin' either. He's digging deep as we speak." Po'Boy stared at him. "Ain't shit happenin' to your ole lady, brother. My hand to God, may he strike me dead if I'm lyin', ain't shit gonna happen to your Penny gal."

Twisted turned his attention to Ragman, considering everything he knew about the man. Long believed to be a dissenter in the Vicar's

Wrath ranks, no one outside Ragman's inner circle had known how deep the hatred of his father ran. Seemed Leswayne liked everything rough, preferred his boy to want rough, too. He'd been vocally disappointed when Ragman didn't live up to the legacy Leswayne felt he was handing down. That disappointment had turned into physical abuse, and for years Leswayne paid that through his boy's blood.

Throughout his life, Twisted had seen a dozen father-son pairings much the same, where discipline morphed into abuse as the frustration grew, wanting the boy to "man up" or telling him "for your own good" or "won't have a pussy in my house." Those boys staying and taking it rather than running, because really, amidst the stilt houses dotting the swamps and bayous, where could they go? Family everywhere, all with the same raising, telling the kid they just needed to "toughen up."

After cutting their teeth on the villagers in the backcountry of 'Nam, Leswayne and Fiddler had been collaborators after they came home, too. And, with Leswayne, it went so far beyond physical torture with his boy; it was a wonder Ragman came out as good a man as he did.

The thin, dark-haired man stared back at him. In the hospital, he had told Twisted that he felt this was a chance at a new life for him. A chance to find peace. He wanted to give Ragman that opportunity, and would, but first, they had to figure out where the enemy might come from next.

Twisted began, "Ragman, need you to take a trip. Got friends in El Paso. We can sort a meet there. They'll have a closer hold on Nogales." He swung his eyes to Po'Boy. "Call Retro, ask him to set a meet with the Soldiers. He's got tighter ties to Las Cruces than me." El Paso hosted a chapter of the Silent Deaths, a club he'd had occasion to deal with in the past couple of years as they worked a transit corridor deal out, granting passage on I10 for their ventures. Las Cruces was the Southern Soldiers, and Retro had a channel through his brother. "You up for that?"

Po'Boy spoke up. "Sure you want him out of reach right now, brother?" Not to be misconstrued as a slur against Ragman, this was Po'Boy's way of saying he thought the man had value here that might not be outweighed by his ability to gain info.

"Then who?" Twisted ran through the short list of people he trusted, coming up dry.

"Me and Wrench," Po'Boy offered. "Sends a loud and clear that us and CoBos are side-by-side on this. Not that anyone would think any different, her bein' who she is. But for folks looking from the outside in, it'd deliver a crystal message."

With a tilt of his chin, Twisted gave agreement. Po'Boy turned away, pulling his phone from the front pocket of his jeans as Penny called from the kitchen. "Is that enough time? Need me to stay out of the way longer?" Po'Boy looked over his shoulder at Twisted, grinning.

"Naw, we're good, baby. Come on back in." Solid. *Made for me*.

Carrying everything on a TV tray she'd taken off the stand, she brought a bag of chips, and a six-pack of beer, along with plates loaded with sandwiches so stuffed with fried oysters and fixings it was a wonder the buns didn't split in two. "Jesus, Yousa," Po'Boy laughed. "You cookin' for an army?"

"Y'all are big boys, need sustenance. I figure this should hold you for, oh, let's say, an hour?" Passing each man a sandwich, she opened the chips and set the beers on the coffee table. "See this?" She pointed to the beers, looking pointedly at Po'Boy. "This is me not holding a grudge, brother." Twisted saw Po'Boy's face soften again and knew there was a story there he'd have to pry out of his brother eventually. "Eat up."

"He picked good. You didn't lie, Penny Dane." Po'Boy's mutter was quiet, but still Twisted knew Penny had heard him when after a moment, she cleared her throat, turning to look away. She laughed aloud when he finished up with, "Yousa not a liar."

Chapter Eighteen

TWISTED, SIX MONTHS LATER

"BELL! Where?" Her shout broke the stillness of the night, jerking him up from a sound sleep. She was thrashing, fighting, the covers transformed to demons in her mind, and Twisted reached out, gathering her close to his side. The dreams didn't often come, not anymore. In fact, she faced them less and less with every passing month, which was good. But, when they did, it took her a while to settle. "Where are you, Bell?" Panting, the question in her voice quavered in a way he knew she'd hate if she recognized it.

"Right here, Penny. I'm here, darlin'." Slipping one hand up her back, he cradled her head and pressed her cheek to his shoulder. "Right here. Safe and sound. We're both safe and sound." Sometimes the dream was about his wreck. He'd made the mistake of talking about it where she could overhear, and she relived the crash a dozen times the first week afterward. Him waking alone, in pain, unable to call for help, then thinking assistance was there, but finding out it was as far from relief as he could get.

Then, once he was off the pain meds, smoking some green to mellow himself, she broke out the tequila one night. Between tokes and shots, he'd gotten blitzed enough to talk about the hours spent at the mercy

of Leswayne and his men. Her dreams were different, then, filled with anger alongside the fear, the two combining in a punch that took her down deep inside herself. Hard to rouse, she fought him nearly every time, making it difficult to contain her until she woke.

Lately, however, the dreams had changed again, and these she wasn't willing to talk about, but she would only settle once she knew he was near. Resting his chin on top of her head, he listened to her breathing, hearing it begin to even out, slow, only occasionally interrupted with a lurching catch. For a time, the dreams had been so bad he hadn't wanted her in the truck by herself. Working was part of her, ingrained deep, and he couldn't deny that need. He just didn't want her by herself if a dream came calling.

He couldn't go with her, with the sling and stitches, and the physical therapy. He couldn't be climbing in and out of the cab without damaging himself, undoing all the work the surgeon had done to make sure he had a 100-percent working shoulder. Which he needed. So when he couldn't go, he had an idea. Given an option between Po'Boy and Wrench, Penny'd laughed at him. Laughed so hard she had to bend over, arms crossed over her belly, trying to keep from busting a gut.

It was no surprise she took Wrench. Twisted and the man had words before he set foot inside her truck, those words being all from Twisted in the form of a reminder who she was to him, what she was to him, and what she would never be to the man who'd given up his chance with her well before Twisted came on the scene. Penny didn't know about that chat, had no reason to know, but Twisted had faith that Wrench had honored every request he'd made. Kept her safe, kept her sane, called Twisted when she had dreams, handed her the phone and let her ole man talk her down from the terror.

"Bell?" Soft now, but controlled, she'd pulled herself together.

In my arms, he thought, tightening his hold. "Yeah?"

Silence for a long minute, then, "Nothing. Sorry I woke you." Not the first time she'd started to ask something, then pulled back, and this shit was beginning to worry him. "Go back to sleep."

"Tell me." He pushed hard, making it a demand and knew she understood he would accept no less than the truth when she tensed in his arms. "Tell me." In his words, he heard echoes of his past, images flashing past in a gruesome slideshow. He tried to deflect those and hold onto what was here, now. She might have nightmares, but he had his own demons. Something he'd bury fresh every day if it meant she breathed easy sleeping next to him, easier to do every time they reared up to try and catch him off guard. Still caught up in the illusion he spun for her in the cab of her truck that first night. Giving her sweet until it was no longer a façade, but how he just was with her.

She changed me, Twisted thought with surprise, not something she'd have wanted to do, but he treasured the differences she brought out in him. The wanting to care for her, wanting to give her the world, wanting to hold onto that love she gave him with both hands. He rolled them in the bed, tucking her slightly under him, pinning her in place, dragging his knee up her thighs. *Won't let her get away. Not ever*. "Penny, tell me what woke you." He fed the illusion.

"I had a bad dream." She pushed at his chest, not gaining an inch of room because he tightened his hold on her. Doc had given him a full release months ago, and Twisted had jumped back into working out in the backyard of the clubhouse with Po'Boy and the boys. It had taken weeks, but he'd pushed himself, regaining all the ground the wreck stole from him. No way would she be getting away.

"Got that, yeah." He gave her a warning squeeze when she persisted in trying to wriggle some room between them. "What about?"

"Stuff." He saw the wince that wrinkled her brow. He watched her lips twitch to one side and frowned.

"Penny, I can't help you if you won't give it to me." She swallowed, that movement giving everything away. She didn't want him to know, but it wasn't because she was afraid he'd think less, but because whatever it was hurt her deep. She cut her eyes away from him. Something to do with him, but just him. So not the wreck, not what happened with Leswayne, or after, but something else. "What are you afraid of, darlin'?"

He began a calculated assault on her senses, dropping his head to her shoulder, trailing tongue and lips across her skin. Slid a hand across her belly, and then back again, curling his fingers around her hip. Tugging at her torso, pressing into her from the other side and with lips to her ear, he murmured, "Tell me, baby. Lemme in." A nip and a lick to her lobe, then he mouthed the sensitive skin behind her ear. "Whacha 'fraid of?"

"Bell." His name a whisper, breathed on an exhale, there was no muscle behind the sound. It was just Penny needing him to know he mattered, that she knew who she was in bed with. She gave that to him every time, and he loved it. Loved so much about this woman. Everything she gave to him, he took with greedy hands, dragging her in deep, deep, deeper with him each breath she took.

"Penny." He gave it back to her, infusing her name with every ounce of love he had inside him. Goose bumps crawled up her skin, and she took her reaction away from him, turning her head to the side. Afraid of him or of something else? "Penny." He tried again, mapping her responses as she shifted in bed, pressing into the mattress to escape a bit of his weight. He leaned in further, keeping her where he wanted her. "My shiny Penny."

That earned him a reaction he didn't expect; a sob hitched its way up her throat. "Mine. My Penny. Shiny." He gave her words, following each with a caress of his mouth and hands, massaging them into her skin so she'd hold them forever. "My shiny Penny. Love you, darlin'."

That melted her, and he knew her fears by the way she slumped into him, even lying underneath him letting him support her. *Why's she afraid of losin' that?* "Love you, Penny." Face pushed into his neck, he felt the edge of her teeth, felt her hand stroke along his bicep. "You know how much I love you?" A headshake and he puzzled over that. He told her all the time, told her way more than was macho, but never wanted her to doubt. Showed her, too, every day they were together, which was every day she wasn't in the truck. "You payin' attention, darlin'?" A nod indicated she was, tension singing through her muscles again, melt done with. "Never get to the end of that love. I feed it out like a line, but there ain't no end to the feed. It's done gone past anything I expected, and I expected a helluva lot. Never gonna get to the end of this love, Penny."

Head turning, face lifting, lips seeking, he gave her what she wanted, slanting his head across hers and taking what he needed, fitting his mouth to hers in a hard, wet kiss. Velvety soft, her tongue stroked and tangled with his. Throaty gasps released into his mouth as he worked her hot and fast. Sliding a hand up her side, thumb caressing the curve of her breast, Twisted's nail dragged across her scarcely-covered nipple. She'd worn one of his thin tees to bed, rolling in about three in the morning, tossing her clothes to the floor as she pulled on his shirt before climbing in beside him. That single act showing a possessiveness he liked to see. He'd known she was tired, known she'd pushed herself hard to get back to him, so he'd held her while holding back, listening to her few words before sleep claimed her.

Now he roused her, ruthlessly playing on every hot spot he'd noted, quickly bringing her to wordless peaks where her only responses were sweet moans painting her pleasure on the air. With tongue and fingers, he plumped and pinched, licked and lapped at her, feeding from every offering she gave. When his name slipped past her lips again, it was on a rising note, sustained as the wave carried her forwards and upwards, *"Bell!"* As he always did, he recited what he knew to be true, *Yeah, I gave you that. Now you're going to give me more.*

Moving over her, he pushed a forearm into the mattress on either side of her head, holding himself suspended, not crushing her, just covering her, gifting himself with the touch of her skin all along his body. Eyes to her face, he watched as her orgasm restarted like an engine when he thrust his cock up and over her clit, heard her shuddering response to that feeling swelling inside her. "God, Bell."

Still he waited, and when her eyes finally opened, she gasped at what he knew was a hungry look on his face. "Want you, Penny." Her tongue darted out, slipping side to side across her bottom lip. "Wanna fuck you." A jerk of her hips told him she wanted that too, pressing against him then away, already fucking in her mind. "Want you to give that to me." A deep breath had her titties rubbing against his chest, which in turn earned him a gasp. He waited a beat and then told her the truth. Something that ran so deep in him, like he'd told her, there was no way he'd ever find the end of it. "Wanna love on you."

Hands to his shoulders, her palms stroked down, down, down, then up his sides, across his back as he gave her some of his weight. Fingers cupping his ass, she'd learned how to ask for what she wanted without words, initiated into sensual pleasure by him. *Always be her best,* he thought, rocking his hips into hers, feeling the glide of his cock up and through her lips. The liquid aftermath of her orgasm granted slick passage. Messy, but she'd never complain about it, she liked it as much as he did.

"Wanna love on you, darlin'." Arching his back, he felt her quiver. "You ready for me?" Leaning in, he grazed her lips with his, giving her a taste of herself, knowing she liked that, too. Knew so much about her, but every time he loved on her. "So much more of you to figure out." He needed to learn everything about her. "Love you, baby." Mouth pressed to hers, Twisted kissed her deeply, then released her lips, nuzzling into her neck.

"I love you, Bell." Those words did it for him, every single time, making him need to be connected to her in a profound way; him inside

her physically, knowing she was inside his heart. So he adjusted, probed gently, lining things up, and then he stroked slowly. A gentle glide, he didn't stop until he was rooted, deep in there where he always found what he needed. "Love you so much." Her words gave him that other thing he needed, verbal affirmation that he wasn't alone in this. *Riches untold*, he thought, *never get enough of what she gives me*.

Her dream was nearly forgotten until she said, "It's you. I'm afraid of losing you."

"Oh, baby, you couldn't get away from me if you tried." He arched, finding and drawing a nipple into his mouth, sucking hard and growling as she moaned sweetly in his ear. "Give it a try. I'll show you how futile an exercise it'd be. Don't try, and let yourself be content here with me. I'll show you how deep we go. Solid as a rock, baby. What we have is writ in stone, ain't gonna wash away with the first waves of trouble." Holding still inside her, he felt the ripples beginning deep, her pussy contracting around him with his words. "Gave me this, can't have it back. Mine." Another ripple and he pressed his face to the crook of her neck, mouth to her skin, loving that involuntary reaction she was giving him because it told him she believed. "Mine. Always."

He moved then, slowly at first, rolling his back, working every angle, finding, as he always did, that every inch of her was beautiful. Tight, hot, and sweeter than he had a right to want, she let him ride her as he needed, knowing he'd get her there again, and again if she just gave in to him. Pulling out to the tip, he played there, thrusting by fractions of an inch at a time, working the head of his cock in and out. Her wordless cry when he again took her deep was worth every torturous second. Unbelievable how good it felt to sink himself into the fiery heat of her, letting all of that wrap around the length of his cock, knowing she gave him that willingly. *Every time*.

Shifting his weight, he moved one hand between them, sliding a finger to either side of her clit, finding the resulting jerk and clench worth exploring, so he did it a second time, then a third before pulling

out, wrapping his fist around his cock and squeezing hard. “Touch me,” he demanded, and before he could repeat himself, she had threaded her fingers between his. “Feel how hard you make me?”

“Yes, baby,” she whispered, and he shivered at the way her voice reverberated through him. She squeezed, and then her hand moved up, palm cupping the head of his cock. “I feel you.”

“That’s all you. Best I ever had.” He thrust into her hand. “Everything you do makes me love you more. Want you more. Always you for me, darlin’. Never losing me.” Her chin jerked to the side, and he leaned down, nuzzling until she looked at him again. “Never. Losin’. Me. Nothing could tear me away from you, baby. My shiny Penny.” Crystal blue eyes looked up at him, and he willed her to hear what he was saying. “My everything. Wanna plant my seed in you, watch our love grow, hold the embodiment of that love. Do it again. Love incarnate, right here in my bed. Never losin’ me, and I sure as fuck ain’t willin’ to lose you.” He moved, forcing her hand away, grabbing her wrist as he pushed back inside her. The heat of her sheath scorched around the head of his cock. With his fingers twined with hers, Twisted pressed her hand into the pillow at the side of her head. “Ain’t losin’ you. Keep you, my shiny Penny.”

“Love you, Bell.” She pressed her lips to the side of his head, hips arching up to meet his downward thrusts. “Love you.”

***

Po’Boy

Po’Boy grinned, staring down at his beer sitting on the bar in front of him.

He was naked, in a hole down in the 9th, waiting on a courier to bring him an envelope from Retro. With his cut packed away in the trunk under his saddle, uncomfortable but necessary in this locale, the only one where the messenger was willing to meet. He hoped that envelope

would be filled with information about a still-breathing Nico, intel they could move on, fucking finally. But he wasn't grinning about that. No. That was business and would be treated as such; the only enjoyment would come at the end of the day when he might have the chance to convince some poor bastard he needed to roll on Nico, tell secrets with the false assurances of immunity.

His grin had nothing to do with business, and everything to do with the woman he'd come to love. Different from how his brother loved her, but still, a bone-deep love for Penny Dane. The grin was due to the conversation just across the corner of the bar from him, where two patched members of an out-of-town MC sat. Good old boys, drinkin' beer and shootin' the shit, telling tales to pass the time until the oblivion of sleep crept up on them. It was just the tale they were telling was one he'd gotten to see up-close and personal like, having the smallest part in the run that'd become known as the route of twisted pain.

"That Penny, heard Bagger had her on a bike before she could walk. Little dirt bike, turning her loose back in the bayous." One man's contribution to the conversation wasn't far off the mark, not from the stories Penny'd told on herself.

His companion, an older man, one probably of an age with Bagger, shook his head. "Heard she faced down the biggest badass in town for the right to ride point on that run. Head high, she took him down without lifting a hand." *Well, that's just insulting. Nothing like that happened*. He wanted to say this, but held his tongue, wondering how far they'd spin it, the run already seeping into legend in the MC world, a place where women had no place, but Penny'd somehow found a way to make one.

The first guy picked up the story. "Troops on either side of the road, she punched through, made it to the yard. Stood toe-to-toe with that bastard, Leswayne, while her man looked on, lettin' her, knowing she had it."

"Foot soldiers of a shit club are bullshit. I heard it was gators *and* pitbulls." Older guy shook his head. "Bagger took her gator hunting about the same time he put her on a bike. She'd handled bigger. Leswayne, what a pussy. You hear what she called him? Bunny FooFoo. Shit cracks me up every time."

The other guy laughed, slapping the top of the bar. "And the shit about him being a little dicked daddy? That's priceless." He reached down, gripping the knee of his jeans, voice rising to a falsetto lilt as he said, "Got way ahead of it." Po'Boy could vouch for that part. He'd been nearby; not close enough to stop the blow that took her to her knees, but close enough to hear her repartee, which was as sharp as her blade had proven to be.

"Gutted him like a fish. Laid him open, reached up inside, pulled out his balls, showed 'em to him." Not quite, but close. "Got done, strolled to her man, him standing there waiting. God, I'd give a fuck of a lot to have someone like that at my back."

Smile dying on his face, Po'Boy thought to himself, *Wouldn't we all.*

FINI

THANK YOU FOR READING *THIS IS THE ROUTE OF TWISTED PAIN*!

I had a great time writing this story, and hope you've enjoyed delving deep into the world of George Bell, aka Twisted, and the beautiful, resilient redhead, Penny Dane. Not a typical love story, but the setting deep in the canals and bayous of southern Louisiana lent itself to provide a rich background that I hope helped set their stage in a memorable way.

In the story, Penny has occasion to make oyster po boy sandwiches for Twisted and a couple of men (thanks for the idea, Kelsi). Here's her recipe, which happens to be one I've used many times:

Oyster Po Boys

What you need to buy

- Fresh shucked oysters, half a bushel or so depending on what you need to yield in terms of sandwiches. Figure 10-20 oysters per sandwich, do the math yourownself. Can substitute mussels or shrimp, if you can fry it, it all works.
- Po boy or sub sandwich buns, sliced longways
- Creole spices like Tony Chachere's, Zatarian's, or King Creole
- Tartar sauce
- Green onions
- Sweet onions
- Tomatoes
- Red chilies
- Lettuce
- Oil or grease

Want to make your own creole spices? Easy 'nuff:

- Combine a quarter teaspoon each of onion powder and garlic powder. Add a dash or more of oregano, basil, thyme, black pepper, white pepper, cayenne pepper, and paprika. Salt to taste.

Make your own tartar sauce

- Mix two tablespoons of mayo, two of spicy mustard, one of a sweet relish or chow chow. Dress that with some cracked black pepper and a dash of creole spices.

Breading for oysters

- One cup white or yellow cornmeal.
- Dust that with onion powder (not salt), garlic powder (not salt), and you can crack a little black pepper on that, too.
- Find a good creole seasoning you like, dash in to taste.
- Mix well in medium bowl.

Preparation

- Coat the oysters in the breading and deep fry in a hot grease or oil. I like a light canola, but use what you want.
- Split and butter a po boy bun on both sides and toast. Can brush with oil before toasting for extra crisp on that bun.
- Dish up your hot, fried oysters, dab on some tartar, add chopped onion greens, fresh sliced sweet onions, sliced tomatoes, diced medium hot red chilies (hotter if you like it that way), and shredded lettuce (if you like greens on your sammmach).

Enjoy!

TWISTED'S PLAYLIST

Born out in the backwoods of Louisiana, it should be no surprise that the music Twisted chose for me to listen to is flavored in the Cajun way.

Twisted's playlist: bit.ly/ntnt-twisted- playlist

ABOUT THE AUTHOR

Raised in the south, MariaLisa learned about the magic of books at an early age. Every summer, she would spend hours in the local library, devouring books of every genre. Self-described as a book-a-holic, she says "I've always loved to read, but then I discovered writing, and found I adored that, too. For reading...if nothing else is available, I've been known to read the back of the cereal box."

Also by MariaLisa deMora

Alace Sweets

A dark thriller, this book is not a light read. Filled with edge-of-your-seat suspense, this intense story commands the reader's attention as it drives towards the explosive ending. Alace Sweets is a vigilante serial killer, with everything that implies and is sure to trip all your triggers. Be ready.

At seventeen, Alace Sweets turned a corner in her life, taking the wrong shortcut home from school.

Resisting the harsh knowledge her attackers will never be made to pay for their actions, Alace takes a stand. Justice must be served, and if fate's scales are out of balance, she's determined to set things right as best she can.

When the laws of men fail, the rules of Alace prevail.

5-Star Reviews for Alace Sweets

"deMora has a superb story-line and exceptional character development. All of her characters have such depth that will intrigue the reader..."
~Turning Another Page

"Hot, sweet, dark thriller."
~Beth D

"It will keep you on the edge of your seat and give you chills."
~Escape Reality Book Blog

"Disturbing, haunting, sickly; yet hot, sexy and heart racing!"
~Amanda L

"From the first page [deMora] pulls you into the world she has created and you do not even try to escape..."
~Little Shop of Readers Blog

"A must read for all those dark, gritty romance fans out there."
~Sweet & Spicy Reads

"You will find yourself so drawn into the story that the outside world is blocked out and your locking the doors and turning on all the lights."
~Danena F

"Don't judge me for bonding with a vigilante serial killer, she's more than what she does."
~iScream Books

"Thrilling...chilling...full of suspense, nail biting edge of your seat excitement."
~Tracey H

"Every time MariaLisa deMora picks up her pen (or opens her computer), she creates characters you want to believe in."
~Gail S

"Intriguing dark storyline, beautiful love story and nail-biting conclusion, what more could a reader ask for?"
~Manda M

"This book takes you a dark and twisted ride that is gripping..."
~Renee Entress' Blog

"This book is dark and gritty and I literally had to take a day off from reading it because it's that intense."
~My Girlfriend's Couch

"This is my favourite book so far from this author ... I recommend this book if you enjoy dark romantic thrillers."
~Cheekypee Reads and Reviews

"There's not enough stars to give this book and 5 just doesn't really do it justice!"
~DeLane C

"I couldn't put this book down from page one! Tried to stop & go to bed but couldn't sleep thinking about Alace and got up & finished the book."
~Debbie M

"MariaLisa DeMora, wordsmith that she is, made this a story of the enlightenment of a woman and finding love in a life where she has had none."
~Kat W

"Whatever deep dark trench [deMora] pulled a character like Alace from should be revisited again and often."
~Confessions of a Serial Reader

ADDITIONAL SERIES AND BOOKS

Please note that books in a series frequently feature characters from additional books within that series. If series books are read out of order,

readers will twig to spoilers for the other books, so going back to read the skipped titles won't have the same angsty reveals.

Rebel Wayfarers MC series:

Mica, #1
A Sweet & Merry Christmas, short story #1.5
Slate, #2
Bear, #3
Jase, #4
Gunny, #5
Mason, #6
Hoss, #7
Harddrive Holidays, short story #7.5
Duck, #8
Biker Chick Campout, short story #8.5
Watcher, #9
A Kiss to Keep You, novella #9.25
Gun Totin' Annie, short story #9.5
Secret Santa, short story #9.75
Bones, #10
Gunny's Pups, novella #10.25
Never Settle, short story #10.5
Not Even A Mouse, short story #10.75
Fury, #11
Christmas Doings, #11.25
Gypsy's Lady, #11.5
Cassie, #12
Road Runner's Ride, novella #12.5

Occupy Yourself band series:

Born Into Trouble, #1
Grace In Motion, #2 (TBD)
What They Say, #3 (TBD)

Neither This, Nor That series:

This Is the Route Of Twisted Pain, #1
Treading the Traitor's Path: Out Bad, #2
Trapped by Fate on Reckless Roads, #3 (TBD)

Other Books:

With My Whole Heart
Alace Sweets
Hard Focus

More information available at mldemora.com.

www.ingramcontent.com/pod-product-compliance
Lightning Source LLC
Chambersburg PA
CBHW070059030726
47506CB00002B/522
9780996748667